R

M000200154

"A sad, shocking, salient story … an incident- and adventure-crammed treasure for Hoosiers, and many others. I admit historical fiction is my favorite genre, but even so, Bunn's uncomplicated style and ability to provide specific examples, will draw in the local-history seeker. 'A failure to recognize and a failure to act' plays throughout the book, as Bunn takes us through Prohibition, the Women's Temperance movement, cave bandits, the KKK, the kindness of the Amish, violence toward women, accidents and illness without the help of doctors, the 'Dirty 1930s' (the drought-caused dustbowl) and many more. But it's not all wretchedly half-healing femurs and bootleggers adding kerosene to extend their moonshine batch. Bunn reveals the magic of seeing another's pain and pitching in, of reinventing a chunk of trash into something useful, of finding the good and praising it. With his focus staying on recognizing problems and failing to act, but also on the merit of helping others, Bunn has captured a big piece of southern Indiana history."

Connie Shakalis, Reviewer
Herald Times
Bloomington, Indiana

"I really enjoyed Jon's book, especially the scenes around Shoals where I went to school. I liked his realistic portrayal of the relationship between Paul and his father, probably because I remember my grandmother talking about men like him. Her own father was not a nice man. I enjoyed the relationship between Paul and Grover and then mention of the Crane Ammunitions Depot, where two of my brothers worked and the gypsum mines where my father worked when I was young. I remember seeing a man gathering clams in White River, although this was a very long time after the button factory was closed. I never knew that kids did this dangerous work. Paul's life reads like a history of Martin County and its families, with enough mysteries and surprises thrown in to keep you reading. Well done!"

Kathy D. Kalb, Reporter
Springs Valley Herald/Paoli News Republican
French Lick, Indiana

"Just finished The West Bluff *this afternoon. What a great read! Thanks! [A friend] brought your new book over,* Shoals Bluff, *as he thought I might like it. It's been a long time since I've been compelled to read a book straight through! I've finished* Shoals Bluff *just now and am full of 'feelings,' as we have roamed that area, of course for me, in pursuit of things to photograph. I don't know if I can thank you enough for such an experience and the ending that made me sad and happy and contemplative and something I cannot quite describe. I'm often wondering about the strength of the people and joke that beautiful things were built before television. You have made me feel rather than know the importance and meaning of such things in peoples' lives that we take for granted."*

> Paula Stapley, Photographer
> Bloomington, Indiana

"First off, I thoroughly enjoyed reading Shoals Bluff. *I liked the fact that you jumped right into the action, with the boys going fishing and pulling in a big surprise. The characters were well developed, especially Paul's, with the relationship between him and his father and mother showing what shaped Paul's whole life. History was interwoven throughout, so those who like historical fiction (like me) will appreciate the book. It takes us through Prohibition, falling of the stock market, beginning of the Great Depression, the Dust Bowl, and the establishment of the Sycamore Land Trust. The character development was especially good. I feel as if I know these characters. Paul's favorite saying, 'Be a blessing to receive a blessing' tells us what we need to know about his approach to life."*

> Judy Stephens Morrow
> Fearrington Village, North Carolina

"I was captivated by every word. It makes me appreciate [the] modern world that we live in and how just a few generations ago the way that rural America had to be inventive and self-reliant. It has stimulated me to research Indiana history about some of our darker moments with the KKK."

> Dennis Long
> Bloomington, Indiana

Shoals Bluff

a novel

JON BUNN

Shoals Bluff

Copyright © 2020
Jon Bunn

Jon Bunn c/o Mayhaw Press
13618 East Cypress Forest Drive
Houston, Texas 77070
JonBunn.com

Published by:
Mayhaw Press

Editor:
Margaret Daisley
Blue Horizon Books
www.bluehorizonbooks.com

Cover & Book Design:
Dawn Daisley
www.morninglitebookdesign.com

Printed in the United States of America

Publisher's Cataloging-in-Publication data:
Bunn, Jon
The West Bluff / Jon Bunn
ISBN: 978-0-578-80398-2

*This book is dedicated to the
Wise sisters from Dugger, Indiana*

*Ester,
Dorothy,
Mickey,
Rose,
Sarah,
Jenny,
Betty Lou,
Mary*

Do all the good you can,
by all the means you can,

In all the ways you can,
in all the places you can,

At all the times you can,
to all the people you can,

As long as ever you can.

~John Wesley

Introduction

~~~~~~

In a backwater place, in an almost-forgotten time, nestled in obscurity and barely one generation removed from the failures and remembrances of the Civil War, the descendants of that conflict have settled back into the wallows as dirt farmers, many of them destined to live and repeat the habits and mistakes of their kin.

Re-baptized with the dust and the silt of bottom land farming, the Chandler family's perspective on life is one of gazing on a grey horizon. But this outlook is at least temporarily brightened by the birth of a child in 1900, a son who will bring two more hands to toil at the unending labor required of their marginally productive land in Southern Indiana.

Can that brightness of spirit grow and renew? A simple faith of constant and enduring belief through helping others emerges and binds those farmers together with a common cause to persevere. Thus, begins a journey filled with wins and losses, truth and lies, theft and murder, charity, and redemption.

PART ONE

Chapter 1

A stunning blow to the side of the head sent him to the floor and he felt his arms and legs hit all around him. The sound of the slap filled his ears and drowned out everything except the voice and the hands that now grabbed him and jerked him up by his shirt.

"So, you want to disobey me again, boy? I'll teach you to remember the things that are important, and the things you ought to remember is what I say. Do you want some more learning at my hand or are you ready?"

Lemuel had the boy by the back of his pants and was pulling him out from under the bed he was trying to crawl under. Another dose of "learning" was about to happen. Flipped over and staring up at the man's angry face, he heard the voice that saved him.

"Paul, it's time to get up now and get ready for school. It's almost daylight." And he watched the angry face start to fade away, back into another bad dream that seemed to be a constant in his young life.

His shoes were dry this morning, which was nice to feel for a change. His habit of wet shoes and wet clothes were an annoyance for him. School was an occasional habit he liked.

When not needed for plowing, crop picking, clearing stones from the fields and such, it was nice to see some of the other kids from his small farming community and to catch up on what was going on in town and around the county.

It seemed that academics didn't have the fun and appeal for kids who attended school in Martin County, Indiana, due to the goings-on all the time down at the river. Ever since someone decided to look inside a freshwater clam shell and figure that buttons could be cut from the pretty mother of pearl shell and sold, the fever seemed to grip everyone to go dig clams and sell the shells. The clamming fever gripped everybody locally about 1903, three years after Paul was born.

Muscatine, Iowa had big button businesses as a result of rivers full of freshwater clams. Thousands of tons of shells processed as buttons were cut and sold to the garment industry. It was a thirst that made a lot of money for the people who would harvest the shell blanks and then cut them into fancy buttons. It could be dangerous work, both on the river gathering shells, and in the factories making the blanks.

The poor farmers and town folk of Shoals, Indiana wanted a piece of the action and the money. After all, the White River went right through their own town.

The past few days of heavy rains had swollen the White River out of its banks and the currents, the log jams, and the snags could take someone's life in a moment. It was always smart to let the angry waters go by, taking the mud and cloudy out of the water, so they could see a bit while swimming and digging under the banks. The water wasn't clear yet. Therefore, it was time to go to school.

Most of Paul's friends were on the river just like him, clamming to make money in the hard times, which times it always was. Money could be made between sowing seeds and the harvesting of crops. His perusal of the schoolyard didn't show any friends, as he came into the building before class. His pals all showed up in time and they had news to catch up on during recess. When the bell rang to go outside, they went to the meet-up tree to catch up.

"My dad showed me this from a paper he got one time when he finally told me how dangerous the work we'uns are doing," Paul said to his friends. "He told me after I been in the river since I was six—all of about four years. Let me read it. It says—" and he read from the newspaper:

> *A French girl, sixteen years old, was caught by her long hair in a revolving shaft at a button factory in Kankakee, Illinois, the other day, and the left side of her head was completely scalped. A severe concussion of the brain was also sustained. Her condition was considered critical.*

"That was from the Jasper Weekly Courier, 1874," Paul concluded, adding, "I'm real glad we don't have to work in one of those factories." He turned to look at the others and they were all wide-eyed.

"Can you imagine seein' that happen—and with her still a-screaming all the way around and around." Jed started grinning and threw his arms around, making fun, pretending he was caught up in the machine, grabbing his hair and falling on the ground. The others backed up to give him some room to really act it up.

Tillford and Arnie jumped up and joined in, acting like they were trying to stop him from spinning around. One of them pointed to the ground and yelled, "There goes his guts, Yiiii! Get back!" And they laughed it up good. Doofus stood there watching.

It looked gruesome, all right. From a distance one of the schoolyard monitors had been watching the goings on and came over because it looked like a fight had broken out. All the dust flying up and the yelling got someone to put a brow on and investigate. They caught Mr. Spellman, the principal, from the corners of their eyes and they were mostly back on their feet by the time he approached. They were hesitant about whether to stay or to run.

After explanations were given for the frolic and they showed Mr. Spellman the clipping, he read it, and then looked up and said, "Well, well, what if that were one of you? Would you laugh at them?" He gazed into each of their faces and they suddenly lost their sense of humor.

"Enough for today, recess is over. Let's head back in."

Having a week of school under my belt was a pretty good feeling, Paul thought on the way home. *I ought to be able to put in a couple more years, here and there. Fourth grade now, then two more, I ought to be ready to get on my own. Sometime after that, maybe a feed store. I'll find a way to get through this life for me and mom, without being beat on all the time and her, too. He can just go to the Devil.*

Going down the road deep in thought, he walked by a bank of the White River on his way to the cut-off he always took through the wood's trails and pastures to get home faster. Noticing a tin can on the path, he tried to remember if that was the can he used to carry worms the last time he fished on this side of the hills.

Deep in thought, he wasn't sure if he heard someone yelling at the river. He glanced over and noticed the water was still too high for clamming and so he continued to kick the can down the road and then cut into the woods at the trail and headed home. He was trying to not think about his mean old dad as he gave the can one final big angry kick and turned in.

What am I going to have to do today, what am I going to miss, and what am I going to get a smack over today? God, does this never end? Still in thought, Paul questioned himself. *Why am I trying to cut through the woods to get home faster? That's stupid. The work will still be there and rushing to get another knock in the head makes no sense. Why don't your dreams never come true? Mine don't. Why make 'em? Except the one I woke up with this morning.*

Chapter 2

Lemuel was at his bedside giving Paul his list of things that needed to be done, plus Lemuel's work he would need to do, as he and Paul's mother, Iletta, were headed away for a few days to take care of some trading. A sudden whack with a hoe handle from Lemuel let Paul know his father was finished giving out his list. It was up to Paul to have it done, without fail.

"Get up now and get a move on." And then his parents left.

Paul watched the buckboard go over the rise at the end of the field and went to the barn and started throwing hay down to fill the troughs before his parents returned and needed to feed the horse. Not noticing at first, Paul heard a horse and wagon on the road and figured they returned for something they forgot, so he kept on forking hay. The barn door swung open and two heads popped through, their grinning faces yelling his name. It was his friends, Tillford and Arnie.

"Hey in here, what ya' doing? We come to get you to go fishing. The river's gone down some and we finished chores early."

"Wow, boys, I just started mine. Where is everyone else, 'sides?"

"We'll help you, won't we Arnie? Go ask your mom or dad if you can go, especially since we're helping. That ought to be good for something."

"They ain't here. They just left and said they'd be gone for a couple of days. Ha, ain't nobody around! Where's everybody else?"

"Jed went down to Doofus's place to help Doofus look for his sister. She's been missing since school got out four days ago. Everybody over there is pretty worried. She's probably strayed over to her Aunt's house, is where they really think she is. She gets girl sickness sometimes and then probably stayed over. Doofus said she was coming into her flower anyway."

The boys threw hay, mucked out the stalls, filled the water trough, and picked okra. Then the three of them dug around for some quick night crawlers, got into Tillford's wagon, and left for the river.

"I know a place I've been checking out and I got it marked with a rusted condensed milk tin can on the road over by those fields on the other side. Go this way," Paul said as he pointed the way. "Back in this little elbow the current falls off and gets real slack. That's where some big old cats ought to be."

All baited up and lines dropped, the boys got bites and a couple of two or three-pound cats for the stringers. Tillford caught a five-pounder, they guessed, and they had a hard time fighting it before it was landed. Tillford whooped.

"Now is the time for me to catch ole Grandpa Whiskers," Tillford declared. He baited a big treble hook with three big crawlers and made a big bait ball and sunk it next to a barbed wire fence post lying down in the water. He watched it from where they were sitting on the ground and waited for it to produce. They waited. No movement.

With expectations running high, they were all watching that line and paid scarce attention to their other lines, as they waited for the big pay-off.

"Don't go messing with it and scare Grandpa off. Wait till

he's got it in his mouth and moves it good, before you strike. My uncle told me that much."

The line moved. All three saw it at the same time and slid down the bank, easing their way to the line. When it started to really move and pull tight, Tillford pulled hard with both hands and the hook set, big time—and then nothing. The hook didn't come back, so it was in there, still. It was heavy but not fighting much. Then Paul noticed that when Tillford really put a strain on it, the barbed wire fence post moved, too.

"Oh my God, we are snagged on something," he yelled. "Quick, we gotta do something, we could lose this fish."

"Keep the line tight. If the line don't break, we can get him out. We'll just take our time and unhook the snag, easy like," Arnie suggested. "Let's settle down, we got him!"

Searching around up and down the riverbank, they all looked for the right kind of stick to poke down into the water and free the river monster. They began jabbing into the water to see where everything was located and made a mental picture of the puzzle, showing what they had learned from fishing this river over the years.

"It's not moving much, guys." Tillford observed.

"Oh, don't worry. With ones this big, they may not know they're really hooked, yet."

"It'll happen soon, so get ready."

With slow and gentle movements, they cleared some of the small brush and a few sinker logs out of the way. It was time to commit to pulling the fish up onto the bank and they got ready.

"Ready—and slowly, let's put some strain on this thing."

As they pulled, something let go below and their catch started to pull up much easier. Instead of a big catfish, however, a girl's dress came up with a bloated, swollen, bluish face attached. The boys were nauseated, especially when they realized it was

Doofus's sister, Ina Fay. She was tangled in the barbed wire fence. She had drowned and had been in the water for several days.

The three of them stood there and stared at the water. *There can't be any more bad than being dead, somehow, and the next thing is to see dead and be right there next to it,* Paul thought.

"What are we gonna do, what are we gonna say about all this to the Laws, guys?" Arnie said, with a bit of a quiver in his voice.

"We don't do nothing. Tillford, you need to take the buggy into town and get the sheriff out here, so's they can see we done nothing but found it—I mean her—or—" Paul said.

The perplexity of it all, the death and everything about this scene was a little bit scary, since most people who died and passed on were taken away, or covered up so you didn't see them anymore, a hastening to the grave sort of thing. That was these boys' experience with death until now—the conjuring up of Bible verses and hearing people speak in strange ways. The mystery that surrounded these events or the causes of it were what they were familiar with. It was a time of speaking in "Church talk."

"Man. I already know that my dad is gonna make something bad out of this and I'll get a whooping from this, I just know." Paul said.

"No, you won't. It weren't our fault none. All we were doing was fishing and she just floated by, that's all." said Arnie. "That's all."

"You don't know him. He'll find a way to blame me for it. He's always twisting things his way and then it's me that gets it. He's especially bad when he's into the 'shine, Arnie."

After Tillford left to get help, Paul and Arnie tried to figure out what to do until the sheriff arrived. They couldn't leave the body now that they were attached to it in some ways. Sitting in the tall grass in the sun didn't make any sense, either. Sitting in the shade was a joint resolution they made and so they went back to the stand of sycamores growing along the riverbank to wait. And wait. Conversation was a bit sparse from then on, into late in the day. Finally, Arnie spoke.

"So, I'm guessing that Tillford will be awhile getting back and my folks will be a wondering about me. Heck, they may be sending out people trying to find me. It might come to me getting a caning next." He laughed slightly. "If we're going to have to stay here, you reckon we might need to find some food of sorts?"

"Well, it's gonna get dark anyway. Maybe we ought to think about it, and some light, I suppose. I got an idea. I can get over the hill, yonder, and go to my place and get us some grub and bring back a lantern, so's we can see tonight. It'll surely be dark before they get back and they'll need to see."

"Well, we should get going, then. Daylight is a wasting."

"What? Wait—you'll have to stay with the body—I mean Ina Fay—while I go to the barn and get us food and a lantern. You can do that, right? I won't be away maybe an hour or so, two at the most."

Paul saw that Arnie was uncomfortable with the prospect of staying next to a dead body, even if it was Ina Fay. But someone needed to go for food and light, and Paul's house was the closest. And someone needed to stay with the body, the dead body which was not even covered up with something. The eyes stayed open and they stared into nowhere and never blinked.

They decided that she had to come out of the water. They just couldn't leave her in the water with just her head sticking out. That was twice gruesome. Being all in the water to her neck gave the appearance that she was still in a mighty struggle to hang onto life and she needed help. They knew her and they were obliged. Being down to her neck in the water would expose her body to start dissolving, which was a new horror they didn't want to fathom or to visualize. Pockets of air in her dress floated about her corpse and kept her dress on the surface of the water surrounding her.

She had to come out. There were things in the black depths of the water, they suspected and envisioned, that ate things that were tossed into the water and devoured in macabre rituals.

It was going to involve smelling. All things smelled after they died and they didn't want that ghastly exposure, where that odor would spread into their noses and go deeper in the body and invade their lungs. It might harbor malevolence and attach itself inside and work on your insides and hasten your own demise.

"Oh, Jesus! She's heavy and won't move."

They had to then lay Ina Fay's body back down on the riverbank. A combination of factors—the slope of the ground, the wetting of the grasses by the dripping water from her body, and their awkward movements, combined with the entanglement in the barbed wire fence—caused their uncoordinated efforts to drop her on the sloped bank, losing their footing as the tension from the barbed wire fence slid her back down the bank and almost put into the river, once more. They were horrified.

Anything that Paul said in assurances was not received with a grain of comfort. For the rest of their lives, it was an experience that would stay with the three boys always. In re-telling the story afterwards, Arnie was close to declaring himself a victim, as well.

The lantern light cast an eerie intruding presence as Paul came back down the road to the tin can and turned into the path that led to the river. Years ago, a large sycamore had lost its footing amidst the bank rocks and fell over the river and was now used by folks as a natural crossing. Paul searched around for Arnie and didn't find him easily. Until he called out, Paul was suspecting that Arnie may have run from the ghosts and headed home at a trot.

Casting the light about and calling, Paul noticed some movement, something all balled up in the large branches of tree, right over his head. It was Arnie, still half-asleep but coming awake with the calling and the lantern light on him.

"Arnie, what in the world are you doing way up there? Come on down, I got some food. Why are you up there, anyway?"

Climbing down and picking his way slowly, Arnie replied, "I was about half asleep and I thought the water was a rising again. I was afraid that Ina Fay would float up and come down the river and get me, so's I climbed up this tree to be safe until you came back. I guess I went back to sleep. Then, I thought I heard someone or something walking around in the woods, rustling like, so I thought I might be safer out of the way."

Arnie was obviously a bit embarrassed about his lack of bravery, but Paul knew enough not to comment on it.

"Well, come get some bread and I found a jar of figs, too."

As they ate the food in the lantern light, they speculated about the events and what was taking so long for someone to come and take over. It must have been well past midnight and it was a moonless night. Soon, Paul and Arnie heard what they thought were footsteps and someone walking about, barely out of lantern light, so they hung it high on a branch and waited. The imaginations of the young boys at night, stressed with the addition of a dead girl's body nearby, stretched their emotions and senses almost to the breaking point.

Paul was the first to awaken the next morning and look around. The lantern was out, and he heard a wagon coming up the road and someone talking. Arnie was awake and stood up and waved to the wagon as they came in. It was Tillford and his dad in the wagon, with another man and the sheriff and the doctor on their mounts following. As they came closer, the folks in the wagon stopped talking and stared at them. The sheriff came around the wagon and headed over to the riverbank and dismounted. The stranger in the wagon started towards the river and the doctor told him to wait a moment and let the sheriff get the first look.

Arnie and Paul figured out the strange man was Ina Fay's father.

As they stood there watching what was going on, another buggy and another horse rider came up the road and joined the crowd that was now gathered. It was Ina Fay's kin and they were all falling apart, crying and wailing. The sheriff came back to their wagon and pulled the doctor and the dead girl's father over to the side for a private talk.

Tillford joined his buddies to catch up and talk among themselves in hushed words as they watched everybody play out their parts in this tragedy. The three boys felt the burden of responsibility beginning to lift from their shoulders. They were now bystanders.

The sheriff pulled the three of them off to the side to talk with them and in a way, let them know that they were heroes for taking on such duties. He told them the family would be grateful they had found their daughter, even under these circumstances. And then another wagon came in.

As the conversation between the boys and the sheriff concluded, Paul looked up and saw his father approaching everybody in a stomp. His brow was furrowed, and he was already directing his anger at his son, before knowing anything about anything.

"Paul! What have you done? I think you and me—"

Paul started towards his father to explain what had happened, and as he got to him, Lemuel put his hand on Paul's chest and pushed him away, almost making him fall to the ground, before turning to the sheriff to speak. The sheriff saw this and locked eye to eye with Lemuel for a flash. Lemuel stopped dead in his tracks, as if he had hit a stone wall.

"What went on here, Lemuel, is that one of your son's school friends has had an accident and has drowned in the river. These boys found Ina Fay and stayed with her till we could round up her kin to get them here, which was a very honorable thing, and you should be proud of him and his friends."

Lemuel stood there, frozen in his tracks beside the sheriff, naked to the world. *He can smell the moonshine I been a sipping,* Lemuel feared. Without even a tip of his hat by way of condolence to Ina Fay's family, he pushed his wife and son along to the wagon. The sheriff already suspected Lemuel had been at the jug.

"Get in the back, and don't disturb nothing."

Paul noticed a bunch of copper pipes, some tin, and a wash kettle under a tarp as he got in. It was strange stuff to be hauling home, Paul figured.

Chapter 3

The screen door to the spring porch was wide open when they pulled up, and a chicken was standing in the middle of the room, drawing more attention to the situation.

Pulling the wagon out to the barn, Paul opened the door and Lemuel pulled inside and had Paul unload his collection of pipes, metal, and two coils. Paul stayed in the barn to unharness the horse, feed him, and brush him before coming inside.

Paul knew it would be an interrogation as to what happened—*Why I was involved, and why was the house wide open? Why didn't I do chores?* He was right, but once inside the house, he escaped getting hit or slapped. Lemuel was not happy about him sneaking off to go fishing when he had work to do at home.

"Did you catch any fish? Where are they, then?"

Paul told him about them catching a few fish, "We didn't think about fish after we found Ina Fay. We thought maybe they were tainted." Paul said.

"How so?" Lemuel wanted to know.

"We caught them right where she was tangled in the barbed wire."

"I didn't hear the sheriff, or nobody say she'd been chewed on, now did we? Sounds like you could go get them when you come back from clamming tomorrow. Right? It's food for us.

How'd she go off and get herself drowned, anyway?"

"After we'uns were let out of school last week, they figured that because the water was down a bit, she took a short cut and tried to go across that big sycamore log that was laid over the river. She must have slipped on that wet log and was carried downstream by the current and got all caught up in that section of barbed wire fencing and drowned. The sheriff said she was mighty tangled in it, so she must have struggled a bit before she gave out and, uh, succumbed."

"Succumbed? She drownded." He chuckled, "and tomorrow you're going back to the river and get to digging. The water has moved lots of sand and gravel around, so you might as well get ahead of it and get some good pickings. School will wait. This is too much to pass up."

"Maybe there'll be a funeral. I was going to see about it tomorrow when I go to school. It was Doofus's sister—"

"Well, you're past that now, son. You'uns are the ones that found her, and you let them say their good-byes. That's how it is. Life is tough. You'll learn about that when you're older. That's how it is. Get your chores going and get to bed. You get on that river at first light? You hear me?"

And with that, Paul went to the barn and found something to do. It helped get him through the days, to have something to do with his thoughts. He missed school, he missed his friends, and missed a kind word, here and there. It was a comfort to hear the sheriff give him and his buddies a nod about staying with Ina Fay. That was nice. Too bad his dad didn't hear it. But even if he had heard it, Paul knew he wouldn't acknowledge it.

Paul crawled around on all fours in the White River for the next several days and late into the evenings, hunting clam shells and getting enough money to bring back to the house and keep his dad's unrelenting pressure off. He got more tired as the days went by.

The days came and blew a little cool air by him and he could feel the change coming. At this time of year, the water would stay warm and the cool air wouldn't be any bother. He would stay warm when he was submerged to his neck. It worked for a while, until the water itself started to cool down. He would work in a slack water, out of the main currents and stay warm. But when he entered the mainstream and current, then he could feel it. It would take the energy right out of him.

When his friends came clamming with him, to get warm they would get on the bluffs at the bends of the river and dig around in the caves along McBride's Bluff looking for treasure, but they wouldn't go too far in. They could get as dirty as they wanted, because when they returned to the river, they would wash off as they worked. All the boys had heard the stories of the Archer gang who used the caves as hideouts from the law, making moonshine, hiding stolen treasure, torturing—and even murdering—people. It was scary stuff for kids to hear about. Even scarier for the people who had lived through the robbing and killing sprees in real life. There was a hanging tree in the middle of town where the gang was said to have met their fate.

Cloudy days were particularly hard on Paul. He worked like a slave, with no letup in sight. He noticed that the scraps they had at the table were all there was. He also noticed that there were many sacks of sugar and dried corn in the barn, but not much else. How was this going to work?

Paul was an excellent swimmer at ten years old, even with his boots on, and he went to the White River daily looking for clam shells. Being tired didn't figure into Lemuel's plans of making a goodly sum selling shells to the button makers. The truth was Paul was worn out and cold from swimming down into deep pockets and holes to get clams. He was hungry most days—he hardly had enough to eat to help him keep warm. He shivered constantly and it wasn't until well after dark that he would warm up enough to stop the shakes. And the next day was no better, as each day started at first light somewhere on the river.

Food? Usually he toted a lard bucket with a biscuit or corn-bread stick with four or five spoons of sorghum molasses. Maybe a few butter beans would be tossed in, when his mother could sneak a few in, hiding it under the cornbread. Whatever it was, it would be covered in syrup, always in syrup. Even some turnip greens or a canning pear or a stick of rhubarb was flavored with syrup. He was grateful for whatever food he had, but he was dressed in torn and frayed clothing, nothing that adequately protected him from the weather.

It got to the point that Paul could hardly crawl up the riverbank, he was so cold and weak. He must have passed out there next to his shell pile, he didn't know. But when he awoke, his shells were gone, and it was pushing dark.

He had to go home. And with each heavy, dreadful step, he walked towards home like a convict going to the gallows. His ragged clothing dried as he walked. He could hardly keep awake to think about where he was going, much less think about what was surely waiting for him when he got there.

It was close to dark, and the coal oil lamp already lit, when he dragged his heavy boots across the front landing and entered the spring porch. Both parents looked up from their plates. Paul made a few steps and fell forward and collapsed on the divan.

Lemuel stood up. "What the hell is wrong with you? Where's your clam money?"

Paul laid there, trying to speak, knowing something bad was about to happen when he spoke. And when he did, he told them about getting robbed of his button shells.

At that, Lemuel flew into a rage, demanding that Paul "Go

cut a big switch log—you got it coming now," and pulled Paul upright and kicked him and slapped his head as he pushed him out of the house to go get the switch. Paul stumbled to his feet and made it off the porch and into the yard, heading to a bush for the switch. He caught himself against a tree trunk and stood there, blacking in and out and trying not to fall, waiting for a blow to come to him at any moment.

Lemuel came at him, "You ain't got no proper switch, boy," and cuffed him on the side of his head and drove him to the ground saying, "I'll pick out one for you and show you about misbehaving. You just let someone come up to you and take your shells without a fight? Damn boy, you just got the weaks, that's what I think. This is gonna hurt me more than it does you."

He kicked Paul towards the house, saying, "Get in there and I'll deal with you proper like and I'll find out what's going on in town and who got your shells. Yes sir, I'll deal with you proper like." And he turned and said to Iletta, "I'm leaving to find out who's got our money and Paul better be here when I get back." He turned and went to the barn, harnessed up the horse and buggy, and left for town.

Paul hardly moved from where he had collapsed after being kicked. He motioned to Iletta to help him on to the spring porch and into the kitchen. He collapsed on the divan and didn't move, shaking and shivering until he fell into a deep sleep. His mother covered him with a blanket.

Iletta was crushed by her own feelings of weakness and cowered at the edge of the kerosene lantern's smoky light. She sat in the corner, waiting for Lemuel's return and his wrath. She was like a trapped mouse, with no hole for escape.

It was times like these, in the rough spots, she would tell herself that somehow she would find the strength from some-where to challenge Lemuel for his rough treatment of their son and of her, which usually ended in verbal and physical assault on both of them.

At such times, she felt her stomach twist into knots and the pain drove her to try and erase what predictions she would think would happen and the bad outcomes. The choices were not good. She could still her mind and drift into aimless nothingness, but the pain that began in her side always persisted by then. She didn't know if it was something mental or a real physical ailment. At some time, she might ask the doctor about it, but it was unlikely because she seldom went to the doctor. It cost money, which they constantly didn't have, but she kept the slim possibility it would come about. If she were forced to tell him, she was always fretting about it and decided to think it could be real instead of imagined. Once the pain got going, leaving her gasping, she decided to tell the doctor that it felt like dripping rain hitting an extremely hot skillet.

During the next several hours, Iletta stayed by the divan and tended to Paul as she fell in and out of her own sleep. Paul stopped shaking and didn't move from where he fell into bed. His temperature was now very high, and she suspected he had pneumonia. Her fretting was useless. She heard the horse and wagon coming up the road.

In the hollow darkness, Lemuel was heard shouting and cursing at the ungrateful animal he burdened and left him in full harness as he headed to the house. She could hear his slurred speech and surmised he had found moonshine in town. The level of inebriation determined the level of conflict that would follow.

Iletta kept the lantern low so Lemuel could not see well in the dim light. That, coupled with a full load of moonshine in him, meant that he was easier to control.

Lemuel entered but stopped in the doorway to adjust his eyesight and leaned against the door frame to steady himself. He held a black buggy whip in his hand. With a surprisingly quick move, he threw the blanket that covered Paul to the floor. Even as Iletta screamed at him and came from the corner, Lemuel began whipping Paul as he slept, greasing the air with his bile.

The first several blows to Paul's chest, legs, and face fell on an unresponsive body. Lemuel was visibly shocked that Paul didn't move at the assault. Iletta pushed him away and shielded Paul, covering him back up with the blanket. She was ready to take whatever came, as she had done so many times, but he stopped in disbelief and staggered to a chair and immediately passed out. They were spared from an increasing barrage of assaults that night.

With calm returned, Paul's mother examined him and wept at seeing the welts on Paul's chest and face when she turned up the lantern to inspect him. Paul still didn't move after the assault and his breathing became slower and shallow. She feared he was slipping away and decided to take him in the wagon with her and make her way through the dark to town to get help. She knew Lemuel would not wake up for hours and if he woke before that, she had the horse and wagon and he would have to walk to town, which would cool him down, hopefully.

The doctor lived on the road towards town and they reached him within two hours.

"What the hell happened to him?" was the first thing the doctor said when he saw Paul's body uncovered. It was daylight when they arrived, and Paul was still in the wagon when the doctor saw him. Iletta explained what had led to the beating.

"I don't cotton to seeing this. This is excessive and I'll get involved if I need to." After looking Paul over and making him comfortable, he told Iletta, "I'm going for the sheriff to have a talk and you stay here. Paul can't be moved yet, so stay put. No. I won't hear any of your pleadings, so, just hold it, ma'am, if you will."

With a furrowed brow, he left for the sheriff's office. The sheriff was a strong-headed man in his own right and not apt to suffer fools and belligerents. He and the doctor were cut from the same bolt of cloth.

It was a Saturday, a day when folks from the surrounding farms came into town to do their shopping and exchange gossip. Rural folks were marginalized by isolation and poverty. Even though Shoals was a town, it was a very isolated community and the population fluctuated insignificantly over the years. Some folks came from Kentucky and settled around this area to find land to buy and work, harvest timber, and find opportunities that didn't exist on the other side of the Ohio River. Some groups of colored folks came across before, during, and after the Civil War to escape the oppression, as Kentucky had been a slave state and Indiana had not. They had a better go of it on the Indiana side than they did living as slaves some sixty miles to the south. They had become an accepted part of the landscape in the Shoals area.

Still, fifty years later was hardly enough time to cool many people's blood and prejudices, and certainly not Lemuel's and others' who had his way of thinking. The trouble was, the War was over, and people like Lemuel didn't have anybody left to fight, so that bitterness spilled out onto those around him, friends, or family. Not being old enough to wear the uniform of the Greys when he grew up in Kentucky, he absorbed the bitterness and hatred of loss from those around him. He was deemed a failure as a boy because he didn't fight, and a failure as a man who had demonstrated no bravery. And so, he took out his anger on his wife and son and tested his son's mettle with brutality and vengeance. Lemuel painted everyone with a wide brush dipped in moonshine.

The doctor and the sheriff rode back into the doctor's office together and the doctor saw Paul was very weak, but awake. Questions were asked and reluctant responses given. Iletta and Paul had no idea what would come of this but expected that it would result in more trouble.

Once the matter at hand was determined, the doctor drove the buckboard with Iletta beside him and Paul in the back, as the sheriff followed with the doctor's horse for their ride back home.

The noise of the steel wagon wheels hitting the stones in the ruts on the way up the road to the house awoke Lemuel from his sleep in the porch swing. Prepared or not, he was confused and surprised to see such a group in front of his house. He moved off the porch to the front yard and pulled his suspenders up. He girded his belt one more notch tighter, in preparation for he didn't quite know what. The doctor broke the silence first as he looked at Lemuel's wife and son sitting next to him. The sheriff dismounted and tied his horse to a wagon wheel. He was holstered up.

"I'm bringing back your family to you, Lemuel, and today we're going to talk with you. Then the doc and I will leave, and you and I will go about our separate business. Do you agree, sir?"

Lemuel was stunned, as if he were about to be hung. "Yes sir, sir."

"The doc has attended to your son that came in. He was in pretty bad shape besides coming in with a full-blown case of the pneumonia. He was horsewhipped while he was unconscious. Is that true? And your wife gets a caning, too. Is that true?"

"Well, I should explain that I didn't intend to seriously hurt—"

"Lem, I know and seen lots of ways, with the man as head of the house and his domain over it. In my Bible, however, the scripture says, 'If you spare the rod you spoil the child,' and I get that. In this world and the next, 'There will be a reckoning and yee shall not know the day on which it comes.' Are you right to that understanding? If so, we—the sheriff and I—want that to be in your thoughts, Lemuel Gulliver Chandler, and all your family, too, that the excesses of your application of the rod needs to change. It will change. Beating your son while he's unconscious with the pneumonia and then wailing on your dear Iletta, the mother of the child, is now over. Period!"

Lemuel nodded.

"An apology would be a nice thing about now. Lemuel?"

Lemuel looked at the doctor and the sheriff and in a moment of contrition, he took off his hat and held it as he told them he was sorry.

With that, the sheriff and the doctor mounted up, tipped their hats to the group, and rode away. Lemuel turned and looked at his family with a blank stare, replaced his hat, and walked into the barn to spend the night.

Once inside the house, Iletta cleaned off a place on the divan for Paul where she could watch him throughout the night.

"I know you're having a tough go of it, son. It'll get better," she reassured him, "but I can't tell you when that will be. I'll pray on it with you, anytime you want to. You should know that. Can I get you a little vinegar water to sip on? It might help clear you up a might."

"Thanks, momma. I need to rest a little and do some think-ing about things. You know, he's getting worse and worse. We ought to think about things. You know, when I get older, I'll—"

With a quick move, Iletta put her finger to her lips, essen-tially telling Paul to keep quiet and not discuss anything, as it was the wrong time for such as that. Paul dully caught on and rolled over to his side. She blanketed him and then went to the kitchen and got a pie tin and put beans on it and two cornbread sticks. She carried it to the barn where she saw Lemuel at the other end, digging into his metal pile.

Sitting down the plate of beans, she said nothing and left to go back into the house. Lemuel glanced over as she turned away, missing eye contact and said nothing. No attempt at reconciliation was made. That was how he would always be.

She glanced back at him and thought, *Let the dead bury the dead.*

Chapter 4

The first night on the divan was restful. Iletta mentioned to Paul that he had night sweats and his only duty was to rest for the day until he got well. His dad would do his chores until he could get them done himself.

"Your dad already agreed. No need to go fretting about it. He agreed this morning when he came inside to eat breakfast at dawn."

Paul looked apprehensive and so she said, "I assure you, son, it will be okay." And with that, Paul went back to the divan and laid back down and got more sleep. As he half dozed, he had thoughts of the never-ending burdens of working around the farm, his mother's treatment and abuse, and his own physical abuse and dangers when he tried to protect her. He needed to think about things, for his mom's and his sake.

I know mom is trying to shield me so I can become strong, but how do we survive? I've seen too much abuse and punches to her, and she can't survive much more, the way he fights her down. She gives me back so much every day and never gives up on me. How long will it take for me to grow big enough to beat him? I don't want him to hurt her anymore. Why is he hurting us?

And then Paul fell into a fitful sleep.

Paul knew what was about to happen when his parents got home, after a few days gone, with the back of the wagon full of pipes. Coils and kettles were the giveaway when he saw them in the back of the wagon all covered up. It was the same when he had arrived at the river, at the drowning. Lucky for Lemuel, the sheriff hadn't noticed anything.

Since the end of the Civil War, on both sides of the Mason-Dixon Line, war survivors were sent home and they were pretty much on their own. The burden was on their families to take care of any disabilities they might have. These facts of history were unknown to Paul, and yet they had a huge impact on his life. In most instances, the town a soldier came from had the responsibility of caring for him.

In town after town after the war, the town square was the gathering point for the survivors and the disabled. Those survivors, however, were damaged and were there as a daily reminder of the terrible tragedies that had occurred and served as a display in courage, resolve, and resentment. Many of the damaged soldiers displayed outward signs of injury. Some did not. Lemuel's father was one of the ones whose injuries were mostly internal—psychological injuries and psychological scars.

The Indiana state government began as soon as was practicable to address the needs of its returning Civil War veterans. The Evansville State Hospital was built to address those with serious emotional disturbances. Abnormal behavior and low levels of economic productivity, as well as substance abuse disorders, were regarded as a burden on society. Involuntary commitment could be sought by a friend, relative, or law enforcement. No one was denied admission because of lack of financial resources.

October 30, 1890, the hospital admitted the first two

patients. Not long after that, Lemuel's father became another of many. Paul would soon learn about this hospital from the teachers at his school. There would be a day of reckoning coming.

Paul found resuming chores was a physical and mental challenge for him, once he got back to walking about, carrying firewood, and hauling stones from the fields. Paul waited for an outburst from Lemuel that would renew his suffering. Maybe the "talking to" he got from the sheriff a month ago had worked. Paul was doubtful and didn't let his guard down.

Now able to go back to school for a while, he also decided to sneak away and go play football at a schoolmate's farm and then sneak back home. If he was caught out too late, he would bring wrath down on himself, he knew. He skipped on home, taking a new way back. Coming over a ridge on a cow path, Paul saw something in the grass ahead of him and started to sneak up on whatever it was. A quick jump through the tall grass put Paul right in front of a large boar coon headed into a "snake log."

His dad had showed him that snake logs had signs around them that foretold if the log had snakes in it. Paul half-believed it but didn't want to take the chance to find out or not if it was true. The coon was in the hollow.

Paul was hesitant. Was it a real snake log? He momentarily wrestled with himself as to what to do, then sharpened a stick and went after the coon, pinning it inside the open-ended log, then clubbed it and pulled out the prize. He headed on home, proud of himself for being brave and being able to bring home some good eats.

Lemuel was standing at the edge of the porch with an ax handle in his hand and Paul knew it was going to be bad. Seeing

Paul approaching the house from the woods, Lemuel rose from his stool and slapped the handle into his palm in anticipation of using it on Paul. Iletta came from the spring porch, saw what Lemuel had in store for Paul, and then saw the big coon Paul was carrying. With a cheerful yell she said, "Well, hello the house!" to Paul as she ran over to him. "That's an awful big critter you got there, son!" She turned to the porch. "Look Lemuel, look what Paul has brought for supper."

"Pretty good, son."

That evening, the three of them sat down to fried coon. Each ate a whole sweet potato and drank tea, even sweetening it with sugar. There seemed to have been a truce of sorts made between all of them that day.

Back to a life of toil, Paul wondered what in the world was next. He watched Lemuel go to the barn and work, leaving more and more things for Paul and Iletta to do. Crops in the field couldn't wait. If rain was threatening, you got them in. If they got wet, then they got mildew and rotted and spoiled. They had to work long into the evening and many hours into the night to keep up. They carried candle lanterns with them so they could see to work. The smell of corn mash in the barn drifted across the fields on many a night. Paul thought about when the sheriff stood in their yard.

Lemuel forced Paul to go back to the clamming business. The water was already cool, and he began to feel weaker by the day. He was off from school more and more these days.

"The bean crop looks good and we'll get a little money for the first time in a while," Lemuel said at the table. "You keep getting those clam shells and we'll do fine."

"I'm not finding much where I'm working, and the water is cold already."

"Let me be the judge of that. A little longer and things will be better. Keep going and I'll tell you when it's time. You're twelve years old, for Christ sake."

"You need to know, Lemuel, that Paul and I have a lot of beans to get in here, very soon," Iletta interjected. "I'll need him to work with me. You know, if we get rain and these beans get wet, we will be in for it."

Lemuel tinkered in his barn throughout the night, cooking mash. He was almost ready to make a run. This was his big money machine, he was sure, and he was ready to cash in. Family be damned.

The next morning was overcast. Paul walked to the river, his mom went to the fields and started picking beans, and Lemuel kept cooking corn mash. The first trickles of moonshine condensed off the coils. Instead of throwing it away, he mixed it back in.

It was overcast and the wind had a definite chill in it. Lemuel didn't notice, as he was in the cozy barn, next to a fire. Paul had gone down to the river though he didn't feel well, so he sat on the bank waiting for his queasy stomach to settle down. He didn't want to get wet. He felt a chill. It started to rain, and the wind started up and blew cold air. Paul headed home, got soaked, and by the time he made the front pasture, he was shivering. A wheeze was creeping into his lungs.

"Dang it, I think I got the pneumonia again."

Iletta came from the lower pasture with half a sack of dried beans. The rain that followed Paul came closer to the house but was not yet in the bean fields. It was going to be touch and go.

"I need you Paul. I'm sorry but we're to be in a jam if I don't get these beans." She watched Paul shaking and knew what was happening, but he went to help her anyway. Her side had that twinge.

As he worked the beans, Paul thought of Mrs. Olsham, his

teacher, who spoke to the kids on a personal level. Of course, she knew about Paul and his friends finding her student, Ina Fay, drowned in the river. When he came back to school, she pulled him aside and spoke to him, offering words of comfort. Paul liked the way she talked with him instead of at him, and he listened hard. She was the source of the information about the state hospital and other things that he had wondered about. As in every small town, people talked about everyone and not much was ever secret. Mrs. Olsham had also heard about Lemuel's evil temper and the beatings Paul got from him.

"Often as not, Paul, things usually work their ways out. It might not always be the ways one wants it to work out, but solutions are usually all around. The tough part is in choosing, and wiser is usually the better way to choose. The simplest solution is usually the right one."

Paul tried to keep those thoughts in his head as he and his mom started in on a row of beans. The dark clouds gathered, and darker clouds were on the way. Lightning would split and streak across the sky and made no thunder. They worked at a fast pace to get the burlap sacks filled with beans. When the sacks were full, they left them on the ground and moved on to the next row. Looking back, they could see maybe two or three wagon loads of beans ready to be loaded and moved inside. The race to keep the beans dry was the next task to get done.

"Paul, go to the barn and get the horse and wagon hooked up and get them out here as fast as you can. We might make it." She had a sense of hope in her voice as she yelled.

Paul tried to run but nearly fell. His increasing weakness was evident. Entering the barn, the smell of corn liquor and burning hay filled the air. At the far end Paul saw a small blaze where the hay loft was catching fire and then saw Lemuel laying off to the side in a stall, passed out. Yelling for his mother to come help put out the fire, he ran to the horse and got the wagon hitched. Once the horse was safely away from the barn and tied, Paul ran back in. Iletta had managed to get the fire out. She was staring at Lemuel's besotted body. Paul couldn't help but wonder what they would have done if the barn had burned down with Lemuel in it.

They left Lemuel on the ground where he had passed out and went back to the task of getting bean sacks loaded into the wagon, and then into the barn, still fighting to beat the rain. So far, it had held and so far, they held to their task.

Though they accomplished their almost impossible goal, when it was all over, once again pneumonia gripped Paul, and once again he was bed-ridden. After Lemuel had sobered up enough to get into the house and come to the table, he began arguing with Iletta, who this time argued back. The farm was going to ruin, the fields were mostly fallow, Paul was being worked nearly to death, Lemuel was drinking constantly, and there was no money from crops, only money to buy sugar and corn to make liquor. It continued for hours. One of Paul's thoughts before he fell asleep that night was, *Does God tell lightning where to strike?* He was surprised at the boldness his mother showed in arguing with his father. He was proud of her. *Good for her,* he thought, smiling to himself.

Chapter 5

The whole gang was assembled at Jed's farm to play football, with a real football—Arnie, Tillford, Jed, Paul, and Doofus. The field was mowed, and the hay was in the barn. It was a cold morning, but it quickly warmed up. All the boys got sweaty, but for a change it was not by doing work and chores, but by having fun for the sake of a good time. But then, eventually everyone scattered back to their own farms and the drudgery of after-harvest work started up again.

Canning, skinning, and butchering animals, and filling the root cellars made long days and tired bodies at the end of those days. Fireplaces were readied and wood was chopped, cut, and split for the winter.

Lemuel was inside, had the fireplace lit, and was listening to the radio.

"He's spent long hours tuned in to the radio," Paul said to Iletta. "Since that time, he almost burned down the barn because his still caught the hayloft on fire, he seems to be more inward, mom."

"He worries me a little, too, son. He don't seem to be talking right. I can't put a finger on it."

They listened to his crystal radio and tried to follow the deliberations of the 1912 Anglo-French Naval Agreement and the discussions of who controlled Egypt, Morocco, West and Central Africa, Thailand, Madagascar, Vanuatu, and parts of Canada. It was too much to take in, and so removed from their own world. Lemuel stayed angry most of the time and moody and took it out on Iletta and Paul.

The next day, both parents left to drive the wagon to town to sell some of the dried beans Iletta and Paul had harvested. Paul talked to himself as they were leaving. *Now that I have a bit of time, I can get back to the Indian caves and this time go deep in and hide my button shell money I took such a beating for. For mom and me, this is money for us when he isn't around no more.* After stashing his clamshell money deep in the Indian cave, he joined his buddies again for another game of football.

Arnie, Paul, and Doofus made up their team and huddled up and talked about how they would run their plays. Doofus had to be the first to be chosen, *because of—you know,* they all agreed. Even as a three on two teams, the way they figured out to make it square was to have Doofus be the center for both teams. So, it worked out and after a period, Doofus chose someone from either team to be the next center and he joined that team and took their place. As far as these boys were concerned, it was all real football rules, and everyone got to play.

Both teams only ran about four different plays they had invented, and everyone figured out long ago what would be the next play because they had played each one so many times before. Today was going to be different. Arnie came up with a new play that was sure to win the big game by the end of the day. During a cool down period, Arnie explained how the play would go.

They tried it and it fell apart because Doofus hiked the ball way over Arnie's head. So, the next play, they changed positions, a move intended to confuse the opposing team. Doofus was to throw, and Paul was to run out to catch it at the end of the smooth part of the field.

Breaking huddle, Arnie whispered to Paul that he would throw it farther out—he always did.

"So, go longer past the smooth ground and turn around and the ball will be there."

They set, then hiked. Arnie blocked and Doofus threw long. Paul had to run out to catch it past the smooth ground and turn to locate the ball. He looked up, stepped on loose limestone rubble, tripped, and then fell on a limestone outcropping with the full impact on his right hip. The leg bone and broken hip snapped loudly, and they all heard it.

Paul lost consciousness for a moment. His air was gone, and when he came to, he struggled to catch a breath, and then screamed in pain and then in terror, because he felt he couldn't move. The fear in his eyes was frightening to the other boys. They were terrified seeing him down.

I'm paralyzed and I'm going to die, oh God. He blacked out again. When he came to, he was still on the ground and the pain had gone away. Both of Tillford's parents were there and they had wrapped him up in blankets. He heard one of them say, "He's in shock. Don't move him."

"What, oh what should we do?" Mrs. Tillford lamented to her husband.

"We have got to get him home and get him to his parents, Margie. I need some rags and a board to bind his legs together so we can get him in the wagon. You boys will have to help me."

Doofus was bawling, as was Margie. The rest of the boys were standing around, not knowing what to do. They had tears in their eyes and anxiety on their faces, as they tried to comprehend what had just happened.

"Is he going to be all right, momma? How bad is it, really?

Will he be all right and get better?"

The Tillfords made a big soft bed in the back of their wagon with hay and blankets and then everyone lifted Paul into the wagon as gently as they could. Every grimace Paul made was like daggers to the boys, who crowded around to steady Paul for the jarring trip home.

Later, Paul said to Tillford, "I remember going down the hill and on to my place, but the wagon ride wasn't too bad. I bet you'uns were scared out of your gourds, too, huh?"

Arnie wouldn't leave Paul's side throughout the whole ordeal. It was Paul who had helped him through that night on the riverbank when they found Ina Fay, and now it was his turn to save Paul, somehow. Once the wagon began to move forward and their apprehensions subsided somewhat, then they felt they could get him home. One by one they began to glance up at the road ahead and tried to identify any rough spots or bumps they might hit, advising Mr. Tillford accordingly.

The grownups were talking quietly among themselves and looked back at Paul to see if he was comfortable. The difficulty ahead for Paul, they knew, was not just on the road ahead. Till- ford began to describe to his parents what kind of family life Paul had and how his dad treated him.

"Dad, he's mean to Paul and strikes him a lot. He's going to be pretty sore when he finds out Paul's hurt his leg and all. He expects Paul to go to the White River and hunt for clam shells all the time, even when it's too cold. That's how he got sick and got pneumonia. I guess they need money bad."

"Shush now, Tillford," his mother admonished. "We all need money these days, as if 1912 is doing us any favors. Let's don't talk ill, especially now. Now is not the time. Your father and I are very aware of those things and hope the best for Paul, don't we Robert?"

Tillford looked at his mother with a question on his face as to how they knew anything at all about Paul and his family. He had never seen his parents ever talking to the Chandlers before. How did they know that?

Arnie propped Paul's head up a little, so he could look over the buckboard and up into the walnut trees and out over the fields he was used to walking through. The walnuts had no leaves now but still held walnuts. Paul wondered who would gather them this year.

The wooden gate across the road to Paul's house was pulled shut and it stayed shut mostly since the doctor and the sheriff had come out and had their Come to Jesus talk with Lemuel over the beatings he had given Paul.

"If it's locked, then he's gone. If not, someone is home."

"It's not, so's we're going in, Paul."

The wagon pulled up close to the porch and Mrs. Tillford called out, "Mrs. Chandler, are you home? Oh, Mrs. Chandler, it's Margie Tillford, we need you here. Iletta—Iletta—"

Iletta came from the barn with a hay fork in her hands and seeing a wagon full of people in front of the house, she started to run down the yard to them. She saw Mr. Tillford getting down from the wagon, putting his hat in his hand, a very ominous gesture.

"Iletta, there's been an accident and your Paul has been badly hurt. It happened up at—" and before she could finish, Iletta doubled up both of her fists and grabbed her chest as she got closer.

"Paul, where are you? What's happened?" She peered over the side of the buckboard and saw Paul laying in the hay, covered up. She tried to climb up and get into the wagon, but Margie held her back and said, "It's better if we take him out."

"What's happened to him? Paul, are you all right?" As they

took the blankets off, she saw her son practically hog-tied to some barn lumber, unable to move. Now, she started shaking and looked bewildered.

Mr. Tillford tried to explain, "What has happened was they were playing a game of football in the pasture and Paul fell onto an exposed seam of limestone, and it looks to me like he's broken his hip and maybe his leg. That's why his legs are tied together."

Iletta backed up a couple of steps and collapsed on the porch step to gather her wits. Margie put her arms around her. The boys were silent and fearful, not knowing what to do or say, waiting for cues from the adults.

Iletta thought to God, *So, what can Thou do for me, Dear Lord?*

"Mom, I need you," Paul called from the wagon and she went to his side. "It looks like I really messed things up. What kind of beating am I going to get now?"

His words were like a dagger through her heart. "With my body and my soul, I give you my word that he will not lay a hand on you ever again," Iletta responded. "Son, I will take care of you until you are well, and you can leave this place for good. This will pass. You must trust me on this."

Her voice was cracking as she spoke, but her strength and determination were fortified from hearing her own voice speak words of commitment and resolution. Gathering her resolve, she began to take over, mentally working out what needed to be done to protect Paul and shelter him through a slow and difficult recovery.

With both his legs bound and tied to the barn boards, the options of where to put him in the house were quite limited. The inner rooms of the old farmhouse wouldn't work. There was no way to maneuver around the small rooms and get him through the doorways. Even if the doorways were wide enough, the rooms were piled high with accumulated things that promised future usefulness—stacks of papers, crates of hand-me-down clothes, broken and used dishes, canning jars, and anything that could not stand to get wet. There were only pathways here and there through this accumulation. The spring porch seemed to be the only option.

The divan was pulled away from the wall and some of the clutter was restacked to other places or carried to another room. A shipping crate minus its lid, and a steel milk can were used to extend the supports to make a platform for Paul to be placed upon. It was November and already cold at night, with below freezing temperatures. Fortunately, the spring porch was on the leeward side of the house. It offered protection from the wind on most occasions.

"Iletta, you and Margie stand aside and let me and the boys get Paul into the porch. We'll be as gentle as these best friends can be, won't we boys?" And they rose to affirm their duty and their eternal friendship with their best friend, who now needed their help. Paul's expression had changed, and his face had the look of bewilderment on it. A veil of uncertainty settled over the gathering.

Getting Paul into the porch was a bit of touch and go, but it was a smooth transition and they placed him ever so gently on the divan.

"That's swell, fellas, I now have a new home," Paul said, as cheerfully as he could. "Hey, you can come over any time and we can eat some hay together." Paul pulled a piece of straw from under him and waved it, trying to be funny and lighten the mood.

Another wagon came up the road and they looked out and saw Lemuel getting off his wagon and coming into the house. No one wanted to take the lead in starting a conversation, as it would be a shock to Lemuel to see Paul strapped down to the barn boards. He entered the porch and looked at everyone with a tinge of suspicion. He had a drop of sweat on the end of his nose. He wiped it and then looked down and quickly surveyed the situation.

"Well, Paul, you must have done some kind of bad thing this time, boy, for them to tie you up and drag you back here. They caught you at something—"

"Mr. Chandler, please!" barked Margie. "He's been badly injured at our place and we fear he has broken bones. That's why he's tied down." Her tears began to fill her eyes, once again. Half of them were for the injured boy and half for the anger she felt at dealing with this despised and ignorant man. Her hands were shaking as she wiped away her tears with her handkerchief.

"You'll need to tend to him right away and get him a doctor, as he's not going to be able to be moved, sir," said Mr. Tillford.

"Oh, we'll see." said Lemuel with a note of dismissal in his voice.

"I've seen breaks like that before on cattle and on a horse. If he's moved about, he could be permanently damaged. He needs medical attention as soon as you can get the doctor out here."

"So, okay then, he'll get right good attention." And Lemuel wiped the sweat still on his face.

"Margie, get little Tillford and let's go. Boys, let's load up."

Margie gave Iletta another hug as she was leaving. "I'll come by in a week or so to check on you, okay? And Paul, I hope you get along well, and get well soon. God's Mercy."

"Amen."

Iletta came from inside the house with another blanket and another pillow for Paul and tried to figure out what else needed to be done. With Paul being confined to a screened-in porch, she knew he must be protected from the winter cold and kept dry. Extra blankets would be needed, and he would need a bed pan of sorts. Nature's call was to be anticipated. However, Paul was strapped down and couldn't move about. It would be tricky to figure out how to take care of all his needs.

Paul wasn't hungry for two or three days after the fall. Everything stopped and Nature didn't get things going until the third day, which was a painful and bloody event. Iletta realized that the waste products needed to be buried away from the house and not around the outhouse. She knew not to ask Lemuel to assist and so she got up on the fourth day and went away from the house with a pick and dug a furrow in the snow. The ground had not had a chance to become frozen and she did the digging. She thought that she better dig a second trench because when the ground froze for good, it would be a real problem.

As she dug the second hole, she thought about digging it six feet by three feet and envisioned she could put something in it like a body, but not Paul's. *God, if I had the strength.*

After the sixth day, Paul's hip area was bruised almost purple and swollen. He was laid on his back and when she examined him, she saw that he was developing bed sores. She chuckled to Paul and called them "board sores." That night she talked to Lemuel at the table inside. Paul couldn't hear what they were saying, as he had to snuggle under the heavy quilts to stay warm. But several days later, he heard Iletta say to Lemuel, "I've been working on Paul's hip and putting hot compresses on him and maybe I can see some of the swelling going down a bit. But Lemuel, we have got to get the doctor out here to look at Paul. He could be hurt real bad on the inside and we wouldn't know nothing."

"You just hold on, let Nature work on him some. That's what all God's creatures do in the wild, you know. The next time I get things loaded and pass through town, then we'll see. Anyway, what do you know about doctoring? You might be doing him too much harm as it is. You ever think about that, huh?"

"Well, I know this much. You can't keep him tied down all the time. He's got to get some kind of exercise to keep his strength up. I know that, and you do, too, even though you don't ever do nothing to help us. He's your son, too."

"Actually, I think he looks good, all tied down to that board." Lemuel chuckled a bit. "What do you know about doctoring anyway? You puttin' all kinds of poultices on and herbs and stuff, maybe thinking you're doin' something just to keep Paul guessing is all."

"I know more than you and you know that, too. When I was a kid, long before you come around, we had the Gypsies that would show up and camp down in the apple orchard and they would show us things, that's how. We learned from them how to solve all kinds of things, healing, and everything."

"Paul is going to learn from this here accident stunt he pulled. And I'm going to teach him a lesson on it, too." His face got a mean twist to it and he continued, "He disobeyed me and run off to that other farm. He missed chores and now I'm going to be stuck with doing his stuff and mine, too. Might teach him a lesson to obey what I say, won't it?"

She looked at him with daggers in her eyes and he shot back, "Like I said, the next time I get to town I can look the doctor up and see what I can find out. I don't want him coming out here and snooping around without me knowing he's coming. I'm not going to be blamed for his accident and have the sheriff out here, again. Get that clear."

The following week went by and Lemuel didn't go to town to see the doctor or even make a move to do so. Iletta was fretful and worried herself sick. She started to do the only thing left she hadn't tried and that was to slowly start moving Paul's leg a little. Nearly twenty days had passed by and she needed to try something. Without Lemuel's help getting Paul in and out of the wagon, she had nowhere to turn. Lemuel had them both trapped on the farm. These were low times.

"Mom, I've had my head stuck out and have been looking around. I looked out and seen him going out to the gate with a lock and chain in his hand. You don't suppose he has locked us in here, do you?"

"He better not. How are we going to know if anybody comes out this way if they can't get onto the place?"

"I've got an idea," Paul said. "We can get a bell. Anybody that wants to come visit will ring the bell and we'll know and can go let them in."

"He don't want the sheriff or the doctor coming 'round, that's why, son."

That night, lying in bed, Iletta had an idea. The next morning, she went to the barn and found a busted wagon wheel that had rotted felloes, but the flat steel tire rim was still good. She got a piece of bailing wire, a hammer, and rolled out the flat steel tire rim and headed down the roadway to the gate. Paul saw her rolling it away and wondered what she was doing, but his ears soon answered the question.

A wagon wheel rim hanging from the fence made a great bell when struck by the hammer and he heard his mom out there striking it again and again. It really rang good, Paul thought.

Iletta worked out most of the soreness over time that was in Paul's leg. The big worry came when she moved it up high, the bones in his leg would move around. Putting weight on it was very painful but he could manage with crutches, which his friends had made secretly with the help of Mr. Tillford. They brought them by one quiet and still morning.

Jed was the one who was going to sneak onto Paul's place and go through the barbed wire, but to everyone's surprise, the gate wasn't locked. Not only did they go in, but knowing that Lemuel wasn't on the place, they rang the tire ring many times before going through the gate. All of them were piled up and bundled in the buckboard as they drove up to the farmhouse. Paul was excited to see them all.

"A month has come and gone, and I could have died, and you wouldn't have known it till spring," Paul said, in mock anger.

"We brought you these. We made them ourselves—with a little help from Mr. Tillford."

Iletta was right there beside Paul and he looked at her, seeking permission, and she nodded and said, "Yes. So, in trying them, you'uns will have to give Paul a chance or two."

Turning to Mr. Tillford, she said, "He's been able to stand a bit using his barn board slat, but only for a bit. This is just what he needed. How swell, everybody."

Mr. Tillford responded, "The idea came from Mrs. Olsham at school and she sent him some books to read until spring gets here. She wants him to be able to come back to school then."

"We'll have to see. We'll just have to see."

Making talk, Mr. Tillford asked Iletta what the doctor had said about Paul's injuries and she looked into his eyes with a sense of profound sadness and replied, "He never was taken to see the doctor. I'm afraid at this point, it's too late. However, it was healed by the Good Lord's hand and that is how it will always be."

She looked back into Mr. Tillford's eyes and he reflected a stare of remorse and angst that unsettled his hopefulness. The unhappy news registered, and he looked away.

Chapter 6

It was a hard winter for the Chandlers, though they managed to get two pigs butchered and smoked and put up dozens and dozens of canned vegetables. Everyone around had a bad winter, too. It seemed the button shell business was in a slump and steady money from that kind of work depended pretty much on young folks and others who didn't have a strong connection to the land. Those who did had to spend necessary time repairing fences, repairing houses, and working on barns, or working in the ground once it thawed out. Collecting clam shells simply had to wait.

Lemuel realized, to his chagrin, that Paul would not ever be able to crawl on all fours in the mud under the banks and sandbars of the White River and gather button shells, ever again, and his disappointment melded to a stab of bitterness every time he thought about it. The more he looked upon the crippled boy, the more resentment he felt, and he soon just stopped looking at him when he talked to him to give him orders about what he wanted done. He started looking away when he ordered Paul about and didn't stare at him with his mean, wrinkled, and dirty face with gritted yellow teeth. Paul noticed, and was perplexed and felt it was just another step of a slow abandonment of any vestigial attachment of kinship.

The tin roof that was on the barn was old and reused from another farmer. It had been swapped for moonshine. Lemuel got some badly rusted tin sheets and the farmer got some bad headaches, but it worked out better for the other farmer than it did for Lemuel, because Lemuel had to slop on some roofing tar on several places of the tin. He put it up over the crib on top of an already poor and leaking roof. Spreading the tar very thinly to save money was costly in the end. The sun heated the tar, making it very soft and thin, so that it leaked into the seams in various spots. The rest of the beans that Iletta and Paul worked so hard at getting in, during the time they fought to keep the barn from burning up, got wet after the snows loaded the roof.

Iletta came into the house. "Paul, I smelled something out in the barn this morning I didn't like none."

"What was it?"

"That tin roof your dad put on is no good. It leaked and got into our beans and almost ruined the whole lot. I smelled something musty when I was getting some eggs and I went to looking. It was the beans. I'll get out there and get some for us to eat, some are still good, but we won't be selling any more beans this next spring."

"We got to do something to make it, mom. With me all busted up, and it don't look like I can get better, I am going to go and get me something."

"Now Paul, you don't have to be thinking about that kind of stuff. We got this place. We can work it and make out okay."

"We're not going to make it very far. We're having to live on half of what we used to and with him always in the barn and drunk all the time on corn liquor, it won't get no better."

They both paused to think about the truth that Paul had just spoken.

"You and me both know that some time's a coming that he'll

be a problem. We won't be able to fend him off or we'll have to fend for ourselves. It's clear like that now, mom, and you know it. I'm a cripple and I can't get away from him, neither."

The words coming from her son were a cut to Iletta's heart, bringing tears to her eyes. *His naivete is gone, but he's building a strong character and it will serve him well, from here on out. Amen, Lord, for answering my prayers.* They would still go down and sleep in a furrow of life once more if change didn't come.

"I'm good for lots of things. I need to go out there and find them. He's not going to stop me, and you're going to be able to count on me real soon, you just wait and see. I can hear you say this, right now, in my mind, 'Be a blessing to receive a blessing.' That's so, isn't it, mom?"

"Yes, it is, son." She hugged him in silence for a long moment or two. It was the holding that brought the healing to both of them. They felt renewed. Iletta saw and felt a new beginning coming for this young man who was emerging from the hard-scrabble ways of a struggling farm life, to an unknown future that might hold promise and a bit of luck. She saw him get up his gumption.

"We're going to have to talk about getting him into a hospital someday."

"But maybe not today, son."

Paul managed to get himself up and out the door, and down to the river to do a little fishing. He watched the bobber in the water, floating, and all his feelings of sadness and hurt came flooding into his mind. He saw another bobber in his mind's eye, the one that was floating on the water before snagging Ina Fay and rescuing her from a watery eternal resting place.

He calmed his stomach and resolved not to heave up the last bit of meal he'd had, to keep his thoughts in the present, and focus on the catfish he needed to catch in order to bring home something for dinner.

The steps up the bank and away from the river were a painfully different experience now because his hip had not healed correctly. And the crutches he had learned to use made him feel awkward. But perhaps this was the last punishment he must endure throughout his remaining lifetime. He was a cripple.

Chapter 7

~~~~~~~~~~~~~~~~

Starting out and taking the horse on trips around the county and beyond, Paul traveled north to Loogootee to see what he could find in the way of work. He could no longer work the farm, but he was somewhat optimistic that he could find something else that he could do. He needed just one break.

As Paul was sitting under a tree on the roadside eating a pear, an Amish wagon came by and he waved to the driver. The wagon went on ahead a bit and stopped, turned around, and came back down the dirt road and pulled up to the shade where Paul was sitting.

"Howdy, there," came from the wagon.

"Howdy, back. About all I got is some shade if you want to share some."

"You looking for anybody around here, can I help you?

"No thanks. I'm out looking for work. I just went through Loogootee and nothing I could bump into was going to be suitable. I'll keep looking. That's how I do it, though."

"Not really any extra hands around here. We got our own community we draw our workers from, but most times we can use an extra hand, here and there."

With that said, Paul rose up, using his one crutch to lean on, "You don't say."

The man in the wagon saw the crutch and paused for a moment, figuring, and then resumed. "How do you get on and off that horse, friend?"

Paul stood tall next to his horse and grabbed the horn and held his weight with that arm and lifted his good leg up and stepped on to the hand bar on his crutch that he leaned against the horse, and then grabbed his bad leg with his other hand and pulled it over the saddle.

"Like that, I suppose," feeling proud and confident about himself in front of others.

"A lot of us Amish have farms around Odon, up the road, and we could use a person like you to come and work with us. Right now, we're doing our mowing and will be raking up hay for bailing. If you can drive a four-up or not, we'll show you how, anyway, but we got lots laid down and dried, ready to bale or for the barn. Come with us, then. I'm Samuel, who might you be?"

"I'm Paul Chandler, sir."

"Yes sir, back. Follow me then. It's only a few more miles."

This day was a good day. Many more followed.

The four-up team Paul was put to work with were large, very stocky horses, much bigger than the one he rode. It took a bit of time over a couple of days to get the hang of how they moved. They weren't mean horses, but they were very, very strong. The first thing he had to learn was how to turn them and get the horses lined on another row. A few Amish men were always close by and when Paul got in a bind, there was someone to come over and get them straight and then give them back to Paul to continue on through the fields. These farms were big places to work and the whole family went at it, without a harsh word. They weren't unkind to each other and they were not unkind to their animals.

He was given a room with clean sheets and bedding and

good solid meals. Before the Amish family broke bread, they gave thanks. He had not been to a table with all giving thanks for quite a long time. After eating, no one lit up and smoked. Tobacco was not used, and neither was alcohol.

He was gratified and his thoughts lingered a bit before he slept and recognized a difference between the bottomland slime in the river and fertile farmland soil. One would stick and seal his pockets together and the other would fall away at the end of the plowing day.

Paul was working like a young man should and finding honesty and respect among people who respected others. He was renewing his soul. After a while, even his bad leg quit hurting.

When Samuel came to him and asked how he would like to be paid, Paul asked about working until he could earn a horse-drawn implement or two, since most Amish were pretty good hands at building farm equipment. A couple of things were of interest and the terms were agreed to and the bargain was struck.

On an Amish farm, the worth of what was done was increased by its utility, such as with sorghum cane. The tall stalks were cut down at the end of the growing season and the seed tops were removed and stored for livestock and poultry feed. The cane was put through a press to squeeze out the juice and then cooked down and made into syrup to use as a sweetener and for canning.

Paul took a trip back to Shoals to bring home a pull-behind hay rake and sorghum seeds so he could grow his own. Already owned but not used was a Georgia stock plow that stayed in the barn. When he arrived home, Lemuel looked amazed and said, laughing at his son, "Why would a cripple bring home such stuff? You was tricked by them Amish, boy. I guess you could sell it to someone that knows how to use such stuff."

Paul was not to be deterred. He studied and learned from the Amish farmers and in turn, he was always treated with respect and courtesy. It was not what he got at home.

Paul needed a walking plow, so he fixed himself a rolling box to attach to the back of the harness single tree. He used it with skill when he got it home. He had come to realize that using one's brain was better than sitting at home getting beat on and losing one's self-respect.

Iletta was happy to see him and noticed that he was a bit stockier. He crawled out from under his covers on the divan on the porch one morning and discovered his mom had left a soap mug, brush, and straight razor for him to use. Being with the Amish where many of the men had facial hair, he had let his own grow, without concern for how he looked.

"You're not Amish, so you can shave, son."

Lemuel turned on the crystal after supper back in Shoals. The Amish didn't believe in electricity, so he hadn't heard any radio while he was gone, which had made no difference to Paul. However, today's broadcast was a serious announcement about the murder of an Austrian Archduke named Ferdinand and his wife, Sophie. They had been shot to death, and the announcement said that several European countries were now at war.

Paul decided to head back to Odon and not let his paying job get away from him. He still had a thing or two to see if he could buy, earn, or barter before the weather turned. He didn't know the Archduke's death would eventually affect him, his mother and father, his community, the Amish, and his country. He did know that he didn't care too much about what happened to Lemuel.

Paul learned every day, or tried to learn something every day, that would shield him and his mother from his dad's increasing meanness. Making moonshine was all Lemuel ever did besides get drunk.

I can't keep doing this, Paul said to himself, repeatedly. As a cripple, Paul couldn't challenge his dad physically. Lemuel put fear into him that ate at his soul and his very being, *but what would work?*

He thought about the many times he was "taken in hand" as his dad said, always adding, "This will hurt me more than it will you." He had been knocked around since before he could remember, and those particularly bad whippings stayed in the back of his mind as a constant reminder of his own failures and the ridicule he endured over the years.

Sometimes he would re-live the memories of his father's brutality in accounting those applications that were delivered by slaps or punches, sticks or limbs, belts or leather harnesses, razor strop, ropes, or even a lamp cord or bailing wire. Now that he was almost fifteen, he was not spared the quirt or a short bull whip, either. "Spare the rod and spoil the child" was the tonic everyone prescribed, and it was heartily endorsed by Lemuel.

"Don't you ever run from me, boy. If I have to catch you, I'll beat you twice as bad, you hear me?" was the standard epithet issued at such times. At school, Paul once stumbled across a word in the dictionary—sadist. *Yep, that's what he is, all right.*

Paul returned to the Amish and got in on the sorghum harvest in the fall of the year. He learned about syrup making from the folks who had done it for generations. With lots of Amish families gathered round, Paul was assigned to keep the cooking fire going under the big pans of juice until it turned and thickened into sorghum syrup and was put in jugs and canning jars and then divided up between all the families that did the work.

Paul got a good sum for his work and he wanted his mother to have it. Riding back home to be with her during the winter, he found Iletta on the porch rocking in a rocker and taking it easy. He was so surprised when he came up the road because the gate was swung wide open, the gate that Lemuel wanted to keep locked to keep everyone out.

He was certainly confused. His mother waved to him as he approached. She never did that before—she looked happy. He turned his horse alongside the porch so that he could dismount without using his crutch for a step-down. He led a pack horse behind him, carrying bundles secured on the frame and it held almost two gallons of sorghum as a surprise.

"Hi, son! It's gonna be good having you home for a while."

"What in the world is going on around here? That gate is wide open, as if you want the whole world to come in. Where is—?" Paul couldn't bring himself to say the word "father."

"He took off to go on a, uh, vacation and left two weeks ago. I've been here by myself since then. Margie Tillford came up in their wagon and visited, and she went home yesterday."

"Mom, what in tarnation! Are you okay?"

"Tillford was with her and he says, 'Hi'."

"Am I missing something?"

"Your father's 'shine business took a turn for the worse. The sheriff and the doctor came out here to call after one of Lemuel's dissatisfied customers turned him in. He's going to be gone for a spell, over a year, someone told me. I couldn't care less, you know. Son, how is your leg doing and are you well?"

And from there, the questioning and the catching-up continued well into the night. Paul was to be home for the winter and would be by her side, without Lemuel around, and he would enjoy life without interruptions or any kind of assaults to either of them. It was going to be a real Christmas for a change.

Paul helped Iletta get a fall garden in with the new walking box and plow and then planted cane for a sorghum harvest the next fall when he would again be home for the winter. They would even go to church!

The following year was a good one for Iletta and the farm, and it was a good crop year, besides. Paul renewed old friendships when he came back from Odon and the sorghum crop was ready to harvest. Tillford got the "footballers" to come around and lend a hand with the pressing of the cane and the cooking into syrup. Paul had enough cash money put back that all he had, he used.

There was a bit more stashed away, money that only he knew about, and that was the money he had stashed in a cave along McBride's Bluff. The local legends said that the Indians used to hide valuables and treasure in a cave at McBride's Bluff. It was sometimes called the Outlaw Cave, because it was where the Archer Gang was rumored to have hidden out and murdered a man, cutting him into pieces and scattering his body parts around. Paul had spent many hours as a young boy exploring McBride's Bluff and Outlaw Cave with his friends.

As a ruse, Paul ginned up the idea of going out there and proposed to his friends that they head to Outlaw Cave to "poke around and see if there would be any treasure still there." They weren't too enthusiastic about the idea but agreed anyway. After all, they were buddies and they could be together again to re-live some of the old memories and the good times.

The first thing they noticed upon arriving at the bluff was that the cave seemed to have shrunk a bit because the openings they crawled through were a little bit tighter.

"Doofus, you plumped up some?" Paul remarked. "I can get into some of those places, so let me try." The others were kind of surprised at Paul's boldness, especially because he had a bad leg. They hadn't seen him in a while and they were a bit apprehensive watching him struggle and get about, but they weren't going to say anything.

Paul was confident and put their minds at ease, somewhat. The old memories of the day the accident happened were still vivid. Since he didn't go to school anymore, he wasn't aware the schoolyard kids had given him a nickname they used behind his back, "Crooks."

They entered the cold, wet cave. Jagged limestone outcroppings protruded into the passageway and Paul said, "I know this place. We've been here many times. I'll lead." So, he wiggled himself in, his bad leg dragging behind him, as he worked his way along. Now the guys realized that this was not such a good idea after all. They had candles and matches and one length of rope, maybe fifteen feet long.

Paul got stuck. He'd wedged into a pinch point and couldn't turn around, due to his bad leg. His candle was close to being used up.

Arnie said, "Well, boys, he's going to come out the opposite way he went in. Paul, we are going to have to grab you by both your legs to pull you out."

It had always been taboo, the idea of touching his bad leg and they assumed it would be painful to pull him out backwards. However, they had to do something. Being trapped in a cave with no light would compound the bad.

"We have got to bind your legs to keep them together and pull you out by this rope. Sorry man."

"Well, get to it, I can't stay in here forever," Paul told them.

"What if the Archers come around here and seal us ALL in the cave and steal our treasure? Ha, ha! We'll become legends like them, huh?"

They laughed. "Killed us for nothing, we don't have no treasure."

"We'll see," Paul said.

They breached the unspoken taboo and despite the embarrassment of it all, they proceeded. Once they got Paul out where he could manage on his own and he turned around, Tillford noticed he was holding onto a sack.

"Hells bells, Paul, why are you so determined to get into such a tight spot anyway? We all been in here before. What you got?"

Paul turned over and sat a gunny sack in his lap.

"Where did you get that? What is that? You *found* that?"

"Here's the surprise, boys—*money!*" They were incredibly surprised as Paul went on.

"I never told no one, but I been hiding money in here for some time. All that time I was out swimming in the river for them damned old shells, I been salting some away. I was afraid if I came home with a bunch of money, Lemuel would beat me up and take it. And I didn't want to hide it on our place. Too risky."

"You're crazy, man. What if we weren't around to get into this place with you, and now that you're—well, you know—you could have lost it all!"

"When I seen you guys, I figured I better do something. Once I saw old Doofus there, he's plumped up a bit and I knew if I didn't go after it, we would never be able to ever get it back."

Once they were all free of the cave mouth, they laughed and joked around. There really was treasure that came out of that cave.

Chapter 8

There was no joy in the day that Lemuel Gulliver Chandler saw the light of freedom for the first time after being released from jail, after fourteen months of incarceration for selling moonshine. The group of law enforcement officials and assorted deputies who had swarmed his farm had seized his hooch and his still. He came home to an empty barn, no corn in the crib, and the ground plowed up and showing cane stubble from the recent harvest.

Paul was home for the winter from Odon and new plows and harnesses were hanging in the barn. He had become used to the unexpected, and so had his mother, who was now in the full swing of canning and putting away crops from the garden into the root cellar. It seemed like a new day and a new change was happening that Lemuel had no part in, and no control over.

This marked the conclusion of the second time in two years that the sheriff and the doctor had been involved in Lemuel's life in a negative way. His footprint had been altered and he was forced to adapt his attitude and actions accordingly. The officials from Shoals had become allies for Paul and Iletta, somewhat unwittingly. But they were firmly determined to have a community that would uphold law and order, a town where people would stay. Joining in that effort was the staunch anti-liquor movement of the Women's Christian Temperance Union, supported by the local churches and the school board.

Iletta was still a somewhat passive soul, not mentally or physically able to stand up to Lemuel's verbal and physical assaults. As a woman in the first half of the 20th century in the U.S., she had hardly an option. Women were often considered persons of servitude, simply appendages of their husbands. However, some changes were beginning, and the WCTU would print out flyers to pass along that information. Their crusade against alcohol was also a protest, in part, by women to make their lack of civil rights known. These flyers were circulated within the community, and even Iletta became aware of the changes in the air when she read their pamphlets:

> *Women cannot vote. In most states, women do not have control of their property or custody of their children if they get divorced. There are no legal protections for women and children, prosecutions for rape are rare, and the state-regulated 'age of consent' is as low as seven in some states.*

Paul had few options, as well. As a cripple, in a day and age long before the word "disabled" came into use, he would always expect to have a hard time finding any work in a rural, agricultural community where one in four were unemployed. Once the 1930s arrived, only half found employment. Paul's hiring by the Amish had been a great bit of luck. As a closed community that was almost completely self-sufficient, the Amish were not overly affected by the community of "English" around them. Paul was a demonstration of their Christian practice to take it as it comes. "We find the good and praise it," was part of their actions, as well as their words to live by.

Once home, Lemuel pretty much milled around and didn't have much to do with his family, other than to let them know, "You want to fight agin me and call the laws on me, see what you get in return. Wait till you need something from me, you'll come a-begging!"

Iletta was at the kitchen sink, cleaning out pig intestines and getting ready to stuff casings and make sausages for the smokehouse. A dog was behind her and had puked up something he tried to eat which she slipped on. She reached forward to grab a hold of something to steady herself, but her hand landed on the top edge of a simmering pot of boiling water that held several half-pint jars of canning tomatoes. The pot of hot water overturned, and she was baptized and scalded in it.

Unable to scream because of the immense pain, she tried to back up by pushing away with her feet. Both legs were scalded. With her left arm, she reached behind her as she continued pushing away from the hot pan and hot water and thrust it into the broken jagged top of a canning jar, severely lacerating her forearm.

Finally, able to fill her lungs with precious air, she shrieked with such sounds of pain that Lemuel heard it from the barn. He casually walked into the house to investigate. Iletta was still on the floor, sitting upright, trying to get her apron undone with the one scalded hand, and to get the burning hot tomatoes and broken jars off her lap with the other. The steam from her clothes rose in wispy fingers. She held her left arm out and away from any glass as the blood dribbled down her arm and poured off her elbow and mixed into puddles of hot tomatoes, water, and blood that was pooling around her.

"Help me," was all Iletta could say. Lemuel stood there for a moment or two, putting together what he saw, as if he was trying to put the events together and thinking about it in backwards thoughts, going back to the beginning before resolution took over and he began to act.

Lemuel saw a towel hanging on a hook and took it down and

held it out for her to grab. With instinct, she reached for it and gasped because she could not get her right hand to fully close around the towel and hold it. It was then pitched into her lap.

He stepped around her and walked over to the screen door where the dog was patiently sitting. He opened the door and let the dog out. Iletta had the towel pulled around her left forearm by this time, to catch the blood and stop the bleeding.

Pulling the wash basin from the dry sink, Lemuel picked up the broken glass jar from Iletta's lap and helped her up to a chair. He adjusted the towel and then noticed two shards of glass still embedded in her arm. He made sure she was looking elsewhere, and then quickly pulled out the shards. She didn't seem to notice. She had gone into shock.

"Let's go and lay down, yes?"

"Sure, let me get to the porch for a minute first," and she was halfway out the door by then.

Paul put up the horse and came out of the barn, unaware of what had happened. Looking to the porch as he approached the house, all he saw was his mother standing there, left arm covered in a towel that was dripping with blood. Most of her clothes were soaked in red, too. It was a ghastly sight.

"My God," he whispered under his breath as his pace quickened.

"Your mom has hurt herself," Lemuel announced. "She's burnt up and got some cuts, too. You might want to help her. I got to go clean up this mess." He turned away and walked back through the screen door into the house.

The steam was gone, though Iletta's clothes were still warm, and she had smaller glass shards on her apron. Paul took out his pocketknife and cut off the tie strings and lifted the apron from her. She sat there watching him, hardly moving, or saying anything. While she was still and quiet, he removed the towel from her arm and saw some bad cuts made by the broken Ball jars.

As he gently cleaned her up, she began to look better and worse at the same time. The red tomato sauce, once cleaned off, made it clear that only some of the red on her clothes was blood. But the cuts looked deeper and more open by her movements, while the bleeding slowed.

"Try and stay still, mom. I got this. Can I get you anything? Would you like a dipper of water or something?"

"I'll be fine in a bit. You keep on doing—and thank you."

"Some of the skin on your arms looks red and very loose. What can I do, mom, tell me?"

"After a bit, you can get some liquid lard and we'll put some on the really red one, then we'll put on some light wrapping over it, to keep the grease from getting on everything, you'll see."

"Mom, we don't have any liquid lard. What else can we use?" She hesitated and then said, "I got a bottle of Hinds Honey and Almond Cream we can use. That would be even better." Paul noticed her hand was curled up and she couldn't straighten it. "What should we do here, mom?"

"We'll have to wait and see what happens with it. It got a lot of hot water poured on it and it might take some time before it relaxes. I hope it does. It won't be a big use to me like that." Iletta glanced down at Paul's bad leg, a sorrowful reminder of what could happen when one loses the use of a limb.

Within the next two weeks the swelling and tenderness from the scalds became less sensitive, except for when Iletta was exposed to sun or wind. Then they became quite painful. She stayed in the house mostly and went to the porch when the sun was on the other side. The Honey and Almond Cream was a godsend. Paul took the horse and went to town and bought eight bottles for her.

The dead skin had to slough off and re-grow. However, her

skin was overly sensitive for months and she knew the coming cold winter would be especially bad. The new skin did not have the elasticity the former skin had. When stretched, it tended to tear open. Hair did not grow on the skin for almost another year.

◇ ◇ ◇

The bleak future Lemuel envisioned for himself was coming to a head. He couldn't make good moonshine with everyone working against him. He had to keep an eye out for a sheriff who knew what he was up to, and the doctor was against him for keeping his crippled child in hand. The WCTU and school board watched his every move and reported their findings to the authorities. *Now, my no-account wife is all gimpy and unlikely to recover her no-account self,* he thought.

And so, with resolve and being fed up with all of them, he didn't say anything to anyone before he left the farm to sign up for the war that had broken out in Europe. "To hell with them back home! They can get along on their own without me!"

What tipped the scales was when he heard on his crystal that it had been discovered that Germany was secretly trying to get Mexico to revolt against the United States. He was always ready to fight someone, so he went and signed up to join the Army.

He was sent to Europe within weeks of completing his basic training, to the front lines with the British troops, filling in openings in the line where a hole was created by the soldier in front of him getting killed. The orders were, "Fill in a hole when you see one and keep moving forward."

It was of no matter to Lemuel that he left his family and community without a word. However, the word got back to Shoals when another local, an enlistee, was rejected during induction because of a bad arm. When he returned to Shoals, he let folks know who from their neck of the woods got in, and the word spread around, accordingly.

Before word got back to Shoals and the whereabouts of Lemuel became known, Iletta and Paul figured that Lemuel was off on a drunk somewhere and had stumbled into a ditch and broke a leg or something. They weren't concerned enough to go out and try to find "old Mister Trouble," and so they let his whereabouts remain obscure, knowing Lemuel would make his presence known when he wanted to. There was no sleep lost worrying about it.

Paul's concern was for his mother's left hand, which didn't uncurl much after the healing up. At the encouragement of the doctor, Paul and Iletta made a trip to see someone at the Evansville State Hospital. The doctor in Shoals had told them, "They do all kinds of things and they may be able to help you."

The response at the hospital was lukewarm. "They may be able to suggest a treatment, but the wounds would need to heal up a bit more and then they said we could come back, and they would look at it more seriously," was the explanation repeated by Iletta to folks who asked how she was doing. It was a treatment facility for those suffering from mental illnesses and substance abuse disorders. With a stretch and a wink, the hospital personnel decided that it was a secondary substance abuse injury and, as such, the cost would be covered by the hospital. That suited Iletta and Paul and they scheduled a return date.

"As green as a stalk of asparagus," was the phrase used to describe the Yanks that showed up to fight in the war that started in Europe in 1914—the Great War, as it was later called. Learning on the job put ill-equipped Dough Boys in harm's way on many fronts. Lemuel's nose was in the wind in some of the heaviest fighting with the combined American and British troops, who were attacking small villages and towns. A mortar shell exploded behind his foxhole and he was sent flying forward, knocked unconscious.

Lemuel woke up with a gravely injured leg. He faintly recalled being dragged away from the foxhole and worked on. He had suffered a concussion and a shattered knee. Having a sense that he would be going to a field hospital and back to the States, he felt relaxed and was resting when a second mortar exploded close by, throwing him out of his tent, and he was again back on the ground wondering about the extent of his new injuries.

This time he was loaded on a transport and driven to a safer location. His final destination, once he awoke and heard everyone speaking German, he realized was a prison camp. Lemuel came to with his ears ringing and disoriented, seeing a new fracture of his splinted leg, and he was unceremoniously thrown atop a pile of bodies, mostly cold and rotted, some warm and a few still moving. He was treated very badly and starved almost to death. With his leg bound to a board, he could get around only by crawling. He became filthy and emaciated. He received no medical treatment. His bandages rotted on him. He didn't expect to survive.

Maybe this house needs a good cleaning and maybe some things need to be thrown away, was Iletta's thought one morning. It had been a time of rest and renewal for her and Paul now that Lemuel wasn't around. No one she knew of had received any kind of correspondence from troops fighting "over there." Maybe they were too busy, or maybe they didn't have a way to get the mail through, or maybe the mail didn't get through because of heavy bombing. After all, it was war.

"What needs to go, mom, do you think?"

"Lumber, for one. We got stacks of it all around, covered in bramble bushes. That stuff has been here since I came on this place. Don't ask me to tell you when. Then, we could bring water into the house and get us a water pump, right there where we would pump directly into the sink. Think of it."

"How much does something like that cost, do you think?"

"You won't believe it, but we have a well pump in one of the sheds. It would need a new sucker washer put in it. Wouldn't water in the house be a nice thing, son? Think of that."

"Pipe?"

"We got enough pipe for *two* wells. It's around here on the place somewhere. Maybe under the thistles. We'll have to look. Want to burn something down? We got some sheds that aren't quite standing now, so it's more lumber to burn. If you want to reclaim some more of the field Lemuel let go to weeds, we could do that. If you want to keep up with some of that sorghum and those grain heads, we could do that. We could have a few more birds, you know, chickens to eat and eggs to sell, maybe some guinea fowls."

Paul was successful as he took a trip around the dilapidated sheds and found several piles of junk that were stacked up with the blue flowered thistle plants growing among the discards. There once was a time when the piles of scraps of wood or tin or wire and such had an order about it and the things were sorted, somewhat. Old, used stacks of cracked and broken leather harnesses, blistered black by the sun, were piled in among pieces of broken windowpanes and broken chains and rotting piles of rope and rusted and crushed tin cans, broken tools and shovel handles that would seldom be sought again.

An old white chipped thunder jar, half filled with nails and covered in rainwater, was rusted into a brownish red mound and sat atop stacks of long sections of steel pipes. These were protected and covered by dozens of large thistle blooms that surrounded the sloping ground, their menacingly large, sharp needles threatening any trespassers. It was a jubilant gift of the moment for him to watch the lightning bugs begin to rise through the foggy mist over the thistles, twinkling and bringing magic to the evening's twilight. In the early morning, the ground fog created a blue ocean of flowers, until the sun burned it off later in the day.

"He let everything go to seed, including this whole place. When he gets home, if he ever does, we'll have everything running. And maybe he'll be about done with all his snortin' and going about."

"Who knows how long he's going to be away or if he'll come back at all. No tellin' how long the war will go on."

"First things first, mom. We got to get your hand fixed first. Can't have you doing all this work if you got your hand not working right."

"In the morning, we'll go back, and we'll see."

They had the wagon ready and pulled out early and went to the hospital to have the exam of her hand completed and get a diagnosis. They both had changed into clothes that were cleaned and washed. They were still stained and soiled, but they were clean. The doctor didn't think it would be a problem to go ahead and see if they could fix it. He explained what he proposed to do—the skin on the wrist would be opened and some of the damaged tendons that had contracted would be severed, leaving some tendons that would promote improved flexibility, but at a loss of a strong grip. It was a radical idea, but one they agreed to. It was a success.

"Do not get into any heavy lifting for several weeks," the doctor advised. "Tendons aren't like flesh. They don't heal back that fast. I'm going to give you a wooden splint to wear for a couple of months. Take it off for cleaning and some *light* exercise every few days and do *not* churn butter or go digging in the garden. This is *firm*. Now go home and take care of that hand."

Chapter 9

Lemuel was still alive, living in the mud, filth, and squalor of a prison camp. The Allied Forces would continually hit the front lines of the Germans and when the German lines were fortified, the Allies retreated and retrenched, pushing on the defensive line in other locations. This wore down the German's ability to maintain the front. Battlefield equipment could not be moved about easily, being pulled by horses, and it exhausted the German troops. It was a losing battle for the Germans.

Saying the prisoners of war were still alive was somewhat debatable. Lemuel, still strapped to a board, his clothing filthy, contracted epidemic typhus. It was identifiable from some distance away. His entire body was covered by red whelps, numbering in the thousands. The organisms that transmitted the disease were the human body louse. He was crawling with them. Food shortages and malnutrition weakened resistance to the disease. He resided in the lowest bowels of the human war machine, surviving by laying and crawling over dead and rotting corpses.

In nearly four weeks of fighting, starting on August 8, 1918, over 100,000 German troops were captured during the period known as the Hundred Days Offensive, along with any surviving prisoners of war. Lemuel was still alive. He woke up to a French soldier lifting him onto a stretcher. He later heard it described as The Black Day of the German Army. At the eleventh hour, of the eleventh day, of the eleventh month of 1918, the Germans gave up.

When the end of the war was announced in a broadcast on the crystal, Iletta said, "Now, we'll find out for sure if he made it or not. In the meantime, we're looking fit, and having a water pump in the house is a real joy."

Paul was able to buy another horse from the Amish, and plowing was still hard work, but easier with a bigger horse. It was a Percheron, a draft horse, not a horse that Paul preferred to ride because its size made it difficult to mount and dismount. Iletta took the horse they had and did some vegetable gardening, after her hand had been healed and the wooden splint removed.

The farm had gone through some changes in Lemuel's absence. The front gate was now almost always open and inviting, unless it was closed when the horses were grazing out front. A nanny goat was a needed addition. When she had kids, she was fresh and they milked her and had enough to make a cheese, now and then.

"You know why I came home with that goat, don't you?" Paul asked, with a smile. "It's a hand exerciser for your left hand to help it get better."

The Allied Expeditionary Forces created hospitals using staff from different countries' military units. Some shortages of medical staff occurred because they were relieved of duty to go to the front lines to fight. American medical staff were dispatched to French and British hospitals by gearing up and creating a way of classifying the wounded that showed up, either by ambulance or by troop train, where casualties were transported directly from the battlefield to the hospital and surgery centers. Most were admitted through the showers because they were infested with vermin. Of all the soldiers admitted throughout the war, American casualties amounted to no more than four and a half percent of the total wounded.

The French town of Rouen, located along the Seine River, had porous gravel under the hospital and it was nicknamed the "pot de Chambre de France," and this was where Lemuel was taken. A special apparatus for the field was used to x-ray his shattered knee and then he went under the knife, was patched up, and remained for several weeks in recuperation in Rouen before he was transported by ship to the United States.

Dressed in drab brown and olive-green clothes, carrying a duffle bag, and leaning on his crutches, Pfc. Lemuel Chandler emerged from the bus. He stood in the road at the gate of his farm and saw a much different place than the one he had left. Even then, the irony almost escaped him as he stood there. The wife who had taken his abuse for years and was injured with a contracted hand, and the crippled son who had taken his assaults and his cursing was going to be his welcoming committee.

His last bit of honor was stripped away, and he was a vessel full of resentment as he surveyed how his farm had flourished in his absence. *Why did I even come home?*

Three of the outbuildings were gone. He could see the ash piles where the buildings used to stand. *They were burned down on purpose, I can tell. I wonder what else has been destroyed around here? I better check the barn.* Upon entering the barn, he was startled by a large horse staring back at him, casually chewing on grain. Well, who in the hell has moved in, is what's I want to know, Lemuel thought, as he crutched his way to the house with a purpose on his mind. No one was home, but he noticed a well pump had been installed at the sink in the house. *Well, who did THAT? Maybe I'll stay after all and sort this stuff out that's happened with MY house.*

Lemuel rummaged around some more but didn't see that something of his was missing. He would have blown his top and stomped around, except he couldn't anymore, because of his wounds. Paul and Iletta would want to be around when it was discovered the still was gone. After he was arrested and taken to jail, the Law returned and confiscated not only the still, but all the tin and copper pipes, too.

In the back of his mind, he was convinced that he could recreate his moonshine business. *I'll still make a good living on the corn liquor, as soon as I can get this leg of mine healed up a bit more and get me back with the folks that can get me the fixins to make a bigger and better still.*

Lemuel returned to the barn and went to the corn crib and pulled a board away from a timber and reached in and got himself a bottle of corn squeezings he had stashed before he'd enlisted. It had been some time since he had a pull at the bottle of Indiana corn liquor, and he had a big one. It went to his head. With the long bus ride and train ride to get back home, he was exhausted and quickly passed out in the barn until the next day.

Still dressed in his drab brown and olive-green uniform, still carrying a duffle bag, Lemuel emerged from the barn the next morning on crutches. They spied him almost immediately as he left the barn and approached the house. The first thing they noticed was that he was on crutches, the same as he left Paul. Lemuel noticed Iletta's arm was in a sling, still bandaged from before the time he left to go fight in the war. Iletta and Paul both had the same thought, although they expressed it differently, *Oh, how the worm turns!*

Iletta tried to say it humorously. "Strange place to go fight the war, Lem," pointing to the barn. "Didn't tell us you were headed out. We never got no letters or nothing from you or about you, so we figured you might have been killed or something. It does look like you survived, though, don't it, Paul?"

Lemuel remained as steady as he could manage on his crutches. He was nursing a bad headache and heard his name "Lem" used, a shortened version that Iletta had used regularly before the love went out of it. Now it was only "Lemuel" and that's that. He was a standing drunk.

"Yes, it does, mom. So, you got crutches, now," Paul said, addressing his father. "Mine are permanent. How 'bout yours?"

Lemuel was washing in humiliation now. "Don't know yet. Depends on what the doctor says in six months from now. I got to go to Indianapolis to see him there."

"When I returned to school, they called me Crooks. I wonder if they'll call you that, too."

The hot sun blistered anyone in the sun these Indiana days, with temperatures in the upper 90's. Paul and Iletta were on the porch, sharing the swing. The undertones of the squeaking chain noise grated on the man in the drab brown and olive-green clothes carrying a duffle bag.

Iletta was in full control at the moment and paused, ever so slightly, as if to extend the temporary exile Lemuel must endure for his self-inflicted fate.

"Not knowing anything about you for almost two years now, we moved on and made some permanent changes. And we're getting used to them, as you might have guessed. Paul took over your room in the house and he doesn't have to live under a blanket on the spring porch anymore, so's there's that. Most of your stuff has gone away. We figured something had happened, and Paul needed a room of his own, instead of the divan and a blanket. What we did save, and it wasn't much I'm afraid, was put in the barn, out by the corn crib. Paul and I moved the divan out there, too. It's still in good shape. I think, considering your injuries, that you'll need some peace and quiet and a chance to heal and all. Don't you, Paul? I'm curious, too, to see if they'll call you Crooks, as well."

Paul nodded, straight-faced.

"Anyway, you'll take the divan for a spell and rest up and heal. Out there. We get up around here pretty early these days and so we don't want to disturb your recuperatin' and restin'." Dripping with sarcasm, she continued, "It will be better for us, too. You know, it may take some kinda time to get busted bones to heal up—when you're all busted up—"

"Oh, and one thing, too," Paul interjected, "That old outhouse behind the barn was starting to lean a bit and show its age, so we dug a new, empty one on the other side of the house for us. Yours will still be good for a while, though. It will be only yours out there, anyway. So's that's that."

Paul would not have been able to physically challenge Lemuel in the past and so had been forced to wait till the "what comes around goes around" time came. This could be the day.

It was the day. Iletta heard it in Paul's voice and understood the effect the years of abuse Paul suffered was driving him on. But now Paul was standing up for himself. He reacted as he should, in her eyes, and she knew he wanted to let the chips fall where they may.

Lemuel was still standing in the yard under the blazing sun, as if he were in a daze when the conversations ended. Paul and Iletta turned and started back into the house. He stood there for some time, as they looked to go about their chores inside. Several minutes went by and they noticed he was still standing there, sweat rings spreading from his arm pits. With added confidence and strength in her voice and certainly plenty loud for him to hear her plainly, she said, "Don't pay him no mind, Paul. He'll get in directly. But it does make me wonder that he does seem a bit slow in not getting on with himself. He might be a bit touched from the war, you know. Time will tell. We'll have to watch him. He's got nowhere else to go, so it looks like he'll be with us for a while. Maybe the barn will be the best thing for him."

For Lemuel, it didn't seem so bad, being in the barn. *I can lay around and I can get better on my own time and I won't have to lock horns with them for now. The boards are hiding my 'shine. I got enough of a stash to keep me going for some time.*

With a halting shuffle he returned to the barn and settled in by opening his duffel bag and getting his war clothes out and hung, to get out the musk. And once situated, he started to take the edge off the memories of the prison camp. He needed food and smelled something coming from the house. Being curious and hungry, he started over and saw Iletta putting out a plate of food on a chair, inside the screened-in porch, to protect it from flies before she returned to the kitchen, where he saw them sit down at the kitchen table to eat. He hesitated and watched them eat. Once they finished and went on to other things, he went up to the porch and got his tin plate and returned with it to the barn and ate it in solitude. Within a few days, his food was set outside the screen door.

In the back of his mind, Lemuel still held the notion that he was going back into the distilling business. He assumed that if he kept it to himself and kept them out of the barn, he was free to pretty much do as he pleased. However, his splinted leg was a problem.

That night, the leg began swelling and throbbed throughout the night. No pain medicine was available other than moonshine. With no way to get to town to have it looked at, other than by wagon, he laid there and endured it. As the leg continued to swell, some of the stitches were tearing open and the only remedy was to drink more 'shine and dab at the festering wounds with his hooch-dipped dirty socks.

Steady and slow healing was what would do my leg the best good, he figured. Exercise was essential to him not losing muscle mass and tone. If he didn't take care of it, the muscles would atrophy and he could wind up being a cripple, too. He had never been concerned about Paul's leg and how he managed with his. He was sure he wouldn't wind up the same way. He prayed he wouldn't, later.

After a few weeks at home, he rode to town with Iletta and Paul, in the back of their wagon, on the pretense of seeing the doctor. But his goal was to look around for copper to make a coil. From the get-go, once Iletta got wind of what he was buying, she knew what he was up to and what kind of trouble he was about to bring down on himself, and maybe them.

Mrs. Olsham, Paul's old teacher, was still close to many of the families and kids she had taught over the years. She kept her eyes and ears open for the latest news and gossip flowing around. Unbeknownst to Lemuel, she was a woman who supported women's suffrage and was connected to the Women's Christian Temperance Union movement. The WCTU worked to stamp out the use of alcohol on moral grounds. It also had supported abolition but opposed foreign immigration because of the belief that "undesirable immigration and those immigrant hoards" brought disease, old world habits, and radical ideas along with them. She also supported eugenics.

Iletta and Paul had seen the changes in the opinions of most of the people around the county and were aware that a shift had occurred. Knowing that, they waited for their own personal troubles they knew were on its way. Lemuel was the master of his own ship that had sailed long ago, and they knew there was little they could do to stop him once he set his course in a certain direction.

Reminiscent of those who came home from the Civil War seventy years prior, the town square was once again a gathering place for the survivors and soldiers who were lucky enough to get back from the Great War. Gaunt, dazed men roamed around the city seeking jobs and a bite to eat. Lemuel soon saw this as a favorite place to chum and seek copper parts for a still he wanted to construct, start up, and run. Customers would be right there, gathered around to buy from him. He was known. He already had a reputation for it. His mind was made up at the first swig back.

Showing up out of the blue, Mrs. Olsham arrived at the Chandler place for a visit. She knew that Iletta had had a rough row to hoe and that Paul's leg held him back from doings things he would want to. But she'd come to share other news in the mix of things. She had only compliments for the look and productivity of the farm, particularly in these rough times. Everyone she knew had pulled up another notch in their belts and looked for better times ahead.

Mrs. Olsham was very busy these days spreading her opinions and gathering support for the WCTU. It was with a sense of friendship and concern for Iletta and Paul that she had to tell them that Lemuel was arrested on the town square, drunk as a skunk, and the sheriff had put him in the jail to sober up and to await talking to the judge.

"I'm so sorry to be bringing you the news. There was suspicion of selling alcoholic beverages, but none were found. How could that be?"

"I've known for some time that he'll do himself in and it's only a matter of time, Mrs. Olsham." Iletta wanted to convey her sense of distance from the man she was still married to but had no control over. "The sheriff and the doctor have been so supportive of us in the past. It's hard to have to keep your heads up and go on," she said.

"We at the WCTU work so hard to rid ourselves of this demon alcohol. We hope you can support our cause at some time, dear." Iletta and Paul both nodded in agreement.

Once she left and headed back to town, Paul hitched up the wagon and Iletta packed food for a bus trip to Madison by way of Bedford.

Madison State Hospital was a dual treatment place for substance abuse and mental illness. They served adults with the worst mental health challenges. Iletta and Paul were on their way to explore their options. Lemuel's return from the European war and his capture and internment into a prison camp were a couple of aces they held.

Filling in the blanks to the staff was a painful recollection of how they had been living their lives for some time. Upon Lemuel's return, they described how "he wandered around the property most of the day. In the beginning, he took food from the porch and went to the barn to eat. Later on, he would eat his food at the steps to the house and then return to the barn, refusing to let anyone inside except on rare occasions, like he was a manger dog protecting something like the Christ Child. He managed to stay drunk all the time, without operating his still that was seized by the sheriff and caused him to be locked up for over a year. That's when he went to the service."

"Any other habits or conditions either of you know about?"

Paul responded, "He wanders around or goes to the barn and sleeps for many hours at a time. One really peculiar thing, though, he won't go into the outhouse. It's right behind the barn, so's its close. Ever since he got back from the war, he's been like that. I see him at the edge of the woods, out in the fields, and at night sneaking around. His droppings are all over the place, so I know where he goes, mostly. He will not use the outhouse. He refuses."

Indiana was able to take soldiers and structure a rehabilitation program for them, particularly those who had combat injuries that required extended stays. These men, like Lemuel, would trickle back to their homesteads and join so many more that were disoriented and shell-shocked. Their experiences of an extended period of disassociation with familiar faces and places exacerbated their difficulties.

"Due to the length of his drinking and the fact that he drinks until he goes unconscious, we suspect he has sustained major damage to his brain and his organs," the doctor told Iletta. "We're quite familiar with moonshine poisoning. Let me describe for you what has probably gone on with your husband. It's been studied because of moonshine's wide appeal and physical harm that occurs.

"So much of what is consumed is faulty and made with all kinds of stuff that's bad for you. The beginning liquid that pours out of one of those coils is really poison and it mixes with the rest of it when it's made. That part needs to be thrown away, but seldom is. The moonshiners call it the angel's share, but it's definitely not that. Sometimes it's mixed with rat poison in small amounts that gives it its kick. Lots of those pipes they run that junk through is a lead pipe—very bad. The brain doesn't know. The kidneys don't either, and neither does the stomach and the liver, and on and on. Some people nowadays have been drinking hair tonic after it's been strained through a loaf of French bread."

The doctor went on with his description. "So, finally the body can't handle all that poison and it goes unconscious. The brain doesn't repair itself, I'm afraid. What we'll be able to do is to send a couple of people from our hospital to your farm and persuade your husband to attend our hospital program and see how well he does. It may take months, at the very least, but very likely, longer. Those other issues with his leg may need to be addressed at the same time.

"Please also understand that he may not want to be here. So, he'll be confined here until he is able to be released and can do well on his own. We don't want him to hurt himself or anyone else. Getting his mind as clear as possible depends on him and his condition.

"You say he's been violent in the past, and for quite a while?" the doctor asked, and they nodded. "So, the road to recovery will be a bumpy one."

Paul and Iletta stared at each other for a few anxious moments. Finally, Paul spoke. "We don't feel like we have any connection to him now. He's been gone about two years with the war and all. We've suffered him for years and his 'shining' has brought nothing but misery and pain for all of us. If he gets well, whenever, and we don't see him no more, it may be for the best. And it'll be for the best for my mother, too."

"This could be extremely dangerous for us, son, I guess you know? We'll advise you periodically of how it's going for him. But for this first round, it's advisable that you do not communicate with him. We want his focus on getting better and not thinking about relations building at this time. You can write to us, all right? I'll be sending you a letter to tell you the day we'll arrive, so you'll know what to expect."

Stepping out of the hospital and looking up at the sky, Paul remarked, "Now I know why it can rain during the sunshine."

❖　❖　❖

Prohibition was in full swing in January of 1920. Carrie Nation had had her heyday of smashing up saloons and speakeasies. Bathtub gin was the rage and money would be made. Thousands of private stills were producing hooch from all kinds of concoctions. In northern Indiana, at the Great Lakes, rum runners were shipping thousands of gallons of booze in from Canada. Chicago was jumping. And just south of Shoals was French Lick, where the gangsters went to gamble in the casinos, and some even partook of the mineral springs there. The road between the Great Lakes and Southern Indiana was a hotbed of traffic in illegal alcohol.

Deliverance came to Shoals, eventually.

The day the truck wagon showed up was a normal day, except for the churning stomachs and anxiety felt by Iletta and Paul. The vehicle itself was an everyday milk wagon that could deliver milk, except it was painted an ordinary brown instead of the customary white. When the attendants emerged from it, Iletta pointed to the barn and then went back into the house.

Three men got out of the wagon after they backed up to the door of the barn. Two of the men opened the barn door and entered. About five minutes went by and the rear door of the milk wagon opened briefly and blocked most of the goings on. Three sets of feet stepped into the vehicle, the rear door closed, and the Model T started, rolled down the driveway and left.

Iletta was alone when they came and afterwards, she walked out to the porch and sat down on the steps. *My, I never noticed how quiet it is out here. It's like someone that's been in my head has stopped talking to me. The silence is wonderful.*

Paul rode in on the smaller horse and saw Iletta sitting on the porch. "When do you think they'll arrive?"

"Done and gone, son. Done and gone."

PART TWO

Chapter 10

"Paul, I think we need to go on a visiting trip. I want you to see the place I grew up in and meet whoever is left alive up there. What do you say? Let's do one. Been thinking it's about time."

"Well, sure thing. When?"

"In a couple of days ought to be about time. I have some things to do before I go and get ready. Have the house to lock up, and all. Guess you should rest the horse for a day or two. We'll take the wagon and I got us a stopping point around Newberry. There are two branches of the First Creek we can stop at. It ought to be nice this time of the year."

The horse was ready, the wagon was packed, and away they went.

Paul and Iletta headed up the road north towards Odon and found both branches of the First Creek and started to follow it west and then settled in for the night. Later they would continue along the creek and head north towards Linton and then to Dugger.

"How come you never told me about your family coming from up here?" Paul asked. "It's all new to me."

"Wasn't much to tell or to talk about. We'uns were all raised in coal country and it's such a hard life, there's hardly much attached to hardscrabble that's worth sharing. I thought I'd get you some bare facts about it for your memory."

"Tell me about your family, mom. What should I know? You tell me."

"Your granddad was a coal miner and worked in the mines is all that I could remember. Sometimes it was in a coal mine, where they loaded coal wagons, and they were pulled out by horses. Otherwise, they were pushed out, usually uphill, so you can see how hard it was. I'd hear stories about someone falling while they were pushing out and the wagon would then go back down in the mine and run over whoever was down there. Usually it was one time.

"I remember my dad coming home nights and washing and trying to get the coal black off him. His hands were almost black. He could hardly get 'em clean and they'd be covered in miner's crud, kinda' like what I've seen you come home with."

"What are you meaning, mom?"

"Paul, I seen that you had been in either coal mines or in caves, because you always had all your skin on your hands peeling. Can't get it from being in river mud."

Paul's eyes got bigger as Iletta carried on.

"Later on, when they found a vein that was close to the surface, they would get a big drag line and cut off the overburden, throw it to the side and dig the seam of coal right there. Lots of seams were cut out that way. The top dirt had to be put back, so they didn't have a hundred holes filling with water. That's where I learned to swim when I was little. Also, where I learned to fish, too. I didn't fish much in a creek or a river, only abandoned coal pits.

"To try and make a little extra money, your Granddad tried to grow things besides vegetables. He got him a tobacco base and grew tobacco and would hang it in the barn to dry and then take it and sell it. He smoked some of it, but mostly tried to sell it. There's lots of fiddling around to grow it, but it can be done.

"So, I was going to ask you some, son. I wanted to know how you feel about seeing him going away. You never said." Iletta paused to see if there was any reaction from Paul.

"He wrecked my life pretty much all along, so that part of it can close tight. I don't need to see any more of him. I want to see that you're all right. I don't know what my life is going to turn out like. I keep hitting the big rocks on the road."

"It will change. You're twenty, now, and remember, I've said it so, so many times—we find the good and praise it. We don't have to have much for it to work. We don't have to have much money to live that way. Take that little girl you found when you were young, Ina Fay. Now that we're on down the road from that you can look back and think about her parents being able to say a proper good-bye. Forever in their hearts, she'll be in such a special place. It's not even about counting your blessings. It's about giving a blessing. If you are giving more than you can remember, that's about the right pace, I'd say." She gave him a big smile.

"But I can't remember to go around giving blessings. I won't remember to do it."

"You might have done it and not known it, so that counts, too, son. It's like remembering someone who you really liked, and you never know how their life turned out. Then, when you remember them years later, it's a good feeling to know you knew them. It's just like this—" and she reached over and kissed him on the cheek, unexpectedly. It almost knocked him out of the wagon.

"MOM—!"

"Here's that place to camp, I told you about. Right here."

◇   ◇   ◇

It was late afternoon when they arrived at Iletta's homestead. She had a place picked out in an old apple orchard where they camped the second night. The house was small, and it still had blue paint on it, but it looked like no one lived there, or at the very least, they weren't home. No lights shown out of any of the windows.

"This was an old orchard your granddad planted when I was a very little girl," she said. "All us kids played and ran around this place and it sure was fun. If you look at it now, you can see it hasn't been pruned in some time. It's a might sad. So, now if you look at all these old apples all over the place you can certainly find wonderful ones to eat. They have bruises and bad spots, but lots of good is here, isn't it?" she said with a twinkle in her eye and a smile. "It's kinda' like that with people."

Paul was astounded at his mother. She seemed to almost be a different person altogether. He wondered how this change happened. He still thought of her as the abused woman she had been, bruised like the apples on the ground. But now that Lemuel had been locked away, and now that she was on her home territory, she seemed to have become someone else. She even smiled.

"Mom, I've heard you a few times say, 'Hello the house.' Tell me about that. You said it happened in an apple orchard. Was it this one?"

"Yes, it was," Iletta replied. "So, to tell you some of what I know, there was a Gypsy queen who died in 1895 and she was buried on April 1, 1896, at the Oak Hill Cemetery down in Evansville. In the early 1800s, the Gypsies had these camps in different places around Crowne Point and they were chased off because the town's people accused them of sneaking in and stealing livestock and other things and having immoral values. Well, some of the Gypsies got sick, somehow, with the plague, and they told the townspeople they couldn't travel with sick people and asked if they could stay around until the sick people were well. The village people refused to give them any medicine to help them and some of the Gypsies died as a result. So, it was said that the Gypsies put a curse on them."

The Gypsies that Iletta spoke about were coming out of Europe starting about 1880, from Bosnia and Romania. They were called the Ludar. From the Chicago settlements, they wandered southward across rural Indiana, into the coal fields around Dugger and Linton, trading horses, and sharpening knives, plows, and shovels, before following the coal seams and mines further south.

They learned about the clam shell business and worked to gather shells to sell to the button-makers. They were prosperity-driven but clannish, staying with their own kind mostly, except when selling things, trading, or looking for opportunities away from curious eyes.

"When the Gypsies died," Iletta continued, "they buried their folk in different places in the woods, which were their traditional burial grounds. The townspeople dug into the mounds, the gravestones were knocked over, and they dug up the bodies and some of the corpses' heads were chopped off.

"The Gypsies would travel around, and they would camp in the woods and then come up to the yard and yell out, 'Hello the house.' Your granddad, back in those days, would go down to their camps and check them out when they would show up. He wanted to find out if they were the good kind or the bad kind of Gypsies.

"I always remember them coming around and your granddad would tell me to go and count the chickens. They would come by the road and yell, 'Hello the house' to talk to whoever was there about doing any work that needed tending to and then they would get paid mostly in foodstuffs, canned goods, chickens, and all. We never had real money around, the folding kind. We only traded mostly like everybody else did. I learned about Gypsy herbs and medicines, as well."

In the early morning at first light, Paul heard a screen door slam, and someone call some dogs, which barked briefly. It was time to get up and Iletta was stirring about and soon they walked through the apple orchard and she called out, "Hello the house."

Someone stirred inside and the screen door squeaked as they stepped onto the porch and looked out in the dim, calling back, "Who's here?"

"It's Iletta and Paul Chandler," she called back. "Who's talking to the apple orchard, girl?" Iletta's sister Dorothy came bounding across the yard and they grabbed each other and started jumping and carrying on.

"Lordy girl, where have you been? Show me your baby," and then, "Lord, he's a man." And joy poured out of the three of them. Dorothy started to cry and so did Iletta. As Dorothy looked at Paul, she noticed he was on one crutch and she said to him, "You only need that one I'm guessin' so I don't need to rustle up another one. Come on in and we'll make some coffee. We don't spend money to drink it every day. Come in, come in."

They walked down the drive at the side of the house and went over to a shady spot with a stone floor and sat down under a tree, next to a gooseberry bush. Paul was delighted to see one with berries in bloom.

"We had to come up this way so's Paul can fix some memories for himself. It was a spur of the moment thing, us coming. Hope it was okay to just show up?"

Dorothy smiled, "Oh, yes, and 'Hello the house.' I haven't heard that in a while."

"I just put Lemuel in the Madison State Hospital for alcohol. He came back from the war and went pretty off there, so he'll be gone for quite some time. No need to dig around it for now. Just know it was the best thing for all of us, me and Paul, so's that's that. You look skinny, are you eating well? How's your garden this year?"

The confab went on into the night. Paul didn't have much to say, but he listened. After the next day's breakfast, he got up the notion to look around his mother's homestead. They had a water pump at their sink in the kitchen, too, and a tin can with water in it for priming the pump.

Going down to the barn, he saw some frames hanging with big dried tobacco leaves on them. It was his first look at real tobacco. He poked into the root cellar and saw the pile of coal rocks and smelled the basement air. The memory of it stayed with him the rest of his life.

Not wishing to be rude, he came right back and sat down and listened to Iletta finish a story about troubled times. But she slowly changed the topic as he approached, and the conversation changed to him as the attention shifted. *Lots to know about, lots to hear about,* he thought.

When they finally took a break, Dorothy suggested they could take a short walk to the back of their fence line and investigate one of the strip mines that was close to their back pasture.

"Paul, I don't know if it's all right for you to be going that far on your crutch or not. We don't have to go. Your mom was raised on this kind of stuff."

"No, I want to see it. We don't dig like this down around Shoals. I'm a little slower in tall grass, but I can make it. Let's go.

"You want to go *now*?"

"Why not? Let's go. I heard about these strip mines. I'm curious, but I'm not going to go swimming," Paul said, laughing. "After seeing into that deep, clear water, I don't think I would have ever learned how to swim. There's no bottom to stand on."

And so off they went, with Paul ignoring his own struggles to get there. It was as they had described it—abandoned to the ages and taken back over by nature. The pool of water that had seeped into the landscape and covered the crevices in the earth was as deep and clear as Paul had imagined.

Back at the farm, everyone took their seats and the sisters continued to visit and catch up on things. It had been too many years since Iletta was home; the last time was to bury their mother.

Paul snoozed on and off in the chair he sat in as they talked, occasionally pausing to enjoy the breezes. They were not very loud talkers and snoozing was easy to do, and comfortable. After a bit, he barely opened his eyes and saw his aunt and his mother sitting very close together, talking very quietly, holding each other closely, and wiping away each other's tears. When he moved slightly, they pulled apart a bit and became quiet again. Handkerchiefs were put away, back into pockets. The share of confidences was concluded.

It could be about anything, Paul figured. There was so much to pick from and so many things were unpleasant and ugly. Those were the burdens carried by the family. The Dugger folks lived in a furrow of their own, too.

"The greatest test of courage on earth is to bear defeat without losing heart." That was on a note that Dorothy slipped to Paul as they put their bags into the wagon and packed up to return home. He didn't quite know what it was when she gave it to him, so he let it rest in his shirt pocket for later.

"Shall we?"

"Let's," and before Iletta and Paul departed, the three of them headed to the meadow across the road and went to pick flowers. Paul watched them amble slowly along, as they stooped and examined the flowers they saw.

"Black–eyed Susans, bittersweet, Queen Anne's lace, phlox, forget-me-nots, dianthus, asparagus, sweet pea, morning glory," and on and on, like they were little girls whiling the day away. Finally, they made their way back to the wagon and Dorothy handed Iletta a bouquet for the trip south.

"You have to write me now that you know how to find your way home."

"Well, Dot, I'm still as bad at it as I ever was. I'll get Paul to jot a note. What do you say, son? Will you write if I can't?"

"Why sure, mom, I'll do it. Aunt Dorothy, thank you for having us."

"So, we're off. We'll want to make the creek by evening."

Paul took the horse and turned him to the road, and they went down the winding path and disappeared. Iletta settled in rather quickly and didn't turn back around for a final wave.

They were on their way back and got to the creek in plenty of time to find a spot down on the bank to use for the night. As they settled into a campsite that had seen some use and still had wood gathered and stacked, Paul said, "Mom, I noticed that you're favoring your right side a bit and you look like you're sore from something. Is everything okay?"

"Yes, I got a cramp in my side riding up here and now that we're headed back, it has decided to join me. Probably too much watermelon. Did you like your Aunt Dot's cooking?"

"It could have used a bit more salt but, other than that, it was fine. She's living alone? Where's her husband? I guess he would be my uncle?"

"Well, he was lost in a cave-in a long time ago and they had to leave him there. It was too dangerous to try and get him out. They said it was coal gas that made the blow-out. Any sparks down in that tunnel might set off another one, so he stays there,

Paul. I know it's tough on her, but it had to be that way.

"I later learned about all them things that would threaten coal miners and send them to the hereafter. Grown-ups wouldn't talk much about such things, but I would hear little bits here and there. Miner's crud was minor compared to problems with ventilation; they could get firedamp, chokedamp, and carbon dioxide—until they killed the canary—or their carbide head-lamps exploded the methane, killing everyone. When men gave up mining, they had stunted growth, crippled legs, and curved spines."

Paul contemplated what she said, thinking that it was a sad way to go, not to be with your kin in the forever after.

Iletta bent over forward from the log she was sitting on and made a groaning sound before sitting back upright. Seeing Paul looking at her, she tried to reassure him. "It's fine, it's fine, son. Just a passing catch in my side, that's all."

I hope she isn't hiding anything on account of me, Paul thought. Probably nothing, like she said. I can't read the signs like she can. I need to get better. I don't possess the vision like some folks have.

As they drove the wagon up the final road to their farm, Paul began to run over in his mind what things he needed to tackle once they were unloaded and the horse was unharnessed and let out to graze. Soon the list grew and his concern for his mom slipped away. He was truly the man of the farm now and he felt he needed to pull a notch up on his belt.

Chapter 11

~~~~~~~~~~~~~~~~~~~~~~~~~~~~~~~~

He looked at the end of his crutch and noticed that the bottom was split. The whole crutch was worn out. Ever since he was forced to use crutches to get around on, he had found it to be awkward, but he had no choice in the matter. Paul had an assortment of crutches by now and various appliances were stuck in corners and crannies, here and there, within easy reach. He went to the barn to unhitch the horse and noticed that the latch on the door had been pried off and the barn had been broken into.

Why in the world would someone do that? We ain't got nothing. He looked around and saw that a couple of things had been moved about, but nothing seemed missing. The tack room door was standing open, but no harnesses were gone. Some of the hay from on the floor had been swept away from a few spots, as if someone had been looking for something. *Very odd.*

When he went to the house, he found Iletta sitting in a chair, all doubled over and crying, and he was alarmed.

"Mom, what is it? Is it that same pain? Maybe we should go on to the doctor and get you looked at."

"I'll be fine, son. But if it will make you feel better, I'll go to town and we can get his opinion."

"I'll need to go catch the horse again, I just turned him out.

Give me a few minutes." And off he went.

Loaded up and headed into town, Paul's concern was dismissed by Iletta. "Paul, it isn't going to be anything. I've had these for a few weeks on and off. The truth is that I'm getting older and older women go through what's known as the 'change,' which is normal when the child-bearing years have passed. So, don't you worry too much about it."

Paul sat in the doctor's office and waited for the doctor to come out and talk with him.

Minerva Fields entered, leading her husband, Adrian, and holding his arm, which was wrapped in blood-spattered rags. On seeing Paul, they looked surprised.

"Hello there. What's got you in here?"

"I was about to ask you the same. Hi, Mrs. Fields. What did he do with his arm?"

"He got it wrapped into some old barn tin and it's a big enough cut that the doc will probably have to put some stitches in it. What's got you in here?"

"I came in with mom—stomach or woman's issues, we think. How's things going over at your place? Saw some nice corn out by the road."

Adrian said, "Hope it's a good year. Last year weren't for nothing."

Minerva added, "My sister is coming to see me, and we need to get over to your place and visit with Iletta. We heard your dad is in the hospital somewhere, and we hope it gets better for all, real soon."

"Evansville."

The nurse entered the waiting room and Minerva said on departing, "Tell Iletta that Lovety and I will see her real soon," and she turned and entered another room.

Iletta came out within moments of the Fields leaving and

her face was puffy and eyes red, as if she had been crying. Paul was startled but before he spoke, Iletta said, "Thank you, doctor, and Paul, we'll be going now," and they left before Paul had a chance to speak to the doctor. They got in the wagon and headed home in silence. He could tell that she didn't want to talk to him right now. His worries grew.

She's hiding something big. I can just feel it.

Sure enough, within a few days a buggy came through the gate and up to the house with two ladies in it. Minerva and her sister Lovety came to visit, after all. After a nice visit and once they left and Iletta was in the kitchen, she said to Paul, "It was good to hear about the goings-on around here with the neighbors. It's been a long time since we got out and about, mainly because of Lemuel. They asked about him and I said he may be along at some time or not. Who knows?"

"Did you see how those two looked like twins, Lovety and Minerva? They are how far apart?"

"If I recall, just a few years. I don't know if you know it but the both of them are working like your dad was. They were both running stills, at least they were the last time I talked to them. Nowadays, people don't talk about their doings, especially not around the doctor, and of course not around the sheriff. They're just trying to keep food on the table to make it past the winter. It's hard enough to be scratchin' by and then to be worrying about who's looking over your shoulder, wantin' to send you to jail or even worse.

"They were saying, Minerva was, that they been broke into three different times over the past couple of years. Nothing seems to be taken each time, but they keep coming back. Both of them suspect it has to do with their 'shining. They're not happy about it, after seeing what happened to Lemuel and all. Adrian needs to be paying some mind to it, Minerva says. All that corn he grows ain't going to go to hog feed."

Paul reasoned, "Well, he's gonna shoulder his full load with doing it, one of these days. But then, Grover and Lovety don't grow lots of corn since they have an apple orchard."

Iletta gave Paul a sideways glance. "Paul, they been 'jacking' their apple juice for years, everybody knows. They seem a bit well off for the amount of land they work, don't you think? That orchard does it for them every winter."

"How so?"

"They press all those apples in the fall, right? That juice is all fermented and it turns hard. What they do is wait for the freezes. That juice water freezes and turns to ice. They take the ice part off, which removes the water. The alcohol don't freeze. It stays behind and that makes the proof go up. Some of that stuff will sit you in your chair," she chuckled. "One time they brought a couple of gallons to a fair we had in town on the square. I think the excuse was that they got it mixed up and brought the wrong jugs. They had half of the town all wobbly before they realized what they had done."

"You know, mom, we got broke in?"

"When was this? I didn't know! You never said."

"It was when we got back from Dugger. I was getting the horse hitched back up to go to the doctor and I found the barn door hasp had been pried off the door. Nothing I could see was taken, but you could tell that someone was in there snooping around."

"Funny thing is, Lovety and Minerva both said both their farms were broke into recently. I have my suspicions. It's a warning of sorts. Those sneaking around and peeking in is the work of the Klan is what I think. They're all over the place these days."

The Klan was there, all right. They had no idea that the Klan had started to grow when D.C. Stevenson came to Indiana and started selling Hoosiers on the idea that Catholics and foreign-born immigrants and Jews, as well as the coloreds, were not American citizens, and were a threat to their very existence. He capitalized on the "us versus them" theme. In addition, people who joined the Klan were against alcohol and believed that government, religion, patriotism, and politics were intimately intertwined. The WCTU and the Klan were soon aligned.

Stevenson was from Evansville and rose through the ranks from his local "klavern" to become the Grand Dragon in Indiana. Those who aspired to hold public office in Indiana flocked to the Klan, which by the mid-1920s could claim politicians ranging from local officeholders all the way up to Governor Edward L. Jackson, along with most of both houses of the General Assembly.

The folks that joined the Klan in the 1920s were Methodists and Baptists and Disciples of Christ. They were god-fearing Protestants. And they were one hundred percent white. In some counties, membership was estimated to have exceeded forty percent of all residents. However, Iletta and Paul were not among them, nor were their friends Adrian, Lovety, Grover, and Minerva.

Although Paul and Iletta had nothing to do with the moonshine business, Iletta knew people around them who made steady money in it, like Lovety and Minerva. Most farms around Shoals were family affairs and the family ran the farm and did the harvesting, occasionally needing outside help. At those times, any other folks who had a bit of free time would naturally lend a hand. But when it came to 'shining, families kept their business to themselves, for good reason.

"I need to know about the doctor and the visits and what

he is telling you. What about your side? You been holding on to it while you're working, and I've seen you crying. That's too much for me and I need to know. So, please?"

"Son, it's my hand I'm worrying over. I am losing my strength and I can't hold on to too much. The doctor said it was because of the operation I had and those tendons that they cut. It seemed like a good bargain at the time, but he says ultimately, it wasn't a good choice. They won't heal up any past what they are now. It's got me worried some, that's all. That big horse is too much for me to handle and I see you trying to keep him reigned short but he's getting out past you, too."

"Maybe he is, and I was thinking about it. When I seen Mr. Adrian and Minerva in the doctor's office, I wanted to let him know I could send him their way, if I got a fair price for him. I think, since you mentioned it, I might ride over to the Fields and Adrian could look him over. He's got an awful lot of corn this year and the weather is cooling now. He might think about using this big horse for this year's harvest."

On the way to Adrian and Minerva's place, Paul was reaffirming the idea that it would be good to get the big horse to someone who could use him. *He's a bit much to handle and with mom's hand getting hurt from reining him, it's better if he goes. We can use the money. It's getting tight and everybody's pinching their pennies, so we gotta do the same. If mom hurts her hand any more, that'd leave me in a bind. I don't get around any better myself. I'm hoping this will be a good day, all the way around.*

Adrian greeted him on the porch. "Howdy, Paul, that's the horse you want to talk about selling, isn't it? Come on and set a spell and let's get some tea." He headed to an oak tree in the yard.

Minerva came off the porch with tea and everyone cooled down in the shade.

"How's your mom, Paul? She doing all right, I hope? I didn't see her when we passed each other at the docs."

Paul noticed the big stitch job on Adrian's forearm, "You got into that tin pretty good, it looks like."

"Pretty good, all right. Let's take a look at this horse."

Opening the door on the barn and starting in, Paul smelled the unmistakable smell of 'shine.

"It's not the greatest of secrets that I have a still back in here, as you probably can tell. Your mom probably told you about it. I'm making a lot more money making moonshine than I can at selling feed corn." Walking on, he continued, "So this horse is what I need to pull my harvester. My other horses are getting strained up pretty good and they're getting too old to be pulling. I did get about three more acres put in this year, not a lot more, but some more, anyway."

"He's been a good horse for us. I got him when I was working at an Amish farm in Odon."

"I do need to tell you that Minerva has been concerned for you and Iletta, because of Lemuel. He was bad enough in the past, but the war done a lot to him on top of that, I'm sure."

"He's been that way since I can remember. He's in the alcoholic hospital now. I don't think he'll change. His mind is too far gone. It was before he ever left for the war."

"Let's settle up on this horse. I'll take him and since you now don't have a horse, Minnie can take you back in the buggy and she'll visit with Iletta some and then head on back. You can throw your saddle and bit in the back and carry it home, if that suits you."

"Why, yes, it does. Thank you. Mom has really enjoyed visiting with folks now that our farm is inviting once again. She's so much different now and full up of life." Paul chuckled with pleasure thinking about the change in his mother since Lemuel had been taken out of their lives.

On the way to Paul's, Minerva pulled up to her sister's place and said to Paul, "I'll get Lovety to come, too. It won't be a minute and Grover won't mind none. We're going everywhere together, these days. We let the men go about and do on their own. Don't you dare tell him I told you. We like the break from them, too." She winked at him as she said it and chuckled.

As they came up the road to his house, Paul saw his mother in the swing. She had a paper pad in her lap and had been writing a letter but had fallen asleep. Paul pulled the noisy wagon right up to the edge of the porch, and called out to her, expecting her to awaken with a start and a smile, pleased to see him home and with two of her favorite female visitors, at that. But Iletta didn't wake up. In an instant, they all recognized she had passed on. The angels had taken her home.

They laid Iletta in the front parlor, and then Minerva went for the doctor, while Lovety and Paul stayed with Iletta. Paul took the letter she had been writing and set it aside.

"Lots of things can be said right now," Lovety said, "but a lot of words sometimes is too much, too. You can give me your hand, Paul, and we will talk to the Lord together, and tell Him about the wonderful person He has called to be with Him."

Paul's throat was seized, and he was unable to speak for some time. He glanced into Lovety's eyes, then glanced up at the high meadow at the back of the farm and slowly pointed there. She knew what he was saying, and that his heart was broken. She looked at the meadow that he had pointed to and nodded approvingly.

Paul, heavy and grief-stricken, gathered his two crutches and walked into the field and made his way to the high corner and to the shade of a large sycamore tree and sat down in the tall grass.

When he saw the wagon return with Minerva, followed by the doctor, Paul pulled his crutches under his arms and made his way back down to the house. The doctor had already examined Iletta and was on the porch by the time Paul got there. They sat down together, while the sisters went out to the well to pull up a bucket of cool water for drinks.

"How could she have been taken so?"

"It was her wish, Paul, not to share all of her medical troubles with anyone, until—"

"Why was that? After all the things that had happened to her and me. I don't understand."

"That's the way it happens so many times, and you'll come to trust her final judgment this one last time. I'll tell you, only if you ask me."

"Please tell me what happened. Why did she die so suddenly?"

"Iletta was a strong and loving mother and she did what she could to protect you from harm, no matter what it was and no matter where it came from. You had your own burden put on you at far too early an age and she tried to carry yours as she could. She had been hurt emotionally and physically too many times. I suspect she was gravely injured during one of those times and her appendix must have been given more than it could have been able to recover from. It was swollen and I told her I needed to take it out, because it could burst at any time and take her life. She knew it all along, but she blamed her burned arm as the cause of her pain and suffering. That's the reason for your trip to Dugger to see her sister. She was hoping to get there to say good-bye before her time ran out. I'm very sorry, Paul."

Within the community of Shoals, most people knew of Iletta's death within a day or two. Once the doctor returned to town, the news spread quickly. Many of the families knew about the Chandler family from the stories that were told and passed around about Lemuel's mean streak. They also knew he refused to get medical treatment for Paul and that was the reason Paul was now crippled. Lemuel was known in the moonshine community and although some people didn't like the idea of buying from him, they did. He became the object of the lesson many parents told to their children, as to what happened when you drink moonshine. Children also knew that Paul was given the name Crooks when he was still going to school. In the community, there always seemed to be a dark cloud that followed the Chandler family around.

Minerva and Lovety were there to take care of many things that needed to be looked after. Paul wasn't in the frame of mind to be of much help and they knew that. On the next morning, they saw Mrs. Olsham, the retired teacher, coming up to the house in her buggy, ready to assist.

One of the first items of importance, Mrs. Olsham said, was to decide which cemetery might be chosen—the one on Chicken Farm Road or the one on Dog Trot? But it seemed it was neither. Paul would be burying his mother on the farm in the high meadow under the big sycamore tree.

The common practice was to inter a body within about three days, unless blocks of ice would be available to place under the torso to keep it cool. Tradition was observed, and the body was washed, and dressed in clean clothes.

On the third day, Paul was astonished to see two Amish wagons coming up the road to the house. They reined in at the barn. One of the wagons carried a plain wooden coffin.

"It's my friends from Odon I worked for," Paul explained to the neighbors who were still there helping him. "It's Samuel Rollins and it looks like he brought a friend and a coffin for my mother. Now that is something really nice, yes sir."

"We heard about you losing your mother and we were really sorry to hear it. I was in town when I heard about it. Paul, this is my neighbor, Daniel Wheatman." The men shook hands. "We came to pay our respects now and our families will be along in time."

"So very glad to see you. This brings me so much comfort. You can't imagine." As Paul looked over to the coffin in the back of Daniel's wagon, Minerva, Lovety, and Mrs. Olsham approached, and introductions were made.

Minerva said, "Let me borrow these men for a few minutes while you stay out here, out of our way." The men brought the coffin in to the parlor and the ladies moved the body into it, arranging Iletta to look as if she was still just sleeping.

Samuel and Daniel already knew that Paul would want to see that the grave was dug properly. It would give him something to keep himself busy. Mrs. Olsham was the first to leave to go back to town and then the wives went back to their farms for a change of clothes and to freshen up. They would come back later to begin the wake. Iletta was then presented in the parlor.

As the men stepped through the field, they made some idle talk. Samuel spoke first, "Paul, you still have that big horse you got from us? Daniel would like one like him, if you ever decide to sell."

"I just sold him two days ago to my neighbor, Adrian Fields. You know him?"

"I don't think I do."

"He'll be here for the funeral and you can meet him. If he does want to sell that big horse, you can be the first in line, I suppose."

"Fair, enough. Paul. We'd like to turn over some sod in remembrance of your mother. Samuel told me about your good nature and willingness to do an honest and full day of work and it would be our pleasure. Why don't you start and mark out the place you want, and we'll follow your lead, how's that?"

"Thank you, both of you," Paul said, looking gratefully at the two men. "I'll need a moment, though—" and he took out a handkerchief and wiped his eyes, then kept his head down. Looking at the ground, and using one of his crutches, he began marking out the area to be dug.

"This will be a wonderful place of remembrance, I do believe. Yes, it will." Paul backed up into the shade and the Amish men began digging.

Chapter 12

As the small town of Shoals prepared to bury another poor down-and-out farmer, the KKK, in discharging their local duties, decided how it was discharged, by whom and why, and always kept the wheels of justice tuned to their wishes and edicts. It came down to who would be accepted or refused burial in which cemetery because of their religion. The Klan preferred to know if they were white Protestants. However, a private burial on private land was not of interest.

A few local folks showed up for the wake, ahead of the grave-side service. Local news traveled fast but didn't travel much out of the county unless it was carried by word of mouth. And as such, word did get to Iletta's sister, Dorothy, but not to Lemuel. If he had known, he probably would not have come. And if he did, he would have been sent away, *persona non grata*.

The Amish families of Samuel Rollins and Daniel Wheatman were present. The sheriff and his wife and the doctor and his wife came together. Mrs. Olsham was there but left early after paying her respects. The Tillfords, Robert and Margie, came with Arnie. Doofus and his mother were present, and Jed came alone. Ina Fay's parents came, too. Adrian joined his wife Minerva, and finally Grover joined his wife Lovety, and they all walked through the high meadow to the big sycamore tree.

It was a shady and cool afternoon funeral, as the fall weather began showing up. The breeze showed in the murmuring tussocks and the meadow larks chirped an occasional call. Believing that a better day is always beckoning, the friends and neighbors gathered and began their singing with "Shall We Gather at the River."

The reflections of a hopeful life fulfilled, "Amazing Grace" was next. The Fellowship of Love sermon was concluding, when a wagon approached the meadow at great speed, the driver shouting, "Fire! Two barns are burning on the next farm over. One of 'em is a big red barn next to a white silo. It's bad! We need everyone!"

"That—that's our place!" Adrian shouted. He looked around to see who could help. "Get people in the wagons and come. Eli and Isaac are in the barn." He ran down the hill to get on his horse and get to the barn as fast as he could.

"Everyone—GO!"

Paul motioned for everyone to get down the hill and he grabbed his crutches and immediately fell and rolled over, before getting to his knees, gathering his crutches, and starting again. "Dorothy!"

"I'm good, you go. We'll come, we will come,"

"Our place is on fire too. We're next to them," Grover said hurriedly. "I've got to go now, Lovety. Help them and then come." He ran down the hill and got to a wagon full of men who had raced to the bottom and were leaving. He climbed aboard as they galloped away.

People were going in every direction and trying to get to a horse or buggy, throwing out questions as they hurried about.

"How could two different barns catch on fire at the same time?"

"Who is there?"

"Who would do something like this? This is not coincidence."

Smoke could now be seen over the horizon in the distance. Black, ugly smoke. As people got closer, they saw two billowing columns of black. These were from the barns that were going to be burned to the ground before any help could arrive.

Adrian raced to his barn and yelled inside, "Eli, Isaac, where are you?" and heard a young boy's screams. Samuel reached the barn next. He rushed behind Adrian and heard the two boys' voices calling out. They were yelling, "We're in the hayloft. Someone get the horse! It's locked in the stall—"

Samuel went around to the back to get into the hayloft to try to get the boys out, while Adrian rushed into the barn and got the horse stall unlocked, freeing the horse. And then, the hayloft collapsed with the boys inside the inferno. Adrian was below them.

Samuel couldn't move ahead into the wall of fire and had to retreat. He fell backwards over something, tripped, and hit the ground, and was knocked out. Screams were the last thing he remembered hearing as he blacked out. He was dragged back away from the barn, clothing singed.

Daniel Wheatman, Robert Tillford, and Grover McCullough reached Grover's barn just as the large wooden rafters were starting to fall. His barn was destroyed. Looking across the adjoining field he saw the back of Adrian's house was on fire. His barn was already done for. It wasn't close to anything else that would burn, so the three men ran over to Adrian's house to help contain that blaze. People were showing up in wagons and were directed to Adrian's house to help. Several people were already gathered around underneath a tree with someone on the ground, wrapped in a blanket.

Minerva arrived and jumped down from her wagon and ran over to the crowd that had gathered to watch the burning house. She sensed terror.

"Why isn't anyone doing anything? What's wrong? Samuel, where's Adrian? Was he with you?"

Samuel looked up into her eyes and dropped his head. He was covered in charcoal dust and his arms were badly burned. "Minerva—" At the sound of the hesitancy in his voice, she collapsed. "Where is he? Where—?"

Lovety said, "Minnie, the barn collapsed on him when he was trying to save Eli and Isaac. All three are dead—my dear God."

"We have to go back and get the doctor and the sheriff to come. We took the last buggy that was available, and they have no way to get here. Someone has got to go back."

"We'll go back with you. They'll need two buggies and we need to get with Paul," someone said.

"Let's take Samuel back to Paul's with us to get him tended to by his family."

The returning wagons showed a picture of bad when they got to Paul's. People were running about again, and everyone contributed to a description of the events that had happened. People were stunned to hear the news that three people were dead. How?

The sheriff's and doctor's wives went with them to the burned-out barns. The sheriff would have to do some investigation. He and the doctor had to go.

Lovety was with her sister and waiting for she didn't know what. She was at a deep loss.

The fire to the back of the house was out, but smoke had gotten into the house and it would need to be aired out. That could all wait. She looked into the pasture and saw that big horse, and yelled, "Someone, take that animal away!"

Daniel spoke, "I'll take it to my place when I go home."

"Fine."

The sheriff arrived and looked around. The doctor had Lovety take Minerva over next door for the night. The men brought Adrian's body and the bodies of the two boys to the parlor of Grover and Lovety's house.

The sheriff's duty was to go to each of the boy's homes and notify the families to come to the farm the next day. The day was getting long, and nothing could really be done at night. Sleep and food were about the best thing till then.

They turned their buggy back around and the doctor looked at Samuel's burned arms. Then the Amish folks had to decide whether to head back to Odon or spend the night in the barn, which they decided would be preferable. They would also be taking back that big Percheron horse and daylight was better for that task.

Paul and his aunt Dorothy were sitting together up in the high meadow by the gravesite. Robert Tillford and Paul's buddies arrived and did the honor of burying his mother for him. And then they left.

The doctor returned to tend to Samuel's burned arms. As he was preparing to bandage them, Paul emerged from the house with a bottle of Hinds Honey and Almond Cream. He handed it to Samuel, saying, "It works."

Chapter 13

~~~~~~~~~~~~~~~~~~~~

Lying in bed before the sun showed a glimmer of light, Paul thought, *Where do I start this day? With my worn out and busted up old self, I need to figure out what this day will let me get on to. I have folks in the barn I need to tend to, a friend with burned arms, friends that have been called to Glory, people that need my help to get themselves back on a better road than they're on. The fork in the road comes at any time, I suppose. Dear Lord, what can I do for Thee? The Lord is the one who gives me work for my hands to do.*

At that point, Paul heard someone rattling around the stove and added, *Thank you, oh Lord, for my Aunt Dorothy.* He rose, got dressed and hobbled to the kitchen. Under the lantern light, sitting at the table were Dorothy and Daniel, having coffee with smiles on their faces and talking quietly. Paul thought, *Thank you, Lord, you have turned this day already.*

Daniel had a ham hock in front of him that he was carving on. Paul saw that Dorothy was making biscuits.

"Daniel, how is your family? Did everybody sleep okay? Peace and quiet for one night was good for all of us, I suppose."

"It was, indeed, quiet as a mouse, as you English say," and Samuel laughed.

"I need to see how Samuel's arms are doing this morning, first off. Then, we'll see—"

"Don't be looking for the harness quite so soon, this day, Paul. It will come along as He sees fit. Your dear aunt is a gem. We may want to take her to our place to be with us."

Daniel was looking at Dorothy with a smile.

"I'll stay here for now, thank you, Daniel. We have our duties to do but thank you. I want those kids out in the barn and your lovely wife taken care of, first off."

"Sarah and the kids will be fine. She's a good woman. That she is."

The Chandler farm was coming awake and people were stirring and getting up and on with the day. Samuel was attended to and his arms, once cleaned of the charcoal suet, looked much better. Dorothy fussed about, preparing a breakfast with eggs, ham, and biscuits with jam for everyone. Without notice, she slipped away and went up to the high meadow to her sister's grave.

Paul began looking out on a new world that first day after his mother had been laid to rest under the sycamore tree. The press of life was pushing down on him and all those around him. Though he wondered when the next bend in the road would come, it was not something he would spend a lot of time dwelling on. He put his hat on and got ready to see his next calling unfold. He felt a little lighter in his spirit. He didn't know why, but he just did.

Paul and his aunt took the wagon towards the burned-out farms. Dorothy fretted. "While I'm here, I'll be going through the things in the house that Iletta would want Lovety and Minerva to have. It seems most appropriate to be able to pass them on now, as a result of the fire, and all. Minerva has got to go on with her grief till she can set it aside and start to see a new day. It will be different for her than it is for you. As a woman, I know what that loss is. I can't tell her how to do it, Paul, but you can help them by passing on some things. Does that sound reasonable to you?"

"Yes, it does. I was also thinking about those young boys from the barn. I wish I had something to pass on to them and their families."

"What was the story there?"

"I only got bits of things during the confusion. The boys were there to help Adrian start to harvest their corn. They were moving hay bales around and getting ready to sack corn because it was dry enough."

"I sold him that horse and he paid for him in cash. I still got the money in my sock," Paul smiled. "I think I should buy him back, seeing how things are now."

"That's good of you to think about getting it back to right," Dorothy agreed. "Yesterday, after all of it happened, Minerva said she wanted it gone and Daniel is to take it back to the Amish folks when they go home. That sounds like it will come out to the good."

Arriving at the burned barns, Paul and Dorothy saw several saddled horses and a few buggies gathered, and many people grouped in the shade. One family was taking their dead child to their wagon for the trip back home. Condolences were given and shared by everyone. A family member spotted Paul and Dorothy arriving and offered their sympathies.

"Paul, Ma'am, we want to say we are so sorry for your own loss and sorry again for the disruption of your service."

Hats were soon returned to their heads and the family loaded the buckboard and followed the boy's body away. The caravan of sorrow left Paul leaning against a hitching post, watching them depart. He lingered there for several minutes in contemplation.

Lovety came over and hugged both of them. "We're glad you two are here with us. It has been a trying time."

"How is Minerva? We want to see her if we can."

"She was up earlier before those folks came and went back to lying down again, until after they departed."

Minerva appeared at the front door of Lovety's house and moved onto the porch. The three of them embraced without words and then sat on the porch swing. Dorothy noticed flower heads on the hydrangea bush next to the house were stirring. "Today starts out with a fresh breeze, don't it, girl?" Minerva gave back a slight smile and then returned to looking out to the road.

The Amish families said their farewells and expressed more condolences. The big horse was already haltered and tied to a lead rope at the back of Samuel's wagon and Daniel and his family came next.

Before they had a chance to speak, Paul nodded, "My thanks are to you, first, because you came to honor my mother and me by all you've done. I so regret that many unforeseen things happened while you were here. May God keep you safe and healthy until I can get to see you again. Please have safe travels, Samuel, and take care of those arms and your new horse."

This day is for weeping, I believe, Paul said to himself, as the other dead boy's family pulled up in their wagon and the events played out in tandem. *To be given the potential for a great life and then to be rushed on out of it—*

After the second wagon departed, Minerva was sent to sit in the shade tree swing and let Dorothy and Lovety begin the preparations on Adrian. As emotionally drained as Minerva was, she did choose to idle some time and reflect on the here and beyond. Grover and Paul went to Adrian's barn to look around and see what presented itself.

One of the first things Grover saw, he commented on. "Look right over here, do you see what I think I'm seeing? This east wall and south corner are burned up to a crisp. It looks like it was burned on purpose. Look here, there's the coal oil can—and here, there's another can in that corner. Well, that's how they done it."

Paul looked on and followed him as they both rummaged around. The floor in one crib was filled with tin cans, crocks, and cases of quart jars that had been stacked two or three feet high but had crashed over and spilled out during the fire. It was sure enough the storage place for moonshine, no doubt about it. No hiding the evidence.

Grover didn't comment and moved on through the rubble, poking and moving things around.

"Well," he finally said, "it will take a good bit of time to clear this site. What can be salvaged I would start there, then gather this back into a pile and light it up again. Then it can be loaded up and taken down to the sink holes at the bottom of these fields and dumped and disposed of. Same as for my place, I suspect. Let's go look at the back of the house and see how that did. Come on."

A look at the back room of the house showed a couple of walls almost burned through that would need repairing and a new covering of wallpaper. A big crop of drying corn was standing in the fields and the silo was already full. Adrian had good planning skills and had made use of his buildings to his advantage. The moonshine business had been tucked inside the walls of the barn so no prying eyes could see in. No more pretense now, though.

The evolution of thought, once Adrian was laid to rest, was to take as much furniture as could be accommodated and stuff it into a couple of rooms in the house and fill the other rooms with corn to save as much as they could manage.

"It might mess up the house a bit, but the structure is solid, and it will take a load, same as my farmhouse next door. The folks that built this place built mine at the same time. We won't save a lot, but we can save some."

"Grover, let's go back over and look at your place. You got some planning and fixing to do, too. Minerva will be living with you for a spell and I'll do what I can to help, you know I will. My place is going to have me working it and I'm not able to get too much done, but I can manage some."

The barn that had burned down on Grover's land was not as big as the one that burned down on Adrian's farm. But Grover had an orchard and he needed grinding and pressing equipment to squeeze out the apple juice.

"You've got a good thing going for you, in a way, Grover. All your apples are still on the trees and getting them juiced can be delayed a little, I suppose," Paul offered.

"Well, that's right. I had loaned out lots of canning jars to Adrian. So that's got me worried, as you can see. I'll figure on it some more and come up with something. Right now, we got to take care of Minerva and lay down old Adrian, God rest his soul. Fine man and I'll miss him. But right now, I need to go to town and check on a few things, if you want to go."

"I think I will. The things that need done around here are being taken care of by the women. I'm just under foot right now. So, what's your thinking?"

"The first stop will be to see Mr. Herndon at the Mercantile and see what he's got in the way of whiskey kegs and barrels. I can use what he can find for me. The second stop is to see the sheriff to find out what he's going to do about our barn burnings. It was clearly intentional, both of them, and I want arrests. It is downright murder. They killed those boys straight out. The death of Adrian counted in that number, as well. This time the sheriff was right there. No slacking."

He got to thinking about the similarities to some local

history. "In the 1880s of course, Patrick Archer and his gang run these hills and hollers for a time and burned people out and murdered many a man for getting in their way. He terrorized farmers all over here. Kept that man tied up in that cave on the bluff and tortured him for days, chopped him up, spread out the body parts and burned what was left. We people of Shoals won't stand for that kind of lawlessness. It's now elevated to cold blooded murder. I'll put a hole in anyone I see from this time forward, I'll tell you that, and if the sheriff won't step up on it, these good folks will. I already got my suspicions."

In town they went straight to the Mercantile. Their first order of business was to get a pine box casket for Adrian and then discuss the other things that hung in the air. Paul decided to buy an Indianapolis newspaper to read later.

Wooden barrels were plentiful, and Grover could come back and get as many as he needed, he was told. After loading a casket on to the wagon, they headed to the sheriff's office. Grover already had a brow set when they arrived, passing Mrs. Olsham as she was leaving. They nodded to each other, as Grover and Paul entered.

The sheriff was sympathetic. "I've seen too many good people in mourning already and am sorry for you and your neighbors with the recent losses that have occurred."

"Thank you, sheriff. I've got a casket now that I'm taking for Adrian's family. But I come on the related matters of who is trying to burn us out and who killed those boys—burned them up alive. And who killed Adrian in that fire?"

"This one is going to take some time to get to the bottom of it. Considering that everyone had gathered at your place for your mother, Paul, it was a vile and dastardly thing."

"Sheriff, you know what happens around here and who is out to do folks harm. I'm a God-fearing Christian and don't look to harm others, but I won't cotton to arson and murder. People will not tolerate that around Shoals. I expect you to find out, somehow, some way. Three murders have occurred, and this won't be kept quiet. You know someone will say something or let something slip. That's how evil works and it'll get out. Come out to the farm and look for clues or anything you need to do, sheriff. In the meantime, we've got to bury two fine innocent boys and a fine man." And with that said, they turned and walked out to the street.

The sheriff seemed to be supportive and understanding.

"He seemed to be sympathetic, but it's what he didn't say that's as much a telling as what he did say. I know it and he knows that I know he seen all them fruit jars stacked up in that smoke room that was full of moonshine. And yet, he didn't say a word about it. He's connected to the Ku Klux Klan in some way and he's got eyes and ears everywhere. What I choose to do with my corn is my business. Things are getting mighty bad and folks are barely making it, at best. And now, we got to make our way with Minerva. The only other casket I ever want to see from this point is my own."

"Why do you say that, Grover? I know this is a heavy-hearted business we're doin' right now."

"Well, you heard this a thousand times, but bad luck happens in threes. That's what the sayin' is. While you were sittin' on this bench, I helped old Herndon there get that casket from his outback shed, where he stores stuff. When we went in to get it, I seem he had four of 'em. I told him about them young boys a dyin' and that he might expect them families to be along, directly. So, I put the thought together and counted up and with their two caskets, and then ours, that's three. Now, that leaves just that one leaning against the wall and I sure don't want it to be mine. It could give me the shivers, so I got out of that shed quick enough. Then, Herndon said he's never thought he would sell three caskets at once—never has before."

Back at the orchard farm, the casket was unloaded. Grover, Dorothy, and Lovety moved the body to the casket with some effort, which they then set in the parlor. Viewing commenced the next day.

Paul and Dorothy headed back to the Chandler farm. Paul went to the high meadow and Dorothy started dividing out women's things for Minerva to have, once the casket was in the ground and the time was right. It was the first real pause they had had since all the tribulations started.

On the way to their farm they talked about their visit to the sheriff and what was said. Dorothy picked up on the part of the conversation about the KKK's eyes and ears.

"I can tell you one set of eyes and ears that nobody's seeing."

"Well—who in the world might that be?"

"From the gitty-up, I knew something was off when we were all being introduced around and the folks started showing up for my sister's wake. She was right under your nose. The person who is sending information on is your old schoolteacher, Mrs. Olsham."

"I can hardly believe that!"

"Well, believe it. Here's how I figured it out. She came out at the same time as the sheriff and his wagon, right behind them. After introductions, she was very interested in where you were choosing to bury Iletta and went cold when you told her we weren't going to go to either of those cemeteries. Another bit to consider. She was here for the wake but left before the graveside and went somewhere. I thought it was odd that she showed back up when the barns were ablaze. The town is in the other direction. How did she know about the barns?"

"God, if that's true—we did see her coming out of the sheriff's office when we pulled up. She seemed a little bit surprised to see us, but acted like we were strangers, even though I know she remembers me from school. Of course, she knew all along about Lemuel making 'shine. She helped me with getting information on the hospitals, so I don't know how to take all of this."

"Take it any way you want to, but there are eyes out there looking to stir up trouble."

Once they returned to the farm, Dorothy began going through her sister's things with Minerva's needs in mind. They were both a similar size and Dorothy found several items of clothing that Iletta had that were of little or no wear. Her life had been a life of hurt and abuse at Lemuel's hands, and consequently, she never had the occasion to dress up in anything nice, and so those few nice things she owned were stored away. As sad as it was, they were going to have to get past it. From now on, Paul's mother's clothes became signposts that pointed towards eternity.

In the barn, Paul found the hay under the loft had been fluffed up for bedding for the kids. As he swept the hay back into the stall, a loose board rattled under his feet and he looked down and found a large compartment filled with jars of moonshine. Under the boards were gallons and gallons of the stuff that Lemuel had hidden as a stash that could be sold for good money.

I don't want to dump it out, Paul thought, *but I could get rid of it and use the money for an emergency.*

Paul settled in on the porch and picked up the Indianapolis newspaper he had bought in town and found himself focused on an article about the fall of the once all-powerful Grand Dragon of the KKK in Indiana, D.C. Stephenson. Stephenson had attended the inaugural ball of the newly elected governor, Edward L. Jackson. It was there he spied the lovely Madge Oberholtzer, who was the head of the state's commission to combat illiteracy. Ms. Oberholtzer was abducted from her home by Stephenson, taken to the Indianapolis train station, and held in a private railroad car, where he repeatedly raped her. He then pleaded with her to marry him and she refused, and instead she tried to commit suicide. Stephenson had her secretly returned to her bed, thinking that she would die from the poisons she took. She did die, but not before making a sworn statement to the police about what had happened. A doctor who testified at Stephenson's trial said that Oberholtzer's wounds appeared as if a cannibal had chewed on her. She died about a month later and the Grand Dragon went to prison.

It was the Roaring Twenties in America, but the roaring went on somewhere else besides Shoals, Indiana. However, moonshine stills were still producing, despite Prohibition, in backwater towns and rural communities. The press investigation that followed Stephenson's fall from grace exposed many Klan members, showing they were not law-abiding, but quite the opposite, ending the power of the organization. As members dropped out by the tens of thousands, the threats that seemed to have come from the Klan looking in on everybody's business abated. Burning innocent people's farms, and the deaths of two young lads and a farmer was enough to drive the local member-ship numbers to fall to almost nothing. Their legal status was soon listed as defunct.

Chapter 14

Riding the wagon back to the funeral at the Fields farm, Paul and Dorothy shared precious times and memories of Iletta and set the mood of promise for the future. Promises to write were made and they both knew the press of hard times were before them. Dorothy would have to return to Dugger and go back to a hardscrabble life in the coal fields and scratch it out as best she could. She was heavy with having the death of her sister on her heart and tried to not show any of her soft side, other than a few occasional tears. She had had plenty of practice and did a good job of it, but Paul saw through it. *God, she looks so much like mom.*

"Here is my last idea I'll leave you with, Paul. Not pushing you on to anything, but that moonshine stored in the barn is worth moving it on. You ever think you could drive a stake bed truck, with your leg and all? I bet you could do it. Hell, you ain't gonna go drink it, are you? Ha, ha. Let's go say good-bye to this lovely man and I'll get on with myself after that."

It was a triple-pronged effort to keep the priorities straight and stay the course of working on Minerva's burned house and setting her place winter-ready, getting the corn out of the fields and into the silo, and harvesting the annual crop of apples for Grover and Lovety.

With Paul's farm now occupied only by him, he found himself lending his hands to his neighbors. His stand of sorghum was the only cash crop he would see at the end of the year, besides the windfall that came from getting the moonshine out from the hidden compartments of his barn. He bought a Ford stake bed truck with the proceeds.

After Adrian's funeral, Grover and Lovety, Minerva and Paul needed to gather their strength and work together with whatever resources they had to try and get by until a better turn in the road could be reached. Three farms to run by four people was a very tall order, indeed. Regardless of the collective and personal sorrows they carried, their conclusions were to be cast by the circumstances that developed among them. They were land rich and resource poor.

"Trying to get this back bedroom cleaned up and rebuilt for the winter. After a week, does seem like we might want to put it off till spring," Grover noted. "I don't see that we're going to get it into the dry and insulated in time to do much more. I know, Minnie, you want to have your place back and to be able to get back into your house a.s.a.p. but we can certainly heat one house a lot easier, just for this winter, by waiting till we can fix it right."

"It does make sense for me to be in your house till spring. Settled, then."

"Well, we got the room, don't we?" Lovety asked Grover.

Grover nodded a "Yes," and then turned to Paul. "So, with you Paul, what's your thinking? You might as well be here, too, since it would be only you up there."

"We had already laid our wood in for the winter, so's I'll be all right there. Food and canning were about done, anyway. I'll still get around, now that I got a stake bed. I like the change of not having to go hitch up the horse every time I want to get out and I don't have to feed the Ford, just the horse!" They all laughed.

The last of the apples were in and the juice squeezing continued. Just as Iletta had described it, Paul watched Grover and Lovety ferment the juice and turn it into apple jack. Then they waited for the freezes to come and freeze the water in the apple juice so they could take it off and bottle the remainder. And yes, it had a kick to it. The root cellar below the house was a very busy place.

The Adrian Fields farm and the Grover McCullough farm were next to each other because both of their wives were sisters—Minerva Pate Fields and Lovety Pate McCullough. They shared duties and rewards of having adjoining farms and they were not concerned if some cows from one place got past a fence and into another's pasture. They usually shared the butchered meat between them. So, it didn't matter that they were about to declare the agriculture conglomerate for the umpteenth time.

Paul was the odd man in, so to speak, and had the advantage on labor. He was always destined to be on a cane, except for short hops between things that were close at hand. The only thing he had to contribute was the land that was all his now, land that came with a middle-aged horse and a couple of hand plows, one that was rigged with a riding box attached behind, that he rode in with the old horse pulling.

Adrian and Minerva purchased a Fordson tractor at just the right time. Some years back, Ford Motors, the manufacturer of Fordson tractors, had faced serious and stiff competition from other manufacturers, such as J.I. Case, Allis-Chalmers, John Deere, and International Harvester. Ford decided to drastically reduce the cost of their tractors, from $625 to $395. Having adjoining farms meant they could plow and put in crops cheaper with their Fordson tractor than doing it with horses. For a while, it worked out.

"Minerva," Paul noted, "I wanted to tell you that when Adrian and I were talking about him buying that big Percheron from me, he let me know about the prices people were selling 'shine for and I was surprised to know it could be sold as high as $25 a gallon. That was what led me to get all that 'shine out of the barn and go sell it. It gave me the money to buy my truck. I want to thank him, through you."

Minerva teared up and turned away. "Look at me, all watery at the drop of the hat. You are so welcome."

"I am so very sorry—"

Paul tried to winter over at his farm. With his three friends staying warm and the corn crop now in, he went back and forth, now that he had a truck, to visit and lend a hand. But mostly he went for the company. Once the Indiana weather dropped to 10 degrees or so, Paul could hardly crank the truck and start it. He had to wait for it to warm up.

He had watched Grover build a small fire under the Fordson tractor to make it easier to start, and it occurred to him he might do the same with his truck. *Maybe it will work or maybe it won't. I'm not too sure that it would be worth the trouble and I don't want the truck to catch fire. Hell, I'll take the horse.*

On a following trip over to Grover's, Paul was waved to come over to Minerva's back door. Smoke was coming from the back of the house in the burned-out bedroom. The three of them were standing next to a fire that was under a moonshine kettle, keeping it and them warm. They smiled at him.

"Come in, Paul. Since the bedroom can't be used quite yet, we didn't want to waste the heat from the fire—and the whole place is filled with corn, anyway." They laughed.

What am I doing? Paul thought. The ugly old memories suddenly engulfed him as he stood in the doorway of the burned-out bedroom, looking, staring, smelling, and re-living the combined tragedies of his young life that were associated with a moonshine past. Within that moment, those tragedies and bad memories washed over him, and a chill reached his inner self, down inside his crippled body, right to his bones, and brought the stab of physical pain to him, again.

His stomach wretched instinctively and squeezed more pain to his consciousness. The memory of little or no food communicated itself to other memories which flooded into him like the venom of a snake bite, burning and stinging as it coursed his veins.

Go get me a switch, I'll teach you about misbehaving me.

I don't want to do this to you, but you just keep asking for it.

This will hurt me more than it will you.

The switch, the rope, the belt, the hoe handle, the slaps, and the fists all delivered the blows from his memory to his mind. The smell assailed his nose and his lungs.

Look at you, you're disgusting, can't even follow simple instructions.

I'm ashamed of you. You're no son of mine.

Get out of my sight, get out. Get out!

You are so goddamned dumb. Do I have to do it for you?

You're just plain worthless.

"Paul, you look dazed, are you all right standing there? Come over and get warm."

The paralysis of his memory lessened its grip and he moved over to the stove.

What have I done? What am I about to get myself back in to? What a hypocrite. I have now sold moonshine for that truck. It's liquor money.

And then he paused in thought. *I did the work of planting, I'm the one that swam in the mud. I'm the one that gathered the clam shells and sold them. I took the beatings and now I will have that truck to remind me of it, every time I use it. I earned it, every last bit of it. It will be my way out—sometime—sometime.*

"Paul, do you want to stay for supper? We're making double cornbread—you like that? The clerk at the mercantile said to me that you should go see him. The Amish over at Odon are going to be ready for a shipment or two of barn tin. They're going to build two big barns soon and he needs someone to haul it from his store out there and he'll pay you for it. We don't need any help, except to get some boxes of quart Ball jars the next time you think of it."

"No doubt about it, times are tough, and I could use the money. I got that last crop of sorghum we all divided up and my share ain't big enough to sell any. I'll go see him tomorrow. With this warm-up, I can crank the truck and take it to town and be back within a day, if the roads stay froze. I'll bring out jars in a few days." *Ain't nothing illegal about hauling Ball jars, I suppose.*

"So, you notice that the last snow has been off the fields for some time now and the earth is warming up?" Grover added. "We need to get those fields broke open and get the ground ready for planting. We better hope the markets don't stay down. It's bad out there—has been bad, too. We need to come up with something, that's for sure. We're about to go scratchin' if we can't catch a hold."

The three of them certainly knew what Grover was talking about. It was an agriculture depression that lasted the decade, all through the 20s. The demand for corn, wheat, and cotton had exceeded the U.S.'s ability to keep up during the war, which had caused inflation to rise and drove up commodity prices. The farmers saw great opportunities to cash in and they were encouraged to buy new land or lease it, and they were encouraged further to undertake new plantings and crops which encouraged new borrowing.

However, after the Great War ended and Europe began to renew their own farming industry, demand for American commodities fell sharply, and markets were severely reduced. Wages were cut and people started seeking work in the cities and going to the factories. The balance for the first time shifted. There were more people living and working in cities than on farms. Food and cotton prices collapsed. Farmers all over struggled with the effects of deflation. The great Chicago migration was underway.

In the meantime, farmers in Shoals and elsewhere were land rich and resource poor, but they didn't quite know it yet.

Having this truck might work out for me. It's a good start, I suppose, Paul told himself. I can maybe find enough to move about; I can stay away from the moonshine. Maybe go back to working for the Amish, since they don't use any gas machinery.

Returning home, Paul unsaddled the horse and turned it out to the pasture. He continued to think of ways to beat the odds and get in some crops that would raise a little money for the future. The trouble was that the farming business was at rock bottom. The idea of changing crops was exceedingly difficult. Implements that could be pulled along behind a tractor cost money. If there was no market, the money spent to buy tractor attachments or implements would be wasted. Only crops that could be put into the ground by hand would need to be considered. *I might be on to something—something besides corn or soybeans.*

PART THREE

Chapter 15

The roads were all drivable now and it was pushing planting time. As Paul went towards the Mercantile, he looked over the fields to see who had been out turning the ground and wondered what had been planted. As everyone was in the same situation as far as trying to make a crop to sell, Paul asked around and at the feed store to find out what kind of seeds were being sown.

He noticed three women at the end of the loading dock sitting around, as if waiting for a ride or a hitch. The clerk said that they had showed up the day before and were looking for work. They came up from the south, Arkansas or Missouri he thought. Paul said that they looked like they could use a meal, and the clerk agreed they were pretty well played out, as he loaded sheet tin into the back of his truck.

Preoccupied with his planting plans, Paul left and went to Odon, dropped his cargo off and headed back to get the other half. He was thinking about the three women at the Mercantile and wondering how they were going to make it when he pulled back into the dock to reload. *Yep, they're still here.* Looking at them a little closer, Paul saw they were more than pretty well played out. They were plainly down and out. Someone needs to help them, he thought, and so he limped over to them while the tin was loaded.

"Hello, there. I saw you earlier today and thought you were waiting for someone. How long you been here?"

One of them responded, "Thanks for asking. 'Bout four days I think," and then she turned to the other two with the question. They nodded in agreement and stared back. Even with a glance into their eyes, Paul knew they were in trouble. He knew that look and what it meant, given his own past troubles. He thought he felt his heart skip a beat.

"I'm taking a load of tin up the road toward Odon. If you're headed that way, I could give you a lift, unless you're waiting for someone specific."

"We were, a couple of days ago, but they never came. We don't know this area. What's in Odon, you say? By the way, I'm Bernice Cauthen, this is Mayvis Bailey, and that is Sophie Melvin. We probably should be getting back on the road, anyway. It sounds like north of here, so's that's fine."

Paul got the tin loaded, and they climbed aboard, Bernice in the cab and the other two in back holding down the tin. At that point, he realized that it was too late to make it to Odon and back, and so considered his options. He saw that Bernice was freely talking and that suited him, someone to talk to. "What's north?" he asked her.

"We're headed towards Chicago to find work in the textile mills. We heard there was work there. We been in Missouri but didn't find too much. Thought we better keep going before our resources get tapped out."

"You folks got a place to go to for the night?" He glanced their way but already knew what the answer would be. "No? In that case, let me have you come with me. My farm is up the road a few miles. I'll not make it to Odon and back here before dark, so I'll start out tomorrow. My mother was all I had left, and she passed on not too long ago, so's it's only me. Got a house that's empty and an empty barn."

All three were bone tired and grateful. Paul felt better about them now. He pulled up to the barn and showed them the hay room. "We'll do very well out here," Bernice assured him. "So, don't fuss. We've had some experience sleeping in barns. This will be swell, thank you."

The three women unloaded what little they had from the truck and started to settle in.

"I'm not the best cook, Bernice, but I'm still living." Paul joked, and then assured her that he would have some breakfast for them the next morning. Back-to-back meals would be fine by them.

Cornbread, beans, and a slice of pork shoulder made the meal. The three women took over cleaning up after breakfast. Mayvis went out on the porch and began combing her hair. Paul watched, somewhat fascinated. *A woman at this place—that's nice to see after the funeral. It's been awhile.*

"Is that real coffee I smell coming from the porch?" a voice from outside said.

"It is indeed. I thought I would make some. I don't usually make it just for me. Come in."

"The porch is fine for me, it's peaceful out here. Far better than the road," Bernice said.

Paul nodded. "I'm headed up the road an hour or so away, then headed over to Grover's place to deliver their Ball jars and then back here. I'll be gone three hours or so and then back. If you want to get a slow start and all, relax till I get back, you go right ahead. Any food you find you can cook it up and I got a well pump and water right at the kitchen sink, so make yourselves at home."

"You are quite a man, Mr. Paul Chandler. We are most grateful. A day off the road is what we really need right now. It's sure nice to know you, sir."

Paul blushed hearing the pleasantries given to him and he headed over to Grover's farm without saying another word. When he returned, the three women were ready to load their belongings back on the truck, but they stayed at the house while Paul headed north for business in Odon and then returned to the farm.

While in Odon, Paul met his friends Samuel and Daniel. They had not talked since Iletta's funeral and the barn fires. Paul found out that the Amish had three or four barns scheduled to be built or repaired that year. Three of the four were pending because the owners had no money to pay for lumber and for the extra workers. There was enough work in their community without hiring extras. The tin was for their community projects. They teased Paul about his new truck.

"It's for hire, fellas. Haul by Paul," he said, with a chuckle.

"I've got three women staying at my farm."

Minerva and the two McCulloughs stopped and stared at Paul, not knowing how to take in what they had just heard.

"Say again, Paul, did I hear you right? You have three women at your place? Who are they? Do we know them?" Lovety laughed.

"Well, when I went to get tin to take up to Odon, I saw these three women sitting on the feed dock, like they was waiting for someone to give them a ride. I didn't recognize them and so went on about my business. The clerk said they came up from

Missouri and had been working as sharecroppers and migrant laborers. They looked mighty spent from their looks and about to get in some real trouble. They hadn't had food for several days, so I took them in and now they're staying at my place."

"Well, what's next? What are you going to do now?"

"I think I can help them. I think we could help them. So, let me tell you an idea," he went on. "Since it's about planting season and they need the work, why don't we put them to use for us? They could help get our crops in the ground and you can finish your 'corn project.' Grover, you could be freed up to get the tractor going on the ground."

"Well, we could. Might make a bang-up year if we had extra hands," Minerva added. "Me and Sis could finish this corn and clean out the house. I'll be ready to get myself back in my place. The quicker we finish, the quicker we can start on the repairs. Might work, Paul, it just might."

"They'll stay at my place; I got the room. And for all them hands, I thought on this, too. What about growing peanuts? It would help out the soil with the nitrogen, from what I've heard. We need about four months of growing, though. Once that's in, we can go after planting sorghum. They can de-tassel the seed heads before we lay down the cane and we can get a bigger seed harvest."

"How are you gonna do that?" Minerva questioned.

"So, pulling the wagon down the row, right next to the cane—it's a matter of bending it over the bed of the wagon, cutting and dropping them tops right into the bed, then cutting the cane after the wagon passes by and laying it out to rest 'till we gather it for the press. Two on the ground and two in the wagon, like a machine."

"If you'uns can keep them women out of our 'shine business,' let's use the help," Lovety decided.

The three women watched the Model T come up the farm road and Paul almost pulled up to a stop at the porch, but the Ford moved on up the yard and over an old milk pail, flattening it. He was a bit embarrassed for them to see that he couldn't quite control the stopping part of the truck. As he got out and retrieved his cane, he saw all of them with big smiles on their faces.

"I'm new at this, so pails better watch it, huh?" He saw smoke from the kitchen stove coming out of the pipe. "I never ever thought I would be able to drive with this bum leg."

"Oh, you do fine, sir," Sophie said. "Those things are a little scary to me."

"I'll do much better if I'm just 'Paul' to everyone. How did everyone's day go? Everyone resting up?"

"We did fine, thank you—Paul," said Mayvis.

"There was a crock of tea already made so we put some things together. That garden you have needed some attention. There were lots of things needing picking. Hope you don't mind, but we see all food as a blessing these days, don't we ladies?" They all nodded. With that, everyone went inside and sat around the table. Once seated, they folded their hands and said Grace. Paul hadn't seen prayer hands for a long time at his place. *I can start a tradition from this day at this new table with new friends, with Mom watching.*

"We are very thankful, again, for you putting us up, sharing a meal, and letting us stay for the night," Sophie offered. "Bernice and I went up to your mom's graveside earlier to pay our respects. Mayvis stayed here and cooked. We miss our families, too, and we know your mother passed away very recently. We're sorry for your loss." And they nodded.

"You folks are too kind to me, every time I turn around."

Conversations were becoming easier, and each in turn told the story of how it had been on the road, and Paul learned that so many others were in hard times, too. He had a farm but not much else. They didn't seem to have more than the clothes on their backs. He felt no need to ask what it was that got them traveling on the roads in the first place, but they felt compelled to tell their tales.

Bernice was first. "Sophie and me were working in Missouri on a cotton field and we met Mayvis. She was coming up from Arkansas. Us two had looked to get our wages from the place, but the man that owned it died and they wouldn't pay us. Most of the other folks were all living on their places and had nowhere else to go. They at least had some food from the gardens they had. They were all Negro workers and they weren't about to share anything with us. It was gonna get pretty skimpy for them real quick, too. Mayvis was traveling with the Mexicans that were headed to the Midwest and so, we hooked up and came along, too. You can tell your part, Mayvis, but we got kinda stuck in Louisville after Missouri and decided to go west a bit."

"The textile mills in Kentucky," Mayvis said, "was near impossible to get on. We had heard that it was even worse as far up as New England. The Negroes and the Mexicans were headed north and the textilers were heading down this way. One out of two were coming this way because of the wages. New England wages they said were over twenty-one dollars for forty-eight hours of work. Now, in the South, they get almost sixteen dollars for fifty-five hours of work. It don't seem right. Everybody is being discriminated against."

Sophie lamented, "We went North, they went South, and now we're about to go sideways."

Bernice summed it up. "Maybe we should walk sideways over to the ocean and all jump in."

Everybody laughed at that and they made another night, together.

◇　◇　◇

Since January of 1920, when Prohibition came into effect, the hard times the women found on the road as farm laborers were widespread. People were played out and they tried any half-baked idea to try to make a buck. Paul's farm was an "any-port-in-the-storm" opportunity for the women. They felt the government was against them and every day seemed to be a make-it-or-break-it day. The heart was stripped out of the heartland, as they saw it. The government had even taken the common folk's common comfort, the right to drink, away from them.

With no apologies, the Federal Government worked extra hard to dissuade America from drinking now that Prohibition was in full swing. The 18th Amendment was purposed to keep America dry. The beautiful new world picture painted by the WCTU—that a world without alcohol would halt crime, erase poverty, quell violence, diminish marital abuse, lessen sickness, and erase premature death—didn't work out.

There was another group that thought otherwise, using violence to control the flow of alcohol—the Mob. Prohibition destroyed the fifth largest industry in America. Bootleggers filled the gap anyway they could and produced moonshine with toxins that leached into their liquor, making much of it poisonous. The result was bootleg alcohol that paralyzed, blinded, and killed many people. Then the real trouble began when the government got the idea to intentionally add poisons to certain types of alcohol that could be used to make illicit moonshine. They wanted America not to drink in the worst way, and they chose the worst way to make their point.

Alcohol was commonly used in medicines, paints and solvents, and fuel. Stealing alcohol and making "hooch" was a quick way to make money. So, the government de-natured it and added various poisons. As many as 60 million gallons a year of natured alcohol were being stolen throughout the country.

"Only one possessing the instincts of a wild beast would desire to kill or make blind the man who takes a drink of liquor, even if he purchased it from one violating the Prohibition statutes," one Senator wrote.

Poisonous additions included kerosene, formaldehyde, acetone, chloroform, iodine, ether, and other chemicals. Bootleggers would re-distill the alcohol to try and remove the poisons. Substances like mercury had delayed but long-term effects. Stills that were constructed using lead solder or that were distilled through old automobile radiators added lead to every batch that left the country holler.

"I can see you're an honest man by how you treat others. It must be hard, now that your mother is gone. I still have both of my folks, I think. We had to bust up because we were all starving to death, and we went our separate ways. I've been on the road for too long and I'm still looking for a break, you know."

"Mayvis, I regret that I didn't make the best of things sometimes, but you know it's the press of the times that has about everyone down in the dirt. I see it from my friends. My neighbors sure got a hit of bad luck, at the time mom passed on."

Paul went on to tell about the last few years after the war but left out the past that included the abuse they had suffered.

"I didn't go with them up to the high meadow yesterday, 'cause I was busy, but I would like to go with you the next time you go up there."

"That would be nice of you. You don't have to go, you know. I was up there when we were putting her in the earth, but we had to get down real fast to go put out the barn fires down the road. I got this bum leg tangled up in the tall field grass and I nearly broke my neck," he grinned. "So, now that I've got me a stake bed, I believe I can now drive right on up there, like that," snapping his fingers.

"Then we can do it," Mayvis said, smiling back.

Before the trip up to the high meadow commenced, Paul talked about a possibility of working right here on his place.

"It's nothing grand, but we've been talking about what we've gotta do, if we ourselves are going to make it this year. If not, we may all be going down the road sideways together and I don't know how to do that with a truck. Now imagine that, folks." Everyone started laughing.

The times so far, since the three women had come to the farm, were at least filled with a few smiles and a chuckle now and then. The old farm seemed to be breathing a sigh of relief from the past years. It would be as hard as ever, they all knew. With the women carrying their own load of sorrow, regret and loneliness, everyone's situations had flowed together. The times of hard living had spread throughout the nation. It seemed like the last resources anybody had left were being played out and it was down to the bottom of the deck.

"Whenever you come up here, what do you think about, Paul? I'm curious."

Paul wasn't sure what the answer should be and said so. Mayvis nodded back.

"I'm not prying but thinking. For me, the road has put me off on a lot of thoughts and a lot of things are not as important as they were way back when. I'm changed, Paul, and I don't spend so much time in front of the mirror, if that makes sense."

"Like what kind of things?"

"Well, for starters, I don't think about what's down the road too much. I've been looking at my feet for so long and watching where I'm stepping, it's not much else that matters. I do like to read, though."

"Do you, now?"

"School for me was on and off until—" Paul sighed and looked down at his bad leg.

"It's not what you don't know that gets you into trouble. It's what you think you know for sure that just ain't so." She looked at Paul and he saw that she was proud of the fact that she remembered the quote, as if no one could take it away from her.

While they talked and dodged the sun for the billows of shade, Mayvis had been walking about, picking a few spring wildflowers, saying as she went, as if in idle thought, "black-eyed Susans—"

Paul's heart jumped.

"These are for your mom, Paul," and she laid them on Iletta's grave. After a moment, she said, "I hope to be able to lay flowers at my mother's grave someday, too."

The breeze across and up into the meadow had quit and it was going to be hotter soon.

"Where did that quote you said come from? That's worth remembering."

"The man's name you might not know. It's Samuel Clemens, but he has a book name he uses that makes him such a rage—Mark Twain."

"Well, I know he was full of 'em."

All four of them loaded into the stake bed and drove over to the burned-out barns and met Minerva, Grover, and Lovety. Paul made introductions all around. There was no smoke coming from the back kitchen at Minerva's, so Paul knew the still was cold for the time being.

As they all sat around under the big shade tree, the three women told the same general stories that Paul had heard earlier about life on the road and where they were headed. When they got to the part where their current path was going sideways, Paul's neighbors were nodding to what they were hearing and the desperate situation everyone present acknowledged. It was becoming commonplace for people to take in boarders, to conserve what little they had left to live on, until times would break their way. The recent election in March of 1929 of Herbert Hoover was a sign of hope to many.

The situation that Paul and the others sitting under the tree were trying to modify had been already thought of and was being tried. They were all hoping that it would work. Ideas had run out.

"I can sure tell you two are sisters, um hum."

"We've always been close."

"With things being as they are, what plans do you have now? Seems like Chicago would be a long trip for nothing, don't you think? Louisville and Indianapolis, from what we hear, are dying and mostly dead." Minerva offered, "If we can get planting, that's what we got to count on. Who knows about peanuts?"

"That was me." Mayvis answered.

"Tell me how they're growing them. I've got a Fordson, but only have a breaking plow and a set of discs." Grover said.

"I had worked in a cleaning shed for a few months on a place where they grew peanuts. A Negro man named George Washington Carver from Alabama has been experimenting on the uses of growing peanuts. The plants are supposed to put nitrogen back into the ground that has been depleted from growing cotton or the same thing, year after year."

"I think we might could try it—depending. How do they plant peanuts?"

"As they did it, they soaked the peanuts and when they swelled up a little, they put them in by hand a couple of inches deep. After the plants get up a foot or so, they run a disc down the side to hill dirt around the base. The plants send down roots from the stems into the ground and that's where the peanuts grow from. Then when they harvest, they disc off the top of the rows and the plants can be pulled up and rolled out and they are stacked and dried. After they dry a bit to keep from molding, the nuts can be pulled off and sacked for sale."

The five women went on for a while under the shade and discussed how they could be paid. Without much money available, having shelter, a job with possible gain, and food to eat was worth something, they all agreed. Usually, sharecroppers got a percentage of the sale of the commodity they harvested. That suited them fine. If they needed extra for clothes and personal items, they could go to Minerva and Lovety for those things.

Grover and Paul were putting a pencil to the guesstimate of what peanuts might bring in at the end of the year. They had no other way of getting out a new crop like this without a little bit of help from Mayvis. "I don't guess we should question their motives, much. After all, they're down on their luck, like we may be soon. They got nothing to gain by running us down a rabbit hole, now," Grover conceded. Paul nodded in agreement.

"It's settled, then. They'll bunk up at your farm, you got the room. That's okay with you. We also need to think about having extra food around, so I better break a little more ground to get more space in the garden."

"I got mine going. They got stuff out of it to eat already."

Agreeing to terms of work and payment was done to everybody's satisfaction. Lovety took over the bookkeeping duties for the year and the first thing they had to do was cut the ground. That was Grover's job. That left Mayvis and Paul in charge of getting seeds. They drove to Madison and back for peanuts.

It was an exciting but busy time. The barn had to be set up like a house, with privacy for three. The privy was close at hand and the old well was over to the side of the barn, away from the outhouse.

Paul decided to finally move into the bigger bedroom, but the room was so full of piled up stuff, he gave up the idea for the time being.

Chapter 16

~~~~~~

The Spring of 1929 started off with possibilities for a better future than the one all of them left behind. In Paul's case, the day that he had bruised his hip when he fell, running away from his mother's grave, the day the barns were set on fire, the day the two boys were found alongside Adrian, all dead and burned alive, was now a day that had receded into the past.

Bernice Cauthen, Mayvis Bailey, and Sophie Melvin were off the road and away from danger. They had a decent place to live, plenty of food, and a chance to get up a little grub stake by harvest time. Their self-esteem was somewhat restored, and they were emotionally on the mend.

The Klan was still around, though they'd lost most of their power. Still, other fringe elements and hangers-on could pose a deadly encounter. The sheriff had been complicit, although no one would say a thing. He ran interference, letting others do his bidding. No other information would be coming out of the investigation over the barn fires, that they knew. All the tongues in town would keep on wagging. In the desperate times that everybody lived those days, gossip was a distraction and a bit for entertainment. It was no different for Paul.

"Who is that man, there, in front of the mercantile, Paul?"

After a quick glance as they drove by, "That man is Alton

Herndon. He owns the mercantile. Him and his wife ran it in the early years 'till she run off and left him. It's just him now. Why?"

"I've seen him a couple of times and he has the shape of an egg."

"He is kinda' short and round-shouldered, a might. Yep. Being short and wide like he is, he can't move his head around much and when he gets excited, he tends to spit a little when he talks. Those white suspenders and striped shirts—yup, that's him."

Paul continued to fill in Alton's story. "He supposedly got drunk at his wedding, even though he was a teetotaler. Fell out of the buckboard and the horse jumped and pulled the wagon over his ankle and broke it. Several years later, she left him for a traveling dry goods salesman and moved to Cincinnati, and he's run the store by himself ever since. That's why he's got that gimp."

There was a thread of callous loneliness Paul and Alton carried that bound them together, somehow, but it was never shared between them, even in conversation. One was lamed because he drank to excess, once, and caused himself and his wife irreparable harm, and the other was lamed by someone with little or no regard for others, someone who caused an innocent child, later a man, to have a lifelong burden.

Something doing or anything doing was the pleasantry exchanged on the street and it did not miss noticing that Paul Chandler was seen going through town in his new stake bed Ford truck accompanied by a woman. He had been seen earlier with three women going about town.

After several weeks passed, Paul went to the mercantile, looking to re-stock the Ball jars early. It was a commodity that would be in short supply later in the year. Mayvis went with him. Now that she was close enough for people to look at, it was surmised she looked pleasant enough, and so her presence was not much remarked upon in future trips to town. She finally got a few passing "Hellos" and nods, acknowledgment of her tacit acceptance in Shoals.

The rains had been on schedule and the corn, peanuts, and sorghum were doing nicely. The food gardens were producing well enough that everyone's hands were putting food away for the coming fall and winter. Because of an early planting and quick picking, they were able to get a second planting in for a fall garden, something Paul and Iletta were not ever able to accomplish. Having more hands to do the work made life not so hard.

Mrs. Olsham died. She was found in her house a couple of weeks after she died, they suspected. However, it was curious that her death was officially attributed to a fall, as her face was sunk in on one side. Nothing was found to substantiate what she had hit her head on. However, she was laying on a rag rug and had bled out where she fell.

"Who was she?" Mayvis wanted to know.

"She was my teacher for a time when I went to school, back when I was a kid. I thought she was a good person and a kind lady, back then."

"Are you going to attend her funeral, Paul?"

"I'll have to think about it. In a lot of aspects, she helped me along when I was hitting some rough spots. But on the other side, I have come to have some doubts, so I'll see. Lots of things doing around here."

"What were some of the good things, then?"

Paul explained in general terms about her kindness to her students and to him, especially, when his mother was still alive and after the war. "My Aunt Dorothy, from Dugger, had a curious comment or two about her during the time the barns were set on fire, the day of mom's funeral. I never gave it much thought but have been mulling over her words ever since. It's given me a bit of caution in my thinking since then."

"How so?"

"This land was full up with the Ku Klux Klan and they were mighty bad to folks around here that didn't believe in their way of thinking, as to religion or color or drinking moonshine or any other alcohol. Aunt Dot said she thinks Mrs. Olsham could have been the eyes and ears for them, with her sneaking around, looking into everybody's business."

Mayvis was now standing straight up by the sink and turned around and looked at Paul.

"You can imagine, we had several run-ins with them and their kind on the road and we know the danger they pose. We heard them stories. When you travel on the roads with the black folks and the Mexicans, we were always on guard. That's all I'll say to that matter. I didn't know her, and I wouldn't go to the funeral if I did. I don't want their eyes on me no kinda way," and she shuddered.

Paul's heart jumped at seeing her reaction.

"Grover, Lovety, Minerva, and me think the Klan had something to do with burning down of those barns."

But why would they do that to you, they got no reason—Mayvis was about to say it, then didn't. *Best to let sleeping dogs lay.*

They had shifted over to Paul's fields and had not so far worked at Minerva's. It was time to get sorghum in the ground and they were waiting for Grover to bring the tractor down and cut the rows.

"Does anyone like to fish?"

"Fried fish is one of our favorites. We don't get much of it, being on the road and all."

The Ford headed to the river and all four of them got places on the bank and set themselves along, two above a prominent waterfall and two below. The women had their toes soaking in the water in about five minutes. It was a needed break from the work.

"What can you tell me, Mayvis, about this Samuel Clemens, the writer? You know anything at all?"

"What struck me, was about his childhood. Apparently, he came up from some poverty, for a while, so's he knew about the rough road. That is why he is really liked. People can relate to what he says."

"I can relate to that. He had a father, just like me he wasn't close to. I read his two books, Huck Finn and Tom Sawyer. He was a steamboat captain—kinda' like me and my stake bed." Paul grinned. "Everybody ready to head back and clean some fish? A good supper is waiting!"

Everybody was sitting on the porch after a fine catfish dinner. Mayvis started combing her hair and the other two women started humming some gospel tunes, finally breaking into a hymn that was new to Paul and Mayvis, "Will the Circle be Unbroken."

"We heard this song several times when we passed through those peanut growers' sheds. The coloreds would sing lots of hymns including this one. Sometimes, someone would get a tambourine and then one time we heard someone play an auto harp and sing it. Oh, Mr. Chandler, it was joyful! I meant—Paul."

"Music around here is a good thing. It hasn't been on this place for quite some time. Mom used to sing sometimes when the times were good, and it was right to do so. Sad, but it didn't happen much."

"Here's one, it's an old Scottish song, 'Barbara Allen.' Let's sing this one, if anybody knows all the lyrics." And away they sang. They followed it with "Amazing Grace." Afterward, they all sat in silence, reflecting on their own families and personal memories.

Paul smiled. "What is it, then, that put you three on such difficult journeys?"

"If we took no risks, our lives would be very poor," one of them said.

Their lives were already poor when they showed up at the loading dock of the feed store. It was not so unusual for a few people to show up from time to time, single men, small groups, and a few families who were passing through. As Paul observed, rightly so, these women were not just "passing through" and headed somewhere. They were "broke down" right in front of him.

Compassion for others was something his mother had cultivated in Paul throughout his childhood. It was a lesson that she had wanted to pass on to her son, as a good Methodist learned and practiced. Until Iletta became enmeshed with Lemuel's besotted ways, they had attended a Sunday service, now and again. It was part of the Quaker philosophy, also, and one of the reasons that Herbert Hoover's election came about was his idea of people solving their issues through personal responsibility. Hoover wanted any assistance for down and out folks to come from the local level and vetoed several bills that would bring direct assistance from the government to struggling Americans. Though he was viewed as being unsympathetic to others' suffering by many, he was seen to be a voice for self-sufficiency by others.

Chapter 17

~~~~~~~~~~~~~~~~~~~~~~~~~

"Minerva? Sister, where are you? Hello, the house!"

Minerva came from the back of her burned-out bedroom and went down the steps into the yard.

"Sit in the chair, I got to tell you something. Your bedroom will have to wait for repairs, it looks like."

A slow frown gathered on her brow. "Why, Lovety?"

"All the money we got to use is about gone. We got to keep money aside for kerosene for the tractor to do the plowing, what little of it we can get by on over the remainder of the summer and we must have it to plow up peanuts and to run the sorghum press. I'm sorry, sis. I can't find anything we can sell to the markets before then."

"In the back of my mind, I knew we were on the knife's edge. Phooey! Don't say nothing about this, but we still have a few gallons of 'shine stored away that could give us a money boost."

"I need to tell Grover to sell it. We may already be too late, with the desperation lying about. We are right at getting caught ourselves. People don't have hardly anything left except cornmeal, lard, and dandelions. With the corn market collapsing, no corn to feed hogs, except what has been stored for the winter, we're right at the end, I'm afraid."

The sun was down, it was the end of the day, and the women

and Paul were loading up the truck, about to pull out and head back to his farm, when Grover emerged from the house.

"You'uns may not have been noticing, but you see our corn is going nicely." Everyone nodded approval. "So, I did some bartering the other day while I was in town and Paul, hold up a minute and you two in the back, come with me, I got something you might get some use out of."

They were curious and followed him into the back of the house. When they returned, each was carrying a box, followed by Grover.

"Lovety and I already got one of these things. Thought you folks might like to take this home with you. It is an Atwater Kent Model 20—a radio."

"A radio! It works and we can use it at our place?"

"It is for your place. Here, I got some batteries for it, too. It's pretty easy to use." As Grover explained how to work the radio, they felt like it was a holiday.

"If you hook it up to the batteries, you'll get WXYZ from Detroit and WLW from Cincinnati."

With the radio wired up as they were told to do, and the speaker attached, the sound from that machine filled their ears and filled the house. Finally, they could get some broadcasts and find out what the world was doing out there, after they had sweated in the hot sun six days a week. It was a way to connect to a world they didn't hear about except by word of mouth in town. This was better than the newspaper they got to see at the mercantile occasionally.

The music made everyone happy but the news they were hearing wasn't good. In fact, the news was a lot worse out there than they had imagined. Soon, harvest time would get started and "We won't be listening to those waltzes, won't be listening to the news."

The news they were hearing of the doings outside in the world shuttered their excitement of getting the radio. Businesses were failing and closing. Sharecroppers were being tossed from their lands and their possessions piled along the roadsides. President Hoover assured them it was not as bad as reports were saying.

"I have no fears for the future of our country," the president announced. "It is bright with hope."

But the radio reported that half of Chicago's people had lost their jobs.

"Let's look at this," Grover reasoned. "We have room for canning in three basements. We can put corn in the silo and corn in the house, peanuts in Paul's barn. We got two hogs to get butchered as soon as the weather gets cooler and into the smokehouse. We got two squeezins to get done, apples from the orchard and then sorghum. Root cellars will be full this year. Potatoes, butternut squash, turnips, onions we can sack and hang. Carrots will be fine in the ground. We still have some hay to get in for Paul's horse. Green beans are canned, dried beans we hang and shell later. We could use two hundred pounds of salt, fifty of black pepper. We need coffee, that's twenty-six cents a pound, white flower, a hundred-pound sack. We can get a barter on sugar, maybe. It's five cents a pound now and we can barter sorghum for it. We need a hundred, at least. Anything left, say something. Personally, I already cut sassafras roots by the creek that's drying. Anybody like sassafras?"

As if they were preparing for war, the five of them worked as a team to get things done and prepared for whatever was to come. All had known about the dire straits everyone around them was in but hadn't realized how widespread it was until they heard about it on the radio. Now, they worked together and independently to finish as much as possible before the weather would turn.

In Shoals, they noticed that a steady stream of unfamiliar faces appeared and disappeared, each group looking more haggard and disheveled than the ones before them. The stories on the radio foretold of more to come. They also prayed among themselves.

Chapter 18

October 29, 1929. The day the stock market fell was the beginning of the Great Depression. The weather at the three Shoals farms was clear and cool. Everybody was at work in the fields gathering apples for squeezing or at Paul's farm, cutting down the last stands of sorghum. The seed heads were being removed into an empty wagon and the stalks were laid out to dry, getting ready to be pressed into juice and boiled down into syrup. That night and the next night, no one knew that the stock markets were collapsing, that millions of dollars were being lost by the hour, and that people were jumping out of windows of tall buildings and committing suicide.

Not until Paul and Mayvis drove to town to get Ball jars did they hear about the panic on Wall Street in New York and in Chicago. It took listening to several people's opinions before the gravity of what was happening began to sink in. They gathered at Grover's place to hear the radio broadcast about the details of what it all meant.

Mayvis said to her women friends, "Grover says that since this is sitting hard over the land without a doubt, we got to start immediately to even reduce what we are eating now and cut down some more."

"Bernice, what do you and Lovety think about all of this?"

"We better get the rest of our provisions in the cellars and into the barn. Who knows how bad this will get, but we don't need people showing up here and borrowing from us, if you know what I mean, right Sophie?" She nodded.

"That sorghum seed can be sacked, and we can start cooking syrup as soon as that's done."

Four days after the last batch was finished and jarred, Sophie heard some rummaging around in the barn and went to investigate. She surprised two people, a man, and a woman, who attacked her. In the house, the others heard her scream and ran towards the barn.

"What happened, girl? We heard you scream!"

"I was jumped by two people that were taking syrup jars out of the barn. They hit me over the head and tried to stuff rags in my mouth and tie me up, but I managed to bite the hell out of the woman's hand and that's when I screamed for help. I couldn't get free quick enough, but I had my eye on that there pitchfork and I would surely have used it. That's too much work going into getting that syrup than to let it go like that and somebody take it from us. It's not going to happen to us out here without a fight."

She was hopping mad.

"Don't think I'll be letting the sheriff know we're having trouble out here. He'll be coming around and we don't need him around or the attention. We might try and go to town in the morning and snoop around a little. My guess is that they won't know who any of us are. We might be able to catch who it is—someone with their hand wrapped."

"Well—then what? We might want to stay here and finish our chores. That might be more important right off. If this kind of thing is going to be going on, this will need our attention more, out here." Mayvis noted.

"Is your hand going to be all right? We might need to wash it good with a little lye soap to clean it up. It looks like a few scratches, maybe. Let's go into the house and look at it. Bernice, why don't you go around there and see what may be missing and how they got in. Might need some repair in the morning."

They went to the house to look at her hand in better light and turned the radio on. Bernice went to check the barn and would have a count soon, as to what might have been swiped. The announcer on the radio was beginning to talk about what was happening in the big cities and drawing some conclusions about what it meant.

"Where's Bernice? She's a bit slow. That's not like her."

Paul was standing by the window and saw someone go around the barn and leave through the front gate.

"Someone's going after Bernice! He's leaving the barn."

Everyone jumped up and ran, yelling, to the barn. They were out in a flash and Paul was trying to find his cane so that he could follow them. He wasn't getting anywhere with any speed.

Sophie was the first out of the house and caught a glimpse of the man climbing over the barbed wire fence.

"That's him, that's the man that was with the woman that grabbed me. He'll get away."

In another instant, the man crossed the front pasture to the road, went over another fence, and mounted a horse that was tied up there and was gone.

Bernice was laying sprawled in a stall, pulling her garments back to her to cover herself. She was crying but seemed more mad than hurt.

"Dirty bastard, he'll remember me," she leered. She swept away her tears on her sleeve, looked up at them with a smile and held up a stiletto as Paul entered the barn. He poked at a white robe and cone hat thrown over the stall boards, lifted them up with his cane and dropped them on a manure pile in the next stall. And then he stood on them. Sophie followed Bernice to the house.

Paul hesitated and looked into Mayvis' eyes with a sense of embarrassment.

"Is she—ruined?" he asked.

"Oh, Lord no," she smiled. "That man is gonna be single for a very long time, I suspect."

Back into the house they all went, and then sat and talked about what had happened.

"It seems that the Klan didn't go away, but some of those elements are still around," Paul speculated. "We've got to be more aware and on guard."

"What can we do? We need to get over to the other place and let them know and be on the lookout for strangers. That's a start," added Mayvis. "I don't know how we can stop any of this. Of course, there are four of us and we could take turns looking out, I suppose. Paul?"

"I do hesitate—but—let me see." Paul hobbled into another room and started digging around among all the boxes, crates, and various piles of stuff that had collected in the house over the decades. He came back into the room holding his cane in one hand and a Kentucky long rifle in the other.

"This was my Grandpa's flintlock rifle that came down to me. It's been around since before the Civil War. I've shot it a few times and it can be a persuader if we need one. I have the powder for it and some mini balls. What do you say, girls? This will help out a ton, don't you think?"

They were all smiling and watching Paul skip about. He handed it to Bernice.

"You get to take the first shot. You've earned it, I suppose,"

Paul said with a grin. "Tomorrow we're gonna shoot *something* around here. Yes, sir."

Minerva's house was getting full again, but this time it was getting loaded from ceiling to floor with bundles of dried peanuts.

Minerva told Paul and the sharecroppers, "Well, here we go again. I have tried my darndest to keep my house presentable all my life and here we go dragging in all of these peanuts and filling every room," she says, feigning anger.

"Well, we got a good crop, anyway, don't we?" Then she smiled.

"At the other peanut farm I worked on, they kept the dried plants tied and bundled into bales. Makes good animal feed, like hay. Paul, I bet your horse would like it. It'll be good to use it up and it saves labor on not having to put so much hay in the loft."

"Once we finish shucking these peanuts and sacking them up, it'll be ready for Paul to get them to the mercantile and see what we can get for 'em," Grover said. I don't want the market to fall on peanuts and leave us holding the bag, so to speak." He laughed at his own joke.

Paul interjected, "We come down to let you know we run into some trouble at our place last night and Bernice, here, got roughed up a bit. Sophie got roughed up, as well."

"What are you saying?"

Sophie started, "I was in the barn and I heard some rustling around and it didn't sound like a horse or anything. I caught a man and a woman. They had pried off a couple of boards and were in the sorghum storage and one of them was passing out our jars through the opening to the other one that was outside.

Me and her had a go around and then this fella came in and knocked me in the head and put me on the ground. I was dazed and they was trying to tie me up and stuff rags in my mouth to shut me up. So, I bit the hell out of her hand and yelled out and then you all came a running and scared them off. I wanted to pitchfork one of them, but they got away too fast for me to get 'em."

"Right after that, we brought her into the house to tend to her hand cuts," Bernice added, "and I went back to the barn to count up how many jars they had gotten away with. I was jumped by this guy in a Klan robe. He must have come back into the barn right after we run 'em off, thinking that no one would suspect he would come back, and we would let our guard down. He was trying to steal more of them jars when I surprised him. Me and him had a pretty big tussle going and he got me on the ground and took off his robe and was trying to do me, when I got him between his legs with this," and she pulled out her stiletto, opened it, and showed its pointed blade with a wave and then put it back into the hem of her dress.

"He's not going to be fit for walking or riding horses for a good bit of time, I think. And now, Paul has come up with something. He's got his grandpa's Kentucky flintlock rifle that can give us some cover if we need it. That'll surprise 'em if they get back our way."

Grover, Lovety, and Minerva stood there, mouths wide open, speechless.

"So, we come to say that you had better keep a sharp eye out. They may be coming up this road looking into everybody's farms for a free hand out. So, watch it."

Without saying a word, Grover left the room for a minute and returned with a big handgun tucked into his waist. "It was a swap for some 'shine. It's a forty-five caliber 1911 Colt."

❖   ❖   ❖

The peanut experiment worked, and it didn't work. Stored peanuts were brought out at the beginning of warm weather and sent to the market. Prices for peanuts and coffee were parallel for a period, at twenty-six cents a pound. Then the overproduction of coffee beans hitting the markets drove the prices downward. The population still had to struggle to survive and they had no money to pay for a luxury such as coffee. The cost went downward to only six cents a pound and peanuts dropped with it, to five cents a pound. It was a tremendous amount of work to produce the crop, without mechanical help.

The first sacks Paul and Grover brought to market brought in eighteen cents and the price dropped from there to twelve cents and then to nine cents and bottomed out at five cents a pound, essentially being harvested mostly by hand. Roasted wheat seeds and roasted peanut seeds were mixed together to produce a coffee substitute. Peanuts could be used for animal feed and people could eat them, as well. They could be ground up into a paste and put on bread for a meat substitute.

In the nation's financial world, banks would lend $9 for every dollar an investor had deposited. Interest rates continued to fall to encourage investment and finally banks went to zero percent to stimulate growth. Nothing happened. Banks in desperate situations began to fail when they started calling in debtors' notes, which the borrowers did not have enough time or money to repay. Mass production and motorized farm machinery created excess capacity, reducing the need for extra workers. Small farmers and their families were driven from their farms in droves, wages fell further, and the work week was shortened even more.

A common laborer working a full-time job, if work could

be found, had it much harder, due to the wages being paid out were already more depressed than most would believe. In the South, a going wage was twelve cents per hour and in the North, it was twenty-five cents per hour. The sharecropper women had it better in Indiana than they would have had it in Arkansas. Still, nobody had a grip on "any port in the storm."

The country was seized by a failure to recognize and a failure to act. In the farmer's situation, they did pretty much as they had always done—grow food and get by. They had no resources to buy the latest fashions and new foodstuffs that were being offered. They stuck it out by preserving the food they had, cutting down on consumption, or doing without. They learned, as did the city dwellers, the new survival motto: Use, Re-Use, Wear Out, or Do Without.

President Hoover signed the Smoot-Hawley Tariff Act, designed to raise import duties so high that foreign countries could not sell their goods in America. As a result, foreign countries would not buy American-made goods at a time America was in desperate need of the sales.

In 1930, severe water shortages combined with harsh farming techniques created what came to be known as the Dust Bowl, and the times came to be known as The Dirty 30's. The drought was thought to be the worst environmental disaster in three hundred years. Giant dust clouds formed and blew across twenty-seven states, due to the jet stream changing directions and removing the annual rainfalls from the Midwest and the Great Plains. The drought killed the plants and the topsoil was blown off the land. Overgrazing livestock ate the last bits of stubble.

The surrounding states bordering the epicenter of the worst-hit drought areas faced widespread economic ruin, too. They practiced their same habits and routines, raising crops or beef in the traditions of their forefathers, and did not recognize what they should have changed until it was too late. The land, once abused and overgrazed, did not recover quickly.

It was not a failure-to-act issue for the Shoals farmers. They were doing what they would normally do, which was to make do. The crushing fall of the markets would be mitigated because they were sitting on their own land that was already paid for. They lived for the day and had truly little vision of any future. This day-to-day struggle happened throughout the country.

As they discussed the issues and listened to the radio, Minerva commented, "We can barely get by, but we won't have to sell any of our land. They wouldn't give us a plug nickel for it anyways, so might as well keep it." The other landowners said as much.

After they ate their evening meal at the Chandler farm, Paul was listening to Mayvis and Sophie talking about how life in the city was going with the drought going on. Sophie got up and went to the barn and Mayvis asked, "Paul, have you thought about your choices you might have to make if this drought continues? You won't have to be pushed off or anything?"

"No. I'll be all right. I learned that I'll be all right in most instances. I hope it keeps happening, that's all." He didn't have a smile on his face, and he didn't have a frown, either.

"Is that your head or your heart that's talking?"

"I guess it's a bit of both," Paul said. He looked up at Mayvis and she smiled back at him. He sensed that she was in need of kindness.

Within their small world, Paul and Mayvis were often together when they needed things at the mercantile, hauling produce and delivering harvests. The ease of companionship and temperament abided between them and they enjoyed their sanctuary. Paul and Mayvis settled into a relationship and accepted the respite. Mayvis began staying with Paul in the house and did not return to sleeping in the barn.

Bernice and Sophie accepted the change without surprise or hardly a notice. Consequently, the two women re-arranged the space vacated by Mayvis and created a private dressing room of sorts, and got a galvanized tub so they could actually sit in it to get clean, instead of bringing a bucket to a stool and sitting out to clean off. Mayvis helped them arrange a place to hang clothes after washing and took turns with the other two for bathing. Thus, as sisters on the road, they were able to maintain their camaraderie. They all knew at some time they would go their separate ways but having a roof over their heads and food to eat was a godsend. Nobody was going to go anywhere; the Ku Klux Klan be damned.

Paul was clearing off a surface space of an old dresser that was wedged into the bedroom. He pushed off a wooden box that fell to the floor and spilled its contents. Mayvis picked them up and gave them back to him to re-box. It was bits and pieces of shell buttons, a jackknife with a broken blade, odd shaped and colored stones, and an old Ingersoll Yankee watch that had no hands.

"You wonder about that, I bet. It was an old watch you could get for a dollar. I found it. It looked like someone threw it away, but I kept it anyway. It doesn't have any hands."

Perplexed, Mayvis said, "Why did you do that if you can't keep time by it?"

Some of what Mayvis knew about Paul's childhood was from bits and pieces of his conversations. She knew it was a very painful time and so never pressed him on it for any details.

"I had it by my bed when I was young, and I used to wind

it up and put it next to my ear and sleep on it. I listened to the ticking at night and it helped me sleep and shut off the bad sounds I would hear. When I broke my leg and laid outside on the porch, it was about the only thing I had that kept my sanity. It helped me calm down. I had demons to fight. Putting that ticking sound into my ear helped me win those battles."

Mayvis placed her hand over his heart., "It doesn't look to me that you have any more demons. Do you think you're ready to throw it away?"

"It's been like the crutch I have now. But you're right—it's time to throw it away."

"You're a strong and sturdy man, Paul. Blow out the light."

Franklin Roosevelt called President Herbert Hoover the "hear nothing, see nothing, do nothing government," and offered the American people a New Deal to try and stop the nation's downward spiral. Voters were looking for decisive action and he was elected. In his inaugural address, Franklin Roosevelt declared, "The only thing we have to fear is fear itself!"

But it was still fearful times. There was barely enough rain to make a harvest in 1933. Yields were down by sixty percent. Apples still grew, but the harvest of the fruit was a lot smaller. Without water in the fall or good snows, the fruit set for the following year would be in jeopardy. The Shoals farmers struggled with deciding whether or not to try and plant three farms' worth of crops if no rains would sprout the seeds.

Paul and the others felt rejected from any balance they tried to maintain with the land that barely produced anything and barely gave back to them any value for all the work and toil they unendingly applied.

Everyone gathered around the radio at the end of the farm day to listen to the Amos and Andy Show, already a hit show for several years. It was broadcast from the north, up in Chicago, on a station that had a good, dependable radio signal.

The cost of entertainment was nearly zero in having a radio to listen to. It was a few pennies, here and there, to buy a battery that would run the radio for weeks, with careful use. No one had money to attend a real picture show and they would have had to travel some distance to see one. But they had plenty of radio shows to keep their minds off their struggles. *Death Valley Days* was an anticipated show about the real Old West, as they knew it. *The Lone Ranger* was a close second. *The Eddie Cantor Show* had the women's attention, especially when he sang his hit song, "How Ya Gonna Keep Them Down on the Farm (After They've Seen Paree)?" Paul figured it stirred the wanderlust in his farm mates.

Paul's interest was piqued by the *National Farm and Home Show Hour*, as were the others of his household. They also gathered around the radio for President Roosevelt's Fireside Chats. The show that almost scared Mayvis was *The Shadow!* "It was his voice," she conceded.

"When Roosevelt was sworn in, and they repealed Prohibition, you would have thought that things in the U.S. would be in a turn-around," Grover finally said one day. "Why didn't that happen? What just galls me to no end was his stunt to get the farmers to kill and slaughter six million pigs to reduce supply and boost prices. America could have used that food." The days of scratching in the dirt and hearing that kind of news hardened their hearts.

Grover decided, "The CCC's that Roosevelt put in this area will help a bunch of unemployed folks have work and some money to spend. They're working up in Shakamak, McCormick's

Creek, and over in the Bloomington area and Brown County. They have an all-black camp in Bloomington. Despite some of the other stuff, I think this Civilian Conservation Corps is a great idea.

"Now, that's a place to go visit sometime, Brown County. Nice forests." After a thinking pause, he continued, "I was hoping that we could get the old cooker going again and try and make some 'shine but now that all the big distilleries can produce, we'll never be able to get into the market again. Maybe we should get us a couple more pigs and turn them loose on the corn. Maybe we should think about a calf. Chickens still make the easiest meat and eggs, though."

The drought came in three waves. In 1936, the recorded death toll from the heat exceeded 5,000 people. It was preceded by one of the coldest winters on record. The previous years of no water had weakened Grover and Lovety's apple trees. They lost half of their apple orchard, and the remainder of the trees were heavily damaged.

"We may lose the rest of them this next spring if we don't get relief," fretted Lovety.

The drought continued and the heat got worse. By 1937, over one in five farmers were on relief. Thousands of farmers and their families migrated to California to find work. Shantytowns and Hoovervilles sprang up and Sooners and Okies clogged the back roads. Broken down cars and trucks that were pulled off the roads were lived in if they hadn't been completely abandoned.

Temperatures in North Dakota reached 121 degrees. When the radio reported it, everyone sat around and no one spoke, contemplating what was going to happen next.

The radio was good at casting their thoughts away from the dire straits they were all in, but Bernice was tired and worn out from the heat. She couldn't help but wonder what was next. She couldn't help but assess her current position, their prospects looking dimmer by the day. She felt stuck on Paul's farm with no money, no transportation, and no place to go. And then she reminded herself to feel grateful that they at least had clean water and enough food to keep them from starving. She wondered how her fellow female travelers were feeling about their situation but ended her speculations by summoning up the hopeful thought that things had to get better, and that they couldn't possibly get worse.

"Well hell, folks, someone go find that bottle of moonshine I know is hid around here. Let's have a drink to better times, what do you say?"

"Leave it to Bernice to be the willow that won't break."

Everyone took a long look at her and started laughing. Sophie jumped up at the command and came right back into a room with an unopened jar and the women started singing "How ya gonna keep them down on the farm, after they've seen Paree?"

The two women started tap dancing, in unison, as if they were on stage.

"What a shindig," Paul exclaimed.

Once Grover got a couple of pulls on the jar, he started acting out the "tough guy." "It might be something we can look into, with the still going, again." He started strutting around and pulling on his dirty shirt like he had suspenders on. "Man needs a little room around here, don't ya think? With Capone in Alcatraz and John Dillinger dead."

He turned around and strutted around the floor as if he was a mob boss. He looked at the women and leaned in to say his next bit with emphasis. "Oh yeah, they got Dillinger right over there at Indianapolis."

The women laughed, not knowing whether to believe what he was saying or not and looked at Paul, who nodded a slow "Yes" for added emphasis.

"We're a pretty rough bunch around here, if the truth be told."

Lovety repeated, with emphasis, "IF the truth be told."

Again, they all laughed.

"Enough of all of this, it's time for the radio."

Chapter 19

Sophie and Minerva were shelling dried peas under the shade of a yard tree at Minerva's house and they began talking about different things, but mostly passing the time. Not steering the conversation in any direction, Sophie addressed Minerva. "One of these days I do hope to get back home and see my folks again. They are hard off, and they must be wondering about me and where I've gone off to. My dad, I suspect, suffers with the black lung from working in the coal mines for so many years. He may have already passed on. I know it's hard to have to say good-bye. It must be hard on you after you losing your Adrian, I'd expect."

"Well child, yes, it has been hard and the burden the Lord has put on all of us certainly don't make it any easier. I can't see any road that's going to be easy for us when the drought finally does give it up. We still got the burden of pulling in the harness till the Lord calls us home. I am comforted, at least, with knowing that my dear Adrian is over there resting under those trees and I will be ready to join him when my time comes."

"Now, Ms. Fields, don't go wishing for a shortening of the road He has given you. It's your path in life that's set, and you want to live all of it. I certainly do."

"You are so young and pretty and your path is full of possibilities, and probably kids, too. You should look to that to keep your spirits up."

"Aw, pshaw."

"I'm serious. What about the other two? How do they figure into all of this?"

Sophie sighed, "Most likely they'll both return to their homes and try to pick up from there on. You know your homestead is always a strong pull, especially if you want a family. Bernice would done been gone but for the drought. She sometimes thinks about Chicago and the big lights, more so than Mayvis."

"I guess we'll have to see."

"The way she talks, I can tell that farm life isn't for her."

The radio was bringing more disturbing news about happenings in Europe. The Zeppelin Hindenburg flew over the Empire State building August 8, 1936 and later crashed in a fireball, at Lakehurst, New Jersey on May 6, 1937. The Japanese invaded and marched into Shanghai, China in 1937. By November, over a million people were involved. Shanghai fell and reported one hundred and fifty thousand deaths. U.S. citizens in Shanghai flocked to the U.S. Embassy there for safety. President Roosevelt addressed the nation from the White House, September 3rd, 1939 and pledged that the United States would remain neutral, reassuring Americans that they would not go to war.

That year, the federal government's program to reduce the loss of topsoil included extensive re-plowing of the land into furrows, development of irrigation systems, and the planting of thousands of trees to block winds. The rains would soon return.

The fall of 1939 was a pivotal year for America. The Shoals farmers, having held on for years with subsistence farming, miraculously made it through the Dust Bowl era. The radio was the single reliable source of their information about the outside world. From reporting on the happenings and events in big cities with food, housing, and jobs, all of them held their beliefs as to what would happen with their personal futures. Sometimes, the most private beliefs were never shared with others but were used as guideposts for possible future plans.

Like a jolt of electricity, once the rains started coming back, the sharecropper women seemed to have a renewed spring in their steps. Each of them at various times would find private nooks to retreat to and compose correspondence to be sent out with only a small amount of expectation or hope that they would receive a response. They were aware of the dire circumstances America's breadbasket had gone through. They knew they weren't the only ones who had been suffering hard times, that Shoals wasn't the only community that had struggled. They were beginning now to see other possibilities for the future.

It became a quirky day, the day they saw it rain. Sophie was out by the barn beating on some clothes that she had hung over a line, knocking some of the dust out of them. She suddenly came running onto the porch, yelling, and holding her forearm, as if she had been bitten by a snake.

"Look at what happened," she squealed. "It got me on the arm."

Everyone came rushing over to see the injury. She held her arm out to show everyone, but all they saw was a dusty arm with hair on it. They kept looking and then they saw it—three big bare spots on her flesh. Three round spots with the blonde hairs all lying flat.

She had been hit by three fat raindrops, sure enough.

Like chickens spotting a circling hawk above, everyone instantly looked up at the sky and searched the cloudy blue. The mid-afternoon sun's rays angled down and each falling drop sparkled as it sailed to the ground. Each huge drop of rain struck the ground with such a force as to send up a mini-dust plume behind it. The air was heavy with the smell of rain.

They listened in awe as the rain hit the tin roof of the barn, and watched, speechless, as puddles pooled in the yard and chickens ran for cover.

It didn't rain long or hard that day. The ground didn't muddy, and the water never formed rivulets that ran anywhere. But the dresses Sophie left hanging on the line had white spots on them, evidence that it had, indeed, finally rained. It brought promise.

Paul was on the hill behind the house and he was looking around a stand of hollow trees, where the trees were still alive, looking to find a possible beehive, and to see if bees were able to make honey. Later, and thinking about the marvelous event, Paul seemed perplexed at himself for not perceiving the impending rain event as he stood in the trees. He thought he smelled rain in the soil for just an instance, but then dismissed the thought because he had been baked and dried by the hot temperatures for so long. He was sure his senses were playing tricks on him.

Paul dismissed the sounds of shimmering leaves, rubbing upon themselves in a breeze in the canopy. He dully glanced up and saw no movement. It was the momentary shimmer of water droplets, scarcely larger than fog that wisped by. His senses seemed to have been broken and he was startled and caught completely flat-footed.

The transformation was slow in coming and, as an occasional shower returned normalcy to them, Paul once again was absorbed back into the land and became an integrated element of the woods and forests that surrounded him, bringing a spark of renewal that nurtured his internal life.

A few weeks and months later, when the rain became regular, occasional flocks of small birds would silently leave the sanctuary of the sweetgums and glide down and melt into the thistle patches found in the pasture's edges to seek seeds.

Only after a light rain fell for a period of time would the small birds flash a moment of their yellow rumps as they dashed among the stems, seeking shelter. The birds began to have voices, chirping as they rummaged about, hardly noticed.

PART FOUR

Chapter 20

~~~~~~~~~~~~~~~~~~~~~~~~~~~~~~~~~~~~~~

The Second World War was said to have started on September 1, 1939. Two eventual opposing sides were coalesced into the Axis Powers and the Allied Forces.

Germany invaded and captured countless other countries either through outright force or by appeasement. The Empire of Japan moved to dominate Asia and the Pacific.

The Allied Forces—France, the United Kingdom, and Soviet Union—began the deadliest war in world history, and they were later joined by the United States when it was attacked by Japan in the bombing of Pearl Harbor.

The fourth and final wave of drought started in 1939 and ended a year later, but the entire devastation seemed to have been one long continuous event. The sharecroppers followed the damage of the drought from the radio broadcasts, especially looking to find out where the effects were less destructive. They had experienced a bit of homesickness but had not yet heard from any of the family they had left behind. In its place, wanderlust to get away had settled in. It was well overdue. They had been living on Paul's farm for years.

They knew they couldn't go west into California. They had heard about the shantytowns, the Hoovervilles, and the ensuing lack of prospects of work to be found there. John Steinbeck's

The Grapes of Wrath, published that year, had given the public imagination a vivid and dire portrayal of the reception the down-and-out might receive if they tried to migrate west. Going south would mean heading into the mouth of the dragon, where the Depression was at its worst.

The migrations of the disenfranchised to the larger Midwest cities such as St. Louis, Indianapolis, or Chicago held no invitations either. Even Louisville held no attraction. The women had the yearning and the desire to go but not the destination—yet.

Shoals held the promise of work and a roof over their heads, unlike every other place they considered, but no money. Unless some new direction could be ferreted out, life would become a dead end—had become a dead end. Michigan, maybe? The automotive plants around Detroit might hold a key, they considered, as they had heard there were possibilities of work there.

As the reality of another European war gripped the United States, the government planned to bring its industrial might to bear in support of the Allies fighting in Europe. The military looked for places to develop within the heartland that would be protected from attack and be defendable, should fighting make it to U.S. shores. One place that was chosen for the development of an ammunitions manufacturing complex was next to thirty-two thousand acres of the poorest land in Martin County, Indiana. Located in the middle of America's heartland and well-protected, it had the right topography of rises and depressions for safety purposes in explosives manufacturing. The land was "sub-marginal" farmland with low living standards in the area.

Twenty-nine cemeteries rested within those boundaries and Boggs Creek was where the progenitor of the Chandlers and other family members were laid to rest. As it became a relatively high security area, the cemeteries were closed to the general public. Visiting a grave in Boggs Creek had to be done by arrangement.

It made a lasting impression on young Paul when he went as a child with his mother to someone's burial, and Iletta pointed to some natural gravestones that were painted black. He never got over the memory of those black stones being scattered about haphazardly and how bad those people must have been. That was his inner reason for refusing to have his mother laid down among such bad people throughout eternity until her resurrection.

The Civilian Conservation Corps, known simply as the CCC, was viewed as one of the most successful programs of the New Deal, but their camps around the nation were coming to an end. As the camps were modeled on a military structure, once the war had begun in Europe, the military called more than five thousand reserve officers to duty from camp leadership ranks and the program began changing from a work program to a training program. Entering recruits became younger and less skilled. Manufacturing began gearing up in anticipation of supporting the war effort and they were looking for able-bodied people to fill various positions.

The word spread about the upcoming construction of the Crane Ammunition Depot. The mood at the Fields and McCullough farms took on a sense of tension, not knowing what would happen next. It was the same at Paul's place. Their livelihoods were inexorably tied to their lands, and to survive, they must eat, and to eat they must work the ground until the tide shifted their way.

When Paul and the sharecroppers rode over to Lovety and Grover's to survey and plan out their next actions, Minerva was already gripped with depression, they could see, as they sat around under the shade trees and stared out at Adrian's apple orchard.

"Anybody remember what we got for those peanuts back when we took to them market?" Grover asked of no one in particular. "Well, it got us five cents a pound, which didn't get us seed money. However—" he paused for effect. "I do have a surprise." He reached into his pocket and pulled out a five-dollar bill that set everyone's eyes to full open.

"Ladies hold out your hands." And then he counted off twenty-five dollars in each of their outstretched palms. "I saved eighteen fifty-pound sacks, which I put in the silo for safekeeping. You may not know it, but the market for peanuts has gone crazy and I brought 'em in and got twenty-five cents a pound. That's twenty-five dollars cash money today for each of you."

Paul observed the joy and astonishment in the three women as they stared at the money in their hands. He smiled to himself, happy for them, happy for Grover and Lovety and Minerva, and happy for himself.

They discussed what they needed to get into the ground. The women put the money in their shoes and later in their pokes. They exchanged sideways glances and smiles among themselves for the rest of the workday.

Minerva's depression slowly returned, however. As they headed back to Paul's farm she remarked—despite the good fortune of the day—"We're farmers and so losing just becomes a way of life." There was nothing anyone could say to dissuade her. That night, with a glance of longing, Mayvis left Paul's side and went to spend the night in the barn with the other women.

"She might think losing just becomes a way of life for farmers, but I reject that, right off."

"Me too, Mayvis. Where do you think—?"

"Soon, I suppose."

For Paul, it was so much to take in and so many thoughts to try and process. Perhaps it was an inevitable conclusion to these past many years. Mayvis and the other two women had shown up at the feed store loading dock in 1920 and had then spent a decade working on the three farms. The time stretched out and was barely marked by the fall of the stock market in 1929—no one they knew had any money in such markets.

As if the plight of their collective situations couldn't become worse, the weather of the Dirty Thirties also bore down upon them. But this time, Mayvis and Paul sought to become united in soul and in body to fight against the rages of the Dust Bowl for another ten years. How could all those years ever be accounted for?

The home garden at Paul's needed to be plowed larger and planted more. They had enough food put up that was dried or canned to get by well until the garden started producing steady. With Paul and his mobility issues ever in the backs of their minds, the three women knew they wouldn't leave him twisting in the wind, even though the road was calling. This was going to be a hard leaving.

The three discussed and debated future destinations. They seemed to be divided between two locations, Louisville and St. Louis, primarily due to those cities having railroads and freshwater ports which could be used to transport goods for the military. It was the opportunity they had waited for. They knew the time had finally arrived and they had to take it. This was it.

The women had been landlocked these past several years, not so much by distance to a waterway, as by being destitute of money, having no way to purchase a ticket to anywhere. The land had been a double-edged sword for them. They had to have it to grow food to live on, but they couldn't leave it, because it never produced any surplus revenue. It was the proverbial case of the dog chasing its tail.

The beginnings of the good-byes were evident. The women were cleaning every piece of clothing they had. They mended some, and they burned some others. The bonfire was big, and the trash pile smoldered for several days.

As they got started, Paul heard about some hiring that was to take place down the road, the beginning construction of the Crane Ammunition Depot, and knew he had to explore the possibilities of work there. He expected to be gone for two, maybe three days. Every farmer around would be there, so Paul decided to go two days early, even though it wasn't ten miles from his farm. Though he had picked up on the clues that the sharecroppers were preparing to leave, he figured they weren't quite ready to go yet.

The road that most took to the job registering site was jammed with cars, trucks, and horse-drawn buggies, and single horse or mule riders. Paul went by way of a logging road that families took when visiting the cemetery and made it close in before the road behind him was blocked off. He was somewhere at the beginning of the line, while the back end was some three miles or so away. The hiring event stretched out for more than six days.

The ones who got jobs were sent on into the woods to work camps to get oriented, assigned, and directed to specific tasks. There were brows raised when Paul showed up. Because he was crippled, they didn't think he would be able to do much. He was also quite dirty, in his raggedy bib jeans, as so many were, but he had his own stake bed truck and they were impressed that he had been working his own farm for over fifteen years. He told them about hauling grain, plowing for the Amish and himself, so they surmised that he could probably be used for something. Others who were stronger could get the heavier workloads.

It was a long-term project and they figured he would shake out or not. They hired Paul permanently after he had been there eleven straight days. He was lucky to have had his own truck bed to sleep in, instead of sleeping on the ground like most of the others looking for work. Before he headed back to his farm, however, he was beholden to others to get even a biscuit to eat.

Lordy be, I thought I was back into another depression, he thought several times. He had arrived with enough cash to purchase three days' worth of food but had to stretch it to cover eleven days on the job. When he got back, he wasn't kidding in describing the ordeal as "living close."

He was never so glad to see home as when he drove up to his house after those eleven days. He noticed that a much bigger stack of stove kindling was stacked on the back porch than usual. The front porch was swept off and the kitchen was neat and tidy. Even the dishes were cleaned and put away. It was a welcome sight at first, but his heart fell as he looked about. A big basket of squash and peppers and some new potatoes were at the sink. There were no signs of the women, but then he heard their talking and a laugh coming to the house.

It was a bittersweet sadness to be back together again, with everyone smiling and seeming happy. The ladies were all scrubbed up, with clean clothes and brushed and pinned-up hair. And there was Paul, standing there looking like he just crawled out of a coal chute. He blushed. He didn't remember seeing them looking this well, ever.

"We've been deciding on going on to St. Louis or to Chicago. Our first stop, really, is going to be Louisville because it's the closest big city. But we've heard on the radio that factory workers are being hired in Detroit." Sophie smiled.

"Having a real, steady paycheck will certainly be something." Bernice added, "If I get a chance, I might even buy me a real wristwatch."

Paul's reaction to this news was to have a sudden cramp in his stomach and he began to realize that the time they would be with him at the farm would come to an end sometime soon. In his mind, he envisioned these three bedraggled women transformed and dressed in finery, going down some shaded avenue carrying a parasol, colored ribbons trailing behind.

The evening meal preparations were longer and drawn out, as the women attended to their duties, wistfully. The radio was tuned to their favorite shows and played in the next room. Paul was served lemonade. Anticipating some goings on, Paul changed into clean clothes and slicked his hair down. When the radio shows ended that night, Mayvis joined the other two women as they slowly strolled to the barn and said good night.

In the morning, Paul drove them to the bus station in Shoals for their departure to Louisville. It was too sudden for everything to be happening the way it did, combined with the job coming up at Crane. It meant real money for things that were worn out or were done without. It meant getting a few steps away from the farm. In time, it might even mean getting electricity.

Of the three, Mayvis was the most torn about their decision to leave. She had developed a special closeness with Paul and hated to leave that bond behind. However, she felt her future was out there somewhere beyond the confines of Shoals, Indiana, and she knew that she needed to seek it out. She valued the independence she had gained since leaving her home so many years ago and felt instinctively that if she allowed anyone else to have control over her happiness, that would be the end of her happiness.

Her emotions stirred her memories of the past many years, as she tried to steal glances over to Paul, and the aura she saw radiating from him. There were very few wrinkles on his hard leather face when she came to the farm, and now, so many years later, the hurricane of struggle had taken its toll and etched the wrinkles into furrows that went deep into his skin. The tender mercies they shared between them were no defense against the ravages of harsh times. The soft tracings of her fingers over his face in quiet moments in the past erased nothing. Today became an emotional bankruptcy.

As they drove to the bus station, Mayvis looked out across the fields, remembering all the sweat and toil she and her friends had put in. *Funny, we've been here nineteen years and it doesn't look like we changed a thing.* Her thoughts continued to idle along as they went. *Funny, the one thing I notice is that the dust doesn't rise very far into the air anymore.*

All too soon they arrived in Shoals and unloaded their meager belongings. The tears crept forward and began.

"We said our good-byes to Minerva and the McCulloughs. They knew you'd be along, and they'll be over to see you soon."

Mayvis had what looked like a mailing package under her arm and gave it to Paul. He took it and could feel it was a book, a very heavy book. On the paper wrapping, Mayvis had written in her neat hand, *Run towards love, you will never regret it.*

As she looked into his eyes and placed her hand once again upon his chest she said, "Perhaps you may want to travel. I certainly hope you get the chance to. My heart has been yours for these several years and—I just won't know how to have it back." With this, she turned away in tears. Paul choked, straining against tears himself, and repeated a remembered quote from Samuel Clemens, "Wheresoever she was, there was Eden."

Mayvis followed her fellow travelers on to the bus, and Paul watched, holding tears in his eyes and sighing, as they disappeared down the dusty road.

Chapter 21

~~~~~~~~~~~~~~~~~~~~~~~~~

The Naval Ammunition Depot (NAD) at Crane was absolutely a deadly serious undertaking. After the trees were felled and roads and ditches and drainage infrastructure were constructed, they established munitions buildings in segregated depressions, and they began production of war materials. It was customary to work on a site and not know about all the details and intricacies of the bigger picture. It was a safety and security function.

Paul was involved in manufacturing ammunition for the M-7 Priest, a self-propelled howitzer that saw extensive use during World War I, though that version had been drawn by a team of six horses to the firing location, unlimbered, set up, and aimed before firing. The traditional wisdom during this period was not to use any motorization because it was smelly. However, having to feed and care for the horses was encumbering.

The new model was self-propelled, and able to carry its own ammunition, which was a plus. At any rate, one hundred-and five-millimeter ammunition was needed. It had to move at the speed of battle, and it could travel at twenty-six miles per hour and carry sixty-nine shells, in addition to carrying a fifty-caliber machine gun on top. Paul was proud to be working on the latest improved model and told his fellow farmers all about it when he returned home.

All in all, Crane developed into a facility with two hundred and nine buildings and over a million square feet. After the initial construction was started, Paul was assigned to the machine shop and went home, occasionally, during weekend work breaks, instead of staying at the facility.

The homestead farm was a quiet and sad place to come home to after the women left. Every return from Crane seemed to reinforce that sense of loss and sadness. Among the desperate times they had experienced, Paul found bits and pieces of small comfort in the memories he re-lived there on the property that had become his own. And after all, his mother was buried under her favorite tree in the high meadow.

His barn stood there, seemingly immortal, waiting for Paul's bidding to bring it back from its slumber. The outhouse behind the barn had collapsed into a pile of rotting lumber that was lost in the field grass and sumac surrounding the barn. The previous snows had mashed the weeds down and snuggled it in for the winter. It looked like a groundhog had taken over and made a den.

The house garden had lost the battle to bring sustenance to the place, ever since Paul had begun working at Crane. The cellar held lots of preserved food, which Paul dug into when he was home. Now that he had folding money, he bought his food stuffs at a grocery store, even though meat was still hanging in the smokehouse.

At the edge of the field, Paul saw that stray sorghum stalks were up and in full tassel and realized that there was no one to harvest it.

There was no snow on the ground, but his stuttering steps still crunched on the frozen ground. *It seems to me that today is the pause between this farm's breath,* Paul said to himself as he turned and went into the smokehouse to get a carving of meat to eat and found a half pint of canned beans to open.

Lighting the stove would heat food and warm a room without too much effort. The extra high stack of stove kindling that was left for him hadn't been used until now and it filled his mind with her memory. *She would have said,* he remembered, *gratitude shifts the consciousness. Mayvis, that is correct.*

On the kitchen table among the clutter Paul picked up his still unopened package, felt its heft and then smelled it briefly for a lingering scent that wasn't there. He opened it and put the paper in the stove to burn.

Following the Equator by Samuel Clemens lay before him. It was a seven hundred-and fourteen-page book of Twain's extensive travels. Paul sat down by the warm stove and opened it and began to read. He soon slumbered and awoke a bit later when the stove had gone cold. Re-stacking his stove, he put his book aside and turned on his radio for a glimpse into the world at large. He heard the President of the United States speaking in a very solemn voice—"… a day that will live in infamy…" The date, of course, was December 8, 1941.

We are at war!

People didn't know what to do and walked around the shop floor, streaming into Crane from all corners, once the word got out that America had been attacked. There had been no formal orders to do anything one way or the other in the event the United States was attacked. It wasn't discussed. NAD Crane was already on a full war footing.

However, the mood was measured, the collective angst among the workers increased as the stories and details of the battles seeped back into the families at home, oftentimes compounding the pain and sorrow that revealed itself as cards, letters, and notifications arrived at America's front door. They built the machinery of war every day. The pride of what weapon would do what type of damage to the enemy was bragged about and touted and became an incessant broadcast from each part of the floor.

The chatter described the workings and effects of the phosphorus grenades, shells, bombs, and rockets being sent to the front lines and its effects in burning living bodies and melting them as they ran, blinding light shooting out of them as they fell and the phosphorus burned through; mind-numbing horror simply tossed aside as the next person's description tried to top the previous macabre aspect of death.

The stories might not be repeated but shouldn't be digested because the poison was too deadly to even sit in the mind. Paul would never repeat some of the stories and descriptions he listened to and overheard. He wanted his sanity to prevail. The dirt farmers of Shoals desperately needed the money. Even though they were not on the battlefields of Europe and the Far East, they nonetheless paid the toll that was extracted from them.

The work shifts were not re-set or adjusted in any way, in the beginning. As munitions were constructed and shipped out, any adjustments would be made on an as-needed basis. "The shop floor had a nervousness to it," Paul related to his friends back at their farms and that was all he would say about it.

"Here we go again," Paul lamented as well. "We'll have to go on rations for the war effort, I suspect. You ought to see it, every now and then you could get a glance of someone going up to one of those howitzer shells and putting a palm kiss on it. Now that we know who our enemy really is, them Japanese, it's become personal."

"Well, Paul, you make sure back here you get one of those palm kisses from us, you put it right on there. As a matter of fact, put *three* on one for good luck."

Through the window, Minerva could see Paul driving up to the farm, apparently on another break from Crane. They were glad to see him and wanted to find out the latest gossip on the shop floor and the goings on around there. To them, he looked skinny and tired as he came in and went to sit by the fireplace.

"First off, Grover, you might as well drop the idea of going to war and signing up for the draft. You'd be too old. Besides, you have to stick around and run the tractor. What do you'uns think would be a good crop to get planted this year?" She said it with a hint of sarcasm.

"We're going to go with corn again. The cattle and the hogs need it, and we'll need corn meal for lots of things. As you think on it, remember we won't have six extra hands this year. In fact, we'll be eight hands short with you at Crane. I got the machinery to get it in the ground and out of the ground to harvest. Another problem is that we may be short of storage. We don't have the stretch to put the barn back up."

"I'm thinking we should use my barn, as it's sitting there empty. What about apples? What do you think you can guess-timate on producing now that we got the steady rains back? I hear they could fetch between twelve and fifteen cents a pound."

"That would give us, let's see, eight hundred pounds at fifteen cents, that would be—"

"A hundred and twenty," Lovety said. "It's something, at least."

Paul said, "Don't forget my ground. It needs to be plowed, too. We need seed money to think about. If the gasoline rationing goes in, they're saying three gallons a week is all we'll be able to get. So, I thought about doubling up with someone else when driving to Crane and that could save a gallon or two, yes?"

"We'll most likely get an exemption for farming. The radio will tell us soon, I'd expect. I don't imagine it will be on the

Voice of America broadcasts, so I'll stick with the farm show," Minerva opined. "It stands to reason."

Grover butted in, "Remember, my tractor will run on coal oil if it comes to that. I just need gasoline to get the converter hot for a few minutes and it'll burn that other stuff just fine. You can go ahead and figure that we can get twice as much, maybe a little more, by burning oil. It's running fifteen cents for gas and I should get coal oil for six cents, maybe four or five."

"Damn glad you have a tractor that's a fuel-convertible machine." Lovety beamed.

It was back and forth with one thing or another for the three farms. It was back to being shorthanded and each person running out of steam before running out of work. It was a steady task to arrange priorities as circumstances and weather dictated.

When it occurred that Grover worked so hard he couldn't sleep, the radio was turned on just to supply some background noise that would help him go back to sleep. He often listened when he was half in or half out of slumber, so it became difficult to remember exactly what he heard or what he knew from day to day.

These shifts in farm life occurred during the period of 1943-1945. After fighting to keep up with the demands of farming and not getting ahead, due in part to improved mechanization and equipment modifications on big farms, the Pate sisters were forced to seek work away from the farm. Minerva Pate Fields and Lovety Pate McCullough went to Indianapolis to find work, as did eighteen million other women throughout the United States, filling in the positions that had been vacated by men who went to war as soldiers.

Lovety got a job in a typing pool and Minerva became a parachute rigger. They lived in the same barracks and occasionally went off base to go to town and see movies. It was Lovety's job to type out a letter, every now and then, to Grover and tell him how hard they worked and how he was missed.

They gained a fair dose of independence during their time away from the farm. The Glenn Miller Orchestra was popular, the Allies stormed the mainland of Europe, and they got to see the news reels at the picture show. The Pentagon in Washington, D.C. was completed, they saw the movie, *For Whom the Bell Tolls*, and bawled their eyes out at the end of *Lassie Come Home* and swooned to Frank Sinatra. *Casablanca* was soon released.

Unable to keep up with all the farming chores single-handedly, Grover stayed home at his farm and concentrated on growing a large garden. He grazed two calves on Paul's land for meat. He canned and dried as much as he could. Paul and Grover worked together on the Fordson to keep it going.

Chapter 22

June 6, 1944 was D-Day, the day the Allied Forces hit the beaches of Normandy. London experienced its first attack by the German's newest weapon, the V-2 rocket. Everyone in Europe was encouraged to grow a "Victory Garden." Grover and Paul laughed it up when they heard the BBC report that broadcast. Minerva and Lovety laughed it up in their barracks, too—a "Victory Garden."

November 7, 1944, President Franklin Delano Roosevelt was elected to his fourth term, but he died in office the following April.

Paul's farm and Grover's farms were almost idle, and weeds had overgrown much of it. The efforts of the people at Crane were unrelenting. As the war went on, the workers stayed tuned to the latest developments and details of the battles that were reported. Grover got fair prices for his crops, but he couldn't grow much single-handedly. His efforts were tied to producing food from his garden for him and not much else.

Events began to portend the end of the war was near.

An assassination on Adolph Hitler's life failed.

Three concentration camps were liberated by the Allies—Buchenwald, Dachau, and Bergan-Belson. The latter camp was discovered to have thousands of dead and rotting corpses lying about among the barely alive.

Adolph Hitler and Eva Braun, his wife for one day, committed suicide.

It was particularly hot this summer, Paul thought, as he returned to his farm and went to the porch to rest in the shade. It was another break that was needed. The ammunition assembly lines seemed to be able to keep up with the demands placed on them and on a few occasions recently, the lines had stopped, sometimes for a few hours. Once, some of the lines had shut down for days. We must be winning the war in some places, Paul surmised.

As he started to enter the house, he noticed that stuck inside the screen porch were two pieces of paper. He sat back down to read them, and as at it turned out, he needed to be sitting down for this. The note was from Tillford's mom, Mrs. Margie. It said she needed to speak to him in person and she would call again. Paul's heart got a jolt. *In person? Why would she need to speak to me in— something bad must have happened. God, I pray not.* The second note was dated a few days before and it said the same thing.

The next day, at mid-morning, Paul heard a car drive up. He looked out the window, but already knew who it was going to be—Robert and Margie Tillford.

Paul was immediately gripped with an unabiding fear to see *both* coming to see him. Without his cane, he hobbled to the screen door as they got out of the car. He was struck by how very old they seemed to have become and how haltingly they moved. For an instant, he remembered seeing their faces from the back of their wagon where he laid that day, when they brought him home with the broken hip.

Margie saw Paul standing behind the screen door. She stumbled up the steps and reached out and grabbed the first chair nearest her. Robert was following, pulling off his hat as he sat.

"Paul, with our heart deeply broken, we come to tell you the saddest news. Our most precious son has been killed in this horrible, horrible war." Margie finally looked up and her eyes met Paul's. The pain and sorrow reached unfathomable depths in their faces and hearts, as they recounted to Paul what they knew and what was told to them by the Army Captain and the Chaplain that came to deliver the news.

"Tillford was fightin' in the Philippines and they were in a rescue mission to get the Philippine people off the island he was on. There was no way to get them evacuated in time and they were captured by the Japanese army. They were put on a death march across the island with no water or food and they—were tortured and—killed as they were marched to their concentration camp. We don't know when or how. But we are certain that Tillford was a brave man. And you were one of his closest friends, well before your injury."

"I know," Paul responded, with tears in his eyes. "My dear God, I'm so sorry." Paul leaned back in his rocker to get a breath.

"He told me many times it was you that made him strong, by the way you saw life and the way you pulled through and your healing," Robert nodded. "It's been almost two years now since it happened. They are *just* now letting us know. We don't know if we'll be able to have him home for burial or not. There are thousands of our boys over there and they said it would take some time because the war is still going on. They need to keep pushing and beat the bastards down."

"I pray we'll have him home. I'm so sorry. Is there anything I can do to help you? I want to do anything I can do to help. You already know that, right?"

"We know that. It'll be awhile before we know anything else, so thank you for your kind offer."

"Who else knows about this?"

"The newspaper prints an Obituary listing, so that's how most people will find out. We heard you're over at Crane so much, you might not know, so we came out to tell you ourselves. It seems like just about all the people your age have gone to fight in the war, so's not many around for the news."

"Yep, I know. I don't get into town much, except to buy groceries occasionally and then come back out here and go back to work."

"Paul," Robert said, "I have some more to tell you, but I don't want to add to your burden."

"That's all right, sir. Please go on."

"What I am about to tell you was a strict confidence I shared with my son, who told me this before he left for the service and I was not to repeat it to anyone, ever, except—as he put it—in the event of his death."

"What is it, Mr. Tillford?"

Mr. Tillford looked at his wife and said, "She's the only person besides me, and now you, that knows what I'm about to tell you."

"Okay."

"Tillford and Doofus and maybe Jed had found out that the sheriff and your old teacher, Mrs. Olsham, had something to do with those barn fires that were set ablaze when we were all at your mother's funeral."

Paul froze in his rocker, astonished at this news. "Good Lord, what?"

"As a prank, Tillford and Doofus broke into the old school-house one evening to gather up a bunch of books they were going to bring out here for you. Thought you would get a big laugh out of it. They were almost caught when Mrs. Olsham came back to the schoolhouse and the sheriff was following her inside. The boys overheard them arguing about what they were going to do and how they were going to keep the barn burning secret. The boys both heard it, loud and clear."

"Tillford told me that it sounded like Mrs. Olsham was the lookout for these two other people, a man and a woman, that went to the two barns and set them on fire. The thing was no one knew about the two boys in the loft."

Margie continued the story, "The boys said that the good Mrs. Olsham got scared and told the sheriff that it was murder and that she didn't want to have any part of it. That's when she and the sheriff got into this big argument and he threatened her and then left the library with her, still arguing. I don't know if you know this or not, but when she died, it was supposed to have been a fall off a ladder and that's where she was found, on the floor at the bottom of the ladder. Someone who discovered her there said that when they found her, her face looked a bit sunken in on the side, too big to have happened by her falling a few feet. They ruled her death an accident, but people know it was pretty suspicious because of the injury to her face."

"Well, you can knock me down! I suspected something was amiss, but never imagined Mrs. Olsham was involved. In fact, I have fond memories of her from when I was in school. She went out of her way to help me out at times and was sympathetic to my situation with my father and all."

And then Paul changed the topic. "I'll tell you this. I have had sharecropper women here, working on our farms for a while."

"Yes, we know."

"Not too long ago, one of them was almost raped by some-one that broke into our barns. She fought him off and cut his crotch up with her blade during that encounter, but he got away. They were pretty bold, all right. One of the women, Sophie, first caught them prying off the boards on the back of our barn, stealing sorghum, and she ran them off. The man came back alone and tried to assault Bernice and that's when she cut into him. His accomplice was bitten pretty good on her hand by Sophie."

"Doofus is still away in the war and he's the only other person that has direct knowledge of what the crimes were, and who played what part. I don't know what we can do about it, other than wait for him to get back here and ask him what he wants to do about it, if anything, I suppose." Robert said.

Margie hedged, "There's going to have to be some care taken here, guys. The Klan is still about, and we don't know who knows who. If the sheriff is in the Klan, which it seems certain that he is, he's got allies and thugs around that would harm people or even worse. Letting the laws know would do us no good at this point. Without Doofus, we would be sitting ducks. We couldn't prove a thing. They would go after him, too, I'm afraid."

"Well, I can tell you this, for sure," Paul interjected, "the sheriff and the Klan are together because that man that almost raped our girl Bernice had his Klan robes with him, throwed over one of the stalls. When he lit out across the field, he left them. So's, I washed them for him in the manure soup and then I burned them." He smiled.

"Damn good of you, Paul." They had a good laugh.

Chapter 23

In December 1945, Paul got a letter from M. Bailey, addressed to General Delivery. He read Marvis's letter privately and did not share its contents. After a few weeks, he responded and received a few letters back. He kept them in the pages of his Mark Twain book.

Japan continued to fight on until the first atomic bombs were dropped on Hiroshima and Nagasaki. The Emperor announced their unconditional surrender in a radio broadcast, officially ending World War II.

Shoals had some prosperity. The town saw economic growth during the war as the townspeople dug in and worked hard, contributing to the war effort, and benefitted from the work provided by government production efforts, such as the depot in Crane. However, as the town prospered during those years, the population shrunk. The requirements of the military drained the ranks of able-bodied men from the towns and countryside. Being on a war footing meant that civil projects were put on hold. Once the veterans started returning, ambition was added to manpower and the wheels started to roll. The contributions of women were certainly noticed, by grit and grace.

The accounting of those who fought filled the pages of the local newspaper and lists of those who survived and those who died were posted at the town hall. Businesses also posted these lists, and shop owners shared their personal stories, adding color to local gossip during and after the war. Many families also put gold stars in a front window of their home to denote their loss of a family member, killed in the war.

An accounting and a reckoning began. Once a list was posted and someone was seen adding something or writing on it, natural curiosity brought people to gather around to digest the news and spread the latest. It became a roller coaster that ran between elation and heartache, a collective sensitivity.

Once the war was officially over, NAD Crane released many of its workers, including Paul. Now that he had time on his hands, he decided to go to town to stock up on provisions. He noticed a small group gathered around the bulletin board and curiosity pushed him to go see the latest. Some editorializing occurred during the posting by a city official or newspaper staff. An article was published by the paper, which would be integrated into the next addition. Someone at the board had posted the complete article. Paul waited his turn to read it, before returning home. It read as follows:

> *USS Indianapolis, July 1945. A Japanese submarine followed a single unescorted Navy ship returning to the United States and attacked the vessel with torpedoes. The vessel was hit at least twice and went down within twelve minutes. The military estimated the vessel carried approximately 900 troops that went into the water with 3,500 gallons of burning aviation fuel. Of the 900 troops, only 317 survived. They were afloat for four days in shark-infested waters. A PBY-5A Catalina Flying boat spotted wreckage and dropped life rafts, landed, and loaded the first 56 men. 7 rescue ships arrived and rescued the remaining men.*

The bottom of the article listed the casualties. Paul's close friend, Doofus, was on the list. He became very morose, thinking about the deaths of his childhood friends. He drove home with the news of Doofus's death on his mind, added to the sadness of Tillford's death. The loss created a sphere of profound reflection within him, something even beyond the contemplation he experienced with his mother's passing. For the first time in many years, he began to question his purpose in life.

Paul was a child of a believing parent who had brought him through Baptism and a personal acceptance of Christ. He had learned and understood that without divine grace man cannot do good works or merit pleasing and being acceptable to God. He would be guided in freedom to exercise his will for good. The rebuilding of himself and working in the community was his aim.

A promise of light beckoned Paul to reach the high meadow and the great old tree where his mother's grave awaited his company. His conflicts between the global calamity and his personal loss of friendships troubled his mind. The sense of finding some justice in bringing the sheriff to some sort of accounting for his involvement in the fires and deaths of three people left a bad taste in his mouth. He would need to tell others about Doofus's death and the lost chance for justice. Someday, Paul felt an accounting would come. Amen.

Having brought his Bible with him, he settled in and turned to the book of Acts and read. His biblical namesake, Paul, drew him in.

It rained that day. The dust didn't settle down, the wind didn't start blowing, and the clouds didn't block out the sun.

The trees' leaves didn't get wet and the ground remained dry. In fact, no actual water hit anything. It became a catharsis as the different aspects of war and losses gathered into his mind and created a torrent of emotions that carried him along.

Paul had tried to dismiss the terrible news that had surrounded him for so long—the unending reports of the war's progress and those who died in the process, including two of his closest childhood friends. He was still missing the women sharecroppers who had kept him company for many years. He was still aching with sadness over the loss of his mother, and resentful of his father for his many years of cruelty.

Paul stood on his porch and faced a starless night and screamed and yelled for minutes into the void, trying to expel the evil and destruction of the war from his body and rid his mind of the sickness of death and loss of innocent lives that were lost. He railed into exhaustion until his mind drew a blank and his voice was broken into silence. Holding his Bible nauseated him, and he flung it aside. He carried no thoughts the next morning when he awoke in his swing. Cautiously, he allowed his mind to slowly regain his body and felt his angry throat. He took a dipper of well water and followed it with a spoon full of honey. He then read some of his Samuel Clemens's book, *Following the Equator*. That night he had a dreamless sleep.

Now that the war was over, Paul sought his renewal from the sickness of war by reuniting with his neighbors, the ones who had become the constants in his life. Grover and Lovety stayed put, replanted their apple orchard, and plowed Paul's field when they needed more ground for extra crops. Minerva's farmhouse had been repaired, some the worse for wear, and she was back at her place, but still dependent on the working collective of Grover, her sister Lovety, and now Paul again, since his job at Crane had ended. Minerva had two houses she lived out of, her own and her sister's, and a bedroom in each. Where she stayed depended on where they quit working for the day and which house was closest. Since they all cooked and prepared food together, they were usually together.

Paul went to seek renewal at the Old Order Amish farms north of him around Odon. These days, when he started his old stake bed truck, Paul crossed his fingers and prayed that it would start. It was certainly dependable, but he felt it was seeing its last days. The new cars that everyone drove had three pedals—accelerator, brake, and clutch. With only one good leg, one day in the not-too-distant future he was afraid he would be stranded again.

As he drove up to his friend's place, he reminded himself, *Breathe in the gratitude you felt and receive life again from that moment. Ha, I am starting to feel better coming up this way and getting out from under the shadows of Shoals.*

On the road into the Amish farms, Paul knew the community would not be in the war business madness like he had been in and they would not have been building ordinances and the weapons for the war. They didn't have need for electricity, like him, and they didn't have radios and would not have been listening to the broadcasts that were filled with all the war news. He felt this would be a time of renewal.

The Amish farms were places with broad sweeps of unbroken pastures containing corn, hay, or other crops that were put into perpetual rotation, and livestock pastures. An occasional pond for cattle to use for watering would, most likely, have been stocked with fish. Wild asparagus grew along the fence lines, where cows and horses could extend a neck to eat the tender shoots in the spring sprouting. Each family would know where the best shoots would be growing and take advantage of the bounty.

He drove over a rise in the pasturelands and absorbed the picturesque waving fields, and looked at the neat, well-kept large barns and houses all in white, each an occasional staccato in the harmonious vista. He felt a touch of envy, thinking about the possibility of having such a wealth of a place of his own. It revived a brief childhood whimsy that had been erased at an early age.

"I can't imagine I was going to see you again, English," Samuel said to Paul as he drove up to the barn, "I figured your government would make you go and fight in the war. That didn't happen, I guess. Welcome. What got you out this way?"

After exchanging pleasantries, they settled into visiting a bit and took the shade of a tree.

"I'm sure you'll appreciate this, but the other day I had to get out my Bible and seek some renewal. You know, this war was almost too much for me and I went to the book of Acts and found me a passage, 'In God we live, move, and exist,' so I thought about you and came over to visit."

"It's too bad you don't speak German. If you did, you could learn yourself some new hymns."

"I got enough of German and Japanese to last me a lifetime, Samuel. How is your community getting along? I know the government don't mess with you folks too much and leave you pretty much alone, but I know there are times—"

"We've been pressed, like in the past. As you know, we practice nonresistance and we won't perform any type of military work, but we're sometimes called to do civilian public service. A few of our community were asked and we have a few who are doing deeds now. Brother Daniel Wheatman, who bought your horse, is at the hospital in Madison, but he'll be home soon."

"Are you taking on any outside work for us English any?"

"Not so much. We've been busy building new dwellings for four new families, where they have chosen to marry."

"No barn raisings, then?"

"Not out of the community, nothing we've accepted. But it's good to see you again, Paul."

"Give my best regards to your wife and your family for me. My sharecropper women have moved on now, so's it's just me again. I can still haul things in my truck, though."

"Be well and hold your faith," Samuel offered, as he waved and walked away.

Returning to the Shoals area, Paul passed by his farm and continued down the road to Grover and Lovety's farm to plan a bit with them about getting the next crops in. Returning veterans were pulling up stakes to go to live in the cities, giving up the hard farm life they came from. Fewer people growing crops meant that more food needed to be grown by fewer farmers. It seemed to be a good opportunity to get better prices for commodities. They figured they might be able to get a new barn out of it within a year.

Minerva saw Paul pull up next door and walked over to speak to him. He could tell she had something on the tip of her tongue to say.

"Might as well get ready for some good news as bad news, don't you think?"

"Minerva, I'm ready for some good news. What you got?" he said, as he stepped down from his truck.

"The town has been shrinking since so many people have been moving on, so the city council has decided to shrink up our local government a bit and share the burden with Loogootee.

So, guess what? They just retired the sheriff and he's out! Out. Of. A. Job."

"You don't say!"

"Yep, Grover heard it this morning on the square. Everybody was standing around, and he says it was like watching a dog die. Everybody had smiles on their faces and a spring in their steps. They were all gathered around across the street from the jail and they see the sheriff go into his office and start cleaning out his desk. Someone decided, one of his half-friends, to go in and see if it were true. They came out with a smile on. So, we knew it was true before he ever got back across the street to tell everyone else."

"Well, isn't that something?"

"He said they called it a long-term suspension, so's if they need to bring someone back, they don't have to get everybody back together and do a lot of meetings and voting. If they need to, they can then lift the suspension and then they can hire someone right off. They would only need a key to open the jail house door. In the meantime, anybody that needed it could be locked up at the Loogootee jail."

"We need a doctor to be here, but if we didn't, he could take the doctor with him. That would take the KKK out of here a might better, still."

"What does Grover and Lovety think about all of this?"

"They both said it at the same time—'We need to plant more corn.' So, I started laughing with 'em."

Paul glimpsed at her from the corner of his eye and said to himself, *it sounds like she is turning into a bit of a wag—maybe, maybe not.* The idea that Lovety would pick up a bit of town chatter was amusing to Paul. After all, rural folks didn't have much contact with many other people in their day-to-day lives unless they had a good reason to. Going to buy Ball jars, feed, cloth, or other staples occurred intermittently. Gossipy exchanges would be out of character. It was humorous to Paul to hear it.

As the four of them settled in for supper and discussed what not having a sheriff around meant, Grover had more news to share. "Since the war has ended, I am proposing we modernize around here, so's I am putting us on the list to get electricity to this farm and we're getting an electric refrigerator. The ice man is always complaining about losing customers and he hardly has enough on his route to keep going. He uses electricity to run his ice business and it won't be much longer and he'll be out of business. Paul, you better think about it, too."

"It's gonna be a problem in that I don't have a telephone pole."

"They're going to put a line down this road starting next month. Then, you can hook-up any time after that when you want to."

"That also means electric lights in the house and we could even put lights in the barn when we get one of those. We also don't have to worry about knocking over a lantern and burning the place down." Minerva quipped and continued, "And the next thing I'd like to see is an electric water pump so's we would have faucet water, too."

"The thing I like in all this is going to be not having those damned kerosene lamps inside the house covering everything in soot," Lovety lamented. "I bet it would be cooler, as well. Grover's moving right ahead, right into the modern times, ain't you, hon?" Then she added as an aside, "They've been playing baseball at night—for over ten years." They all had a laugh.

PART FIVE

Chapter 24

~~~~~~~~~~~~~~~~~~~~~~~~~~~~~~~~

The importance of winning the war could not be overstated. A can-do attitude gripped most of America, once they got back to living, working, and growing their families. The small community of Shoals began to change as well, and its people began to change, too. The distant, outside world became closer, for better and for worse.

It was the beginning of what was much later described as the Baby Boom era. Everybody paid attention to everybody else's attention and some groups in the U.S. began to fear a secret Communist takeover was going on throughout the government. Although President Truman didn't believe it and thought it was ridiculous, he nevertheless created, through executive order, the Attorney General's List of Subversive Organizations. Seventy-one organizations were listed as adjuncts of the Communist Party, including the Ku Klux Klan.

As far as the Shoals farmers were concerned, it was another nail in the Klan's despicable coffin. Prejudice was still around and followed the G.I.s home from the war. It was a situation of separate but not equal. When church doctrines were examined by some faiths, the congregations were blind to recognizing their own shortcomings.

Jackie Robinson began playing baseball for the Brooklyn

Dodgers in 1947, and even the Shoals farmers followed his progress with interest, by radio. However, one week after Robinson joined the Dodgers, players for the Phillies shouted abuse at him across the field, calling him "nigger" and advising him to go back to the jungle.

Besides radio baseball to listen to, music was a very popular pastime, especially The Grand Ole Opry, and the farmers tuned in on Sundays for the Gospel Hour. The only church in Shoals was a bit closed-minded and accepted new congregants with a bit of suspicion, until they could be investigated, and rumors were debated and settled. As a result, the church never grew and Christian fellowship was best exercised at arm's length, except for school functions that brought some together for those who had kids of school age.

Music shows held in the fall in Bean Blossom, Indiana, the Brown County Jamboree, were worth several trips north during the fall season. The Shoals farmers would roam around the nearby town of Nashville, occasionally go to dinner at the Nashville House, and get black licorice candy from the coffee shop there. Or occasionally they would make the trip over to Bloomington, where Indiana University was. Paul never went very far. The "old timey" bluegrass and gospel music they heard took them away from the daily drudgery of year-after-year farm work. These infrequent excursions always marked off cider making time when the weather cooled off and the leaves started to change colors in the forests of Brown County.

Farm work and planting and harvesting pulled them away from the social events others enjoyed who were living a more urban life. Moving away from the rural life came about only when some form of livelihood was secured that gave a financial base to the change. Without that security, it was only a gamble if there were no close friends or relatives to lend a hand. Paul didn't have those connections, other than his closest neighbors. His closest relatives were buried and scattered about in rural areas away from commerce. Paul did try, like most of the surrounding farmers did. A better income was always needed. Farmers were usually on the lower end of opportunities. For many, the ground stayed idle.

An expectation of hope and opportunity arose when he learned, like everybody else, by way of the radio, of the invasion of the North Korean Army into South Korea, in June of 1950. The United States Army was heading into Korea to bolster South Korea. China was heading into the conflict to bolster the North. Paul thought it wouldn't be long before they started up the ammo production at Crane and he would be back to work and away from the farm once again. It was money he could always use.

It didn't happen. Expectations grew but the reality of working again at Crane never materialized. Instead, the facilities that would be involved in the war effort were located between Charleston and Jeffersonville, Indiana, nearly eighty miles away. Jeffersonville was the site of the Civil War era shipyards that built paddle wheelers. It was located across the river from Louisville, Kentucky, a major port. Paul thought, *not a chance in Hell.*

However, although shrouded in secrecy, National Gypsum drilled some exploratory holes searching for gypsum on farmland by the White River near Shoals and found a large vein and a water supply that could be combined to make gypsum wallboard products. The Shoals newspaper, right after Christmas in 1952, announced the plans to build a plant and develop mining for the extraction of the mineral at Shoals. The local farmers were torn between staying on the farms and being covered in the dirt or going to work for the national company and being covered in gypsum dust.

The gypsum dust came with a steady paycheck if they could

get on, and they would have medical benefits. Very few farmers had medical insurance of any kind. If medical attention was needed, paying for it came out of their very shallow pockets or their very great promises to pay sometime in the future. There was just so much bartering that could be done. Healthcare was most frequently dispensed by the untrained family in the form of folk medicine and natural remedies.

The Shoals farmers continued to work the land and divided up the planting between corn and soybeans. Crop prices stabilized and the idea they come to rely on in the Depression days, planting two different crops instead of one, seemed to be a decision that was well-founded. One crop was a hedge against the loss in price of the other crop if the market for the other crop dropped.

Traveling around through the farmlands in and around Shoals provided all the proof they needed that the two crop plantings method was better than one. They were always watching the neighboring farmer's crops grow and looked for signs of plant diseases or blight that might be carried on the wind to their crops, which might then need a preventative application of a dust or spray. Once the crops got put into the ground and then came up, the Shoals farmers were always reluctant to get back into the fields with the tractor unless it was really needed. It cost money to run the tractor.

"Like we know, it cuts down on the overhead, which is the insurance on getting it to market and gaining a fair price," Grover said.

"If it weren't so, it still wouldn't make any difference to argue the point with him," Minerva added.

The sisters went on about their business. The gypsum mine started up and produced the first load of gypsum board in 1954, making the front page of the Shoals paper.

"Seeing that it's a god-send to have that mine located right at our doorsteps, directs me to tell you sisters to come here. We should talk." Grover beckoned. "I'm headed to the mine with Paul tomorrow to talk to some folks about getting on."

"We got the corn in, so I guess we'll be good for a spell, won't we, Sis?" Lovety said to Minerva.

"It shouldn't be that bad. The crops are in the ground and growing. You two can sit back for the most part and watch them grow. Just keep a sharp eye that we don't get blight in the corn, I guess."

The women just rolled their eyes at what Grover said, as they all knew there was always things to do on the farm. It was always a catch-up for something. They stared at each other as Grover continued to talk.

"That damned old Fordson tractor is getting harder and harder to start. I don't know how many more cranks I got left in me. Since Ford quit making those things in '27, I hope it don't get a breakin' spell and go acting up while you're over at the mine, that's all." Both sisters nodded in agreement.

Lovety thought there was going to be more 'tough road' for the two of them now that he was going to go to the mines. The women couldn't get on over there. They certainly wouldn't be hiring women. That left both women to run three farms.

"I'll work myself to death and be dead by my next harvest, I just know it—" Lovety sat in a chair with her arms tightly crossed, gritting her teeth.

◇   ◇   ◇

Grover and Paul arrived back at Grover's place well after dark. Grover had powdery dust all over him and a smile on his face.

Jokingly, Lovety said, "Grove, did you fall down in the parking lot? You look mighty dusty."

"No, I didn't do no such thing. I got a half a day of actual work and the other half day was signing and filling out all kinds of papers. They took my picture and I'll get a work badge in a few days. I'm going to be driving a front-end loader, it looks like."

They had smiles on their faces and were happy to know that Grover would have a paycheck. They looked at Paul, who was not dirty, with questioning looks.

"I didn't make it, at least in this round. In a few weeks, they said to come back, and they could do some more hiring. You'uns know they looked at this bum leg of mine and raised an eyebrow over it. They didn't ask me any other type of questions to see how good a worker I was and then they went about their business. I stayed around in the truck till Grover finished his shift and we come on home."

"Well, Paul, it will surely work out, won't it? It always does," Lovety said. "We expected you men earlier, but we got supper on the stove waiting, so let's eat and give thanks. What does everybody say? Grove, you could do a washing to your elbows, at least."

After supper, Paul got in his truck and headed back to his farm. They could tell he was disappointed at not getting hired, as he had been subdued at the table.

Grover explained, "I didn't want to say anything while he was here and didn't want anything hurtful passed. I kind of supposed this, and I might be wrong, but I was watching all them mining hands sorta watching Paul through the front windows where he was outside. After a few hours of him milling around, I thought they were getting uncomfortable with him being out front, like he may have been one of the mine workers that had got hurt on the job and it was reflecting on them and the company, in a negative sort of way, just saying."

Minerva nodded, "I can very well imagine it. Of course, Paul is aware of how others see him, and he has taken it in stride all these years. It's hurtful, I know. We don't pay it any mind because he's a man of strength and dignity. Once any of them get to know him, he'll be a great friend and willing to do anything for another man. I wish there were more men like him. That's what I got to say on it."

Changing the conversation, Grover went on, "I have to say though, I got a lucky break, getting that driver's job. Everybody would want that one and there were not but a few of them to be had. Most everybody else will be on the ground working. At least, I'll be above the ground a bit, maybe the dust won't be so bad higher off the ground. Naw, it's damn dusty, no getting around that."

The work of the farm consumed the women, like always. Grover settled in to working at the gypsum mines and driving a front-end loader and Paul came around to help the women with the farm work. Lovety or Minerva drove the tractor. Paul couldn't because of it having too many pedals for a one-legged man.

Towards the fall of the year, the corn was standing tall and drying well. Everybody was working, like always, but they seemed to not be getting as much done as they used to. *Maybe it's an age thing,* Paul thought. *We're just getting older and moving slower.*

One Sunday afternoon, not a workday, Grover had an idle comment about the corn standing.

"There seems to be a lot of it that hasn't been harvested—"

"Well, Grove, I got myself in gear just as much as I can."

"Oh, honey, I didn't mean that. I was thinking and hoping I could get it all done *for* you and we could have an early year, that's all."

"I'm just tired. I can't seem to get enough sleep and when I get up, I'm already wore out before I even can get the tractor started. I'm just tired."

"Take it a bit easier, if that helps."

"Minerva and Paul don't get no rest if I don't pull my load."

Somewhere in the back of Grover's mind, he sensed a twinge of concern, but nothing that aroused any further thoughts.

A few weeks went by, and they were once again on the porch on another Sunday and Grover looked at the corn again and saw only ten more rows had been taken down. Now, a concern was awakened in him. Without a comment to anyone, he went over to Paul's farm and looked at his fields. They were all standing, and no corn had been taken down. Now, he became genuinely concerned. There was lots of corn standing.

Grover and Paul were in Paul's barn where the tractor was parked. Grover wanted to look at it to see why it has been so hard to crank. As they worked on the carburetor, Grover asked Paul how Lovety was doing and Paul replied, "We're all working but the women need to take a breather now and again. I guess the time gets away from us. Both of them are so tired. Me too, I suppose."

Treading lightly at the dinner table, Grover talked about the mining job. "I think this mining business is going to go on for quite some time. I heard some of the white hats talking about the veins of gypsum we'll be chasing, and they're very deep. It's good for our family I got on. We're sooo fortunate to be able to get real insurance. By the way, Paul, there is talk that they're close to opening up another shaft in the mine and they may be bringing more people on. That's good, huh?"

Until the mine was developed further, and more buildings were completed, the health insurance aspect was offered through the company doctors, who came and set up a clinic at the mine, and operated Tuesday through Friday. If Lovety didn't feel well within a week, Grover decided that she would go with him to work on a Friday and go to the clinic and wait for him to get off at the end of his shift.

That Friday, a white hat came out to the mine to get Grover to come to the clinic to see about his wife. This alarmed him, but he cinched up his resolve and they went in. There were lots of people at the clinic waiting to see someone.

"I'm Dr. Fenton, Grover. Come in, and don't get all concerned. Your wife is okay, just so's you know. She has a condition called anemia and I suspect she has a touch of food poisoning, which has aggravated her digestive system, okay? I'm prescribing her some medicine to take for the next ten days that ought to clear things up. If not, we can have a look again, but I expect her to be much better in about three or four days."

Grover was wearing a brow. "You're going to get better soon, honey," he said reassuringly.

"So, I'd expect that the food poisoning came from eating something that wasn't fully cooked or maybe not eaten quickly enough, maybe it stayed around too long, or not refrigerated properly, something like that. It's a matter of looking when you get home and if you suspect something, throw it out. You can do that, right?" As if trying to add a bit of humor, he added, "the Depression is over, so splurge and get new food, huh?"

"We'll do it."

The doctor remarked, "You don't need to get back to work for this afternoon, I'll take care of that. Just go on home and enjoy the weekend."

Getting to the parking lot, Lovety said, "I can't imagine what it was we ate that was bad. But Minerva has been feeling the same as me. My guess is that she might have the same thing."

Half in jest, Grover said, "Maybe you can share some of them pills and doctor on her, while you're getting better."

The Martin County census where Shoals was located reflected a poor county affected by grinding poverty that put one in four households below the poverty line where development and healthcare severely lagged other communities. Running water and electricity were primary components that were missing in large part. Food poisoning, poor hygiene, and malnutrition were common.

They discussed the importance of getting an electric refrigerator once they got electricity down the road and could string power to the farmhouse. In the meantime, Grover saw lots of money standing in the fields. After they got home and Lovety was settled in, he drove over to Paul's farm and got out the tractor and started in on harvesting corn, finishing for the day at 11:30 p.m. He started again the next day at 5:00 a.m. It was going to be a hump, but it had to be done, and he was not going to quit the mine during harvest or any other time. This instance of having to go to the doctor proved how valuable it was to have insurance. Lovety shared her medicine with her sister.

Grover mounted a mighty battle to get the crops harvested. For days on end after he worked in the gypsum mines, he came home and ran the tractor till midnight or 1:00 a.m. until he could hardly stand. His supervisor at the mine warned him to pay more attention to what he was doing, or he could get someone hurt or worse. Grover then cut back and worked every other day in the fields after he got home and Minerva, Paul, and Lovety took up the other days. It might work, Grover thought.

Minerva was still weakened by her illness and even though she took some of Lovety's pills, she didn't improve much.

"Grove, I'm feeling bad for my sister. She doesn't have the insurance like we do. Is there anything we could do to help her get some?"

"I've tried, but I can't get help from the company. They

will only insure immediate family, and that means just wife and kids. I know, I feel it too, but she doesn't have any money to pay on any insurance. We don't either. You see what comes out of my check. We'll have to do what we do and get by the best we know how."

Some of the crops were left standing. It was now cold. The ground was hard. Lovety was still puny. Minerva was, too. They were all wearing brave faces. The winter coughs and runny noses started.

The women drove the tractor. It was Minerva's turn on the seat. However, this morning, she couldn't get the tractor started. It might have been too cold. Paul didn't show up till mid-afternoon and he immediately saw that something wasn't right. The tractor was in the same place it had been the day before.

"Paul, I can't get that damned thing to turn over. I'm not that heavy. Maybe you can give a crank or two. It's a little warmer now, maybe it will go."

The fuel bowl needed to be heated first to evaporate the gasoline before the engine was cranked over and the fumes pumped into the cylinders and ignited. Then when the engine was hot, the diesel fuel would run smooth and no more gasoline would be needed.

Paul got the bowl hot, like Grover always did. It started strong but sputtered to a stop. It was too cold, yet. He tried it again and grabbed the crank to give it a throw. It fired prematurely and the crank flew backwards and caught Paul mid-chest, driving him to the ground. He was gasping and trying to yell as he turned over onto his back. When the women got him laid out, he could not bend forward to sit up.

"Wait—wait, let me lay here for just a second to catch my breath—I definitely have a couple of broken ribs."

As they waited for Paul to regain his breath, Grover surprised them by arriving home from work early.

They got Paul up on his good leg and he slowly hobbled into the parlor of Grover and Lovety's house and laid him out. Paul looked down at the bed, thinking Oh my god, another divan.

Broken ribs were not an unusual injury to farm life and Grover went to the drug store and bought elastic stretch bandages to wrap Paul's ribs and hold them in place for a quick, though somewhat painful, healing.

Adding more pain to his injuries, Grover announced his news at the dinner table that night.

"It was a run of bad luck that will go by, Paul. The white hats announced today that they'll begin advertising for more mine workers, come next week. Probably twenty or so men will get hired on. You can make the next one, that's all." It was the second round.

"Yes, you will," chimed in the women.

Paul settled in to recouping on the real bed they had for him and with a little help, he could get to the outhouse by himself and avoid that humiliation. A radio by his bed gave him lots of rest time and he got warm under the collar to hear Senator Joseph McCarthy spewing accusations of subversion in the Red Scare hearings in Washington, D.C.

Crops were left standing.

Hard freezes were coming with more frequency and everyone stayed inside except for a little "apple jacking." The women were still puny and stayed close to the fireplace.

"I'm tired of cussing that tractor. It's going into the shop, while the ground is hard," Lovety declared at the table one night.

During the coldest parts of winter, a few slackers working in the gypsum mines decided to stay close to a warm fire at home, have a corn drink or few and miss work. An occasional absence from work was allowed for true family situations, but by and large, employees who missed work were let go and openings arose now and then. On such a time, word of mouth was all that was needed to get new hires to come in and fill the vacancies. Paul was ready. Grover found out about two or three positions coming open and took Paul with him a few weeks later.

It wasn't a glowing welcome, but an opportunity nonetheless for Paul. Most of the work was underground and not so cold, just dusty, always dusty.

"What can you do?" a foreman asked, seeing Paul's leg and his cane.

"What do you need done? Let's see."

"Well, I'll show you." They walked into an electric tug tractor area and the foreman pointed to one of the tractors. "I need someone to drive this around and pull full trailers over to where they would be dumped to an assembly line. You think you can do it? It's mostly sitting and driving this thing back and forth. It's lots of sitting and driving. Where you go is into some of the smaller spaces to pick up ore and it's not an area with a lot of headroom, that's why you're sitting. Get it?"

"I think so. If you can get me a two-by-two, a saw and hammer and nails, I can put me together a brake stick for my bad leg and then I can push it with my shoulder to stop. I've done it for years. I'll show you what I can do—I think I can do it. Yes, sir."

"Well then, hop into this thing and I'll drive us around to a shop and let's see what you want to put together. 'Sides, we can tour around as you go. Get in." Away they went.

So, the "stick brake" worked. The foreman was a little surprised at Paul's ingenuity, but it worked out and he became a dependable employee.

Chapter 25

Back at his farm, Paul continued to live a quiet existence, without much disturbance, which allowed him to get some reading in on the Samuel Clemens book that Mayvis had given him years ago. The letters of hers that he saved, which were all of them, were always falling out of the book and he opened them up and re-read them occasionally before placing them back into his big book. Whatever page or passage he was marking was invariably lost for a while and then rediscovered and remembered anew. It kept her remembrances alive.

The good fortune of having a steady paycheck was a marvelous thing to Paul. He wanted to experience the joy of having electricity in his house, so he directed some of his precious money towards that end. When the utility poles were ready to be set in, he was ready. Maybe he would get a refrigerator.

Grover and the sisters couldn't wait for a refrigerator. They were delighted to have cold milk to drink, which was much better than keeping a glass bottle hung down the well for chilling. Butter was another marvel—they could use a knife to cut it, rather than just spread it. It was so different. The light inside the Frigidaire meant that they could see what was in that space, even at night with the lights turned off.

It was a Friday evening after dark when Grover drove over

to Paul's farm. He was concerned. That day at the mines, when he went through one of the tunnels where Paul was hauling, he noticed his tractor plugged in and charging, but no Paul around. "Hello, the house," Grover called out, as he got out of his truck. Paul was inside and opened the door. Grover entered, saying, "I didn't see you at work today and didn't know if you got sick or not. Both of the women at my place are still puny. Don't want you catching anything they got."

"It could be better. Come in."

"Your house is pretty cool—"

"I haven't lit a fire in the hearth yet or the stove. I just got home. I was laid off today."

"Why, what for? You've only been there about a couple of months—"

"I had a wreck with one of the tugs and ran into a roller line assembly. It wasn't too bad, but they did have to stop the production for almost an hour."

"You're not hurt any?"

"No, I'm all right. Hurt my ego is all. I got a three-day suspension, but I can come back next week. I nailed up a stob on the end of my brake stick and I didn't nail it tight and it came off when I went to stop. I didn't get my good leg over there in time."

"I'm sorry to hear that, Paul. Those things happen, though they get jittery pretty quick. You ought to see them when they're around me and my big bucket—" Grover rolled his eyes. "Well, we got our electric hook-up to the house and we got the refrigerator going. It's pretty fine."

"Mine is coming in the next day or two. They're gonna do the drop to the house and into the kitchen."

◇   ◇   ◇

Paul had to go meet with the Safety Coordinator and his foremen before he could get back to work. They had to go over what had happened and the details of the accident. Once Paul showed them what went wrong with his stick brake, they told him to go back to the shop and redo his stick and make the piece that fell off sturdier.

It was a mobility issue they were concerned with—a short-term re-hire. Paul heard it but figured he would be let loose within a few months.

In the meantime, Grover and the sisters wanted to go to the town square on Saturday for the Sheriff's Auction. It was a way to get rid of unused, unclaimed, unwanted items and they had an auctioneer to do it for them.

The street was blocked off and discarded possessions no longer needed were stacked, dragged, or piled up so anyone could look before the bidding began. Walking by the auctioneer's table, Minerva spotted the old sheriff, sitting off to the side, looking out over the crowd. She bumped the others and they spotted him as well.

"Well, that old cuss is still around. He must be mid-seventies."

The sheriff got up to say hello to someone and they noticed he was using two walking canes.

"Well, whatever it was that chased him, it must have caught him," Paul commented, "and him with two canes. I done beat him, after all. Ha!"

And then, as they looked in the other direction, they were surprised—all but Grover—at what they saw.

"Right in the middle of the street—you put our tractor in the middle of the street!"

"That's where it needed to be. I sold it and the dealer that bought it from me is going to sell it. I hope he does well."

"What in the world? What are we going to use, pray tell?" Lovety asked, looking at Minerva. Minerva looked pale and out of sorts. "Are you all right, sis?"

"So, so, I guess."

"So, so, I guess, really? You aren't feeling well?"

"Not so well. We can go if you'uns are ready."

"Sure, we are. Paul?"

"I'm ready, sure".

There was something amiss, although they didn't talk any more about it on the way home. They drove back in silence.

Minerva sat down in front of the evening fire to warm up. She had gotten a chill. And then she went off to bed. Lovety was going to go check on her sister, but didn't want to disturb her, so let her be. Pretty soon, Paul drove home, and the house was quiet.

The next morning, Lovety made coffee for Grover and went in to see her sister. Almost immediately, she emerged from the room with tears streaming down her face and looked at Grover. "My sweet Jesus, the Angels have taken my sister away, and she is with the Lord."

Grover dropped his cup of coffee and went in to see Minerva, and it was so.

A church funeral was arranged for Minerva, and Lovety wanted a minister to say words over her because it had been Minerva's wish since they were girls growing up together. Minerva had also wanted to be wearing something with lace. Some nice things were among Minerva's clothing, gifts that had been passed on to her from Iletta's camelback trunk, after Iletta had passed away.

Paul felt it was his duty and contribution to drive his stake bed to Herndon's Mercantile and get the coffin, which he paid for with his mining job's savings.

He remembered when Grover got the shivers over being there the last time they went for Adrian's coffin. Paul now saw the last coffin, covered in dust, leaning upright against the wall that Grover had shivered over. Paul did the same.

Pulling up to the loading dock, Paul and old Herndon came close to floundering in trying to move the coffin about and situate it to load it. Exposing their vulnerability and dignity with their personal disabilities, both men carried and moved their end of the wooden box as best they could, Paul having to manage his cane in an awkward manner and Herndon gimping along.

A sense of misplaced guilt surrounded Lovety's heart, she said later, so at her insistence, a church service was provided. A minister delivered the service and the eulogy in the Methodist Church in Loogootee.

Pastor Leland concluded his sermon with his remarks, looking and speaking directly to Lovety and those seated with her.

"It is when a person of characer in a long slog through a rough and trying life comes to a sudden and abrupt end, the closeness of family and friends are emotionally squeezed and pressed with the sudden grasp of uncertainty and loss. The familial bonds that were woven throughout a lifetime of caring and love seemed to have been dumped and discarded as a visage that soon will not ever be recognized again. It was a sudden talon of death that carried her away without warning or preparedness. The autumn life will be covered in the white snow of time. Let us bow our heads and pray."

The cemetery that Minerva Pate Fields was buried in was located inside the NAD Crane Ammunition Depot. The Pate Family plot had five gravesites. Three of them were occupied by Minerva's dad and mom and a still-birth infant child, name forgotten. That only left one spot open. The parents had planned to have all the children in the family plot, and they didn't figure on any marriages, grandchildren, or spouses to come in the later years.

Grover and Lovety had decided after they buried her mother to purchase plots close by, so that Lovety wouldn't take the last spot in the family plot, with Grover having to get buried elsewhere. Because the cemetery had been closed to new development as a national security issue, it had made it easy to adjoin one additional plot at the end, where Grover could be next to Lovety in the end, at Lost Creek Cemetery.

About a dozen friends from the community went to NAD Crane for the graveside service and internment. They offered their respects and condolences to Lovety and Grover because of old family connections from the past that were too tenuous to retrace. Paul was nodded to, mostly because of his mother's family and life tribulations.

A pleasant courtesy provided to the grave sites by Crane was that they were responsible for the mowing and care of the cemetery. Paul, noting how tidy the graveyard was kept, noticed three random black rocks half buried around a cedar tree. He wasn't sure why, but they gave him a chill.

Then Lovety spoke before anyone moved away, addressing Grover. "I had a premonition for the two of us girls the day you went off to work in the mines that I would work myself to death and be dead by my next harvest. I never spoke about it and got my first vision of it when Paul got them busted ribs, which was a sign to me it was coming. When me and my sister took sick, I thought my time was near, but it weren't for me. I was mistaken, it was Minerva that was took."

Grover laid his arm across his wife's shoulders. Paul patted her on the back. The other mourners murmured soft words of sympathy.

Chapter 26

The Allis-Chalmers Tractor Company emerged from a crippling strike at the end of the Second World War, though during the war, they had produced equipment for the Manhattan Project. They had introduced an improved version of an earlier model tractor, the WD, in 1948. A better version was the WD-45, a diesel version, introduced after the war. Grover made the purchase, on time payments, and used the multi-fuel burning Fordson tractor as a trade-in, in 1953. That was the one they had seen up at the town square.

When the Fields came home from the burial service, they saw the new tractor sitting under a shade tree. It was to have been delivered in another week, but it had arrived early. Lovety stared blankly at the new machine.

Grover knew she was having some painful thoughts. "I'll get you all settled in and then I'll take it down to Paul's and put it in his barn for now."

"Why would you do that? He's not able to drive it—"

"I know, I'll keep it out of the weather, and it'll be ready when we—uh, I—will be ready to use it on those fields first. Are you going to be all right, Love?"

She nodded and went inside to change from funeral clothes to field overalls.

Grover drove his "alley charmer" down to Paul's and into the barn. Paul was still a bit morose as he drove Grover back home.

"Minerva looked very pretty today. I saw she wore one of mom's fancy dresses."

"Lovety wanted her to look nice and it was a way to honor your mother, as well."

"It's gonna be sad around here. Their whole farm is gone away, it seems, with them both not around. It's gonna take some getting used to."

Lovety and Grover soon had the duty to put Minerva's affairs in order, as they were going to have the farm deeded over to them. It had been talked about when Adrian had passed on, so they knew what to expect. When Adrian died, not much needed to be done, as the farm went to Minerva. He had only one brother who had died in the First World War, so no one was left on his side of the family to pass anything on to. It would be a little more involved, now that Minerva was gone, too.

Ever since they were married, Adrian had handled all the farming decisions as to what was to be plowed up and what was to be planted. It generally followed what others in the county did. Crop succession, seed variety, fertilizer applications and such was his wheelhouse. At one time he had worked nearly two sections of land that was broken up into several fields because the land was not tillable or the slopes weren't right. However, when the auditors looked at the papers, they discovered Adrian worked a fair amount of land that was leased instead of being owned. Lovety was shocked, as was Grover, to discover that Adrian and Minerva had been land poor and debt rich. They were stunned.

What Grover and Lovety thought was going to be a simple land transfer did not occur. The leases, four of them, had not been paid on for several years. The absent owners didn't have the wherewithal to follow up and attend to their land holdings like so many that had suffered, lived, and survived the Great Depression years. The specter of struggle and poverty reared its ugly head and grabbed them once again.

Flushed with sorrow and the specter of imminent poverty, they left the bank feeling broken and down and out.

"I can't imagine what Minerva would have done, God rest her, if she would have found out what we now know," Lovety observed, ruefully.

The dilemma certainly was not new. It was a chain of circumstances that whipsawed countless farms, small and large. Like reading tea leaves in the bottom of the cup, Grover and Lovety could anticipate how the events would play out. Once the true owners of the land were pressed for back taxes, they would come calling for their money. If they didn't pay it off or make arrangement to "settle it on paper," they would lose the land. They would then demand back payments in full, so they could hold on to their own assets, which even they could not afford to keep. The only saving grace for Grover and Lovety was to hope the bank didn't call in the taxes from the owners of record.

A quick action plan was to at least get the corn off all the fields, the sooner the better. If the bank was aware of the taxes being in arrears, they would seize all of Grover and Lovety's crops as partial payment on taxes due. They were in a no-win situation.

"My God, we just bought that tractor. Well, we got to have it now, even more," Grover stressed. "As soon as we can manage it, we got to go and clear ALL the land they have and hope we can get it done before any of this is discovered."

Once they told Paul about the situation they found themselves in, the first thing Paul said was, "Let's slow down and think. Three heads are better than one. It isn't a good choice, but we are all in desperate times. So, if you don't push for the land to be transferred to your names, you have some breathing room. That will be to our advantage. Since nothing is moving under foot, we'll catch a break, I'm sure of it."

"Everybody that's of any account knows that this is your land," said Paul. "They know that you got it when your sister died, so no eyeballs will be on you for a while I expect. The land is where you use and generate money from. So, working the land, however you want to, is up to you and your business, right? So, here's my idea. Don't ask me how I come up with this, just listen.

"The first thing that needs to be saved is that tractor, period. Second thing, if you can generate income without incurring more debt, you'll be way ahead. Simple." He smiled.

"Paul, what in the world are you thinking about?"

"You've already generated the profit. You haven't seen it yet, so here it is. I had a dream the other night about the time when I fell and broke my hip and I was riding along, headed home, in the back of the wagon. In the midst of all that bad time, I laid there thinking about how I could see any good in it. It was something that my mom taught me to do. It was one of the things that has always gotten me by. It was that dream I have held onto, sort of waiting to use it somehow, and it comes to me today—Joy cometh in the morning." He stood there and smiled.

"I laid there, without any pain, which was remarkable. I was looking up into the sky and the sunlight was a glistening through the trees as we went along and I thought that was remarkable in itself, too. I thought about all those walnut trees and all of them walnuts I would never be able to pick up anymore."

Lovety suddenly blurted out, "The walnut trees!"

"Yes, indeed, the walnut trees. There's been a number of folks that have seen where some big truck or tractor or another have driven down and went over someone's fence and drove up into a pasture and have been cutting down walnut trees, poaching them, and selling them to the sawmills. If they're worth selling and you know they are, then you could go in and harvest them and make some good money. It's your trees, so you can do it as you want to."

"Mr. Paul Chandler, you constantly amaze us."

"That could pay off the note on the tractor, right off," Grover smiled. "Yes, it would."

"So, you got anything else up your sleeve, while you're ruminating on things?"

"Yep." And Paul was smiling. "When I went back to Odon to see my Amish friends, I passed an Amish sawmill that was operating close to the road in Cannelberg. They would be glad to cut and plank up walnut for us to dry, I would think."

After such agony of going through another funeral and Lovety losing her only sister, the heartbreak of finding out about the dire straits they were faced with, the mood was suddenly switched to a mood of euphoria.

Without any further hesitation, Grover went to the stand of walnut trees with his chain saw and felled several of the biggest trees. The gorgeous walnut logs laid on the slopes and started slowly drying out as Grover and Paul drove to Cannelberg and discussed having the logs sawed into planks and found out what sized lumber would bring the best prices.

After the logs were brought to the mill and the initial cuts were planned and executed, they were hauled back to Paul's barn to be stacked and air-dried before going to market or having a timber buyer drop by, grade the wood, and present an estimate of the value. Most of the process was completed.

However, the buyer told them the wood needed to be cured a bit before he would offer a price. Until it was cured, it would be a gamble. The green wood was subject to splitting if dried too fast, so, "slow and steady as you go" was the plan to be followed.

There were two options to be considered. One was to sell the wood before it was planked and still green. The buyer would assume the risk of the logs drying out too fast and splitting. The price would be a bit lower, but it would be firm. Option two was to plank it and wait for it to cure out first before selling it. It would be a longer time before the payout, but they would gain substantially more money for the cured wood. Since the money did not need to be in hand yet, the value of the lumber would continue to rise, like interest from a banking account. They chose the second option and covered the green lumber with canvas tarps to slow moisture loss.

Grover returned to work at the gypsum mines after the funeral and Paul rode with him, sharing transportation. Both men worked steady at the mines for a time and Paul decided to go ahead and have an electric line installed to his house. Over a week or two, he managed to run the wire from the pole box at the front porch brace to his kitchen at the back of the house. There was no hurry; Paul took his time wiring everything in, and Grover was there to help him.

"I'm new to knowing about electricity, Grover. Are you sure that we're doing this right? I'm talking to the electrical man in the shop about it, so's I'll know."

"I think we're doing it right. My house is running along fine, okay?"

At the end of the work week, when paychecks were passed out, there was a note stapled to his check directing Paul to go to the payroll office after the Labor Day holiday. Paul didn't like the notice. Grover didn't care for it either. Even the weather was rainy, and the day was gloomy, which foreshadowed their anxiety.

Grover drove Paul home and as they arrived at the farm, they saw steam rising out of Paul's house through the rain.

"How odd—"

Grover stomped on the brake and they jumped out of the truck and ran to the front porch. It had caught fire. The flames burned across the front of the house, which was now smoldering. Grover reached the front corner, where some flames still danced about, and grabbed some wet burlap sacks that were piled on the porch and began swatting out the flames. Nearly the entire front of the house was charred. The rain had stopped the spread of the flames.

As if things couldn't get any worse, Paul thought. "How did this start, do you think?" Then he noticed that the box and wires at the corner of the house were fried into charcoal.

"Look at this, Paul," Grover pointed to where the wires from the pole went down to the box and attached to the porch. "See here, that wire burned up, all the way to the pole. You know what, that looks like this pole was hit by lightning. It wasn't the electric service at all."

"Seems to be right. Hmmm—my house hit by lightning. Jesus Christ."

"Thank God it rained. It stopped it from catching the whole house on fire. That's a good thing, huh?"

"Suppose so. But I could do without this one thing in my life—"

As they checked the house, they discovered that the inside hadn't been touched, but it smelled of smoke and charred wood.

"It'll go away. I'm not worried so much about it." Paul shook his head and told Grover good-bye as they both stepped back outside. Paul needed to figure out what he might have done, as good and bad kept pouring out in constant measure around him. Every day was a surprise of something.

Back when the drought was finally passed, Paul had seen an occasional thunderstorm and watched the sky flickering with electricity. Just such a thing occurred before the porch was set on fire by a lightning strike. Paul later remembered that it was a strange moonrise the night before.

So, what can be done? Paul asked himself, while speaking also to heaven. Wh*at can I do that I haven't already thought about? In this time of toil of testing, what shall I do for Thee?*

Paul didn't wait for an answer to his prayers. "I am ready, Amen."

Well, it rained that whole Labor Day weekend and his house got hit by lightning. That's two things, and Paul knew bad comes threes. He entered the personnel office and a few other people were brought in beside him and he saw it all unfold, just like his premonition.

"Gentlemen, we appreciate your good work and we thank you for your service. If something comes along that fits your qualifications, we will notify you. We wish you the best and you'll be paid for the full day. Thank you and best of luck."

"It's gotta be taken in stride, Grover. You can't wait for the road to be smooth before you travel it. I'm not headed over any cliff and the boat ain't got water in it and everything is still floating. You know, Grove, sometimes I wonder about why I'm all gimped up and sometimes I think the reason is that I was slowed down on purpose, so's I might think about things more, instead of rushing off and tripping over something and hurting myself. I'm thinking about things all the time, so's I'm busy right now. Let's drive home. I got to get something initiated," he said with a grin and a wink.

Paul felt he had to get Grover faced in the right direction. He had a burden he was trying to bear with Minerva's passing and knew that other burdens waited for them all.

"Paul was always like a cat tossed into the air," Minerva used to say. "He's always landing on his feet."

"The boards on the front of the house need to be replaced. I don't think they'll hold up well. They're charred too deeply, and they'll let in too much cold air unless I cover the inside with tar paper. If I'm gonna fix this, I ought to do a better job of it," Paul explained to Lovety, when he was there next. "How are you feeling, girl? You're getting along better now?"

"I'm with the living until my turn is called, I suppose. I want to ask you when you get started on the front of the house, let me know. I'll give you a hand since Grover is still at the mines."

"I'm getting them good materials brought in right now and I'll let you know when they get there. I'm about ready."

A few weeks went by and when Lovety drove up the drive to Paul's, the boards that had been on the front of the house had been pulled off and the frame had been stripped to the studs. Replacement wood was started in one corner of the porch.

"I brought you some canning goods for your cellar. We got plenty already put up so's I brought these down for you. I'll put them in for you. You keep at what you're doing, and I'll join you shortly."

Once the outside boards and the inside boards were nailed into place, a slot across the top of the inside wall was left open and Paul and Lovety filled the wall between the studs with sawdust, a common practice, and the last planks were nailed in. It was a good use for worthless sawdust, and it made for great insulation. In addition, it didn't cost anything.

"These floorboards on this side of the porch are gonna need replacing."

"They can wait for now. I'll find something to use later. I just won't walk over there." Paul smiled.

"What about your electric line to the house?"

"Waiting on that, too. I'll get around to it."

"Well, okay."

"We're finished for now. How's it lookin', Lovety?"

"Fine, I suppose—for an old bachelor." She laughed. "You know Grover will like it. It looks like a man's job, all right. I see him coming up the road. He can tell you what he thinks of it himself."

"Fine job, there, Paul—and Love. I guess you'll feel snug this winter with that insulation. You never had it in your walls when this place was built, so you'll notice it right off."

He motioned to Lovety, indicating that it was time to leave, and they headed for his truck. Lovety turned back to Paul. "I'm gonna leave Minerva's car with you. I'm sure she would want you to have it."

Paul looked up, surprised. "What for?"

"Well, for you. It's a '54 DeSoto Firedome. It's only about two years old and it doesn't have that many miles on it. You need a new vehicle. That rickety old antique truck you drive is well past putting out to pasture. But you need to register this one, as it's a real road car and you can really travel in it."

With a skeptical face, Paul said, "That's good and all, but I won't be able to drive it, you know. I have one good leg. That thing will have too many pedals for me. Thank you, anyway."

"You might want to look at this car a bit closer. It's got the new automatic transmission model and you can drive it with one foot. It shifts on its own."

"Really?"

Bill Monroe and his music was on Paul's mind in quick order. With spring emerging, he had wanted to go over to Bean Blossom for a while, and now that he had his own car, he could go wherever he wanted, whenever he wanted. Word of mouth had spread about the possible sale of the Bean Blossom campgrounds to Bill Monroe in 1952. He was already popular in Central Indiana, when his reputation spread because of his appearances on The Grand Old Opry. After that, his weekend shows in Bean Blossom grew in popularity.

Since no one wanted to jump up and go, Paul took a solo run and drove over there by himself. It was refreshing to get out in the countryside with the windows down and smelling the spring air and watching the autumn leaves turning to green. He decided to break the bank on this trip, and he went to the Nashville House, found the candy shop, and spent a whole nickel on licorice.

On his way home, he met teams of bicycle riders trudging up the rolling hills around Nashville, practicing for the Little 500 race that was put on by Indiana University's sororities and fraternities. It was coming up on the 10th Year of the races. *College frolics I call it,* as he drove past them. *My next trip will be to go over and see my Aunt Dorothy in Dugger.*

The car had a nice, smooth ride. He felt rather proud of himself, driving around in his Firedome. He tried out his horn a time or two, when he was off the pavement and back on the dirt roads. He scared a few cows on the way home and drove a murder of crows off a dead rabbit that had been hit. If he would have had a hat, he probably would have lost it in the breeze.

Chapter 27

It seemed like it wasn't any time at all before the "Black Tide," as Paul and others called it, came rolling in. It came by mail. "What are you saying, Lovety? Slow down. Why are you crying so and why are you all upset?" Lovety handed Grover the letter from a legal firm in Indianapolis and he sat down and read the bad news.

The legal firm represented a bank in Chicago that had received a foreclosure and was deeded land in a settlement to notes that were in arrears for several years. "You are hereby ordered to vacate, and surrender said property in 45 days, unless payment in full is received within that time by certified check."

Grover sat there, stunned, and speechless, and Lovety did, too. Minerva's entire farm was going to be lost. No one had money to save it or enough labor available to generate money to pay on a monthly note if those terms could be granted. They were failing at their own place and felt the hot breath of those "Revenuers" down their own necks.

"All those years we worked so hard and were so proud of what we raised and the people we fed. It's all gettin' wiped out." Minerva began to cry.

The repairs on the house with the burned-out bedroom came to an abrupt halt. "We need to get all the canned goods out of the cellar and over to here, I guess," she sniffled. "The furniture in the house is ours, we ought to take it out, as well. And you know, I'll go to them flower beds and dig our bulbs up that came from my parents' homestead." Now she was getting angered and ready to go fight someone, but she didn't know who to punch in the nose. Not yet.

"That porcelain sink belongs to us." Grover growled with an edge. He went around the property, picking up anything he could possibly use or salvage, dragged it over the property line, and dropped it on his own property. After a while, looking back, he saw another line of junk in his front yard. He stopped and realized the ridiculousness of what he was doing, just piling more junk in the way.

Returning to the front porch and looking back at the trash line, he shuddered to think that someday soon, this might be what it would look like as the beginning of the demise of his own place.

Seeing Lovety sitting quietly on the porch swing, Grover pondered out loud. "It is through, over there. We got to keep our wits about us and not let ourselves get down about it. We have our own affairs we should tend to. As I look on it, that place was pretty worn out. That place and this place have about worn us both out. We should save our strength, I suppose."

Lovety glanced out towards Minerva's house in a blank stare and conceded, with hardly a breath, "That don't make it right and I don't have to like it. Grove, you might as well go on and bury me with my sister and you'll be along in due time. I guess I'm saying—I'm done."

Grover looked at her with a tilt on his head but said nothing. There was no need to say anything more. There wouldn't be a point to it. A wispy chill passed through him. From that time on, Lovety didn't talk much.

"The purpose in her has left, I believe," Grover mentioned to Paul.

I'll be swore, Paul thought when he noticed Lovety later. She didn't even seem to be wearing her clothes. She had them on, but they hung off her and she went about like she was waiting to be called to the Great Beyond. It was her overwhelming sadness that hurt him the most.

The Revenuers came, once the last date for paying off the farm's arrears went by, and brought in a Caterpillar and knocked down the farmhouse. The way they did it seemed to indicate they had some interest in doing something with the land, but it turned out to be a bunch of bluster, Paul thought.

The day before the demolition crew started, Paul went over to the house and removed the front door glass because it had colored glass panes that framed the center glass. He thought the window might have been put in the house way back when they built the church in Shoals. It looked like it was some of the same type of glass they used in town. It looked pretty and it was the sort of a memento that Grover and Lovety might enjoy later, when the dust settled, and they would be in a better mind.

The big Cat knocked down the house with ease and pushed it all into a big pile of wreckage, as if they were going to load it into dump trucks and haul off to the land fill. However, they didn't do that part of it and instead left the pile in the middle of the lot.

Paul got up early on a cold spring day and started a conversation with himself. *Since this is 1960, it also means I'm sixty. Lordy, lord. So, that puts Lovety about seventy-five and Grover at near eighty, I think I need to spend time on thinking. Maybe thinking about thinking is even better. All in all, Lovety isn't doing so good, to my way of thinking. She don't need to be staying with her sad thoughts all the time, moping around. Grover and me are tired of her dragging herself around. She don't eat, she don't talk to hardly a soul, and she's in a daze. What can I do to get her out of that sort of feeling?*

Paul went to his porch to survey things—things he could say something about to Lovety to get her focused in a different direction.

He started scanning about. *Those persimmons out there. I'll get her to give me a recipe. That sassafras tree. I'll see if she could blend it up and make a new food concoction or something. Something to get her thinking. Look at this place. It's about seein' the good. So, let's see—*

He suddenly stopped and took a good look over his land, as if he was seeing it for the first time. It had been awhile since he paid attention to his own concerns.

My pastures are so overgrown, I don't know if I could get Grover in here to plow it or if it needs a bush hog on it. If I don't take better care of my place—whew, being 60 is more of a burden than I ever thought about.

Paul went to the wood pile and got a couple of pieces for the fireplace and returned to the house. He was reading his Samuel Clemens book when he abruptly stopped and had a thought. *I think I can recall some of this song—I think.* Digging through a few piles of cardboard boxes and then in a chest of drawers, he located his harmonicas and found the words to the song, "Barbara Allen." Satisfied, he sat back in his rocker by the fire and read the lyrics. He was soon asleep.

The Sheriff's auction for Adrian and Minerva Fields' farm hardly drew any serious attention. The townspeople already knew about the misfortune and it was a sale that put the owners in dire straits. What was the point, most thought since both had passed away? The other farmers took that as a sign to play their own cards a little closer to their vests.

Spread out in the yard around the central lumber pile were remnants of a life that had gone by with few results now showing from it. Mostly, the curious would pick around. Lovety decided to go ahead and sell the remaining pieces of furniture that were left—a couch, an upholstered punched leather settee, a Hoosier cabinet, a porcelain top kitchen table and three chairs, a punched tin pie safe, various clay crocks from the local pottery kiln, a treadle Singer sewing machine, a few large clay moonshine jugs, minus the contents, a butter churn, and some linens. The rest was going to be offered as "buy one, get one free." After that, anything left and burnable would be thrown onto the lumber pile and hauled to the dump. The only things that Grover and Lovety kept were the canning jars salvaged from the barn fire.

An angry flock of Blue Jays sat up in the cedar trees and finished off "the penny pinchers" and the "rag pickers," scolding and yelling at the human scavengers, as if wanting them to leave.

Once the auction and "penny sale," as Grover called it, was concluded, he went down to Paul's place with the tractor to help him with the overgrown pasture situation and shape up the ground for planting something.

"You still got the notion that this onion idea is going to produce?"

"Grover, I spent time with the County agent man at the mercantile and he has assured me that getting out of planting soybeans, corn, and milo is not only good for the land, it's good for the pocketbook, too."

"Onions?"

"Yes sir, onions. I'll give it a try if you are willing to open up the ground. I'm going back down there and order the sets and get them in. While I'm there, is there anything for you, or are you set?" And then Paul laughed at his own pun.

He ought to hear more jokes now and again. He's getting as gloomy as his wife. He should loosen up. If he gets any worse, I'll have to communicate with them by pencil and paper.

"Onions, are you sure? One last time?" Grover caught the

spark of whimsy and Paul saw it come over his face, especially when Grover added, laughing, "I hope this field don't get you down none and the only thing you get to harvest is a field of tears."

As Paul reached his car to go order the onion sets, he turned back to Grover with a point of seriousness about this year's planting, catching him before he went back into the house. "Grover, the agent says this is definitely a big decision we're making because it will affect what other crops we can grow afterwards. We're going to be limited."

Grover flashed him a look of indignance, affronted that someone would presume to tell him what he could grow or not grow, after his eighty-four years of farming.

"What do you mean? I never heard of such—"

"He said, 'like potatoes. You can't grow them next to onions."

"And why not?"

Paul slapped the leg of his dirty overalls and the dust puffed out as he guffawed, "Because Grove, the onions will make the potatoes cry their eyes out!"

Paul doubled over in laughter, dropping his cane as he fell into his car, still laughing at getting one over on old stuffy Grover.

Within a week, Paul arrived with four big boxes of onion sets that were to be put into the ground as soon as possible. The ground was still a bit crunchy with the last bits of ice and snow that was soon to melt off. After cutting the furrows, Grover and Paul devised a dragging sled for Paul to ride on. Grover would pull the sled as Paul put the sets in, and then the sled dragging over the top of the furrow would cover it in. Paul thought it went surprisingly quick the first two days.

A drenching rain came and settled in the hills and gave them a good start. Just a few more days' worth of planting was needed, and the spring planting would be done.

After the rain finished, Paul was expecting Grover to come back over and get the last bit of sets in the ground, but he didn't show. *Probably had stuff to do. Maybe let the ground dry another day to keep the tractor from bogging in. I might as well work in my food garden and finish that off.*

The next day, Grover again didn't show, which Paul thought was a bit odd. He had a bit of news to share about an announcement he'd heard about the building of a new reservoir and lake south of Bloomington that they planned to call Lake Monroe. It was going to be a big one and take five years or so to finish. The lake would be surrounded by forest.

After the third day, Paul worried about Grover, as well as Lovety. *Grover is needed to run the tractor and get the onions finished up. I can't do it myself. What could it be?* He set his cap and went to see.

As Paul drove up to their farmhouse, he noticed the front door was wide open and Grover was not around. He thought it was odd, knowing that the open door would let the heat out. He went to the door and called out and saw Grover sitting in the kitchen, drinking coffee. He hardly turned towards Paul when he called out his name.

"Well, that field of tears is waiting—" Paul jested as he came on in.

"I know, it's right here."

"What do you mean, Grove?" Paul suddenly became alarmed. He looked quickly around for Lovety. "Where's Lovety? Grover? Say something."

It must be her.

"I found Love yesterday about mid-day, laying on the ground out by the little place we put together, where we used to bury our dogs. It was the place where she and Minerva wanted."

"Grover—"

"I know. I must have missed her last moments. She had a jar of iced tea she had sat down, and the cubes weren't hardly melted. Maybe a half hour at most. God, I loved her." He put his head down on the kitchen table and cried. Paul backed up and sat in a chair and let Grover have his time. The two old men were starting to mark the passing of a fine woman.

A duty and responsibility, but a source of anxiety, worry, and hardship, was spread before them. Paul left Grover in his chair at the kitchen that day, but the next day, he found him in the same place. With coaxing, Paul got Grover to join him in eating some food and then they discussed what Grover wanted for Lovety. Paul would make the arrangements and consult Grover when needed.

Upon Paul's arrival the following day, he first noticed Lovety's shoes and feet extending over their divan. She wore the usual work dress and apron. He also noticed her clothing had been tenderly hand-brushed free of wrinkles and dust. Her hair had been lovingly combed, and her hands were placed just so.

"I want it like Minerva's was," he kept saying to Paul and Paul tried, which meant to him that he should find that very esoteric minister, Pastor Leland from Loogootee, to conduct the service and deliver the eulogy. His first stop was at the Methodist church for information and help in Shoals.

Upon setting the wheels in motion and affixing the specifics, three women from the church came out to Grover's farm to assist and move Lovety to town. They had some news that would be unsettling to Grover, they imagined, so they spoke to Paul confidentially.

It was left to Paul to tell Grover that the two burial plots at NAD Crane were no longer available, for whatever reason, and another location would need to be found. Upon hearing the news, Grover seemed distracted and nonplussed. "Anywhere we could afford is all right."

No money was all the money they had and so she was to be buried at Dog Trot cemetery. The grave marker would just have to come later. With that being solved, Grover came out of his lethargy, and his spirits were brighter when Paul returned from the church. He had a church program bulletin he had found on a pew from the earlier week's church service and handed it to Grover to read. Paul thought it might be soothing for Grover to know Lovety would be with Christian people.

A message from the Lord will be delivered in Martin County style and the music might be bluegrass. This is a loving church in a small community. We are very warm and friendly and desperate for others to know our friend Jesus, as all our 31 members will testify to.

The cortege of Lovety Pate McCullough wound its way down the dirt road through the hardwood forest to the cemetery. Since the church service was noticeably short, Pastor Leland gave the concluding remarks at the graveside, speaking directly to Grover.

"Starting to tell the story of someone's passing was begun by those friends who didn't know what the story was or how to tell it. It was a grasping of the bits and fleeting moments that were gathered and captured, ever so incompletely, by someone, brought together by the accounting of impartial memories and recollections. Those noble moments were laid in an ever-widening emotional gap that bridges love to eternity."

Within a few days after the burial, when the emotions had settled down, Grover was wistfully recounting happy remembrances to Paul. "Her sister Minerva and her, since way back when, were young ladies who always had a softness and tender spot for their dogs. They weren't just dogs, they were pets. We always had one or two that laid around for them to be sweet on and one time when one of those dogs died, they wanted a special place to bury him in. So, Adrian and me got our shovels that day and went out to go looking for that special spot, a regular pet cemetery."

"That's got to be the place that's over by those trees where the three little gravestones are placed, isn't it?"

"Yes. Bel and Jug. He was the last one buried there. Before him was Bel. She was a special one. The first one of all of them was Hurricane Flotsie. She started all of it. After a while, they were getting familiar with the notion of how emotional it was to bury a pet, as they get buried a lot faster than a person would be, and I guess the pain eventually became too much and they quit keeping dogs around. Hurricane Flotsie was the first dog they named together. After that, the other ones came along. They would lay around and take life, as much as the Lord would give 'em, and they would be petted up, I swear, until them girls pulled the hair off their backs."

Paul noticed a slight smile that came to Grover's face.

"If it would be all right to say it, Grove, I know Lovety longed for the Great Hereafter, I do believe. She was ailing in her heart ever since her sister passed away. I know it and you do, too."

Paul glanced around the rooms and could see that the tidiness and fastidious ways the sisters kept their farmhouses had been abandoned and neglected for quite some time. The placement of prideful possessions and things was messy and haphazard.

For Lovety, as when her sister died, the old families from around Shoals came to the funeral home to pay their respects and wished Grover their condolences. Since he had a bit more land than a lot of others, he was known for good deeds and pitching in to lighten the load of people for whom fortune didn't always shine on.

It was generally known throughout the county that several people had dabbled in the moonshine world in the past and so the transgressions to others' sensibilities about moonshine were overlooked. The zeal that a lot of fundamentalists had for crushing the practice and sale of the illegal hooch came to an abrupt halt when they learned that a grown man and two children were trapped and burned alive in the barn fires.

"If you are agin it, just don't drink it. The fires of Perdition will burn those that needed the cleansing," was how one of the townspeople put it.

The thought of the sheriff and his involvement with the Ku Klux Klan was another sore spot, tempered or agitated by the mysterious circumstances and death of Mrs. Olsham by his minions. The townspeople prayed this chapter was finally dead and over.

The "Black Tide," as Paul named it, came rolling back in. However, this time it came by The Divine Hand, he felt. Some things said or spoken had a duality to them. The "Black Tide" meant more than a singular thing.

Grover's providence was dulled by his wife's death and his future became cloudy. Paul noticed the change in him after the funeral and the bouts of melancholy. To keep him up and buoyant, Paul kept him busy as he could. What money Paul had gone to diesel fuel. Work was the tonic that Paul thought would keep Grover on a steady path. When Grover went back to the gypsum mines after the funeral, Paul thought it was would improve his outlook.

Right after the onions were harvested and before the weather got hot and the spring rains ran out, Paul and Grover sold the onions and got good prices for them. Immediately, Paul planted pumpkins. The loose soil worked well for the fast-growing plants and the water came when it was needed. It looked like the crop was going to be even bigger than they anticipated.

And it was. The pumpkins were heavy for their sizes and a few grocery brokers got in on the bidding. They made money selling by the pound instead of selling by the number.

At the gypsum mine, the working pocket where Grover was digging became smaller and smaller. The bosses made the decision to collapse what was left of the pocket and dig it later. More production could be had in other parts of the mine, and since those other parts were almost overstaffed, decisions were made to lay off two shifts of miners. The third shift was being distributed to other parts of the dig. Grover was on one of the two shifts that were laid off.

No one paid much attention to the comings and goings of common miners into and out of the mine. Work gangs, equipment haulers and maintenance people going about made the mine feel like the inside of a beehive. The lights never went off, so it was always going full tilt inside. With the dust covering the men like it did, everybody looked pretty much the same.

When Grover and the rest of the work gang went to the clean-up area to get the powder off, their faces were once again recognizable. It happened that several supervisors were doing excavation planning in the clean-up room and one of them noticed that some of the men were awfully "old looking, I mean, senior fellows." They went to the office and investigated personnel files and discovered that Grover was over eighty! That was the day the mine bosses decided he wouldn't be re-hired.

He was stopped by one of the foremen and told the bad news. However, since he was such a hard worker, they decided to terminate him instead of laying him off. He would lose his insurance, but he would be able to draw unemployment. He was told he could file for it in two days as soon as they could get the paperwork completed and to the unemployment office.

After a day of resting up and licking his wounds, Grover went to Paul and told him his story of woe, and then began figuring his next plan to make a few dollars. Never concerned much with "paper business," he began looking through the growing stack of papers on the piano stool, only to discover that he was a few months behind on the tractor payments.

"Yikes, Paul, I'm almost in hot water. I got to get this handled and those payments up to snuff or you and I will be out of business, permanent like."

"What money I have, I'll get quick and let's look at it, say, tomorrow."

The next day, without hesitation, they pooled their greenbacks and calculated the situation.

"One more field of pumpkins to harvest and I think we'll make it."

It was during the "great pumpkin harvest" that the unexpected happened. The last flatbed left the fields and headed for the distribution hub. Grover and Paul were counting their money that they had in hand. Grover was up on the flat bed hooked to the back of the tractor and Paul was sitting on the bed to ride back to the barn. Grover jumped for the back of the three-point hitch on the tractor, but the wagon had been unhitched and it rolled in the opposite direction as he jumped. He fell almost straight down and slammed his right shoulder and collarbone onto the power take off, breaking his arm and his collarbone.

It was all Paul could do to get Grover up from being tangled in the three-point in the process of getting him away from the tractor and sitting on the ground. He could see Grover was badly hurt. Paul was unable to do much, with only one good leg to use. He dropped his cane and crawled underneath the flatbed to get to it, so he could maneuver for himself. Two grown men with extensive injuries struggled, trying to help each other out.

"You stop that hobbling along at full speed, Paul. I'm not going anywhere. Take your time. I'll be laying here when you get back, okay? Thank God, you got Minerva's car."

Paul ignored the old man's words and loaded Grover into the back seat.

"All kinds of things are moving around inside this shoulder, Paul. This ain't gonna be a quick fix, I'd guess."

"Probably not, but at least you get to go to the doctor, and I didn't. So's you owe me one."

Grover laughed and Paul could see that it really hurt him.

"Don't you go getting me to laugh. It hurts too much, Mr. Paul Chandler."

"Yes sir, Boss, I'm on the way."

Grover was laying down in the back seat as Paul drove to the highway and looked up and out of the window. "Where we going?" he asked.

"Oh, this is going to be special delivery today. You're going to go up to Loogootee for this one, you old coot. What do you have to say about that?"

Silence from the back seat. Paul looked out the rearview mirror. "That's fine, just like that."

The Loogootee medical facility did not have enough of the medical equipment needed, so they were sent on to Daviess Community Hospital in Washington, Indiana for treatment. Grover was in obvious pain as he attempted to get out of the back of the DeSoto. Paul saw someone standing outside of the door and yelled for them to get someone with a stretcher, then hobbled around to the other side of the car and opened the door.

Two medical people came out of the hospital, asking "Who's hurt?" and looked at Paul, who was struggling on one leg.

"Oh, it's not me. I'm old hurt. It's him, here," and pointed to Grover lying in the back of the car.

"Okay, we got him now. What happened?"

Paul hopped along behind on one leg, trying to follow them into the hospital, and then out of the blue, an orderly approached Paul with a wheelchair, saying, "Sit, we can go faster in this thing," and rolled him in, too.

Paul talked to the admissions nurse, telling her what had happened, and answering her questions. It was only the third time he had ever been in a hospital. The other two times were when he and his mom went to get "him" committed for the alcohol disease.

Paul was happy that Grover was getting good treatment like that, and right now. They had their own x-ray machines, which was handy. *Boy, I hope he is all right—for the both of us.*

"Are you Mr. Chambers? You can come with me this way, sir, and you can see your friend in just a minute. He's coming out of x-ray and the doctor will be in shortly. You can stay in that wheelchair if you want. Can I get you anything?"

Paul decided to test her offer. "A Coke?"

"Sure."

Two people wheeled Grover inside the room, and he was sitting up, having a Coke, with a straw in his. Paul didn't know what to say as the doctor came in, right behind the rolling bed, with x-rays in his hand. He introduced himself.

Paul heard the doctor talk to the nurse first, and heard him order medicine, some kind of "cee-cee's," and then he turned to Paul and Grover.

"I'm Doctor Titman, and your friend here got banged up a bit. The only thing I can say is I'm glad to know the tractor wasn't moving, otherwise he might have come in here with a tag on his toe." He laughed, and Paul and Grover tried to laugh with him.

"To get you up to speed, this is what is going on. He has a lateral tearing of the rotator cuff, a broken collarbone, and a shoulder dislocation. In other words, he's pretty messed up. The healing will be slow. Do you hear me? s. l. o. w. And unfortunately, it will be a bit painful, but I can get you things to keep the edge off, for the most part. Once the healing has started and things are stable, we can look to do a corrective surgery on that shoulder to fix the muscle tearing and get the arm socket to moving again. But for now, no baseball." At this, he made both men smile, putting them at ease.

"We'll get you back over here in two weeks to look at your progress and then send you back home for another six weeks of healing before we look at that socket and see what needs to be done. It could get healed up and do well. Or it might need an additional surgery if things don't go as well as they need to. You understand, gentlemen? Okay, my last question is who is driving home?"

"Short, sweet, and to the point." Paul nodded on the drive home.

"Very much to the point. And those little pills he gave me, they're working. I feel like I'm on an airplane, although I've never been on one. But I bet you this is what it feels like. And then when I close my eyes, it feels like I'm on a roller coaster."

"Grover, you sound like one of those California hippies."

"Oh, yeah, what would you know?"

"I know you're in the back seat of my car and you're taking drugs. The next thing you'll want to do is go out crawling around the farm looking for some loco weed."

"Old Doctor Tit Man, nice fellow. I like him."

This was all unexpected. The way circumstances stacked up, Grover would need some close attention for quite some time. In the next several months, Paul found a new calling. Grover's bandages and arm sling were somewhat problematic. Paul was hardly able to change out his shirts without much discomfort, on both sides, for both men.

Paul brooded. *Yes, he's every bit of eighty-four and he don't move around too well without being strapped up in a sling.*

Now that Paul was Grover's caretaker, he wanted to get him healed and well. He sat in Lovety's chair and stared at Grover, as he slept in his chair, thinking about what he needed to do next for him—fixing food, helping him up and out of his chair, and so on.

Paul fretted. Then, the crops may need tending. He paced back and forth, stewing over what he might be missing that needed to be done. After a while, Grover had to shoo him off to go do something else, so that he could get some peace and quiet.

Over the weeks that followed, the old men worked out a daily routine that suited them. They barely acknowledged the fact but realized that Paul, crippled as he was, was all that was left of two farms. But they had to make do.

The two men barely noticed it themselves, but they became what anybody else would call "gamey." Washing clothes had to occur and it was something they had to figure out. It was only so long before throwing soiled and dirty clothes in a pile on the floor, in the corners of rooms, had to come to an end. They kept the windows open during the day.

Paul figured how to use the ringer washer on the back porch. When wash day was unavoidable, he took the two big washtubs down from the walls and set them on the floor. As Paul agitated clothes in the washing machine and ran them through the ringer, he threw them in one of the tubs until the tubs were full. One tub for one man's clothes, the other tub for the other man's clothes.

The tough part for Paul was hanging the clothes to dry. They were wrung out but still heavy. With him still on a crutch or on a cane, he moved around with caution when he had dripping clothes hanging over him as he headed to the clothesline that was strung off the porch to a pear tree in the side yard. When the clothesline got full, it would stretch and sag till the clothes would touch the ground. Grover told him where the clothesline pole was, and Paul learned where to attach it to prop up the line. Clothespins weren't used much. Flung and sun, a new wash day tradition.

When the washing wasn't finished because other chores needed to be done, or other clothes filled the clothesline and weren't dry, the next load of wash to be dried would wait in the wet tubs till the next day to be hung, or maybe, the day after that. After two or more days, the garments began to smell sour, as if they were dipped in old buttermilk. They had to choose one odor or the other.

Another solution they considered, instead of washing more was to wash and use less clothes. That didn't work out, either. Overalls were the preferred attire. Pull up, straps up, and done. In Grover's case, one strap and done. Paul liked the look, apparently, and he adopted the one and done, as well.

Grover's arm and shoulder healing went slowly, just like the "Tit Man" had said. It was a painful start and Paul had to go over to the mercantile more than once to use the phone to contact the hospital in Washington for pain pills. He was also the one who got the medical bills, instead of Grover. Just as well. Grover would stay sick if he knew the situation. Losing insurance coverage occurred at the worst time. *But it's too late to cry over spilt milk, Paul told himself.*

As he slowly learned the truth about the medical bills, Paul knew he needed to go to the store to arrange selling all the slabs of walnut in the barn. *To get money coming in steady, he told himself, I could go up to Bloomington and get on at the RCA TV plant and get some good money. Or I could see if I could get on at the Sarkes Tarzian plant.* He realized Grover wasn't going to make it without him and wondered if he could leave him alone for that kind of time.

Simple fare for simple men. "Grover, come on, we'll eat now."

"What does the chef make today?"

"Pinto beans, *with* ham hocks, a double batch of cornbread, and Jell-O for dessert. Then we need to talk about that shoulder and what you're thinking about. Doctor Tit Man told you that the shoulder wouldn't get much better unless you had him fix it with an operation."

"I know that, Paul, but we ain't got the money, that's plain to see. Besides, it's getting better and I can take it easy for a while more and see what we need to do after a few more months. I can go most of the day without wearing that sling, most days."

"Grove, can you do it?"

"I believe so. I'm gonna try it first. It won't cost any more money to try. And if it don't work, then I'll let the Tit Man have a whack on it, then. What do you say?"

"We can do another year planting onions and then pump-kins. That worked out and we got good money for the pumpkins. It will give us two paychecks instead of waiting a whole year for one measly check. I don't know if you can make another year. Your arm may not hold up that long, Grove."

Paul drove to the feed store to buy some salt licks for his back pasture, and ran into the game warden, Ollie Jordan, who was buying scratch for his chickens. When the game warden noticed Paul's salt licks, he offered to put them out behind Paul's pasture in the next week. The warden was doing vegetation surveys and gathering data before the weather got cooler and the deer went into rut. All indications were that the populations of deer were very plentiful.

"Paul, I know you. You ought to get out there early this fall and set up a blind. I know you'll be rewarded."

"Thank you, Mr. Judson, for that information. I might have to do that. I've been spending a lot of time over at Grover McCullough's place. He fell off his tractor and got busted up pretty good, and you probably know he lost his wife before that. He's hit a pretty rough patch."

Ollie Judson nodded his head. "I knew about his wife passing and about the Fields farm next to him going back to the bank. Is Grover's farm holding steady? Is he going to make it, now?"

"Ollie, I hardly know at this point. I'm about to try another year of planting onions and then pumpkins for a second year. The yields were all right, and it hasn't put too much of a strain on the harvesting process. But I'm looking to do better, you know."

"Yes sir, I do. Let me share an idea with you. I know you would at least give it a good consider—"

"So, run it by me. Let's hear what you think." Paul was eager to hear.

"How about turkey? You ever think about them as a food item? I mean to grow them for food?"

"Well, Ollie, I have a few chickens for eggs and some dumplings now and again."

"What I mean is for you to think about raising them to sell. Paul, you can make more money, acre per acre, than by growing two harvests of corn, just about."

Paul was paying attention.

"It hasn't caught on down this way yet, like it did up state, say around Anderson and New Castle. I've seen some of the Amish farms that have taken up raising turkeys for Purina. They're doing very well, indeed."

"You don't say. You're serious, though?"

"Mighty so. If you see them and how they do it, everybody will get in on it. Basically, Purina comes in with the young turkey poults and turns them out in the pasture. They go into the fields that haven't been mowed and start eating bugs and scratching for worms and grubs. They roost in at night to your brood house and eat the grain and supplements that Purina brings in. They furnish the grain and when the turkeys are of a good size, Purina sends out a big cattle truck and shoos them into the trailer and they take them to the slaughterhouse for processing. What you wind up doing for the most part is furnishing the land. You can put a lot of turkeys on the ground, compared to pigs or milk cows. They need some good shelter. You don't even have to grow the feed. How 'bout that?"

"Between Grover and me, we got enough land for it. He's got some better out-buildings. I don't know if my fences—I would have to do some patching."

"Purina will sell you the fencing. They don't turn out all those young birds to lose them. They're into making a profit and keeping them birds on the farm."

"It sure sounds simple."

"It sure is," said Ollie. "Here's a little trick I saw the Amish using when I was working that area. Those Amish, right off, plant the entire field in sunflower seed and let the plants get two feet or so up, and then let the birds loose. The hotter it gets, the more the turkeys go and hide under the shade of the sunflowers. The sunflowers grow big and bigger, right? No doubt you've seen sunflower heads growing two feet across. They're loaded with fresh seeds. When the flower heads bend over and face the ground, the turkeys start eating the seeds that fall, and eventually the seed heads. It's like they're being finished off right before they take them over to the processors. Some of the fastest weight gains on the turkeys happens right then. Right when you want it. Pretty sweet, huh?"

"Well, I guess so."

The game warden, like he said, came by Grover's place and stopped to visit and put out a salt lick for the deer. In discussing the turkey situation, the two old men began to see the advantages of trying to grow farm-raised turkeys for the market. It was nice to think about having a partner to work with. After all, they were down and needed a hand, though they wouldn't have said a word. They were out of investment dollars and didn't have a nickel to spare on infrastructure. They were tapped out.

They could pay for the wire needed from the proceeds and didn't have to front the money. The only thing they had to front was their land. They could float the costs of the poults and the feeder barrels until they settled at the end of the contract. All birds were guaranteed to be live upon delivery.

They began to look at fences that needed attention. Purina brought in farm hands to staple wire. Paul didn't have to hobble through the pasture, and Grover didn't have to try to drive the tractor with one hand.

"Two old men trying to make it," everyone said. They were described by others as the "one with a bad arm and the other with a bad leg." They were a pair of broken-down old men, but they had a plan that gave them hope.

When they got close to paying off the tractor, they bought two calves at auction to run on Paul's farm. But Grover's arm was giving him more trouble. The money they earned, minus their Purina notes, was to pay for Grover's rotator cuff surgery. Their heads were down, and their tails were up. Was it too little, too late?

The old men drove over to Washington to the Daviess Community Hospital to see Doctor Titman. Grover and Paul went into the lobby and waited for Grover to get the examination that would tell them which path they were taking with the shoulder.

Paul stayed in the lobby and read a *National Geographic* magazine. When the exam room door opened, Doctor Titman invited Paul in. Grover was sitting on the exam table, fully dressed, but with a fresh arm sling. Several x-rays were posted on the light box. Paul knew it was Grover's arm in the x-rays.

"Paul, how have you been? Grover says you two have been raising turkeys. Is that so?"

"Well, yes. Yes, it is." Paul looked at Grover for a clue as to what was going on. Grover looked clueless.

"I'll review for you, first, how you were when you first came in and we'll look at the current x-rays and look at what progress you've made so far." The doctor reached for the first picture.

"The collarbone has finally grown back together and healed sufficiently. So, the healing is going satisfactorily, barring any heavy lifting. At this point I'd say surgery will not be recommended."

"We'll take that bit of good news, doc!" Grover grinned at Paul, and Paul grinned right back.

"You'll still need to wear that sling, here and there, to rest those muscles that were torn. If you go grabbing something heavy and tearing that muscle—" the doctor pointed to the x-ray where the muscle was attached to the bone at the shoulder joint—"you may damage it permanently and I can't go in there and re-attach it. You'll have a limp arm that will mostly hang there. You might use a spoon or fiddle in your pocket for some change. But beyond that, it won't be good for most else. I guess we are straight with the necessary truth on that, Mr. Fields?"

That revelation came as such a blow to the two of them that they both froze and were unable to respond. Suddenly confronted with the totality and the sum of the injury, they immediately didn't like "good old Doctor Tit Man" as much as they had a few minutes previously.

"It's one of those things that we get to realizing at some juncture in one's life. We do, in fact, get older. That's a good thing. The good thing is that it lets us enjoy the results of our life without having to work hard all our lives and gives us a break from life's toil.

"You men need to put down your tools and pick up the fishing poles. That will cure lots of aches and pains, you'll see. Another obstacle we can't, or I can't get over, is that you are now over that threshold as a candidate for any more surgeries. Paul, you need to tell him, so's he'll listen to you. He is too old for surgery. If I needed to get you onto the table and carve on you, the chances are really good that you would never wake up. I can't put you to sleep. You're going to live without any more surgeries. That's it."

The air of anticipation expelled from the two of them. This burden was lifted from them on many levels. The grip of a life's struggle seemed to evaporate for them. Somehow, they felt liberated.

Was this getting old a good thing? Grover and Paul both wondered.

Once home, Paul pulled out the Samuel Clemens book and read a bit and then ruminated about his closest friend. There was something about Mark Twain that kept him going back to re-reading the man's impressive writing. These were words that

Paul absorbed and was comforted by. Thinking back to Grover's whole trying ordeal, Doctor Titman seemed to be a heroic character, and in Paul's mind, he connected the two, Twain and Dr. Titman. Such an admirable visage on both.

PART SIX

Chapter 28

As was his custom, Paul got up whenever he felt like it and went about his day as he chose. He lived like he wanted to and had for many years. Not a hermit, but perhaps a recluse. The house was now close to falling down by all appearances—no paint, only weathered natural brown planking. All the windows still had glass with maybe a cracked pane here and there. Tar paper squares were cut and inserted over a few places where the windowpanes had been damaged. It kept out the wind.

The good-sized fire that had occurred and burned the porch flooring had been put out, but the porch had never been repaired. The charcoal planks were still in place. Consequently, the front side of the house had been repaired and the wall was rebuilt with surplus ammunition crates that fitted together. They were interlocked in greenish/brown patterns. Identification numbers and codes on the lids were block stenciled in contrasting yellow spray paint. It made the front of the house a bit speckled looking. It was a fine gift from the Crane Ammunition Depot for free. He'd just had to haul them off.

A couple of large trees were either felled or blown down and laid in front of the house and they were gradually being cut up and used for firewood. No work was being done to split large cuts yet, only drag-and-burn sized wood were being used. The downed trees had laid there for over a year. Both trees were well seasoned. One of them had a hollow log for the main trunk. Paul would have described it as a beech tree.

On the property were three outbuildings. One was partially blown over, but still standing. In the barn, the rear end of an automobile could be seen through the brush and red sumac that covered the stall. A big, heavy canvas tarp covered most of the car, and the tarp was covered in dust that fell through the cracks in the floorboards from the hay loft above. The barn was erect and standing straight. The third building was used for storage in the back and wired up in front as a coop for chickens and turkeys.

Paul was at the back woods behind his house when he heard voices—bits of laughter and talk. He limped back to his house and got his Kentucky long rifle and headed back out. As he got to the fence line and entered the woods, two young men walked up, both carrying weapons. Paul stepped from behind a tree and surprised them both.

"Boys, you should hold it right there where you are. This here's all private land and the both of you don't have a right to be here without permission." His dark pupils were all that showed through his squinted eyes.

One of the trespassers carried a shotgun over his shoulder. He took it down and rested it, leaning it against a tree. The other one un-notched an arrow from his bow and held it hanging down.

Paul stepped from around the tree.

"We've been walking this fence line to see where it would come out and never expected it to run this far. We wanted to ask someone around here if we could get permission to hunt."

"Looks like you are already been doing that, don't it?"

"Yes sir, it does. We jumped three does already, but we never thought to try a shot. We don't know the woods and didn't want a bullet going where it shouldn't, you know."

"Well, I know where all mine go. Who are you folks?" Paul relaxed his grip on his rifle, and they settled in for less straining talk.

"Yes sir. My name is Oakie Stillions and my buddy, here, goes by Tex. Nice to meet you."

Paul didn't extend his hand yet. He was still a bit hesitant about meeting up with these strangers on his land.

"Again, we didn't mean any harm. We've been looking for trespassing signs and didn't see any, until at the top of this hill. We came so far in, we decided to walk it on out and see if we could find someone to ask."

"You won't be hunting here. I keep them deer around and put out a lick for them. I eat them."

The one called Tex addressed Paul. "Yeah, I saw it back in the clearing and I could tell it was a spot."

Paul leaned on his tree to take the weight off his lame leg. "You said your name is Tex. Does that mean you from Texas?" He continued to look at them cautiously and barely moved.

"Yep, that's right."

"What you doin' up here?"

"I came up here to live with my Aunt and finish up high school. Now I go to college at Indiana University."

"You're college, too?" Paul asked the other one.

"We both are." They nodded in agreement.

"Well, come this away and I'll show you the road. This is the end of a section line, so you can walk on back, taking the road."

Paul turned around and repositioned his cane, so his leg bent around the crook in the wooded stick. He held the gall knob on the top of his stick in his palm and pushed down as he stepped forward. They slowly moved up the gentle slope and noticed the roof of a house.

The two young men followed and wondered about this

crippled old man and what he was doing in the woods, especially because his bad leg obviously made moving around through the woods difficult for him. All sorts of questions came to their minds as they followed Paul.

Tex asked, "How much of this land out here is yours, sir?"

"Well, it's a lot. I got it passed down to me through the family."

"It's a pretty old forest, I can tell you that. That's a big old sycamore up here on this hill. We don't have many to look at where I come from in Texas." They walked on a bit without talking.

When they reached the top of the hill, the young men noticed the knob of the hill was mowed short and they saw a natural limestone slab standing erect that was carved into a headstone marker.

Oakie looked at Tex and started to say something, but Tex looked back with a quick glance and a shake of his head. They walked on, following Paul, who said nothing, as he picked his way down the other side of the hill toward the house in the distance.

As they descended, Oakie remarked, "You have a lot of hay in here. Are you grazing anything in this pasture?"

Paul kept walking for a few more yards, picking his steps, and then stopped to reply. "I got back from the auction barn and bought me a couple of yearlings that's in the barn. I'll be turning them out as soon as I can check the fence line for any breaks. I haven't run anything in here last year, so's it needs a chew down. I'll butcher one of them and hang the meat once it gets cold enough. That's about all I can handle these days."

"Well, the fence line we walked this morning looked pretty good, didn't it, Tex?"

Tex nodded and then offered, "If it's this pasture you're

planning to use, Oakie and I could walk it for you and see, couldn't we? We already have our brush pants on. It would be easier for us to do."

"You'uns could do that, I suppose. If you want to sit here on the porch, there's water right there in the well. I'll get some staples and a hammer for you to carry, just in case. Makes sense, don't it?" He looked back at them and smiled. He was pleased with the opportunity to have that chore covered.

As Oakie and Tex walked the pasture fence line, they talked about their chance meeting with a crippled old man in the woods who toted a Kentucky long rifle.

"Talk about an antique! When's the last time you saw someone hunting with one of those things? Maybe in a Revolutionary War reenactment is what I think." Oakie laughed.

"You thinking what I'm thinking? If we could help this old man some, we might be able to hunt on this land. That's what I think."

"I think the same thing. It certainly looks like he could use a hand. Did you see his place? This whole thing is falling down, and yet he's still around. You notice he doesn't even have electricity."

They re-walked the perimeter and went past the headstone and around the barn and back to the house. Paul was sitting on a stump next to the two downed trees in the front yard.

"We had one spot, it was the top strand we had to staple down," Tex reported and then said, "Oakie, we ought to get to walking now that we're warmed up. You think?"

"We should, I suppose. Mr. Paul, it was good to meet you."

"Same for me. Sorry for not allowing you to hunt here. Things are pretty tight these days and that's meat I count on, plus them calves, you see."

"Absolutely, we understand. My grandfolks in Texas lived

pretty close to the land too. Grandpa never had a motor or a car on his place. He plowed with a horse his whole life. Bob was his horse's name. I wish you all could have met. We'll keep looking for a hunting spot around here. Maybe we can drop in on you again the next time we come this way."

"Sounds fine with me, I'm almost always home or roaming around here."

Oakie and Tex shook hands with Paul and walked down the section line road towards the truck. As they walked, they talked about Paul. Oakie said, "If I could get in good with Paul, he might know of some neighbors that would let us hunt on their place."

"I've got an idea. If we find someone who lets us hunt, we could swing back by old Paul's and give him a quarter from what we get. Did you notice? He seems pretty close to scraping along. How in the world does he do it, all busted up like he is? And that cane? That's an old crooked sycamore limb he wraps his leg around. I don't believe I've seen anything like that before."

They returned to their truck and instead of driving on and looking around for other farms to ask about hunting rights, they turned back and pulled up the drive to Paul's house, where he was still idling along on the porch where they left him. He seemed a bit surprised.

"Hey, Paul, we did say soon!" As Paul approached the truck, Tex got out with several unopened beers in a cardboard box and handed them to him.

"They were cold when we bought 'em."

"Since we're driving back to Bloomington, we don't need to take them back warm, so thought you might cool them down and drink 'em."

"I don't have any electricity for refrigerators, so I'll just drink 'em like that. Thanks, boys."

"See you sometime."
"See you, too."

"The next time we go by Paul's, let's put a box of stuff together for him and all of us could eat without putting a strain of any sort on him and his house," Oakie said to Tex two weeks later. "Let's take our guitars and go down there and play some music and see how that old man is getting along. How do you think he's doing?"

"He could be doing good. You think about it, it looked to me like he's been there for quite a while. I would think he's *just* getting along."

"We need sleeping bags. That old house looked cold as a grave. You know he's not going to go chopping much extra wood. He probably doesn't keep a fire for much comfort, other than heating the kitchen when he cooks. That old leather-skinned man is sure something, isn't he?"

"I think we could take some of those big cans of Dinty Moore Beef Stew and all we would have to do is pull off the lid, heat and eat. I bet you old Paul would like that for a change."

"Let's take our guns, anyway. We might get a chance, but better to have them and not need them, than to be without them."

"You're probably right."

Putting together a carton of food to take began with a box of saltine crackers, cinnamon rolls, pork and beans, canned corn, beanie-weenies, a loaf of bread, instant coffee, oatmeal, packets of instant hot chocolate, two tins of smoked oysters, a canned ham, and a bag of Pecan Sandies cookies. Tex had to get a pack of chewing tobacco, so he could chew, spit, and spin a story, he thought. He got a 12-pack of Stroh's beer and a six-pack of

Coke to take, as well. They picked a time to go, adding a five-pound sack of onions and a five-pound sack of potatoes, plus a can of Crisco, at the last minute. They were packed and ready to go to "Paradise."

Arriving at Paul's place, they found him down at the road, checking his mailbox and both parties were happy to see the other one. Oakie pulled up close to the house and they waited for Paul to make his way back. They shook hands and sat down on the front porch and caught up on things.

"You'uns aren't out hunting, are you? You don't look like you're dressed for cold weather."

"No, we aren't. We thought we'd take us a Sunday drive and we swung over this way to say 'Howdy'."

Paul chuckled. "Seein' that this is Tuesday, you're a might early, I'd say."

"So, how you doin, Paul?" Tex asked. "We've been thinking about you. We were wondering about those calves and how they're doing. I can see they aren't making much progress on grazing your field down."

"Well, it beats doing all that work to cut and bail that hay." Paul glanced at the back of the pick-up and the tarp that was covering stuff in the bed.

"What you hauling? Did the school run you two off?"

"Oh no, school and us are taking a break. We can take a few days before I have to be back at work."

"Tex, you never said. What kind of work?"

"I'm a bartender at Nick's English Hut. It's a college bar right off campus. I get three or four days a week and I can fit it between classes, so it works out well." After a pause, he asked, "What have you been up to yourself?"

"I shot a doe last week," Paul said with a raised brow and a slight squint in his eye, "even though it's a little before season.

I got a man at the processing place that's going to make it into mostly sausage for me, so I'll get it in about a week. I give some of the deer as payment for what he does for me and I can keep mine in the locker with his meat. It's pretty good, and it don't cost me any money to do it."

"Sounds sweet to me. I got my last deer with a logging truck."

Paul looked at Tex, as if he knew Tex was pulling his leg.

"Really, I did. I was out in the woods with a couple of buddies and we came over a ridge and saw a pulp wood truck coming down a grade. There was a deer not twenty feet away from us, and I guess we scared it, because it went across the road in front of that truck. It broke its neck and was thrown into the ditch on the other side. We went over there, and I got it hung in a tree and skinned it out, right there. The truck never stopped. We came home with a little something. I'm living in a house and there are six of us. Some of my buddies were not thrilled about eating deer meat, but I eat it."

"I don't pass it up, neither," Paul said.

"I knew a man when I was younger," Tex said. "His name was Dick Jackson and he got a deer with a rope. He's this man that lived on a river up in the swamps, on a houseboat. He was out on the bank and he heard his dogs barking and they jumped up a deer and chased it into the river and it started to swim across. So, Dick jumped in his jon boat and caught it in the middle of the river and roped it by its antlers and drug it along till it drowned. You ever hear of someone getting a deer by drowning it?"

Paul was satisfied with the story and shot back, "Well, he saved a bullet."

"Exactly. Paul, we got our sleeping bags with us since we didn't know where we were going to sleep tonight. Do you think we could—"

"Sleep in the barn if you want to. I used to have women sharecroppers staying in there, so, it was good for them and they did all right. You're welcome to it."

"Thanks, man. That would be cool."

"Women, huh? I suppose you got a story on that to go with it?"

"Yes, sir. Three of them, to be precise." Paul realized he sounded a little smug and started to turn away.

"Let's bunk up, then. Paul, we brought some eats in this box." Oakie set the box on the porch and while Paul rummaged through it, the two young men took off the tarp and moved their sleeping bags to the barn.

When the guitars came out, Paul became interested. "Now, I could have a little music around here. It's been too long since a happy tune went through this place."

"Paul, I'm a fairly good cook. I cook at Nick's so let me take over."

"Tex, you go right ahead. What do you want to cook?" Paul asked.

Tex reached into the box of groceries and produced the canned ham, "Voila."

"I sure like your cooking, Tex," he said with a wink.

Afterwards, Tex opened the canned ham and they cut pieces from it, directly from the can, and they made sandwiches, and opened a big can of pork and beans and ate without having to mess with a fire of any kind.

"So, you boys both play guitars? How did that happen?"

"I played guitar in a bar a couple of times a week," Oakie said, " and when I finished playing one night, I went over to another one, The Royal Oaks, to get a few drinks and listen to someone else's music and watch them play. This guy, Tex, was bartending there and we got to talking about music and guitars and what kind of music we played, and so forth. We played the same type of songs, so we started playing music as a duo in the Oaks one night a week."

"We got thirty-five a night and all the beer we could drink," Tex added. "By our third set, we would really get into it. I guess we played over there for about a year."

"So, play me a tune, boys. I like gospel and old timey blue-grass music. I'm fond of Bill Monroe's tunes from over at Bean Blossom. He started buying the land at the old Brown County Jamboree in the Fifties and now he owns the whole thing. I've been there, boys," he said with a smile. "He just had his big first annual get together time two years ago and I went to that. It was mighty fine. They said it's gonna be a regular thing. Nashville is sure going to grow, I bet ya'."

As the two young men got out their guitars and started to tune up, Paul saw Tex's twelve-string and commented about it.

"Well, Tex, what kind of special guitar is that with all them strings on it?" He looked and read the neck. "A Harmony—"

"Oh no, Oakie's got the special one, a Martin. That one is special. So, let's do 'Leaving on a Jet Plane.' Peter, Paul, and Mary had it as a single this year. Here you go, Paul."

After that, they played some Bob Dylan, then "John Henry," and then Johnny Cash's "Folsom Prison Blues."

With each additional song they played, Paul seemed happier and happier. He sat on the front porch in his rocker and kept time with his foot.

Music and stories went around that day and for the whole weekend. Paul seemed curious about their talents and curious about Oakie's background.

"Where did you get your music background, Oakie? Any of your family music inclined?"

"Well no, other than singing in the church choir. I took lessons for a while and then quit. I found I could learn more by playing with other folks. Tex is that way, too."

"Why do you go by Oakie?"

"I was born in Oklahoma and my nickname just stuck on me."

"It was ironic," Tex began, "I always thought it was funny, me and him, Tex and Oakie. I really was born in Oklahoma, too. They call it the Cimarron Strip. It's that little sliver of land that goes across the top of Texas. It was the no man's land, full of outlaws. It was where they marched the Indians to and off their lands on the Trail of Tears. But my life until I left home was always in Texas. I may go to see it again sometime, to see what it looks like."

"Any music background in your family?"

"That's the funny part. I have an uncle that lived in Bloomington that I learned about, mostly, when I came to live in Indiana. He had a country and western show on TV for many years called the Indiana Hayride. He was known as Uncle Bob Hardy. When everybody talked about Uncle Bob Hardy, he was my Uncle Bob. My classmates in high school all knew him and watched his Hayride show. He knew this young singer and talked to Ernest Tubb in Nashville, Tennessee, about him and Ernest said he would give him a shot and that singer hit it big with a recording—'You Are My Special Angel.' The man was Bobby Helms."

"I'll be darned, I sure know about him. He was big around here, too."

"My Uncle Bob threw a big country show over at the park in Spencer, at McCormick's Creek State Park, and hundreds showed up and the traffic closed the roads. I lived with my Aunt Mary Hardy when I first got here from Texas and we used to talk, and she told me about all the musicians that would come in with Uncle Bob when they got off the road from touring around. They would be sleeping all over the house. It must have been quite a scene back then. And so, what about you, Paul, can you play anything?"

"I can play the Jew's harp, the spoons, and I have a harmonica or two around here—" he pointed to the front door— "if I could find them some time. It's probably in a drawer or something."

"So, I have a curiosity, Paul. Did you ever have a horse around here? I suppose you did at some time?"

"We did and I plowed with him for years. That was back around the Depression. We always had them on the place. I bought one big old Percheron from the Amish and used him for a while, but he was too big for me or my mom, so we sold him back. Now we got tractors to work the land."

"You got a tractor Paul?"

"No, my neighbor down that away got one and does all the groundwork now. Tex, you said your granddaddy never had a tractor and had a horse, that true?"

"That's so. Bob, my favorite horse, he plowed with him for as long as I could remember. And then one day, my dad backed the trailer up and we took him to our ranch, and he stayed there for a few years, until one day he was gone. Someone took him away. I'd feed him watermelon rinds and black-eyed pea hulls and he would love it. Granddaddy would saddle him up and we would ride to town once or twice a week to go check the mail at the post office. We, really everybody, had a little box at the post office. There wasn't any route delivery back then. Hey, I got a question for you—did you ever see or hear of your horses being bothered by witches?"

"What do you mean?"

"When I was around ten, I came home from school and got off the school bus and saw my dad in the yard with my big white Jenny mule. He was cutting the mane back and trimming out burrs. He had cut the mane down the back, from the ears to the shoulder, and he left a shock of hair on the bottom uncut. He called them the withers. He said it was left for the witches. He said on full moons, the witches would fly into the barn and tie up little loops they would use for stirrups and take the horses out and ride over the moon with them. He swore it was true. Back in the olden days, he would go to the barn to harness up the horse and the horse would be in his stall all broke out in a sweat from being ridden all night. It gave me the shivers."

Paul sat there, still for the longest time. He was thinking about Tex's story and then budged a bit. "I don't say or not say what is or isn't, but if my mom were still with us, I would ask her about it. When she was younger and a girl, they used to have Gypsies come around their place and if they were the good kind, her dad would let them stay in their orchard for a few days and she was able to learn some of their ways and about the folk medicines, how to make them and use them. I got doctored on a few times from her by what she learned. I know she did talk about some of them having the 'vision' and being able to see things. That's why some of them did the fortune telling and were able to cast spells for different things. It was long before me, though."

Tex and Oakie thought of some more tunes and played for another hour. Oakie had a small cooler with some beers on ice and he brought it over and put it on the porch and they all had cold Stroh's beers. They could tell Paul enjoyed a cold beverage.

"Paul, what about your garden, what are you growing these days?"

"I'm growing a bunch of foolishness right now," he said

with a wry smile. "This garden is pretty much played out. I do need to get in there and get a winter garden put in. Squash and sweet potatoes, and carrots."

"Peanuts?" Tex offered.

"Lord, the peanuts! We used to grow them here back during the Depression."

"My parents in Oklahoma had a garden and they used to raise things, but they lived almost in town and nobody seems to have gardens anymore," Oakie went on. "They used to grow a big garden and can and all, but it was too much work and they went to the store. My mom used to tell me about their victory gardens back during the war. The Second World War certainly must have been something. You didn't go, I guess?"

Paul smirked and motioned to his bad leg and let the subject die. He got up and went over to the edge of the yard and wet one of the bushes. "Gooseberries, they like a little fertilize," he said as he sat back down.

They heard a rifle shot in the far distance and Paul noticed it. "Sounds like someone is sighting in a gun, getting ready for hunting season, I'd expect. Did you fellas ever get a place to hunt on? You never said."

"Not so far. Tex here thinks he wants to try and shoot a deer with a bow and arrow."

"You ought to be pretty good to do that, Tex."

"I figured I would give it a chance. I see that bow hunters get a month at the beginning of the season before gun season comes in. I guess black powder folks get to hunt, too."

"I can lay one down with mine—in one shot," Paul boasted.

"God, that gun must be old, huh?"

"It came down through the family when they came to this region from over in Kentucky. That rifle has got a curly maple stock on it and that will tell you where it came from if you know about rifles. Back then, we had another one that was Bird's Eye maple. Now, if you are good at tracking, you can go out and get them by hand." He laughed at his own joke.

Tex looked at Paul with doubt, which cued Paul to go on with his story. "My neighbor, old Grover, the one that owns the tractor, used to hunt black panthers around these hollows as a kid and he got one."

"How?" Oakie blurted out.

"He had been hunting around in the hollers for this big cat that had been robbing his chickens. He seen the back side of him from the barn one evening, carrying off a pullet. So, he started to hunt it down and spent three or four weeks at it and could never find it. One morning, it was pretty nippy out, Grover come around a trail that went up to a flat and saw the big cat's tail, where he was a sleeping on a rock in the sun. He found him a big seasoned limb and stayed on the rocks and was able to creep up on him without making a sound. All he had to do then was step out from that outcropping and knock that cat crazy in the head. That was that."

"That's just too lucky. I would never get a chance like that, and if I did, I would probably crap my britches," Oakie confessed.

"Paul, you ready?"

"I believe so. These cold beers are something else. I might have one more."

"I'll tell you a black panther story from my childhood," Tex said. "When I was little, like four or five, my granddaddy would sit me on his lap in his rocking chair and he had this big old tube radio and we would listen to The Grand Old Opry. That's where I remember hearing Ernest Tubb sing. At some time or other, granddaddy told me the story of a big old black panther that would creep around, and then he would make it all dramatic and then jump at me with his pretend panther claws on my stomach. It scared me and my sister, and right before bedtime, for a bedtime story.

"My Uncle Charles was going to tell me that bedtime story one night, instead of my Granddaddy telling it. He was a *lot* more dramatic in his telling and when he got really close to the climax, I guess he didn't know that I knew the story and I had these big old wide opened eyes and I looked at him, he looked at me, and I jumped in his face with my claws out right before he got to that part. We both came flying out of the chair, I scared him so badly. Everybody that was sitting in front of that radio howled with laughter. At the family reunions, they would always bring up that story to embarrass him and he wanted to live it down."

"They don't have any big cats around here anymore. I guess they were hunted and trapped out a long time ago. I can't remember the last time I heard of one."

"The man I knew, Dick Jackson, who lived in the swamps where I came from, is the last hunter-trapper I have knowledge of. Someone ought to write a story about him. He was such a unique man. I did some hunting with him when I was a kid. He lived on a houseboat in a swamp."

As they sat there on the porch watching the day and talking about anything that came to mind, the time seemed to have become suspended, and the usual anticipations of chores needing to be done did not seem to tug at any of them.

A white pick-up with an official medallion on the door entered the driveway and drove up to the house.

"It's Warden Ollie. He comes over this way to check on things and keep me up to date with the doings around here. He checks on us woods people and brings me anything I need from town. I don't get out so much and he's a good friend. Hey there, Ollie, what shakes?"

Paul went out to the truck and talked for a while with Ollie. The game warden stayed in the truck and soon left.

Tex and Oakie watched the old man come back to the porch. To them, he was such a delightful person, always with a sparkle in his faded blue eyes and his white stubbled face. He had fly-away white hair, and he invariably wore the same pair of bib jeans, with a rather stained pair of long johns underneath. His worn-out boots were giving up the stitching that held them together. His right boot was turned over to its side because of the twisted foot and he walked on the side of the boot as much as the bottom of the sole. The lacing that secured the boot was untied or about to come loose and dragged along the ground as he returned to the porch. He sat back down and returned to looking across the yard to the barn, seemingly lost in contemplation, as if no visitors were there. His pace of life seemed to baffle Tex and Oakie.

"We're invited to a sorghum making tomorrow. I want you to take them guitars and them folks will make some music afterwards and we'll have some fun. You two will join in for all the music-making. I know you'll like it. Most of the neighbors that are still around will be there."

Chapter 29

Early the next morning, they heard Paul let out a big "ah-choo" sneeze and they knew he was up. They looked out and saw him taking a leak off the porch into the yard. He didn't have his overalls on yet and was standing in his long johns.

"His long johns are pretty raggedy, Tex, maybe we should buy him some new ones for a Christmas present."

"Sounds right to me."

As they walked to the porch to sit down, Paul came out and met them.

"Come in, why don't you, and I'll make some real coffee, instead of that spoonin' coffee you'uns brought. I need a hand with something in here, anyway, and you can move it for me."

It was the first time they had been inside his house, and as they entered, they saw the inside of the house was stacked and crammed full of sacks of "stuff"—boxes, crates, a bicycle with flat tires, furniture, assorted pieces of mechanical apparatuses, and burlap sacks containing "things." They entered and followed Paul through the maze and tried not to look too much at his "things," so as not to appear to be snooping around.

There were beds in two bedrooms that could have been slept in at some time in the not too distant past but were now relegated to being "storage units." They were stacked with clothes and wardrobe items, some with coat hangers still on them.

"This is what I need a hand with." Paul pointed to a tall black bureau with a dark marble top and mirror.

"This needs to move over to here, so I can get behind it, to get to them drawers on that one."

Tex and Oakie re-arranged the furniture and cleared a passageway for Paul to get to the chest of drawers. Paul started rummaging around and from one of the drawers he pulled out two harmonicas and a folder full of papers.

"I might need to step in on the music today or tonight, so I needed these." He slipped the harmonicas in his jeans and looked through the papers.

The papers were a combination of hand-written song lyrics and some letters he saved for reading later.

Coffee was made on the wood-burning kitchen stove. A combination of coffee aroma and charred pine smoke assailed their noses.

"This is some good coffee, Paul."

He knew it was good and glanced at them and nodded, approvingly.

"Before we go, you might want to go to the barn and get a jacket. It might get cool this evening. We'll be there after dark, I'm pretty sure of that."

They both went to the barn and got jackets, while Paul wetted his hair and ran a brush through it haphazardly, pushing half to the left and half to the right.

A bit of teasing got started when Tex said to Paul, "My word, who cuts your hair? You got it mostly pushed down on your head. I might need to find you a hat—"

"And you and Oakie—two longhairs, yourselves. Don't let the barber catch the two of you. Why, they'd charge you five dollars to cut your hair—five dollars apiece! Let's go before tomorrow gets to us."

The farm Paul directed them to drive to had cars and trucks pulled up in the pasture and adults and children here and there. It looked like it was a farm auction. Wood smoke was circling in the air and two tents were erected and people were busy.

In the pasture at the back of the house was the cane press circle. Large stacks of sorghum stalks were waiting to be run through the press, to squeeze out the juice. It would be cooked down. Large mounds of pressed out cane were to be carried off and burned later, once they were dried.

A nice-looking woman in her fifties perhaps, came out to the truck as they got out and came right over to Paul and gave him a greeting and a big hug. He made introductions.

"This is Tex and Oakie. They've been staying with me, on and off, and they play these guitars they brought out today. This is Anna Katherine. She's my barber you were wondering on earlier. You watch her, she might get a hold of the two of you and then we might be able to see your eyes." He spoke as if was making a formal announcement, and the woman shook her head in mild embarrassment as she greeted them. She knew Paul was a kidder and the boys could see that they were close.

"Just call me Annie, and you're welcome here. I'm the one that carries him around, everywhere, so's I'm used to him. Paul tells me you've been driving out from Bloomington and have stayed with him a few times. Come up to the house and meet everyone else."

The introductions seemed to go on and on for most of the afternoon. As they got to be accepted as "family," no further attention was paid to them and they found a shady spot under a big tree, off to the side of the active workers, a place to keep the guitars out of the sun. Later someone brought out two chairs for them to sit on and left them in the shade when they went for beer.

After half a beer, they started wandering around, assessing what was going on and discovering what everyone was doing. Tex didn't know about syrup-making, so his attention in the activities was more absorbed than Oakie's. Before long, two of the men who worked at stirring and skimming motioned them over and started explaining the process. It was clear they had a sense of pride in what they were doing.

Most of the pressing was finished up. The horse that walked the circle was unhitched and syrup cooking and bottling were all that was left to be done. Food was being set out and everybody went to the tables and formed serving lines and then spread out to go find a place in the shade to eat.

"Well, I'm glad we got a shady spot, don't you?" By the time they got food and went to the shade, however, the chairs were missing. So, they used the tops of the guitar cases for tables and sat on the ground.

About half of the participants in sorghum making took their full jars of syrup with them after eating and loaded up kids and old folks and left. Cooking and pouring jars continued and Paul stayed under the shade tree with Oakie and Tex and responded as lots of people came over to visit with him, hug him, and shake his hand. He was a popular man. He seemed to be everybody's grandpa.

Most of the grown-ups found their way inside the house, where the lights were turned on, right before dark. The kids went to chase lightning bugs and play hide and seek in the barn.

"Bring those guitars on in here, so we can hear you play." Orders were shouted out and people started moving furniture out of the house and onto the front porch. Someone started rolling up the big rug. A banjo man came in, followed by a fiddle player, then another fiddler showed up and they started tuning. No one took the lead, other than calling out a tune and taking off with it, leaving those who wanted play along to join in where they could. Some knew some parts and that's all they played. It was loud and there was a rush to get going and keep going.

Tex and Oakie gradually joined in. The more organized players seemed to know several traditional tunes which, they could tell, were played at regular intervals and were well-practiced. Some players were "called out" as featured performers. Some were damned good!

Paul got up and walked into the house and dug around in his pockets and pulled out the two harmonicas he found earlier. A chair was pulled out for him to sit on and he stomped along with his good foot and made musical noises. Another old man, about as old as Paul, came over with a fiddle and they paired up on several tunes, sounding well-rehearsed. It was obvious the two had known each other for some time.

Oakie and Tex had stumbled into a nest of bluegrass lovers and players. Then someone said, "Tex, you call one out."

"How about, 'Will the Circle be Unbroken?'" His twelve-string filled the living room like an organ filled a church. Oakie took the intro and several church women fell into that tune, as surely as they did on Sundays at their places of worship. Someone joined in with a tambourine. A musical tabernacle was formed.

Then the songs and tunes came from many suggestions. "How Great Thou Art," started everyone on gospel hymns, and Oakie and Tex decided they would have to steer the selections in a different direction. Otherwise, they felt, the gospel tunes would kill the evening's enthusiasm for singing.

"John Henry," "Folsom Prison Blues," "Henry Martin," "Stewball," "Leaving on a Jet Plane," "House of the Rising Sun," "Barbara Allen," "Wildwood Flower," and "Old Blue," capped it, and changed the mood of those gathered. The two young men made sure they did not get anywhere close to playing "Amazing Grace," which was too sacred for several. Some Bob Dylan was thrown in by Tex, but the fiddle players retreated earlier, and no slights were intended or given. "St. James Infirmary" closed the night.

When Paul got up the next morning, he found Tex already up and out on the porch. Paul invited them to sleep in the house on the other beds, as it was getting down into the high '30s at night. The wind coming through the cracks in the boards in the barn made for a cold sleep. The sleeping bags they were using were a bit light, but very comfy when used as a blanket on the bed.

"You'll need to rest up your fingers, Tex, from all that guitar playing, I believe." Paul jabbed him, as he came out on the porch in his long johns to take a pee off the porch.

"We sure had the music last night, didn't we?"

"Yes, we did. We used to do syrup making regularly, but nowadays everyone is off doing everything else. The young 'uns hardly know about such stuff these days. You seemed to know a little bit about it, though."

"I never did get to do much of it. In the South, it's kinda different. The syrup is called black strap and I never liked it. I mean, Paul, it is black syrup. It reminds me of horse liniment, the kind you put on a paddle and swab on a horse's throat to cure him of the cough. In rough times we did that stuff."

"Well, son, I know about rough times."

"I know you do. I know you went through the Depression just like my grandparents did. Sometimes, though, you don't need to go through a Depression to have rough times. You ever heard this—'This is going to hurt me more that it's going to hurt you?' Or, this one, 'I hit you because I love you.' Did you ever hear such shit?" Tex repeated, not expecting a response.

Paul stood there, looking down on Tex sitting on the porch and staring out over the pasture. He was momentarily startled by the abrupt response from Tex.

I am as deeply rooted to my patch of ground as he is to his, Paul thought.

"For me, I got it all," Tex blurted out. "Hand, fist, belt, rope, stick, and whip. After so much of it, I could either kill him or go, so I hit the road and made it up here to Indiana."

"I learned this a long time ago, Tex, when it comes to crazy, everybody stays hushed up."

"Ain't *that* the truth, man. I *hear* you."

Paul mused, "Learning about life is like living like a pencil. You can put it all down until you want to change, so you try to erase and write new. The marks from before are still visible and you can squint and look back on what was written there before."

"It feels like mine was written with a pen and right now, it does not erase very easily."

"Give it some time, my friend. It's a matter of perspective. A twig is a limb to a hummingbird."

Paul rummaged around in the dresser they had moved earlier, and he was digging in another pile of papers when Oakie got up and wandered through the house in his long johns, and then wandered out on to the porch and peed into the yard, like Paul had done earlier.

Paul found something in the stack of papers he was going through and came out to the porch and sat down and began reading. He gave the letters his rapt attention.

After Paul took a break from reading, he returned to the house for a bit and started digging around again. This time he came back on the porch with a fiddle in a case and opened it up and the hair on the bow was quite frayed. It looked like the head of a dandelion.

As Paul turned his fiddle over and was about to put the bow to the strings, something broke off or came out of his instrument. Paul then shook it back and forth and they could hear something rattling around inside, as if a piece of something came loose. He then picked it up from the floor and showed it to Oakie and Tex.

Paul held out his hand and they saw that he was holding rattlesnake rattles.

"What in the world, huh, fellas?" Paul asked them as he showed it off.

"Those are real rattles?"

"Yes, indeed. Lots of fiddlers in the old days put them in their fiddles. The old preachers didn't like the fact that church members would get out to a hoedown on Saturday nights to listen to fiddlers play mountain music and spend their pennies and nickels on such stuff and then come into church on Sundays with no nickels for the offering plate. So, them preachers began telling everyone the music that came out of them fiddles was the voice of the Devil.

"They didn't even want fiddle music to be played inside town. They didn't want the Devil roosting inside them instruments. So, somehow anyway, someone got this idea so's at least they could run off the Devil out of their fiddles. Why, after that, just about everybody got them rattles stuck inside. I seen lots of people go up to the musicians and ask them if they had rattles and you'd see 'em shake their fiddles."

"We didn't know you were a fiddler. We might have used you last night. Since we both have seen your rattles, we now know you are a sanctified, authentic, and bona fide fiddler."

"It wouldn't have mattered. A Jew's harp would have suited

me better. I haven't had this thing out for years." Reaching for some papers, Paul showed them the handwritten words to "Barbara Allen" that someone had written out.

"This was sent to me long ago," he said wistfully. "You know I told you about some women that were living in my barn? This was sent back to me after they moved on, by one of them, Mayvis Bailey. It was so long ago."

"You can tell us about her if you please. All the women we know back in Bloomington don't have any history. They're always new," quipped Oakie.

"Someday fellas. That's all I got to say about it," and Paul went back to the drawer in the house and put the letters and the papers up.

"Onions and watermelons, boys. That's' what the last crop of things I had planted in here," he said next. "I grew turkeys for a while."

"Turkeys, huh? Did you make any money off them, Paul?".

"It saved our bacon, me and Grover. He's the one that's got the tractor to do the plowing. I can't do it," and Paul looked at his leg.

Tex looked to change the subject. "Paul, I'm learning how to skydive."

"Tex, what in heaven's name are you doing?"

"I know—bird shit and fools and all that—but, here is what happened, talking about turkeys. I went to Anderson to jump at a fairground for a Fourth of July air show and we all got into the airplane and took off to get up high and the pilot told us to look out the window and he showed us a big turkey farm that we were going to fly over. It looked like snow on the ground, there were so many of them. Ha, you should have seen it! The pilot flew over the farm and the shadow of the plane went over the ground where those turkeys were. Boy, you should see them scatter. They must have thought it was a hawk circling overhead to get one of them. It was a big white wave, parting on dry land."

Paul and Oakie thought that was funny, as they visualized the scene. The three of them sat around most of the morning like that, swapping stories. Oakie went and got his guitar and sat back down and picked around some.

During a pause, Tex asked Paul, "Do you ever do any fishing? I do when I'm back in Texas. I go to the gulf and fish and I'll go to some big lakes and catfish. When I fish, I want to catch something big, so I don't try and bass fish much. If I catch a bass, it's usually by accident."

"No, I don't do much fishing anymore."

"I've been living out at the new Monroe Reservoir, past the dam, and bow fishing. I shot some big old carp, but I gave them away. In Texas, they frown on you if you ever admitted that you ate carp. But why not?"

"There's some big fish in the White River, I'll grant you," Paul said. Me and a couple of buddies snuck off to go fishing instead of doing chores one day and we went to the river and got in some bad trouble. One of my buddies hooked what he thought was a large catfish and we all got a hold of the line to pull it up on the bank. It turned out that we hooked one of our classmates that had drowned. I don't think I could describe to you what we felt that day. Even though it happened a long time ago—"

Tex and Oakie groaned when Paul told that story. Obviously, there were many more details to the story they didn't get in his telling. They paused their idle conversation. Tex found some cold Stroh's beer in their cooler, and so they had a beer.

At one point, Oakie walked over to one of the downed trees that was periodically chopped on for firewood and went over to it to pee away some of the cold beer.

Paul casually said, "Better be careful over there, you know

that's a snake log." Oakie stepped back, mid-stream and looked about, cautiously.

"Now Paul, are you trying to scare me? I never heard about a snake log before."

"My dad told me about snake logs when I was very young, so's I'd stay away from 'em."

"How so?"

"I learned later, he just said that to keep me from going to the bathroom in tall weeds, is all it was. You would think he would have just told me instead of spooking me half to death."

"Makes sense, I suppose, but I bet you remembered, didn't you, Paul? You just now proved it. Everybody watch for me while I go."

"Well, it's a bear log, at any rate, so's you would know." He snickered because he got Oakie to stop peeing twice. He laughed again.

"So, now what about this log?"

"I learned about these when I was young, too."

"This here's a bear tree. So, look, and you notice the whole inside of that tree trunk is all rotted out and it got hollowed out, but it still grows.

"Them two trees are beech trees and they grow really big, but they tend to get hollow when they get old. A big old boar bear will get to chasing a sow bear to mate with her and he'll kill her cubs and she'll then get into heat and he'll be successful. She calls out to her cubs to flee and they'll run and get up inside one of them beech trees where the boar bear can't get to them. Later, they'll run off. I've heard stories about hunters checking beech log hollows for bears and they've been found. It may also be that they're crawling inside the hollows to dig out the honey from a beehive."

Chapter 30

A day after Tex and Oakie went back to Bloomington, Grover and Paul planned out what to put into the ground and whether they should raise another round of turkeys. It didn't take a lot of work to cash in on the deal Purina had been offering. The fields were fenced in, they brought the birds out, dropped them in the pasture, brought out and replenished the turkey scratch, picked up the grown birds before Thanksgiving season, and delivered the check! It was a mighty fine program, they thought.

Another advantage for Grover was the fact that with turkeys, he didn't have to spend so much time on the tractor. His arm was puny, and he complained about it often. The big chore was to get the field plowed up and get the sunflower seeds in the ground and growing before Purina delivered the birds.

It took either money or hard work to survive and Grover faced tough choices. He still had the expenses of running and operating his Allis-Chalmers tractor, plus the expenses of food and electricity.

Paul, on the other hand, had his land and he still put in a modest garden that helped him eat, plus he was shooting game, occasionally, which the game warden was aware of but not mentioning to anybody. If he found game, things would remain good. His luck could go either way.

The squeeze had a strong grip on Grover, and with no cash flow, he began to "Rob Peter to pay Paul." Without mentioning anything to Paul, he had been quietly selling off "excess" acres to make his tractor note, pay his electric bills, and buy store-bought food. The arm's occasional aches and throbbing continually reminded him how much he hated to go back to the garden, and so he refused. For the coming year, he would manage to plow up the ground and get sunflowers planted.

The left hand didn't know what the right hand was doing.

It was an offhand thought, but Oakie and Tex put a quick road trip together and ran down to Shoals to see Paul. This time, they went in Tex's old truck, a 1949 Chevrolet Suburban Panel truck, "the black Zephyr," his pride, and joy. He worked as a scene carpenter, stagehand, and curtain rope puller at the IUMAC, the Opera Theatre at Indiana University. The house painter he bought the truck from had owned it for many years and when the painter got tired of the color of the truck, he would take out his paint brush and paint the truck. Where the paint was chipped, Tex at one time counted five or six colors.

Tex loved his truck. He put three different engines in it over time by going to the junkyards and buying replacement engines for seventy-five or a hundred dollars and swapped them out over a weekend. So, he was dismayed to see Paul standing at his shed, looking at the back of his 1954 Firedome De Soto, with the automatic transmission.

"Tell me it's not on life support, Paul," Tex yelled out his window as they drove up. Paul turned around and didn't know which was the bigger surprise, the big old black panel truck or seeing Tex and Oakie getting out of it.

"Is my funeral all ready, or do I get in line?" he shot back. As he approached the truck, they noticed Paul had added an additional walking cane, besides his usual stick. They started to say something and then checked it.

"I had been using this to get back and forth to town in and when I was at Grover's last, I hit a limestone rock he had marking the edge of his drive. I've been told I may have bent a tie rod, so it drives with a bit of a pull."

"I can look at it," Tex said. Hell, I've put three engines in this one. I've got my tools in the back. I keep them handy when I travel on long trips now, just as a bit of insurance."

Oakie beckoned, "Cold beer, here. Get your beer," and everybody settled into their usual places and relaxed. They noticed the field had been freshly cut into rows and planted.

"Got the field tilled and planted, that's good. It's getting warm."

"Grover just finished plowing it. He looked all broke down and tired. I don't know what's the matter with him. It's not like he's been working too hard."

"Hell, Paul, how old is he? He's got fifteen years on you, anyways, doesn't he? You're mid-seventies?"

"Yeah, it's something I can't put my finger on. Well, this was a surprise seein' you two."

"We're out looking in junkyards. Tex is trying to find some parts for the Zephyr out there."

"You can find parts in Bloomington," Tex said, "but a couple of junkyards are starting to take the old cars and sell them off for scrap iron. Old parts are getting harder to find than they used to be. But we'll look around for parts for you, while we're looking."

The next morning, Paul and Tex pulled the tarp off the DeSoto and pushed it out of the barn so they could look at it in good light. Indeed, the tie rod was bent. They also noticed that Paul didn't have the other cane with him.

"We might be able to find a new tie rod, but not many of these DeSotos were built. Nineteen fifty-four was good for beer, but not DeSotos. But I bet it could be heated with a torch and bent back and we could get it close. After all, you're not driving it back and forth to French Lick every day, are you? Okay then."

After they sat on the porch and had another beer, Oakie said, "Paul, we have a surprise for you today. Show him, Tex,"

Tex went over to the Zephyr, climbed into the back, and pulled out a chainsaw and a can of gas. He handed the chainsaw to Oakie.

"I'm gonna pee wherever I want to now. Tell that snake log goodbye."

Paul and Tex just about fell over backwards, roaring with laughter, watching Oakie swing that chainsaw around.

After clowning around with the chainsaw, Oakie and Tex tore into the front end of the DeSoto. They removed the tie rod and put it in the Zephyr to carry around with them to junk-yards as they looked for a replacement. Highway 37 north of Bloomington had a couple of places that might have promise, they thought, as well as Stinesville and then Bloomfield.

Eventually, they found a replacement tie rod for the DeSoto, but it was bent as well. So, the solution was to take the two bent rods to a welding shop to get them heated and straightened, and then see which one came out the better one. Returning, it was a quick fix up and Paul had a functioning car to drive. He needed a little air for the tires, but other than that, he was ready to go.

Within a month of his leaving Paul's place, Tex's house caught fire and he lost most of his possessions, including a brand new six-string guitar he had traded for his twelve-string. He salvaged the clothes on his back and his parachutes. He looked to his Zephyr for shelter and transportation.

The generosity of others kept Tex on his feet after the fire and he lived in and around Bloomington on friend's couches, spare rooms, boarding houses, basements, and trailers. After several years of attending classes, Tex would need to be close to the Indiana University campus, as graduation would be within six months or so. He decided to drop in on Paul to see how the old man was doing.

"I couldn't find Oakie around anywhere," Tex told him, "so I thought I would come down anyway. How have you been, Paul? Have you seen him?"

"He's not been about here. Come on in."

They sat on the porch, relaxed and swapped stories, as they had done before. Tex noticed that the "snake log" was no longer there. "Paul, we cut up that snake log from the front of the house the last time we were here. It was some good burning wood, wasn't it? And old Oakie swinging that chainsaw—"

"He didn't waste his time with it, now did he?" Paul chuckled. "I was waiting for you two to show back up, 'cause I figured out a home project you and him could do. But since he's not about, we can't wait on him. Calves' tail."

"I used to hear that when I was a kid in Texas and my Granddaddy finally explained what he meant. When we went somewhere, to the drive-in or something, I would hear it—calves' tail! Paul, did you ever go to the drive-in? They're almost gone now."

"Never had a car to go in. Went to the nickel show a few times. Very few times."

"How's the DeSoto driving? I see you have it back in the barn again. Are you not using it that much?"

"The starter's out on it, so I stored it back in the barn till a later time."

"I'll go start looking for one for you. I'm still going around to the junk yards."

"Well, Tex, I haven't had a need to use that car for two or three months, ever since I put it back in the barn. I don't seem to be needing it much," Paul said dismissively.

Tex thought, *I wonder about this. He's not too interested in using the car. He may not have money to spend on the starter, if he's let it go for so long without getting it fixed. I better leave that subject be, for a while.*

"What kind of project did you think up for us, Paul?"

"You know about my friend, Grover, the one with the arm in a sling? He had some dogs he made a little cemetery for. That's where he found his wife dead, you know. He wants to dig them dogs up and their little headstones and move them closer to his house. When his sister-in-law's place went to the sheriff's auction, they were kinda left in place on the other land. I figure he seems attached to them three dogs and was getting sentimental about them. He's doing it in memory for his wife. They've long turned to dust, so it would be just the gravestones. I don't have two good feet and he's still got that bad arm he wears in his sling. It's about giving a blessing, you understand."

"I'd be glad to do it myself and could do it in fifteen minutes by the way you describe it. Sure. That reminds me of that swamp man, Dick Jackson, I was telling you about. He loved his dogs, too. He had this dog that would always follow me around when I was out to his place on the river. Heard him bark 'treed' and I knew what that meant. I ran down the riverbank to see what the dog was after and he was riled up. He had something up in a tree full of moss, and at that point, I saw that dog run at that tree fast. He jumped on the trunk of that crooked old tree and ran right up into it, after whatever the hell it was. I thought I was going to get into trouble because I got his dog stuck up in that tree. I ran down to Dick's houseboat and he came back with me to see and then he laughed and said the dog has done it several times. I never learned how to get a dog out of a tree. That was something new to me. You ever hear of something like that?"

"I had a beagle about ten feet up inside of an old hollow beech tree once that was chasing something, probably a rabbit, and crawled in after it. I had a rabbit about ten feet up there, too."

"Changing the subject, I brought a loaf of bread and bologna and cheese for sandwiches or a couple of cans of beef stew. Are you ready to eat anytime soon?"

Paul jested, "I'm ready to eat anything soon."

After they ate, Paul said to Tex, "I can see that you have a liking and a draw to old barns and things, don't you?"

"I do. You know that old saying, 'Were you raised in a barn?' Well, it sticks with me. I see all these old barns all over southern Indiana, and I love them. I particularly like going in them, they have a smell to them that tells me they are alive. Honestly, I miss my granddaddy's barn something awful. I've played in the loft, chased mice, ate raw peanuts that were stacked for drying, and poked around between the log walls to see what he put there—old butcher knives, nails, trace chains, and Morton saltshakers. You said you had women living in your barn? Really?"

Paul wanted to be mysterious, so gave him a sly smile and left it at that, not taking the bait. However, Tex had a sense that something was off kilter. Later in the day, Tex noticed that more of the back of Paul's house seemed to have fallen in.

It was the back porch awning that had fallen over and now almost an entire back room and the ceiling had collapsed, in addition to the back porch. It wasn't from a tree falling or storm damage. It looked rotted and no attempt had been made, by what

Tex could see, to arrest any further decay. It could rain freely into the room. It didn't look like there had been any attempt to go into the room to salvage or rescue anything. All the mounds of boxes of "stuff" Paul had stacked throughout the room were still there. It was just as well. Tex didn't look to find out how fit the flooring and foundation joists were holding or if significant rotting had occurred.

Tex noticed that Paul looked frail and he was back to using two walking canes, which he kept close.

"If you want to make some coffee and sit a spell, I'm going to go out and look over the car and see if that's all that's what's wrong with it, while I'm here. I'll be back in a bit."

Tex walked out to the old DeSoto and raised the hood. He almost got stung but realized in time that wasps had built a nest on the car's radiator near the hood latch. He had seen the buzzing wasps flying in and out, so gingerly opened the hood, which had already been popped. He could see the fan belt was broken, but it was still there.

Without the belt, he couldn't try the engine to see if the starter was still good. Without any of his tools, Tex couldn't loosen anything to get a fan belt off and get a replacement. Since the battery would be dead, he would need to bring a set of jumper cables also when he came back.

It looks like first things first, I need to swat that wasp nest off that latch, so Paul won't get stung. And I need to get Oakie out here with me. We'll get this DeSoto running. But he's not depending on the car right now, so it'll give us some time, anyway, Tex figured.

Looking for a hoe handle or a long stick to use on the wasps, Tex's mind was carried back to childhood memories of his grandparents, John Marshall and Bina Electra. It was like entering a sanctuary. Everything in Paul's life and every object had a story, as Tex saw it—the ground, the trees, the well, the barn, and the hills. They were touchstones to know. They were to be seen, to be stood on, to be caressed, and handled. The worn-out plows, the boards of the buildings, the pulley on the crossbar above the dug well, the corn crib, the old butcher blocks, the worn-out and cracked leather harnesses that hung on the walls and in the stalls, the saddles, the medicine bottles of Honey and Almond Cream and Murine for Your Eyes, the rusted tin cans, the dried corn cobs on the ground, the turkey feathers, and the broken barn door hasp on the ground.

As Tex tromped back through the high weeds on the way back from the barn, he remembered what his own granddaddy had said to him—"Always be able to look back across that time."

Back on the porch, drinking coffee, Paul seemed upset to hear about Tex's house fire and losing all his possessions. Paul talked about his own house fire and the lightning strike.

"What about you? You're always getting into some project yourself or doing some project with others every time I see you. What have you been up to?"

"I haven't done anything to make another human being remember that I've lived, so I want to go on."

"A positive mind sees opportunity in everything, that's what I've heard you say. That's a great one I'll take with me. I'll put it in my gunny sack and carry it with me, all the same."

After more coffee, swapping stories, and having beef stew for supper that night, Tex was rolling out to get back on the road the next morning. He looked for car parts on the way to Bloomington, where he had to work the night shift at Nick's. He would be looking for his friend, Oakie, who used to show up on the weekends after 9 p.m. They would catch up, discuss what was happening, discuss Paul's doings, and make plans to get Paul's DeSoto running again.

Chapter 31

It was many weeks later before Tex and Oakie met up again and were able to talk about Paul and his situation out at Shoals. The crowd at Nick's seemed light, as it usually did when it got close to the end of a semester, and especially before the summer. Tex poured him a draft beer and he sat in the front section at the bar. Oakie had a long face. It seemed dismal, whatever it was.

"Tex, I was out to see Paul and I should tell you what I found. Before I even got to Paul's farm, I noticed from the road that the grass in the front pasture was high and I didn't see the two calves out grazing. I saw nothing. The gate was latched, so I know they didn't get off the place and out somewhere."

"I went to the house and I saw it from the road, the whole back of the house has now collapsed and fallen into the basement. It took out the steps to the root cellar, so there is no way old Paul would be able to get into the basement to get the food he stored there, especially the way he is. By the way, the leaves were piled up over everything, I could tell the roof must have collapsed over the winter. It didn't look like anything had been moved around, like to salvage anything. The only thing I saw was that the kitchen stove that was down in the cellar was missing. There is probably a foot or more of standing water down there.

"I went to the barn to look around and saw the hood of

the DeSoto up, so I looked and saw the starter was missing and that broken fan belt was, too. The battery was gone. All four tires were flat, and the trunk was popped open and catching rain. The tire jack and the four-way lug wrench were lying in the back, like someone had attempted to change the flats. The only spare was gone.

"I didn't see anything out of the ordinary in the barn. The dust that covered everything hadn't been moved around, except an area that was disturbed on the floor. The loose hay had been moved around some and I notice small wheel marks in the dust. So, it didn't look like anybody had been in the barn, other than that, and the barn was still latched with the hasp from the outside."

"Here's a refill." Tex gave him a cold mug. "I'm afraid for Paul, Oakie. He doesn't have anything to fall back on, so to speak. He looked very thin when I saw him last."

"Tex, this is the next part you aren't gonna like. I didn't know what direction to go in at that point. I went back to the house and went in the front door. It was so full of junk I had to pick my way around just to move. I could only get so far into the house—say, to the back of the living room and that was where the roof came down and it stopped me from going any further unless I crawled on my knees, but there was no point. I went back and rummaged around and decided to get into that dresser Paul dug around in all the time. Remember that time when he got those harmonicas and that big Mark Twain book with all those love letters in it? They were there."

"I didn't know what to do with them. Those were obviously some of his prized possessions. I didn't know if I should take them and try and save them from getting wet and ruined, but they were his and I didn't feel it was my place to take any of his things. I mean, I could have, and then when we met up with him later, we could give them back to him, but I didn't think I should."

Tex said, "We don't know if he's got any clothes or not, or if we should try and save some of them for him, or what."

"He could take it very unkindly if we were to take any of his stuff and then he sees that it was us that took them. You know how he is. I know he trusts us, but still—"

"And you know how that place is, if we go in there," Tex said cautiously, "and start trying to save stuff that he hasn't cared about or not able to get to. More than likely, we'd be digging into his private life, which we don't have a right to do. He's shared a lot of himself with us these past three or four years, but you know there were some things he didn't want to talk about. Either way—"

"It's got to be bad, Tex. And I haven't told you the whole story." Oakie had tears in his eyes.

Tex was about to tear up and leaned toward Oakie apprehensively.

"The only thing I thought of was to get in the truck and drive down that dirt road and look for that other farm, where his friend had their place. I found it and I could tell that was it from what Paul had said about it. There were a couple of trucks in the drive and one of them was the game warden that Paul knows. He was talking to a couple of men and when he saw me, he stopped and came over to me as I got out of the truck."

"I saw these cardboard signs those other men were putting up—No Trespassing signs. They had them on the door and on the sides of the house and on the fence posts, everywhere. They definitely wanted them seen."

"I asked him what was going on and he told me the man that lived here had died and the bank was repossessing the property. He said the sheriff would be the one to get any information from him if I was interested."

"Is this the Grover McCullough property?"

"Yes. I told him I was looking for a friend of his and he asked me who. I told him I was looking for a Paul Chandler. He turned white as a sheet and said he was the game warden that checked on Paul now and again and asked me who I was. When I told him, he said we should sit down and talk."

"Oakie—?" Tex murmured back.

"The game warden dropped in to see Paul and how he was getting along and if he heard from his friend, Grover. The bank official was at Grover's place and serving eviction orders for him to vacate but he wasn't around. The warden knew he and Paul farmed together, so he went down to Paul's to see if Grover was around there and bring him back around."

"He told me when he went to Paul's and saw the collapsed house, he found Paul crawled up in the back of his collapsed bedroom and he was scrunched down and preoccupied with things in a box. He got him out and Paul was dazed. He asked him how he was, and Paul said to him, 'The Lord is the one that gives me work for my hands to do' and then 'Dear Lord, what can I do for Thee'?"

"He asked him again if he knew where his friend Grover was, and Paul told the game warden that he was in the barn and they could go out and see him. He gathered Paul's two canes and got him steady and they slowly walked out to the barn.

"'He's in there,' Paul told him. The game warden bumped into a pair of boots with his face as he entered, and he looked up and found Grover had hung himself in Paul's barn."

At that, Tex got someone to take the front section over and they went to a booth. They both sat there, trying to absorb the news together.

"Where's Paul?" Tex implored.

"He didn't know. When the ambulance was called, the game warden said he waited with Paul on the porch, until they came. They put Grover on a stretcher and were about to leave. He said he asked Paul if he wanted to go with Grover in the ambulance or go with him, the game warden, but Paul told him no. He said he would be along after a while, that he would drive in, and he pointed to the DeSoto. The game warden didn't know it was disabled and didn't run, so he left him on the porch and accompanied the ambulance to the funeral home."

"Where is he?"

"They just don't know. When he didn't show, they went back out, partially because he wasn't very coherent to begin with, and you know, he doesn't get around very well."

"Do we stay, or do we go?"

Oakie responded, "Tex, I didn't know what to do at that point. I couldn't go looking. Where? He hardly walks. The only thing I knew to do was to give the warden my phone number and my address. I gave him your address, the only one I knew. I told him he could reach you at Nick's English Hut. Don't laugh, it's all I could think of."

"Boy, I don't see how this will work out. We're both fixing to leave college and move away. I won't have a forwarding address, and I don't think you will either. I think we both need to at least drive back over. Maybe we can find the game warden. He would be the best central contact for us."

Oakie grimaced, "I in *no* way could go until next week. I've got finals and I graduate or not, depending upon me passing."

"I've got two that I have to take, no way around it." Tex said. "It has to be next week, then."

❖   ❖   ❖

The game warden and the old sheriff were at Paul's farm when Tex and Oakie made it to Shoals the following week. They were sympathetic to the convoluted situation and glad to see the "college hippies" coming around to help solve the dilemma.

Tex and Oakie had picked up bits and pieces of information about the old sheriff from Paul here and there. They thought he had moved on some time ago. When they drove up and looked at him, half-stooped over and carrying two canes, they realized he was somewhat older than Paul. However, they weren't sure they could trust him. They were picking up on uncomfortable vibrations from him like Paul did, even though they didn't know about his Klan connections and his complicity in the deaths of four people. If they had known, they might have asked why the people of Shoals still tolerated having someone like that around. But sometimes small communities live with the evil they can see and know, rather than try to face the evil that might be hidden and unseen. The two hippies and the backwoods sheriff looked at each other, still sizing each other up.

As Tex and Oakie got out of the Zephyr, the sheriff shook hands with them.

"I see you put up Posted Keep Out signs at the gate," Tex said. "What's that yellow tape doing, wrapped around his house—or what's left of his house?"

"Well, it might be a stretch, a little, but I thought that at least it might keep some of the curious out for a while, or until we can get on firmer ground. Come over here, we've got something to tell you."

They all went to the porch and sat there to discuss the situation. The game warden said, as if reassuring the sheriff, "I've known both of these men for several years and they're both fine, fine gentlemen that would do the world for another man without even stopping to think about it. I think we may at least return that effort in some way by trying something out here."

The sheriff nodded, accepting this explanation and, as if to demonstrate his authority, launched into the story of Grover's demise. "As the sheriff, I knew that Grover was in financial trouble a long time ago, back when the Field's place was seized for not paying taxes. It was the same for Grover as it was for the Fields. But for him, he began quietly selling off land just to keep up. The fact of the matter was that he didn't own the land under his own house, and he was about ready to lose it, when his wife died.

"They were both struggling, and they had been for some time. What I did get out of Paul when we sat there waiting for the ambulance to come—" the sheriff paused and looked at the two men sitting there. He drew a deep breath and delivered the final piece of news to both. "Grover's arm never did heal, and they were going back and forth to the hospital in Washington to see the doctor, Titman I believe. Then Grover became ill and he was throwing up a lot, and so he left Paul and went to get some medicine. That was the last time Paul saw Grover alive.

"As it turns out, Dr. Titman found bone cancer in Grover's shoulder. Paul never knew. It was too much for Grover to handle, with losing the farm and having run out of money. He had no way to take care of himself and didn't want to die slowly and painfully. So, he came back home and wrote a note and then went to Paul's barn to die.

"So, in fact he had no land. There was only his wife and her sister, Minerva. No other family. And so, there was nothing they would've inherited if he would have died before Lovety and her sister. I'm almost certain Paul wasn't aware of that. They were willing, at least, to cut some of the walnut trees off the land that raised enough money, so he was able to buy that tractor.

"Last year, 1972, after so much lumber was being poached

from farmers, the state started licensing timber buyers for poplar, maple, cherry, ash, and walnut. The buyers had to pay farmers market prices for the timber. The Germans were here buying walnut and Grover made a killing. I'm telling you this for a reason."

At this, the sheriff thumped one of his canes on the floor, as if adding a period at the end of a long sentence. He then sat back in his chair, seemingly self-satisfied that he had given the full and official account.

The game warden took over talking at this point. "And so here's the situation. I got a letter sent to me by mail, from Grover, and it arrived after he hung himself. In the letter, he admitted that he had nothing left of any value and acknowledged he knew what would be left would be all forfeited at foreclosure. He knew he would leave Paul in a terrible bind without a tractor to plow the land. I've been getting poached deer and road-kill meat for Paul for quite a while and I guessed that was just about all he was eating. He looked mighty poor the last I saw of him."

The sheriff said, "Paul had the land, but no tractor. Grover had the tractor, but no land. Now, Paul is going to inherit the tractor."

The game warden added, "What we, I, or whoever, will do is to cut down a few of Paul's walnut trees and we'll get them cut and planked and stored in that fine old barn, yonder, and let them season for a few years, so the lumber will draw top dollar when it's sold. The expenses of cutting and planking can be paid back and taken out of the profits when it's bought. It will keep the taxes paid for many years and Paul won't have to worry about someone coming and taking his land from him. Grover's tractor has already been driven over here and is sitting in the barn. Let's go look at it, why don't we?"

The men walked down the hill to the barn to look. As they

walked, Oakie recalled the impressions Paul got from reading Mark Twain. "And he said to us, 'When Huck Finn talked about old Black Jim, he made him a better man to others, just by talking about him.' I hope I can do that for someone myself someday."

"You certainly have done it for Paul and Grover," Oakie and Tex affirmed. "Thanks to the both of you."

The sheriff and the game warden smiled at each other as they all looked over the big diesel tractor that was now Paul's. Then they gave their farewells and left Oakie and Tex sitting on the ground, staring up at the machine.

Oakie looked at all the pedals. "How in the world is Paul going to drive this thing with one good leg?" As he glanced at the gauges, he saw a note attached to the gas cap and he took it and read it to Tex. "The greatest test of courage on earth is to bear defeat without losing heart."

At that moment, they knew they would never see the old man again. "The earth and time always keep moving. Most times you never know it, and sometimes you can feel it move when you stand on it," Paul had said to them once. This day they looked at the ground they both stood on and felt it had moved for them.

Driving back from Shoals and headed for Bloomington and their graduations, they thought about it all.

Tex repeated Paul's often spoken phrase, "He made him a better man to others just by talking about him. I hope I can do that for someone myself someday."

PART SEVEN

Chapter 32

"Again, Paul," said Anna Katherine, "as soon as the word got out about Grover, I came right over to your place looking for you. I didn't see you anywhere and I didn't see the car, so's I thought you were at the hospital or somewhere. I didn't know you spent the night in the barn. You should have driven over here earlier and spent the night with us. Why did you do that?"

"Can't say right off. I was just dazed by it, still am."

"Well, you'll be here with us tonight and sleep here, in a good soft bed. And we'll all go to the funeral together, so don't worry about that part of it. When you get a clear head, maybe we can talk about it some."

"We've been friends, and close friends for a long time. When Lovety passed on, I thought that would do him in, but Grover persevered. I wanted him to be of a good mind. I was a hoping I'd be able to talk with him and keep him in a positive way. After all, we've both been through challenging times and living close."

Anna Katherine heard a gravel in his voice she had not heard before. She knew there was a weight on his heart. "I know it hurts you to have this happen to your friend. He was my friend, too. But you must know he did not do this to himself to get back at anyone, I feel sure of that. Whatever it was that got him to take his own life must have been so heavy a burden, he couldn't fight it anymore. We will know the truth of it and over time, it will settle with us. I know we will."

Paul nodded back and Anna Katherine spoke again.

"I've noticed something about you, Paul." Paul glanced up at her. "When we get into some of these life binding situations, you've just about always been able to express the feeling with words that settle the head with sayings from the heart. What can you say, or can you feel anything that can lift the fog that we're all feeling?"

"My only thought that comes to mind is this— 'Be a blessing to receive a blessing.' We can hold onto to his good memories and testify when we get to the church about him and praise his journey to Heaven. I think God will be able to do the rest." After a pause, Paul added, from the Scriptures, "And I shall rest from my Labor."

They spoke in unison, "Amen."

The night before the day of Grover's funeral, Anna Katherine let Paul sleep in the back bedroom, away from any of the house noise, as she went about getting some clean clothes for him to wear. His old bib jeans were always tattered and frayed, almost to the point of uselessness, so she regularly gathered clothes for him and had several things on hand for him to wear. His old worn out boots would do fine in the present situation.

As he finished coffee and a sweet roll in the morning, she got him to the back bathroom that had a tub and shower and a sitting stool in it for him to sit on while he showered with hot and cold water. He had showered there on two previous occasions more than a year apart. She showed him again how to get the water faucets to switch into shower mode and left him alone.

After drying off and fighting to get into clothes with some struggles, he emerged, and she got him to the porch and performed a quick comb and clip with scissors while his hair was still wet. He wasn't overly pleased to have himself in front of a mirror, where he could see himself close-up. Anna Katherine acknowledged that he was a man who lived without vanity. She went about her barbering as if he weren't there and that suited him, too.

The choice again would be between the Chicken Farm Road Cemetery and the Dog Trot Cemetery. The Chicken Farm was the newer of the two, twice as big, and twice as full. The older Dog Trot was a bit more "casual and relaxed," as described by the funeral director and seen on their pamphlet.

Without much at all in terms of money, the internment of Grover would be next to Lovety and the service would be a graveside only, to cut down on expenses. A church service and burial site rite had been given for Lovety's funeral but wouldn't be extended to Grover.

"Why not?" was Paul's question to Anna Katherine. Later, out of others' earshot, he added, "My guess is that some of these worshipers think it's a sin to die by suicide, so they didn't want their precious clean church to be soiled by his body."

As Anna Katherine drove to Dog Trot, she spotted the hearse coming from the mortuary and she followed it to the open grave. The hearse backed up to the opened ground and the driver shut off the engine. The sheriff and Game Warden Judson drove in and joined them at the site. The pastor came with the body. He stepped out of the hearse and waited a few minutes until everyone stopped milling about. He then moved to the rear, and the others joining him.

It was a small gathering. The clergyman's spoken words were few, casual, and without much empathy. After all, several mounds of disturbed earth in various conditions of settling could be seen in the cleared pasture, which was now claimed as church ground. In other times, it would surely have been a pauper's field. The collapse of the economy from the Crash of '29, and the decade that followed, the expansive droughts, the war years and its aftermath, all left the ground sterile and pockmarked with the accounting. Some meager markers were placed about when the resources allowed remembrance. To the more prosperous, it was simply known as Desolation Row.

"To all gathered here, I'll begin by saying the virtue and the vice, the happy and the sad, and all the days of marking one's life, all come to rest this day, and the journey to Glorious Heaven begins, and Grover McCullough will now rejoin his loving wife, Lovety Pate McCullough, and be with our Lord Jesus Christ. Amen."

A few more words were spoken, and they rang hollow to those who heard them. Each of the attendees were in self-contemplation and arose from those places in their minds when the clergy spoke and repeated the words from the first verse of "Amazing Grace"—

Amazing Grace, how sweet the sound,
That saved a wretch like me,
I once was lost, but now I'm found,
Was blind but now I see.

The hearse driver stepped forward when he recognized there were not enough able-bodied people to remove the pine casket from the back. He and the other pall bearers stepped forward a few more steps to place the box on the elevator frame that would lower the casket down. The old sheriff, the game warden, and Anna Katherine joined him as they stepped up together and rested the box on the frame. They then stepped back and away.

With a glance to the group, the clergyman could see that no one was planning further comment or needing Scripture, and so the body was lowered. After a pause, Anna Katherine reached for and held Paul's arm. As they moved away, Paul commented, "He'll do just fine. Character is destiny."

"I see those fellows over there heading this way to speak to you, so I'll excuse myself and go over to the church men for a word and give you some privacy." Anna Katherine winked.

The two old county officials came over and began sharing information about Grover's death and what had happened with the barn and the tractor, Grover's land, and his cancer. The conversation was not long, Anna Katherine observed from some distance. She continued to make small talk and glanced back over until the talking concluded. She knew the information he was getting and felt for the old man, her friend of many years, and expected that she would become a shepherd to him from here on out.

She met him as he got to the car and she didn't attempt conversation, as she knew he would be flush with emotions. Before he got into the car, he paused and looked at the billowing clouds in the sky and watched the purple martins happily chirping and sailing around. Anna Katherine watched him give one final glance back to where Grover and Lovety were laid to rest.

He summed it up, "A charity wrapped in dignity."

She looked at him and saw he had the most beautiful smile on his face.

After leaving the cemetery and going through the hardwood forest about a mile down the road, Paul seemed hesitant about talking to Anna Katherine.

"If I could have only imagined what was going on with old Grove, I would have tried to turn him away from the path he chose. I would never have guessed he had the cancer. I know he was scared of even the word. Me too, seeing how it's so very bad and when it takes hold of people, they seem to suffer right to the end. It's really bad."

"It scares me too, Paul."

They traveled on some.

Paul motioned to Anna Katherine to turn on the road to his place, as they reached the bend in the road.

"What kind of plans are you fixing to make, Paul? I want you to be with me for the next few days, for a bit."

"Why? I'm going back to my place to start sorting out and salvaging some things. I was thinking about that when we were standing over Grover's grave. I've almost lost my stove—it's in the water in the basement of that wore out old house, and I want to get it up in the dry and to the barn."

"Well, you won't be doing that today. That's too big a haul for your old wore out self, without some extra steady hands. Day after tomorrow Ollie will be coming by and we can take him over to your place. He can help us get that thing up out of there. Don't that sound like a better plan than you standing in the water on your old bird legs, wishing it would just fly in the sky over to the barn?" She had started to tease him a bit to break his thoughts from returning to any low mood.

He caught on quickly and got situated to make a good comeback. They had done this tit for tat for a long time. The verbal exchanges validated their closeness and caring towards each other. He shrugged off his melancholy and showed a twinkling eye to her by the time he got out of the car.

"Well, so take me on to my place. I got some small things to look after and you know where I'll be come tomorrow, then."

"No sense arguing with you. Your hearing is so bad, I can't hardly get you to rise to a fit anymore with those little mouse ears. Ha, ha to you."

"Ha, ha to you, back!" Paul said to her as he got out of the car and passed a smile.

She left him at the door of his barn and knew that leaving him to himself was the best thing for him. After all, that's the way he had been living before he went over to Grover's house and after the sharecropper women departed and moved on.

He's good at living with himself, so I got no complaint to give him that would cause him any more upset than what he is going through, now, Anna Katherine thought. *If the roof on that old shack gets any lower, he'll be living subterranean!*

Several days later when Anna Katherine went to see Paul and look in on his salvage project of getting useful things to the barn, she was surprised to see all the things that had been removed and laid out all over the place, in and out of the barn.

"Hey there, lady," Paul hailed her as she got out of her car.

"I see you got the stove over here installed and put back into use. How did you do that?"

"It was Officer Ollie that did most of the dragging and the set-up for me." Paul beamed.

She saw the stove flue had been attached and rigged to vent out the side of the barn. Paul had evidently been cooking on it, as evidenced from the leftovers in the skillet.

So, you old rascal, you're planning on moving into the barn and not planning on staying at my place, she thought to herself. *No sense in fighting him over it. He needs to just go on and do what pleases him from now on out, I suppose. Guess he will be comfortable with all his things around him.*

"I see you saved some of those sitting chairs from the house and got the kitchen table, too. You better slow up a bit, you'll work yourself to a frazzle. I know you."

"Well, it keeps me from thinking so much, is about all."

"I know you're always full of thinking but put that away for a spell and talk to me," Anna Katherine coaxed.

Paul took the longest pause before he responded.

"When I first saw those women sitting on the edge of the feed dock, I could tell, I could see that she was a unique but somewhat complicated person and it came from her smile, I guess."

"Go on, then."

"So, they loaded up in my stake bed that day and I watched her watching me. It wasn't a glance or two that showed any fear of me or the unknown as to where she was going in my truck. She seemed to be able to look into me and understand that I was able to give kindness without any expectation or obligation and she was pleased. It was like we had this connection and an instant friendship was formed."

The fog of age seemed to momentarily clear from his mind and, with a lucid reckoning, he was able to articulate his thoughts and reclaim those moments from that past.

"In this story of my broken heart I found a hope and a promise that our love gave us a better vision of a greater life to live."

"You seem to be describing a unique person, Paul."

"Yes, she really is, or was. She and I shared our thoughts freely between us after just a short time and we trusted each other with our secrets and gave each other privacy when it was needed."

"From the people I talked to, they told me you and her were almost always together after those three came to your place. The townies would see you and her together a lot in the truck, going about. So, then what, Paul?"

"After we made it past all the Depression years and then fought through the droughts and we could get back on our feet, I could sense it was ending and she had to go and find that next bend in the road that wouldn't include me. She had the yearning to travel and Mark Twain took her from me. I was tied to this land and she wasn't." He paused. "We were together almost twenty years."

"So, what happened? What went on with her companions? What about them?"

"The other two, Sophie and Bernice? They had the yearnings to go as well, but I don't think it was as strong with them. From what I overheard, here and there, they seemed to be determined to head home first and then see what was going to happen with the war coming on. After being here almost twenty years, there was the fear of coming home and finding a parent had passed away and having to accept the grief and the guilt.

"They were quite a pair, I can tell you that," Paul remembered. "They would always initiate something and had no hesitation to jump into anything. They seemed to keep Mayvis shaking or scratching her head.

"As they say in that song, 'How Ya Gonna Keep them Down on the Farm'—they suddenly jumped up and formed a line and started a sort of tap dance routine, in unison, mind you, like they had practiced it fifty times. They would stomp their feet and spin around like they was on stage or something. They were quite amazing. We were amazed! The moonshine lit everybody up."

Anna Katherine was puzzled, "How could they do that kind of dancing and all, just like that?"

"They met each other in Columbus, Ohio and formed a great friendship. Sophie's dad was a coal miner in West Virginia, and he came over the Cumberland Road with the family and worked in a carriage factory in Columbus. Her mom worked in a rooming house that had college students boarding there.

"They met when they were both in that boarding house, and the boarding house was going to put on entertainment for the students. So, that's how they met. Bernice and her family left

Baltimore to go west and traveled by packet boat to Cincinnati. Then they went on to Columbus."

After a somewhat stoic pause, Paul ruminated. "At times, I feel that I didn't grieve my own mother's death enough, because of all the turmoil that went on at her passing, with fires, the deaths that occurred, and all."

"I understand you and I can see it's all these times that's slowly worn you down," Anna Katherine sympathized. "Paul, you do know you are getting long in the tooth? With Grover going the way he did, it puts extra strain on you. It's done that to all of us. That's why I want you to stay with me for a bit. I want you to change what you been seeing. That old house is almost flat and so are you, old man." She chuckled. "Agreed, then?"

"I am now as old as a child again, and I understand nothing, Anna."

"That's what I'm saying. You're getting my house or no house."

Chapter 33

At morning coffee in his office, the old sheriff and the game warden reviewed what had been going on with Paul since they found him after Grover's suicide, burrowed again, inside his collapsed house.

"I did get someone to repair Paul's DeSoto and it's ready to be taken back to his barn. He can use it again. My knee is acting up with arthritis and I can hardly get around. Maybe you can take it out there, the next time you go that way."

Ollie responded, "I'm actually headed out that way today to talk with him about deciding what he wants to do, as far as land use."

"Well, we did go over some of that with him before, and I thought he might go for the idea of cutting some walnuts for tax money."

"I'll put it to him again and see which way he may want to go. I'm also going to suggest to him to let the state have access to his fields to cut hay and use it for cattle feed if some farmer gets short during the winter. His place does back up to the state forest and my crews can easily cut his hay when we're cutting right of ways."

The sheriff injected another idea.

"When you go over to Anna Katherine's house, why don't

you take these two jail trustees I have here at the jail with you? One of them can ride with you and the other can drive Paul's car over there. They need a bit more community service before the judge will let them go free. You can use them for something or another."

"All right then." He motioned to the two jail trustees to load up. "Follow me out and I'll get you into some fresh air, at any rate."

Anna Katherine was on her porch when the game warden drove in, followed by the DeSoto and the two jail trustees in their county coveralls. They waited as the game warden went to the porch and talked.

"He's getting slow and barely gets around, Ollie. You better hurry up and get him to a decision. Paul has changed so much since his friend died. Have you noticed that?"

"Yes, he's just worn out, as I see it."

"Well, sir, let me put a point on it. I've known him for years and I know you have, too. He didn't have much of a perspective on anything when he was younger. He would find a saying or something and then just go on about himself. But now, he's way more reflective and seems to have a wisdom beyond his seventy-four years. I wonder where it comes from."

"Be a blessing to receive a blessing," the game warden said, citing one of Paul's frequent sayings. "You should ask him about that."

She responded, "I intend to. He's over at his place, so you can get him to his car when you drive past, on the way back to town. He's supposed to be staying over here with me but he's always putting up a fuss. Without that car to use, it's me that has been driving him back and forth."

◇   ◇   ◇

As they pulled into the driveway, they spotted Paul with a small wagon full of things he was pulling to the barn. Ollie honked the horn to warn Paul he was behind him. When Paul turned around in response to the noise, for a moment, Ollie recognized the old man's movements revealed how old Paul had become. He seemed much older, just as Anna Katherine had described him earlier.

"I'll take a day or so to decide if and when I'll want to cut some of those walnut trees down and plank out some boards for curing."

"That's fine with me. I want to discuss land use with you, too. I see you're not running or grazing any more calves in here, so I have an idea for you, and you tell me what you think. Since your land backs up to the state forest, I suggest we, the state, could get in here and regularly mow the pastures that are close to the road when we mow the right of ways. If you let us mow and bale the hay, we could take that hay as payment for the work and swap out even, if you would like to."

"I can see that would work out for me, all right."

"I brought these two fellows from the county lock-up with me and I can get them out on the fence line to walk it and take out the barb wire so's it doesn't get caught up in the mower equipment ahead of any cutting. They would pull out all the fence posts that are still standing and it would make the forest and the meadows all go back to the way it was, as the Lord set it up in the first place."

Ollie smiled at Paul and he nodded gratefully. And with that, the two men left the car and headed back to the jail house.

Minutes later, Paul became dizzy and fell on the ground and laid there for a few minutes to get his bearings. Once stable, he got back up, got his cane, and left the wagon where it was and went to the barn and laid down. He felt odd but soon was okay. He laid there the rest of the day, even though it was mid-afternoon, and he awoke the next morning still in the bed he hadn't left.

"When you didn't come home, I thought you might have had trouble with that car, even though they said they fixed it," Anna Katherine said to him, as she found him lying on the bed in the barn the next day. Her suspicions were raised.

"I'm just waiting for Officer Ollie to come back over this morning with them two jail trustees and do some work on the fences around here. I'm gonna allow them to cut hay."

"Well, buddy, I'm taking you with me this morning and get you a good meal and let Ollie and those two turnips take over their own job. We'll take the truck back and leave your car till later."

On the way back to Anna Katherine's farm, she continued her conversation with Paul about his life.

"You said to me the other day, 'I am now as old as a child, again, and I understand nothing.' What did you mean by that?"

Paul was sitting next to her, looking like he was in a daze, until she spoke.

"I'm thinking. And thinking back, I seem to think that I've lived a life that's divided into two basic parts. You know, like the yolk and the egg, but I never have stopped to diagnose which part is which. Sounds funny, huh?"

"Depends. You've got to give me more to go on."

"From the beginning of everything I could remember, from my earliest time as a kid, I wanted to capture my own youth. It simply was because it was all I had. I was always thinking about how I was going to do it. I had my mother's love but my dad's wrath. It was kisses from one and slaps and punches from the other. It's hard trying to find a path when it's always just a circle."

"So, tell me about the other part, the egg, or the yolk part, or whatever."

"I'm always traveling, and I never was having to start." Paul suddenly stiffened and blinked. "Well, I never have thought about ever describing it in terms of using words. Hmm, this is unusual. Yes, that's what it is, I think. Anna Katherine, what do you think?

He is honestly asking me that question that I don't know how to answer, but he won't be concerned with anything I give him back. Like usual, he's already moved on in his mind and will be on to something else, here in a minute or so.

Game Warden Oliver Judson signed an agreement, as Agent for the State of Indiana, with Paul Chandler to allow the state to cut hay from Paul Chandler's fields and remove any fencing and barbed wire, and any other obstructions that would interfere with mowing.

The sheriff arranged to use jail trustees to do the debris clearing. The days started and ended approximately eight hours later. Fencing was removed from the turkey brooder days. Then the barbed wire was cut and rolled into bundles that could be handled and loaded by two men.

Felled and downed trees surrounded most of the pastures. The dead falls were slinged and pulled by tractor to the fence line to keep the field open for plowing and mowing. In the years before everyone working the fields got too old to keep up with the maintenance, the downed trees offered easy access to cutting firewood that could be loaded and skidded down the hill to the house and burned. The remainder rotted away and became shelter to birds and other small animals during the winter and places for nesting at other times in the brush.

Shoals Bluff was a tranquil place and it was anchored at the end of the high meadow by the huge open-boughed sycamore that was the eternal resting place of Paul's mother, Iletta. The slope down at the tree line descended and followed along a limestone ridge that protruded and formed a bluff at the road. In earlier days, before barbed wire came along, a split rail fence stood proud across the low end of the meadow and served as the containment for livestock. A few fence posts remained, and some wire was all that was needed to be removed to clear the field. A small game trail followed the protruding rock face along the ground and then turned and went inside an opening in the rock.

Chapter 34

~~~~~~~~~~~~~~~~~~~~~~~~~~~~~~~~~~~~

"I'm here to check on your patient. How is old Paul today?"

"He's not as chipper as I would want him to be, Ollie."

"I came by to give you'uns a progress report on the clearing work we're doing, and it should be finished in another few days. We have some barbed wire to remove from the bluff side of the high meadow and get the hay cut off from around the big syca-more and then down to the road. Paul's doin' poorly?"

"It's like he's out of gas. He's on the back porch in the rocker and just wants to sit there and be left alone. He's into one of his thinking spells. I'll pass it on to him, though."

"I guess I'll let him be, then, and see him in a few days."

"I'm going to take him back to town to get him a checkup and see if he'll take a flu shot. He's never had one that he knows of. With it getting cool already, I don't want him all puny going into cold weather and be down all winter. The last time the doctors saw Paul, they gave him an iron shot and said his tonsils were swollen from infection. It was common in earlier days to get them out, but he didn't ever have much doctoring. His bone density is way down and he was told to drink more milk, but he doesn't have a way to keep milk from spoiling. Since he's been with me, he's drinking it some. And now he's got arthritis. Well, we'll see you whenever."

The next morning, the sheriff started the trustees working, beginning at the top of the high meadow, at the big sycamore tree. The two men noticed the grave of Paul's mother and went about their work to get the barbed wire free from the posts in the ground and pulled it off the occasional big trees that it was nailed to. That saved extra work when digging fence posts. Here and there, they found short pieces of an earlier run of barbed wire that was much older and different. It confirmed that this pasture was being used a long time before the stringing of wire.

Working their way down the slope of the pasture and pulling wire where it ran alongside the limestone wall, they noticed the rabbit trail went into an opening in the limestone face. It could easily be large enough for a person to enter, except for it being blocked off with stacks of old lumber, barn rafters, cut logs, and a young sassafras tree with some sprouts growing up in front of the sealed opening. It was nailed up all kinds of ways with lots of incredibly old barbed wire holding it together, seeming to make the point that no one was supposed to go in there. The same type of wire they found earlier had been used to seal up this entrance.

It may have been constructed to keep livestock from getting into it and getting stuck, or to keep kids from getting inside. It was a curious location to find and the jail trustees were mildly anxious to see what was there and why it was sealed. It could always be rebuilt if it needed to be.

The trustees managed to get a lot of it pulled out of the entrance, but the end of the day came, and they needed a flashlight to do a little exploring. At least this was better, they felt, than sitting on a cold steel bench all day in the jail.

"So why do you need a flashlight? You're not trying to tunnel out and get away?" The sheriff laughed at the absurdity of his own joke. After they explained to him what they had found, he became curious enough to go with them to see the hole in the ground. After all, it was boring to sit around the barn in the shade and watch them working for eight hours a day.

"On second thought," as the sheriff saw the sealed entrance up close, "this may have something in there worth giving a look." He beckoned for them to open it, but first had them cut down the sassafras saplings around the entrance and get them out of the way.

"If you can get enough of it roped up, let's pull it out with the truck and make it easier on everybody, what do you say?"

Most of the heavy timbers stayed together and came out. The opening was a bit larger than they had originally imagined, once it was unblocked. Clearly, a man could fit in the opening, though barely.

The sheriff saw a moment to have some fun with the trustees and held out the flashlight for someone to take it and said, "If that hole is that large you might find you a bobcat in there. They like to get scrappy, I've heard, when they get cornered. So, who wants to go in and take a look?"

Both men hesitated and then the braver of the two took the light and walked cautiously to the entrance and stepped in.

"What you got in there? Can you see something?"

"Just a minute for me to adjust my eyes. Yep, there's stuff in here. It looks like somebody's been living in here, but a long time ago. It's bigger in here than you think, that's for sure. I'm gonna bring you something." He came out holding what looked like a leather pouch with something in it.

The pouch was an old and very brittle hair leather, with a stiff strap. The sheriff reached in and pulled out some cards, which turned out to be several tintypes, old metal square plates that were used to print photographs before film was produced on glass or paper. Some were rusted and stuck together and two or three were loose and remarkably well-preserved. They were pictures of Civil War soldiers. These pictures from the cave told him that the site had some significance and it should be looked at with a better pair of eyes than he had, and by someone who was a bit nimbler, as well. And perhaps a little thinner, too.

This was going to be right down the game warden's jurisdiction. Occasionally, archeological sites were discovered and artifacts found that could offer historical relevance to the state's history. Being a game warden kept him outside and in the woods a lot of the time. When things like this came up, it was the one of the more interesting aspects of his duties for the county and the state. Hunters, campers, and trappers usually made most of these types of finds.

"Officer Oliver Judson will now oversee this place and we'll pull off of here. Besides, he's a bit younger and he'll be able to get in there and have a better look around, do some inventory. I kind of thought it might be an Indian campout, but I guess not. So, we'll just leave it to him."

"Well, that's a bit of interesting news," the game warden commented, after hearing about the find. "I need to get up there and look at this and let's see what we've uncovered. Once I can see what it all is, I'll go ask Paul and Anna Katherine if they know anything about this."

When he arrived at Paul's farm, he didn't see anyone around. There were no cars and the sheriff's truck wasn't there, so he continued up into the high meadow in his vehicle and drove down the sloped field till he saw the rock abutment. The old lumber and timbers were restacked in the corner, covering the opening. He got out of the truck, thinking *this looks like it could have some secrets or something in there, so let's have a look.*

Officer Judson was not as old as Paul or the sheriff, and he was able-bodied and fit from walking the woods, roads, and steep banks regularly. Pulling some of the boards aside and looking inside, the mid-afternoon sun cast a bit of light well inside the opening and he could see lots of things all around the floor and on boxes, crates, and kegs. He decided he would return for a closer look with a light and probably a lantern. *There's enough stuff in here I'll need a notepad to write some of this down.*

He left the entrance open and found his notebook and a flashlight in the glove box and re-entered the cave. He was delighted to be the first person to be in such a place that certainly was older than a hundred years, he thought. *Those tin types will date to the Civil War, so that'll be a hundred and ten years, right there. This place may be even older than that.*

Slowly going around the cave with his light to see how big the place was and how much stuff was in there, he decided to begin his listing and do a cursory sketch for the time being. The list wouldn't need to be very detailed. Someone else would need to come in and cover everything in more detail later.

He began listing the different items he was seeing with his flashlight. More light would be helpful, and his batteries were already weak. He started talking out loud, as if noting his list of finds to someone writing them down.

"Bundles of pelts. Yeaooow, a family Bible! Crocks. Two rifles—Civil War, no doubt. Trace chains, glass kerosene lantern. Shovel heads and ax heads, whip saws, splitting wedges, sledge.

Ah, horseshoes! Wise man. Steel traps, about eighteen or so and a fire ring. Come on flashlight, keep going.

"WHOA, whoa, whoa! I do not believe this!"

It was unmistakable. There were three bodies. They were wrapped and bound in burlap and laid on an outcropping shelf in the corner of the cave. Ollie assessed the situation, noting that two of the bodies were adults and one was a small child, he surmised not more than two years old. The bodies were wrapped in burlap, which told him that these bodies were not Indians, and so must be settlers, whether on this land or settlers just passing through on their way West. If that were the case, he was hoping the Bible would provide clues about their identity.

He returned to the truck, made some notes about his findings, and then went back to the cave and picked up the Bible. It was big. He looked through it carefully and discovered many letters between its pages. In the front and back of the Bible, Ollie saw a handwritten family tree with names and dates of many people, though several branches were blank.

Without hesitation, he drove down out of the field and went straight to Anna Katherine's farm to show her what he had found. He wanted to tell her about it first and then give her the Bible. It had to be given special care because of its age and handled delicately.

When Anna Katherine came to the door, she saw a curious and happy look on Officer Ollie's face.

"What in the world's got you here with a big grin on your face? Are you going to get married?"

"Something just as exciting. Sit down, I have a story to tell you."

"Well, go ahead and tell me something. You are going to bust a seam if I don't."

"The sheriff had those guys out at Paul's to clear off stumps and barbed wire and such for mowing and they found something—a cave over on the Shoal's Bluff that's down from the high meadow. The opening was blocked by boards wrapped in barbed wire and they found a hole behind it. One of the men looked in and found a hanging pouch with some old tin types in it, soldier pictures from the Civil War—" he paused.

"Well, where are they? I got to see 'em!"

"Where is Paul? He needs to hear this, too."

"Well, he's back out there, over to the barn. You didn't see him?"

"I didn't see a car or anything, so I didn't think anyone was around."

"Well, I took him this morning and he was probably sleeping or something. So, tell me about what?"

"I uncovered a cave full of things—and three bodies."

"Lord above, you cannot be serious?"

"Oh, yes I am. I'm guessing they've been there since the Civil War, maybe earlier. I saw some strange tools and all kinds of things. I have one thing that's more important than anything. It looks to be a family Bible."

"Oh, my word!"

Ollie went to the truck and opened the door and gently lifted the large book and brought it to Anna Katherine. She held it carefully and then sat down with it in a chair and gently opened it up. The inside flap showed the drawing of the family tree and lots of signatures and dates.

"Officer Judson, you are an amazing man to have found this and have handed it to me. I'm overwhelmed. This is so much information that it's gonna take a while to even uncover it. Look at the letters in here and it's got pictures, as well."

She took a breath and sat back to think a moment.

"I can't wait to tell Paul about this and see what he knows about these people."

"First I want to ask him about that cave and to see if he knew about it. As a kid, he must have known something. He was all over his farm and must have known about it. Until he was injured, there was no reason he wouldn't have known. And with all the old lumber stacked in that wedge, someone had to have put it there, especially because it was all nailed up with lots of barbed wire. There are questions about it, all right."

"Well, first off, I'll go over to Paul's and fetch him home and we can explore what this thing is. I bet he might get excited over this, too. So, what about you? What are you going to do?"

"I'll go back to the district office and file a field report and I think what we should do is let the DHPA know we have a site they could look at—that's Indiana's Division of Historic Preservation and Archeology. They do the accounting and tracking of sites for the state. They have professionals who'll know about the artifacts in the cave. They have computers."

So, off they went in different directions, each with curiosity and a bit of excitement. When Anna Katherine pulled up to the barn, she honked her horn to let Paul know she was there, but he didn't come out of the barn, which she had expected, so she went in.

What she found did not make her happy. On the table that had been moved from the collapsed house to the barn were various recovered items from the house. It was obvious to her that Paul had been into the collapsed house to recover more things, even things that he wouldn't use. His "stuff" was accumulating again.

She started looking for Paul. He wasn't in the barn. He couldn't walk very well these days, so she knew he was close. She checked the house—the collapsed house—and found him somewhat stuck, under an old dresser that had shifted over and pinned him. He looked up and smiled at her as she called out his name.

"Lordy Paul, what happened? How long have you been like this?"

"I'm okay. I just let this dresser shift on me, that's all. You don't need to worry."

"I need to tell you that all of this stuff you have here doesn't need to be brought over to the barn. You're spending too much time and energy on these things. They can just sit here where they are. You're spending too much time thinking about your past when you need to concentrate on where you're going."

It wasn't hard getting him out and he could have done it himself except for his bad leg and not having any leverage or strength left. He might have been there overnight, but he wouldn't tell her. His clothes had a smell that told her he had been "caught short" and would need to change clothes and take a bath.

Once she freed him, Paul could hardly move. He was very weak. She saw him looking and smelling the mess he'd made. He needed a shave, too. *All that old white stubble on his face—he's going to be a handful to get into my truck.*

Once she got him home and cleaned up, Anna Katherine put him to bed for the afternoon. He ate some soup, then got the chills and so stayed in bed and remained there until the next day when Officer Ollie showed up.

"He isn't well," she started in, as Ollie entered the kitchen porch. "I found him stuck in that old heap of a house and from all the signs, it looked like he'd been there the night. I think he may be close to pneumonia, so I'll have to watch him. I had to dig him out."

"Anna Katherine, I'm sorry you were the one to have to find him. And I know he can be quite a handful. Can I do anything? Let me know." He took off his hat and sat down and had coffee with her.

As she returned from the other room, she was carrying the big Bible, and sat it down on the table. "I haven't had a chance to look at this book, with chasing him around. Maybe we can look at it a little ourselves. How did you do with contacting the state office? What about those dead bodies and what happened with that?"

"So, you know it is legal to disturb the ground in a cemetery to find human remains when you have a license or a permit. I should be able to get that, but have you been up there to look?"

"Not really. I been chasing Paul around. I would like to go

up there and look around for myself, but now that Paul is down, I may need to stick around. I know him, and he's not goin' to let pneumonia and one bad leg keep him down!" They both laughed.

Looking at the Bible, on the inside cover was the family tree, and something caught her eye as she read through some of the names. The ink was weak or dissolved or smeared in spots, due to water and mold, and the sheer passage of time.

At the bottom of the tree, where the newest entries would be, were the names recording a new marriage.

Anna Katherine had a magnifying glass handy and used it as she read,

"Something, something 'of marriage between Balcom Hitches and Norveena News—' It's smeared and unreadable, this part. News, something."

She looked up at Ollie with a questioning brow. "That's funny, but I remember that name, I've heard it at some time, probably when I was a kid. Norveena. You wouldn't get that name mixed up with any other, now would you?"

He chuckled, "Yes, it's rather unique. What else does it say?"

"Boy, I don't know. This will take some time just to try to get the bits and pieces from it and see if we can, somehow, put them together some way to make sense of it. It's already got me curious."

"Well, go tell Paul that you and I are going out for a while, and get a flashlight. No, get a lantern if you have it. It will throw more light. I want to see it with more light, anyway."

They left Anna Katherine's farm and headed out to the high meadow on Paul's farm and drove down the hill to the stack of old boards and timbers leaning against a limestone wall.

"This is it?"

"It's behind all that lumber. It sure doesn't look like much from here and you can't tell from this junk that anything would be there, but it is."

With some anticipation Anna Katherine squeezed into the dark crack. Ollie handed her the lantern and they went inside. It had an old musty cave smell and the same smell some people knew from childhood of their own dirt-floored coal basements.

Now that they had light, they could see there were two rooms that stored lots of things used for living and surviving—two stacks of stretched and dried animal furs that were partially disintegrated and brittle from age, and old sacks that had held seeds, flour and grain which had been eaten through by animals. There were steel traps and two Kentucky long rifles and one Civil War cap and ball rifle. There were small kegs for whiskey, black powder, or nails.

Ollie whispered, "Over here, this is where they are," and he pointed to a ledge that revealed three somewhat decomposed burlap cocoons with a body inside each one. She was anxious but not scared and looked at them carefully for a bit before she stepped closer.

"I wonder why they're here, instead of being buried out somewhere else. Ollie, do you think that's odd?"

"I don't know that yet. I don't quite know how to figure a lot of this stuff out. I'm usually around animals and people that are alive."

"Look at this, Ollie," She pointed to the flat rocks that held the corpses. At one corner of the flat limestone point sat a perfectly whole, five-armed petrified starfish. It was as if it was a toy placed there by the deceased child. It was about four inches across.

"It's rather eerie, but it looks kind of natural," Anna Katherine whispered.

The two of them climbed back outside the hole and squinted into the shining sunlight until their eyes adjusted. Ollie said, "The state can get a qualified professional to assist us and do research. That's what they're equipped for. They can do historic, prehistoric, and even underwater discovery."

Chapter 35

In the passing weeks, Paul began recovering from his bout with pneumonia. Ollie and Anna Katherine sat with him and Ollie asked what he could remember of the early days of his farm. With some hesitation, Paul thought about the questions they had asked him.

"Ollie, I'm going back on an old memory, but I do seem to remember a time when we used that upper pasture you're asking about. We had a shed up there that we kept old harnesses and such in. I was told it was a place where the Indians used to go, and it was dangerous to be up there after dark. It scared me so I hated to go up there."

"Is that all?"

"Well, no. Like I said I was very young. I do remember I had to go up there and help tear it down because it was going to rot away. We stacked the boards all up in that crevice and left them. Later, I saw it all wired together with barbed wire, but it was just left alone. Never saw anyone around it. Beyond that, that's all I know."

It was time, Anna Katherine and Ollie agreed, to tell Paul about the cave behind the shed and what they had found. The things of importance such as the Bible, the tools, and the corpses made Paul ask a few questions, which they tried to answer. Yet, it remained a mystery. Having the state's Department of Historic Preservation and Archeology division working on it would hopefully yield some answers, they were certain. They also felt the big Bible and its family tree held a lot of clues that would be important.

Paul thought Anna Katherine and Oliver Judson seemed to be awfully close. He saw them as they got out of the Game Warden's truck with papers in their hands, heading towards her house. *It's the laughter that gives it away.* He winked and smiled to himself.

"We got the scoop from the state on the Indian Cave, as you call it. Here's what they have to say. To begin with, Paul," Anna Katherine read, "your great grandfather, so to speak, Iletta's grandfather, Balcom Hitches, and his father, worked in shipbuilding in the Jeffersonville and Louisville area in the 1830s and they bought the land you've been living on. So, what you were told all those years by your no-account dad that the land was his was a lie. He claimed it was his by marriage to your mother, which it wasn't. He never owned anything.

"They were here in the 1830s and probably a bit cautious about the Indians living in the area. It wasn't until 1846 that the Miami Indians ceded their land. That cave was the Hitches' place for protection. It had water in it at times, and it would have been nearly impossible to attack them or dig them out. They stayed in there for quite some time while they worked the land, dug the well that's in the front yard, and then built the house and barn."

"In 1846, this says, the Miami Indians signed a peace treaty and gave up the land. That was before the Civil War. Some of the tools in the cave were commonly used in shipbuilding, is how they confirmed it. They found a poke wedged in a pocket, in the cave, and the coins in it were dated after the War."

"The two bodies they suspect are your mom's grandparents. They were put there for safety, before anyone could find a place to bury them. They may not have been buried on purpose because of the Indians. That cave would be considered a burial ground and it couldn't be disturbed."

"The small body is a female of about eighteen months to two years old. Likely, it was your grandmother's sister, which would be your great aunt. Obviously, she didn't live very long and probably died of some sickness. She may have died before your grandmother was born, but just not buried."

"Now, you may not realize this," she continued, "but my grandmother was another sister of your grandmother. So's that's got you and I being second cousins. I knew we must have been family somehow, but I didn't know until now how we were connected.

"The state people noticed, also, that all of those walnut trees growing below the bluff were most likely planted there by your great-grandparents. All or most of those trees are of the same age. The walnut trees that you all cut down not too long ago at Adrian's or Grover's, I can't remember, were planted there at the same time, too. There was a long-time connection between that place and yours. And they mentioned that the big sycamore at the top of the hill, where Iletta is buried, was maybe over three hundred years old."

She looked up from her papers and exclaimed, "Isn't that something? You can look at the trees and they can tell us a story about what was going on way back then. It's like they're talking to us." She looked at Ollie, "We need to listen to what they're saying to us."

Paul remembered looking up at the walnut trees from the bed of the wagon on the way home after his accident. He was moved by this news and then again, he was still somewhat weak from being in bed for several days. Hearing what the state people had put together, he was ruminating on the details, which mentally pulled him back to the tumultuous times in his life.

"Well, Paul, what do you think about all them apples?" Anna Katherine asked. "I think it's exciting to know we got straight connections to our land. Having those people in that cave set it all straight for me. I never knew about any of my kin like that. Back in those days everybody just traveled around and saw lots of country and lots of places to throw down wherever to make their own place. Boy, what would it have been like to travel around this glorious land like that, huh, Paul?"

"It worked out. You said that he took all the land from my mom and she got nothing. You mean he swindled her somehow?"

"It was a bit of stretching, I guess, on my part, but the conclusion was spot on. I knew from Indiana history when I was in school that women were denied rights of ownership of land, even inheriting it from their family, in the nineteenth century. Your mom's granddad would have had their land purchase passed on to her or her sister, except she was a woman and only had rights to a third of it."

"We'll never know. So, let it stay."

"Well, it's yours now, full up and around the world, you might say."

Paul pondered. "I didn't have to travel far away; my adventures all came to me."

Anna Katherine and Oliver Judson left Paul alone and went arm and arm to work up a little surprise project before Paul got well enough to get out and about. Ollie knew where the ruins of an old homestead was located. It had a little family graveyard at one time, though the caskets were re-located off the property. But the decorative wrought iron fencing was still there, and he bought it from the landowners with the intention of erecting the new wrought iron fencing and establishing a family cemetery on Paul's farm, on the hill where the big sycamore stood. It would then be ready to inter the bodies from the cave to join Paul's mother. Anna Katherine thought it was a marvelous idea and confirmed what she had already suspected about this man she was growing fond of, that he was very generous and kind-hearted.

They made a trip to the high meadow to measure out the fencing and plan how to plot the perimeter. Once they got the specifics, they left and went to downtown Shoals.

Just after they left and started to town, the old DeSoto pulled up to the barn. Paul got out and went into the barn to start a fire in the cast-iron stove. His intentions were to stay the night.

Ollie and Anna shared an agreeable afternoon and evening together. They drove to the neighboring town of Washington for a sit-down dinner and some cozy conversation. They had not afforded themselves that type of luxury till that evening.

Around nine-thirty the next morning, Ollie's office phone rang, and he picked it up and listened for a few moments, then drove to Anna Katherine's house with his emergency lights on, honking the horn as he drove in. She was standing on the porch with an apprehensive look on her face. She had just discovered that Paul was not at her home. She ran to his car.

"Don't turn the car off. We must go now. It's Paul."

Anna was truly frightened, and Ollie had additional bad news. The two jail trustee workers at the farm had found Paul lying face down on the pathway leading up to his mother's grave. And that's apparently where he died. They found him there about eight a.m. They also called the sheriff on the two-way radio but got no answer.

Ollie and Anna drove up in the meadow and saw the two workers come out from the shade of the sycamore tree, then stop over the body to wait for them.

"Paul—" Anna pleaded with him to be all right and Ollie reached down to him and lifted his head and felt that his body was cold. They were both full of tears. As Anna sat with Paul's body, the workers took Ollie down away from the hillside several yards and showed him something in the grass. Ollie picked up a lard bucket with the lid off and saw beans and cornbread in it. It had syrup drizzled over the food.

The men pointed out to him a broken bottle of beer on the path. Paul's burled-top walking cane was laying close by and it was snapped in half. Ollie looked closer and surveyed the scene. He noticed Paul's bad leg was awkward as he lay there and saw that his bad foot was broken above the ankle and completely snapped.

The hillside was strewn with loose papers that were scattered and blown about by the wind and captured in the tall grass.

"It looked like Paul had tried to climb the hill yesterday evening," he said to the group, "possibly before dark, to eat the supper he brought with him and read his big Mark Twain book he carried along. The signs show that he must have stepped on a big rock or tripped over one and his bad ankle turned and broke, instead of making a sprain because of the weak bones in his foot. He went down and maybe crawled towards the headstone for a bit. He probably just became exhausted and was unable to move further. He was there for some time and probably went into shock and died from exposure sometime between last night and early this morning after sunrise."

Ollie used his radio to contact the sheriff's office. The sheriff himself was on medical leave, and so a deputy was sent to investigate. After a brief meeting and conference and two photographs were taken, Paul's body was wrapped and secured in the bed of the truck. The deputy offered Anna Katherine a ride home, but she said she would ride with Paul's body, as Ollie drove them to the funeral home.

The game warden had the authority to issue a death certificate in circumstances like this, and so he issued the document and the body was received. The mortuary had the duty of preparing the body according to its own schedule. The embalming would be delayed by a few days and Paul would be interred in his family graveyard, next to his mother and their kinfolk from the cave. Anna and Ollie would cover the costs.

Ollie took the two trustees back to the abandoned cemetery to erect the cast iron fence. A grave site had to be prepared and dug for the body. Some maintenance mowing was needed and that was completed, too.

The three of them had been bound together and now a blanket of grief covered Anna and Ollie. The event of Paul's death by default fell to them, and so they wanted to honor this fine old man with a funeral service.

Several families from Anna's church came to show respect that day of the funeral, at the sycamore tree. These were people who knew Paul from the times he attended the sorghum makings. Many senior citizens living in and around Shoals attended, having known the family over the years. Several Amish families came also, as Paul was remembered from those early days of working on their farms before the World War II years. It was a gathering that supported both grief and celebration of a hard life well-lived.

EPILOGUE

~~~~~~~~~~~~~~~~~~~~~~~~~~~~~~~~~~~~

The inscription on Paul's headstone read *I Wanted to Capture Youth Because That Was All I Had.*

Paul Chandler, before he died, had deeded all his land holdings and earthly possessions to Anna Katherine. Not much later, she became Anna Katherine Judson. She and Ollie became stewards of the land, and many years later, they began making arrangements to hold the land in a newly formed non-profit organization, The Sycamore Land Trust, designed to protect the large grove of black walnut trees and the large sycamore tree above the family cemetery.

And the cemetery became the momentary vessel that marked the passing of its family moving into the future and beyond. The gravestones temporarily scribed the ground in a cluster that begat remembrances.

Geological interests and historical curiosity blended, and speleological groups went to explore the caves of Shoals Bluff. Spelunkers, under supervision of the Indiana DHPA, were allowed to access the opening, and what they found was a semi-connected cave system with periodic open seams that emerged into three more caverns. Two of those had been habitations in those earlier times. It may have been one of the earliest colonies that were able to survive in the area that helped to establish the town later known as Shoals.

A lot of interest was generated because of the adjoining caves and the additional artifacts found. Because of this, the cave gained a notable significance and the state wanted to create a formal historical site for public visitation and viewing.

Anna Katherine and Ollie settled down after Paul's burial. They counted their blessings as newlyweds and spoke often about Paul and missed him greatly. Their love deepened between them and they regretted the fact that their age would prevent them from having any children of their own and starting a family.

They felt something was missing but didn't know what it was. There was a longing in their hearts, and they missed seeing Paul at his house. Looking at the collapsed house and rubble pile that greeted them when they were on the land, they decided to build another house using the foundation of Paul's old one, leaving the fieldstone walls and the dirt floor. In less than a year the house was finished, with porches on three sides. It was empty but filled, they said, with Paul's presence. A year passed.

A serendipitous encounter occurred at the general store when Ollie and Anna bumped into the same clergyman who had married them, the same person who had spoken at Paul's funeral. He was with a young woman he introduced as Sharron. Axil, her twin brother, came over and introductions were extended. After pleasantries were exchanged, everyone departed on their separate ways.

The clergyman confided to Anna the next day by phone that he was desperate to find a place where the twins could live. They had lived in foster care for many years and were never adopted as a pair. They had been recently discharged from the home and it was closed, due to the death of the facilitator. The clergyman lived by himsel in two rooms, as it was.

That night was a time for decisions, and, as the new house was finished and sitting vacant, Axil and Sharron moved in. Axil could work with Ollie as his helper and Sharron had a surprise, unbeknownst to anyone.

Anna learned, with a bit of digging, that the twins had just turned 15.

The house and the property were to be inherited by the twins and they were to be the ones to decide what the perpetual use would be allowed and managed by the state as the historical site's guardian.

Sadly, Sharron lost her life during delivery at childbirth. The unnamed newborn lived almost three weeks. Ollie and Anna were ready to accept the infant as they would a grandchild, but it was not to be. Oliver built a small coffin with Paul's walnut lumber and the infant was placed to rest between Paul and Sharron. At the infant's feet, two favorite spotted dogs were buried. To her open side, Axil's headstone was next to hers. His body was never buried there, but the place was marked. Pfc. Axil Judson was killed while on active duty. in 1991 in Operation Desert Storm. His body was never recovered.

The house with three porches was changed into a Visitors House. The artifacts from the caves were moved inside to help preserve them: Kentucky rifles, knives, traps, froes, hammers, drills, utensils, and tintypes were displayed.

There were always questions about the money that was found inside the cave, partially because of the stories that were passed down about the Archer Gang bandits that hid out in caves and robbed people. For that reason, the display of the money was put behind glass, lest someone wanted a personal keepsake for their own. The coinage displayed was of interest to many people—forty 1916 Walking Liberty half-dollars, two 1871 Seated Liberty dimes and Liberty dimes 1916-45, 1910 Silver Pennies, Liberty Head nickels, and an 1899 Barber dime.

The wildflowers and meadow grasses had long ago covered

the cemetery and a gentle hand was needed in maintaining the pastoral venue. The black painted wrought iron fence would eventually return to a weathered rust.

Chicory, dandelion, ground ivy, wild violets, speedwell, henbit, chickweed, heal all, and shatter cane grew with multiflora rose and Johnson grass, blanketing the rolling hill.

Immediately upon receiving the transfer of the Chandler estate, the DHPA went to work to eradicate the Canadian thistles, cockleburs, and the poison ivy that abounded.

The interment to the family's final resting place was believed to be concluded. All the family preceded Anna and then Oliver to eternity.

Twelve marked graves were inside the wrought iron fence—seven adults, one child, one infant, three dogs. The docents had general information and answered questions from the visitors. Some information was posted on placards next to the displays and dioramas in rooms at the house and at the cave's entrance.

The most frequent question from visitors to Shoals Bluff was to ask if anything of treasure or high value had been found in the cave. The docents always gave the same response: "The most treasured things on this property rests within that wrought iron fence under the sycamore tree up on that hill."

Author's Note

As mentioned, this book is dedicated to the Wise sisters from Dugger, Indiana—Ester, Dorothy, Mickey, Rose, Sarah, Jenny, Betty Lou, and Mary. The eight Wise sisters and their three brothers grew up in the hardest of hardscrabble times in a town that measured a half-mile square. Living very close and scratching every day for something to eat and wear, they were as resourceful as they possibly could be, raising food from their garden, canning what was extra, growing tobacco, and looking for that turn in the road to find prosperity, as their dad worked in the coal mines that produced two million tons of coal before it closed.

The Old Dugger Mine started up in 1879 as a shaft mine, then came others. Some were open pit strip mines—City Coal Mine, Little Betty Mine, Baker Mine, and Redbird Mine. Bear Run Mine, owned and run by Peabody Energy, pulled eight million tons of coal annually. Money was made by the owners and the miners themselves got subsistence wages.

Charlie and Stella were the parents of this astounding brood. When their house burned to the ground, they shared space in the barn and in the smokehouse until they could rebuild. One strip mine behind the homestead nearly claimed the house, barn, and the smokehouse. Land behind the barn was sold off to the government before the war.

As kids, the Wise sisters would all try to pile on top and ride their sway back mare, ramble about their orchard, and swim in the abandoned strip mine pits and fish. But the crushing blows of poverty and hardship to the Wise family began before the events of the stock market crash of 1929 gripped the nation and the Dust Bowl years pulverized and destroyed so many. The exodus of the young women began before the start of World War II as they left the dire straits of home and found their beginnings elsewhere.

They were well-educated women, aware of the world around them. They had a love for reading that illuminated the horizons before them. They grew up reading lots and lots of books and sharing excitements among them.

Some of the Wise women had a great sense of humor and delivered one-liners like seasoned vaudevillians. Some worked for municipal governments, several worked for newspapers as proofreaders, one worked in Seattle for Boeing during the war, installing 50-calibre machine guns in the nose turrets of B-17 bombers. Some worked construction as carpenters. One went to work for Indiana University.

Some of them became barbers, some worked as waitresses, one married a Country and Western singer, and one worked for decades at the Mayo Clinic in Rochester, Minnesota. Another Wise sister made moonshine. One sister possessed a superior recipe for making persimmon pudding. One had a shoebox stuck on a shelf in the closet, with a label on it that said, "pieces of string too short to use." All of the Wise sisters eventually became mothers.

About the Author

~~~~~~~~~~~~~~~~~~~~~~~~~~~~~~~~~~

Living in a violent and dysfunctional alcoholic family forced the author to confront ultimatums that pushed him to leave behind a Texas home at 15 and seek sanity and opportunity elsewhere, without much of an education and no money.

As a kid Jon Bunn grew up in and around honkytonks from his pre-teen years and had little chance of finding a bright future, a mentor, or a pathway forward as a high school dropout. Then came Indiana and a distant family that took him in and told him he had worth, something few others had ever said to him.

Jon re-entered high school with nominal paperwork for the Registrar. The only work he had done before leaving Texas was hand sanding cars at an auto body shop, helping a welder build highway billboards, and cooking on a seismic exploration ship in the Gulf of Mexico when he was 14. He never dreamed he would complete high school and was told he would only make it by working with his hands and his back. On a dare, he applied to Indiana University and was accepted. Financial aid was his friend.

Finally, he could do what he wanted to do with no one to tell him "No." In hard times, which were frequent, he had high school friends who provided the food that kept him going. He wore clothes he found in restaurant's lost and found. He did